James Maw's first novel, HARD LUCK, won the Betty Trask Award, and was hailed by the *Literary Review* as 'a brilliantly evocative novel – as colourful and unique as *Oliver Twist* and *Huckleberry Finn*'. He was a producer at Granada Television responsible for comedy before spending a year travelling in Latin America, where he began writing YEAR OF THE JAGUAR, his second novel.

SCEPTRE

Year
of the
Jaguar

JAMES MAW

*To Mars,
with very best
wishes.
love
James Maw*

SCEPTRE

First published in 1996 by Hodder and Stoughton
First published in paperback in 1997 by Hodder and Stoughton
A division of Hodder Headline PLC
A Sceptre Paperback

10 9 8 7 6 5 4 3 2 1

A CIP catalogue record for this book is
available from the British Library

ISBN 0 340 67497 0

Typeset by Palimpsest Book Production Limited,
Polmont, Stirlingshire
Printed and bound in Great Britain by
Cox & Wyman Ltd, Reading, Berkshire

Hodder and Stoughton
A division of Hodder Headline PLC
338 Euston Road
London NW1 3BH

Thanks to those people whose moral and financial support made this adventure in Mexico possible:

Jenny Dodd, Sally Marsden, Lynette Carol, Rob Allen, Tim Sullivan and Yair Teasdale

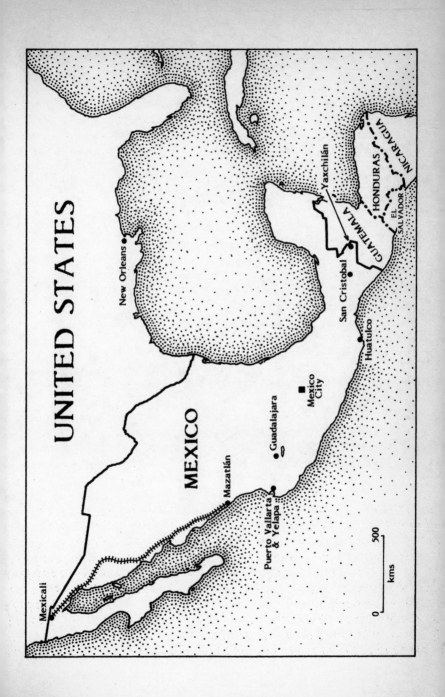

Year
of the
Jaguar

SCEPTRE

England, 1st January 1993.

It was a crisp winter's day, with the mist still hovering above the frost when I arrived, nervously, at Lucinda's house on the edge of the Forest of Dean.

I hadn't expected the place to be so grand, and I stared at its white Palladian façade for a few moments. Then I ran my hand through my hair, cleared my throat, and began walking up the long gravel driveway, my rucksack pulling at my shoulders.

I'd hitch-hiked from East Sussex down to Hampshire. I was twenty-two years old and nervous about meeting my girlfriend's, family for the first time. I was two hours late for lunch.

As I stood in the driveway I expected huntsmen in red tunics to come over the hedges at any moment, or a fox to come tearing across the gravel to take refuge behind my legs. There were classical statues rising above the clipped box hedges with icicles dripping from their breasts and private parts. They seemed to be staring at me.

An elderly man in a dark suit answered the door and I remember thinking, my God he's a *servant*. I didn't know whether I should tip him or not. He took my rucksack for me.

Then he led me through a grand hallway to a long corridor, hung with dark oil paintings and low glimmering lamps.

'I'm afraid, sir, the family have already sat down,' he said, 'some time ago.'

Then he pushed open a great creaking door and abandoned me, turning on the soles of his shoes and plodding his way heavily back down the corridor. I stared into the dining room as the family looked up from their conversation and fell silent. For a moment their faces were perfectly blank until Lucinda jumped up.

'Here's Jay!' she screamed excitedly. 'We thought you'd changed your mind!'

'Sorry I'm late,' I said, still standing in the doorway. 'No trains of course today. Had to walk.'

'Oh but you've made it. Come over here and meet everyone.'

I walked over to her. She kissed me on the cheek, and got up to bring another chair over to the table. Everyone was nodding and smiling. There was no place set for me and so everyone moved their cutlery around and I was put in between Lucinda and her mother. Her mother made no attempt to disguise the fact that she was eyeing me up as a prospective son-in-law.

'I'm afraid we're at the end of lunch and just about to attack the pudding. Can I get you a plate? There's plenty left on the goose and there's pork,' said her mother.

'No, no, really, I'm not that hungry,' I said, hoping that my stomach wouldn't rumble. I hadn't eaten at all.

'Oh you must have something – you'll at least join us in pudding. We save a pudding for New Year's Day.'

'Yes, thank you,' I said. 'I love Christmas pudding.'

As we began eating the pudding Lucinda asked me how my Christmas had been. I smiled and said that we'd watched the BBC programme from Stoke Mandeville Hospital and had then played cards eating my mum's pickled onions.

'It sounds really fun!' she said, turning to the rest of the family, and I really think she meant it. In our final term at university together she'd been experimenting with roughing up her accent to match mine, and wearing second-hand overcoats from Oxfam. The irony was that I'd spent my whole time at university trying to acquire a public school accent.

We'd graduated the summer before and were planning to set up house together in London, not that her parents were aware of this. Neither of us had shared a home with a lover before and we were full of plans and terribly excited. Nor had either of us decided what we wanted to do with our lives, but we were confident about living on love and fresh air.

I was glad to meet her family finally, and felt it would make me her lover *officially*. She tried to get me into conversation with Piers, her older brother. He had the most perfect teeth I've ever seen. The product, I suspected, of too much good food and sport at school.

I can't actually recall what the conversation with him was about because I spent the whole time enjoying the sensation of Lucinda's stockinged shin smoothing the back of my leg, and the smell of her perfume rising from her open neck. A smell I directly equated with wild and wonderful sex.

I looked around the dining room and I was in awe of it all. They looked the most wonderful family to join.

As I ate my Christmas pudding my teeth hit a metal object. When no one was looking I sneaked it out of my mouth and into my palm. I opened my hand under the table and looked into it. It was a solid-silver teddy bear that had been planted in the pudding. It was about three-quarters of an inch high. I was delighted. Others around the table began producing silver trinkets from the pudding as well. Lucinda's younger sister, Claudia, screeched and held a little horseshoe aloft. 'Oh look everyone!' she said 'It means I'm going to get married this year!'

The family laughed.

Lucinda's mother waved a small silver boat in front of her husband's face.

'Ah, *travel*!' she said. 'Are we finally going to make that trip around the world this year?'

He grinned and took another slice of pudding. While the family was laughing I showed my teddy bear to Lucinda under the table.

'What does this mean?' I asked. She smiled and kissed me lightly on the lobe of my ear, whispering, 'It means you're going to get pregnant. Or at least I am – you're going to be a father.'

After lunch we staggered off, port glasses in hand, to a white drawing room with french windows looking out onto a frost-covered lawn, flopping into armchairs and patting our stomachs. I was enjoying it all enormously and feeling relaxed now.

'And what is it that you read at university?' said Lucinda's mother, offering me a menthol cigarette.

'The history of art,' I told her.

'Art?' she said, and thought for a moment. 'It must have so much history.'

Everyone chatted away amicably and then Lucinda's father walked across the room towards me. He was an incredibly tall man, mid-fifties, and very obviously a captain of industry. He stood in front of me for a moment.

'I take a walk after lunch,' he said, 'just a light trot across the lawn. Helps the digestion. Like to join me?'

I stood.

'Certainly, sir,' I said, 'I'd be glad to.'

As he headed towards the french windows Lucinda flashed me a look that said 'good luck'. Her brother looked up briefly with an expression on his face that suggested I was being led to my execution.

Sir Ian was the chairman of the Confederation of British Industry. I'd seen him before, but only on the television news when he sat behind an imposing desk barking his complaints about the government's economic ineptitude. In the flesh he was considerably more terrifying.

We walked for some time, striding across the frost-brittle lawn, with a semblance of purpose. We passed the walled kitchen garden, the tennis court, and the oval pond. Then we drew towards the edge of his estate, with the Forest of Dean beyond.

He turned to me and snorted a laugh. I stared into the pines of the forest. The frost was melting on their needles and everywhere there was the gentle sound of dripping.

'You know,' he said, 'I had an awful time of it in the garden this morning. Had to telephone the RSPCA.'

'How absolutely dreadful,' I said, quivering a little from the cold, and a little from nerves.

He poked his stick at some loose ivy drooping from an oak tree.

'Well, who else could I call?' he said. 'I had a lost baby deer, a fawn, skitting about on the lower lawn.'

'Awkward.'

'Exactly. I asked them if they could send a chap over to pick it up, or whatever they do with them.'

'Quite.'

'You know what they said, insufferable patronising bastards?'

I hazarded a guess. 'Wouldn't come out on New Year's Day?'

'No. They said to just leave it where it was!'

'Outrageous.'

'Exactly, and me with a bloody fawn running amok all over the show.'

'So what did you say, sir?'

'Well I said that in that case I'd have to make alternative arrangements, lodge it in the stables or something until they could get one of their boys to raise himself and come and pick it up.'

'Quite right.'

'And you know what the jumped up little sod said to me?'

'I can't imagine.'

'Leave it where it is, he said – the mother will come out of the forest, find it, and take it back of her own accord.'

'Oh,' I said.

Then he laughed. 'Of course,' he said, 'I didn't have the heart to tell them that I'd shot its bloody mother this morning after breakfast.' He laughed loudly. I stood silent for a moment.

'So,' he said, turning to me seriously, 'are you sleeping with my daughter?'

I coughed and looked towards the house.

'Well I'm terribly fond of her. We didn't meet until our last term really . . .' My voice trailed away.

An hour before dinner that evening everyone went upstairs to dress. I caught Lucinda's arm on the stairs, a slightly terrified look in my eyes. She pulled me into her arms, opened her mouth and kissed me.

'What's the matter, Jay?' she said, as I leant miserably back against the oak carved balustrade.

'Well, this is it,' I said, looking down at my clothes. 'I'm dressed for dinner already, just as I was dressed for lunch.'

She laughed and kissed me on the forehead.

'Oh don't be so silly, nobody cares. Daddy likes to dress up and my priggish brother thinks it's smart, but it's you I want them to meet, not your wardrobe.'

I was still looking worried.

'There's something else isn't there?' she said.

'Yes.'

'Tell me.'

'Well, I know this sounds stupid, but I suppose there'll be quite a lot of cutlery to contend with at dinner. I saw how much you'd used at lunch. I'll get tangled up. I've no idea which fork goes with what.'

'Oh, don't worry about that,' she said. 'There's a very simple golden rule. You just work from the outside in.'

She held her arms out wide as if demonstrating the size of a fish that had got away.

'You just start out here and work your way inwards course by course, it couldn't be simpler.' She smiled at me. 'You are daft to worry about these things.'

She went on up to her room. I felt encouraged and wandered back downstairs. I seemed to gravitate naturally towards the kitchen, where I felt more relaxed. I wandered in hoping to grab a Coke or a mineral water.

Lucinda's mother was in there looking over the dishes that her cook had prepared.

'Oh hello there,' she said brightly. 'Dressed already?'

'Well,' I said, 'I could only manage a light bag as I hitched, so I'm afraid this is it. Hope that's okay.'

'Oh, absolutely,' she said. 'It's all a lot of nonsense these days, don't you think? But Ian and Piers like to fuss about with their studs for an hour before dinner. Gives them something to curse at.'

I laughed. She smiled at me, and I felt that I was approved of.

'More truly, of course,' she said, 'it gets them out of having to give a hand in the kitchen.'

She had a bunch of freshly cut chives on a wooden board and was slicing through them with a Sabatier. I guessed she liked to take charge of the garnish.

'Is there anything I can do to help?' I said.

'Oh that's sweet of you,' she said. 'We've let the help go as it's New Year.' She went over to a dresser and opened a drawer. She pulled out a great wooden box. 'Would you be an absolute marvel and just lay the table for me?' She handed me the canteen of cutlery.

We all retired to bed just after midnight. I was exhausted by my attempts at being scintillating company while Lucinda's mother plied me with port. Dinner hadn't been an entire disaster, despite the placing of fish knives for the dessert course.

This time Lucinda caught me on the stairs. She put her arms briefly around my neck.

'You don't know where my room is – it's just up, left and left again. Give them all half an hour to settle and I'll be waiting for you.'

'Right,' I said, giggling, and went back to my room to shower Sir Ian's cigar smoke out of my hair. I got into the white fluffy bathrobe that had been laid neatly on my bed. I sat staring at my watch on the bedside table deciding that it would be safer if I gave them all at least forty-five minutes to settle. Then I set off for Lucinda's room.

The trouble with old English houses is that they creak at night, great wrenching sounds, as the house is cooling. I let my bedroom door close behind me in stages, with a gap after each great crack of the hinges on the door frame. I was holding my breath.

The wooden boards of the passageway were uneven and rather unpredictable. Those that looked the most solid had somehow been booby-trapped by puritan deathwatch beetles. I cursed the damned floor.

I took to the stairs, which were more solid, and got a bit of a spurt on. I paused for a moment and then went for the last push, taking a turn at the top of the stairs and another after that. I could see the door at the end of the landing and a slither of light beaming out across the polished oak floor.

I got to the door and breathed again. I pushed it open and leapt in, flapping my dressing gown around me, like a swan after a long flight landing on a lake.

Before me was a huge Chinese four-poster bed, designed for an entire family. Sitting up in it and staring at me was Lucinda's mother, reading an historical novel, and Sir Ian beside her with a whisky and soda and the *Wall Street Journal*.

They both looked at me over the rims of their glasses. Lucinda's mother returned to her book. Leaving me to Sir Ian.

'Young man,' he said, 'you should have taken a left and then another left.'

I spluttered and retreated into the passageway.

'What kept you?' said Lucinda, when I got to her room. 'I was almost falling asleep.'

I was panting heavily.

'What I don't understand,' I said, 'what I really can't work out, is why they're not supposed to know that I'm going to sneak to your room when they don't particularly care in any case?'

'Well, that wouldn't be the done thing, would it?' she said giggling at my state of shock. 'It's all about preserving certain double standards.'

'Then why', I said, exasperated, 'did they have to shove me all the way down the other end of the house and make it almost impossible?'

Lucinda rolled over naked on the bed, laughing into the pillow. I lay down beside her and squeezed my face into the soft skin of her back.

'I've got something to tell you,' I said.

'Uh huh?'

'I wanted to wait until we were together. Over Christmas I've had the most extraordinary piece of news. I've been doing a bit of digging.'

She rolled over onto her back. She could hear how serious I was.

'Yes?' she said.

I looked into her face and smiled.

'It's about my father,' I said. 'I think I know where he is.'

Lucinda opened her eyes very wide.

'Are you sure?' she said.

'Yeah, I'm sure.'

'But after all this time . . . ?'

'Uh huh.'

She was startled and shook her head slowly from side to side, and looked back into my eyes.

I reached into my dressing gown pocket and pulled out a long thin parcel wrapped with a ribbon.

'This is your Christmas present,' I said.

'You're full of surprises tonight.'

'I know.'

She unwrapped it, excited. Then her face took on a quizzical expression and her nose knitted up. She looked up at me again.

'It's a map of Mexico,' she said.

'That's right.'

'Mexico . . . ?'

'I want you to come to Mexico with me. Will you?'

'What about my job?'

'Give it up. You're only filling in for them.'

She giggled again. 'You're mad.'

'The old bugger ran away.'

'To Mexico?'

'Mexico!'

2

It was completely dark now. It was that absolute darkness you can only experience when you are crossing oceans or deserts, and the sky is heavy with rain clouds blanking out the stars.

It was the first week in March, 1993, and I was in California heading towards the frontier with Mexico. I was excited, but tired from the long journey, and sitting at the back of a Greyhound bus. I was talking to an American kid that I was sharing the seat with.

'You're crossing the border tonight?'

'It looks like it.'

'How long have you been crazy? It'll be midnight by the time you get there. You're carrying a gun, yeah? At least you got a baseball bat or something?'

'Well, no, not on me.'

The youth looked at me and shook his head slowly from side to side clicking his tongue against the roof of his mouth. He was sitting between me and the chemical toilet. He was making it clear that he thought I was one of the biggest fools he'd ever met. He shook his head again.

'You're bound to get rolled,' he said, 'maybe even murdered.' He screwed up his face as the floodlights from a set of billboards shot across him in eerie flashes. He had a pale face and dull grey eyes and his skin looked as if it were made from wax or white rubber. He was working his way through a large pack of dry-roasted nuts.

We'd left Los Angeles five hours before and we'd only just got talking. I wasn't glad that we had.

'Well you know,' he said, 'whatever you do don't *walk* across.

Don't walk down that damn concrete tunnel they got under the defences, not at night. Take a cab and you might make it. Make it, that is, if the driver isn't Mexican and he smells your money clip and decides to take you on a scenic tour, takes you to visit his brother's house . . . You know what I mean?'

'It's an awkward border, Calexico to Mexicali?'

'Man, don't you know anything? The frontier with Mexico here was designed by the devil. It's the Wild West. We had a Mexican who came to clean our pool once. It was bad, man. You can't trust them as far as you can kick 'em. Two days after he cleaned it the water went green and it filled with frogs.'

'Is that so?'

'Yeah, it was so. The bastard had stashed drugs in the filtration. I reckon he figured he would pick it up later. And you know what? If that ain't bad enough our neighbour saw him take a swim in our pool in his jockey shorts. Disgusting bastard. It was a surprise to my dad that the damn frogs wanted to get in after.'

'Your dad's not keen on Mexicans, I take it?'

He screwed up his face again and thrust his hand into his bag of nuts.

'Man,' he said, 'all they want to do is come over here. Even *they* don't like their country. It beats me why you all wanna go down there. You must have some real big reason to be going across is all I can say.'

I looked out of the bus where the darkness outside was broken by the sudden dramatic flashes from the billboards. He stared at me keenly.

'Yeah,' I said. 'I've got a real big reason.'

He narrowed his eyes again. It seemed to be the only facial expression he knew.

Every night about five thousand Mexicans try to cross the border, he told me. Most are turned back at gunpoint by the US border guards, only to try again the next night at a different spot.

'Sometimes they just run up the highway fifty at a time. Man, it's just a crazy situation. You just shouldn't have the First World bordering on the Third World. It should be better organised. Now we've got this stupid NAFTA thing coming up. North American Free Trade Agreement. Biggest free-trade zone in the world.

They get all our top industrial plants and we get a truckload of nachos.' He spat a nut out into the aisle and studied it for a while. He offered me a nut.

Am I going to get this all the way to the border? I thought. Hour on hour of drivel as blank and featureless as the road ahead. Maybe I'd go and sit in the chemical toilet. Perhaps the fumes would knock me unconscious. Everyone else on the bus was asleep. We were the only ones who still had a reading light on.

'Why are you wearing a suit?' he asked me.

'Why not?'

'What is it, polyester, viscose?'

I looked at the label on the inside pocket to oblige him.

'Claims to be cotton,' I said.

'Shit, man, you're intending crossing over in a cotton suit? You'll damn well get rolled for sure in a cotton suit.'

'Well, I didn't want to get it crumpled in my suitcase. Cotton crumples.'

'Suitcase?' he said, almost screaming the word. 'You can't be serious. You got a suitcase with you too? Now that is definitely a liability.'

'It's on wheels,' I said.

He shook his head.

'You sure got some balls. Doubt that you'll still have them in the morning though.'

The bus pulled into Palm Springs.

'Here we are,' he said. 'God's waiting room, nothing but retirees here.'

I remarked on how Palm Springs is a miracle of irrigation.

'Also a miracle of medication,' he said. 'God, I hate old folks.' He looked out into the street and snarled. The street was deserted.

I breathed a sigh of relief as he told me it was his stop. He worked on Saturdays in one of the luxury rest homes as what he called a 'pill nurse', pushing a trolley load of drugs around all day. The medical equivalent of room service in Palm Springs.

When he got off into the gentle desert rain he turned to me and called from the front of the bus. 'Just remember, don't walk it, not if you want to see tomorrow with a neat suit and balls.'

I laid my head against the window pane as the bus headed back into the wilderness. At the side of the road there were billboards for mile on mile. Most of the ads were for rest homes and spas, with smiling old people on them. They had their arms around each other and they were beaming out at the highway with sparkling dentures and fuzzy-perm hair. It added to the whole unnatural atmosphere of the evening and I felt that I'd already died and I was on the road to the hereafter.

I sank back into the headrest and tried to enjoy the sensation of the silver bus cutting through the darkness, with its great headlamp beams, heading south, further and further south. I was excited.

I glanced over at Lucinda. She was a few seats down on the other side of the aisle, curled up asleep. Her face still had the look that she'd had when I'd gone to sit at the back of the bus. Her brow was furrowed and she'd made her hands into tight fists tucked beneath her chin. She looked incredibly uncomfortable. It was as if she was enduring a dream in which a terrible argument was taking place.

She'd sent me to go and sit with the kid from Palm Springs almost as soon as we'd left Los Angeles. She hadn't been impressed with my travel arrangements from the moment we'd left England. I'd failed to get direct flights, so we'd had to begin in Los Angeles. We'd had to stay in a small motel in Santa Monica and suffered an attack of sand flies. Now instead of getting us onto the *directo*, which would have got us to the border for early evening, I'd mistakenly booked us onto the *locales*, which stopped at every small town and shopping mall.

The bus pulled into the border town of Calexico just before midnight. I walked down the aisle to Lucinda's seat and kissed her on the forehead. Then I woke her up and told her that we'd arrived. She opened her eyes slowly.

'Thank God,' she said, rubbing her eyes. 'We're actually there? We're in Mexico?'

I helped her to her feet and went to kiss her again, but she brushed me aside and looked at her watch.

'It's midnight!' she said. 'It's bloody midnight. I've never been on a bus so long in my life. All my joints have locked.'

I smiled apologetically. She pulled a comb from her bag and began brushing her hair furiously. It was sticking up at the back of her head where it had been moulded to the shape of the seat back. The buckles of her handbag had made a strange impression on her cheek and there were the remains of some tortilla chips just above her ear that had been dropped on her by a passing drunk. She wasn't best pleased. I tried to help brush them out, but she pushed me aside.

'Well, we're here,' I said. 'It's going to be fun, It'll be an experience.' She glowered at me. We got off and walked towards the bus station in silence.

I cleared my throat. 'Well, of course we've still got to cross the border. This is, in effect, just the American side.'

'I can see that – I'm not blind,' she said. I shut up.

We watched anxiously as an odd little game was played with our suitcases. They came out of the luggage store in the bowels of the bus and were dropped on the tarmac a few feet from us.

'For God's sake get the bags,' she said.

I could easily have picked them up but the bus driver wouldn't allow it. First they had to be put on a trolley, to be wheeled twelve feet or so to a hatch in the bus station wall. Lucinda sighed deeply. I smiled at her and shrugged my shoulders. Then the suitcases disappeared and we joined a queue in silence, while the night wore on.

In the hiatus before the border crossing I spent the time trying to organise my passport and my wallet, shoving my money deep into my breast pocket. Lucinda began tutting and sighing. I laid my hand on my chest and felt the acceleration of my heart. A tantalising stash of bills could easily be seen through my jacket pocket and I began visualising the way I would be shortly and inevitably rolled by the Mexican taxi driver's brother. I considered dividing the wodge in half, taking my shoes off in the lavatory and stuffing my socks with it. I asked Lucinda what she thought I should do.

She thought I should shove it up my arse. She hadn't woken up well.

The Mexicans who were lying asleep on the floor of the bus station looked travel-tired and harmless. They clutched their sleeping children to them. They looked forlorn. The sight of them moved me. The baby children looked like cherubs that had fallen to earth and landed on the station floor after having been slain in some heavenly war.

'What a pit of a place,' said Lucinda as she glanced around. 'Are you concentrating?'

'Yes,' I said, pulling myself up to my full height and trying to look as if I was still in charge.

We queued for twenty minutes. She got her comb out again. It hardly seemed necessary – it was a thing she did when she was irritated and I knew it was probably best right now if I kept very, very quiet.

We got to the hatch and I reached into my wallet.

I stared into the wallet for a while. All the money was there but I'd lost the luggage chits.

'Look, why don't we check into a hotel here for the night and cross over the border in the morning?'

'I'm awake now,' she said. 'If we don't cross over now we'll never get the bloody train in the morning. Don't piss about any more, Jay. Let's just get going. Just tell them you've lost the chits.'

I combed my hair with my hands and wiped the sweat from my forehead, reminding myself that travelling can fray anyone's temper. She was tired and needed to sleep. She didn't really mean what she was saying.

The business of our lost luggage chits was embarrassing. We had to make a list of what was in our cases and then they were opened and our underwear displayed to an interested crowd. I could perfectly understand why Lucinda wasn't at all pleased about it. I nodded and agreed with her, but it didn't seem to do me any good.

My suitcase had two wheels and I pulled it noisily behind me and we walked through the concourse, out of the terminal, and into the street. It was busy outside, for midnight. Cab drivers came up offering to take us to cheap hotels in Calexico and offering a 'goodtime' but none of them were willing to take a fare across the border. It didn't seem possible to drive across the border by cab at all. It appeared to be against the law.

'Well there was no mention of it in the guidebook,' was all I could muster in my defence when Lucinda rounded on me.

The rain was pouring and we stood under an awning trying

to get our bearings. The rain coursed along the pavement and plunged into great iron drains.

'I've had absolutely quite enough of this,' said Lucinda. 'For God's sake, the border's only across the street. What are we waiting for?' I braced myself and followed her as she stepped out from under the awning and made for the concrete border post. It was a huge structure in grey brutalist concrete, made dark by the torrential downpour.

It was not the way I had imagined the frontier and our crossing of it to be. The border post was topped with high twisted iron poles, sharpened and facing Mexico like lances. On both sides high fences stretched away from the building into the distance.

A sign on the wall, a crumbling cardboard thing, pointed the way to Mexico. There was a short ramp and in the brightly lit immigration hall I could see the American border guards. Smart in their uniforms, drinking coffee, playing Nintendo Game Boys. No one else was heading across the border tonight except us. I looked again at Lucinda, but she was stoutly resolute and offering no support whatsoever. She was now looking perfect, her hair exactly as she always wore it, despite the rain – which seemed to have the wisdom to glance off her – as she strode towards the border post.

The guards looked up as we arrived. There was no doubt that the appearance of a drenched man in a suit with a suitcase on wheels, and a young woman who looked as if she was about to make a complaint in a department store, was a surprise to them at this hour of the night.

'Well hello, sir, hello ma'am, and how can we help you?' One of them said with a smirk across his face.

'We'd like to cross over into Mexico, if that's okay,' I said, waggling my British passport.

'Well sure, sir, that's okay, sir. Just walk on through the turnstile.' He indicated the sort of thing you see in a fairground. The rain was beating down on it outside the immigration hall.

'We just walk on through?'

'Yep.'

'There's no Mexican border control?'

The US guards laughed. 'There's just the turnstile right there.

You didn't have to come to us. You can just walk right on into Mexico if you really want to.'

'Right, thank you,' I said. 'That's what we'll do then.'

'Be my guest.'

'So, no passports needed?' I asked.

'No, sir, but when you come back, sir, it's different. You better have those passports with you then, sir. And whatever you do, kids, don't try smuggling anything past us here. Remember, no fruit. No bananas, no oranges, none of them strings of hot dried chilli, no animals, no chihuahua dogs, no damn donkeys, nor any agricultural produce as prohibited by United States Federal Law.'

'And what about drugs?' I said, being carried away precariously by the bonhomie.

There was a moment's silence from the border guards. I turned to look at Lucinda, she was smiling painfully.

'We don't recommend it, sir,' said the guard and they all stared at me with cold suspicious eyes while I stepped from one foot to the other, regretting an attempt at late-night humour with uniformed Americans.

'So we just walk on through?' I said, finally.

'That's what you do, sir.'

'Right, well we'll be seeing you then.' I stared into the long darkness beyond.

'God save the Queen, sir,' said one of the guards.

'Yeah, God save her, and the best of luck to Bill Clinton too,' said Lucinda. She was already marching out of the immigration hall, much in the way I imagined her taking to the hockey pitch at school.

The turnstile was encased in a high wire cage. Except for the machine-gun sound of the turnstile ratchet it was completely silent and deserted on the Mexican side.

Stupidly, I suppose, I was still looking for a taxi rank to get us straight to an hotel. But there was no rank, just a long corridor-like cage, getting darker as it went along. I touched my wallet in my breast pocket. It felt like a definite liability now.

The cage gave way to a flight of steps. It was obvious now that we were going to walk over the border and into Mexicali. I caught up with Lucinda.

At the bottom of the steps the cage ended and Mexico suddenly began. On the wall was their red, white and green flag sloppily painted in thin paint onto white washed concrete. The plaster was peeling as if the flag was trying to remove itself from the wall. There was a mural that looked like it had been done by a class of school children each with a different idea of how it should turn out.

The contrast between the two countries was instant. In front of us a long concrete subway stretched under the road and the US defences.

I walked steadily but the plastic wheels of my Delsey suitcase made one hell of a noise, echoing against the walls and signalling our presence like the transport of artillery. I tried to ease off on the wheels, and avoid the more major cracks and dips in the hard floor. I could feel my heart beating faster. My legs quivered and the backs of my knees felt wet. Lucinda was humming to herself, sounding like the low growl of an irritable cat.

Then from behind a pillar two dark figures stepped out. I glanced quickly towards them. They were broad-framed burly Mexicans in shiny bomber jackets with their caps on backwards and they were staring at me. There was still about five hundred yards of subway to cross, and these guys to pass in about twenty.

The men began moving moodily, then they started making heavy steps towards us.

A low dark voice echoed against the walls.

'Hey . . .'

I pretended not to hear it. 'Just let's walk a little faster,' I whispered to Lucinda. I really didn't fancy any 'amigo' business quite yet. There was a sudden look of worry on Lucinda's face. We tried not to quicken our pace visibly, but the men began to follow us, first slowly and then at the same steady rate as ourselves. They began whistling, imitating, I think, the squeak of the wheels of my Delsey suitcase. Oh my God, no, I thought – I know exactly what's going to happen. I'd felt this awful fear so many times before in the streets at night when gangs of pissed-up lads were looking for someone like me, someone who wouldn't resist, someone who was easy game, to kick the shit out of. Here in Mexico, and with Lucinda along too, it was even more terrifying.

We hit a stretch of passageway where the overhead bulbs had been shattered, and I could feel the cloying stickiness of congealed blood beneath my shoes and under my wheels. There was the smell of excrement. My body was becoming insensitive with fear.

I cursed the country only a hundred yards into it, for not putting any guards, or officials, into such an unearthly stretch. I could hear the warning of the nurse on the bus loud and clear now. There were still no signs of life from the end of the tunnel.

We got to the steps at the far end and looked at the concrete ramp ahead. We got up them as fast as we could with me bashing the suitcase behind me. It was at this point, right at the beginning of our journey, that I hit one of the steps badly and one of my wheels dropped off. It sheered its pin and clattered back down the steps behind us into the infernal darkness. I watched it spin into oblivion and then suddenly we were up into the hard light of the street.

Mexicali at night was everything the kid on the bus had said it would be. Dark figures of men hovered in the brothel doorways, and the pot-holed street was filled with lakes of water glowing red like blood from the reflection of the neon signs. A town designed on the drawing boards of hell.

There were electric cables loosely lashed across the roads to power the late-night bars where the tourists go to find cheap sex.

Here on the border it was still every bit the sordid frontier town created in the days of the American prohibition, when they came over the border to drink and gamble. A town still clinging like a leech to the foot of America.

The guys from the tunnel had given up the chase. Perhaps after all they were only trying to sell us drugs. Lucinda stood in shock for a moment, and then turned to look at me.

'Where the hell have you brought me, you bastard?' she said, simply. I couldn't answer.

My suitcase cut a swathe through the mud of the main street as we dashed like jackrabbits to the doorway of the nearest hotel.

'Let's dive in here,' I said breathlessly. 'It doesn't matter what the rooms are like.' Lucinda nodded and we went in.

I cut a fine figure in the lobby: hair in stripes down my face, my suit covered in splatters of mud, and a wild, terrified look in my eyes as I sniffed and wiped my nose. Lucinda collapsed into a red plastic-covered sofa and lit up a menthol cigarette with shaking hands. She'd recently given up smoking.

Our check-in was held up by two policemen who were evicting a couple of prostitutes from a room. All hell broke loose as the prostitutes screamed and the American tourist, a middle-aged man in a lumberjack's shirt, complained that they'd robbed him.

Otherwise the hotel seemed fine, I thought. It was better than the street. The electricity was working and they had a room available. It hadn't been cleaned yet but that didn't matter.

I put our passports down on the bare reception desk to complete the check-in. The man looked up at me, and down at my trousers, and at the battered Delsey. Then he opened my passport. He looked suddenly surprised.

'*Ingles,*' he said, '*Ingles?*'

'*Si, Ingles,*' I replied. '*Buenos noches.*'

We went up to a room, to its hard twin beds and its bare bulb. A room, I suspected, that had become suddenly available. There were bedclothes everywhere and the smell of tequila, or something sweeter. We looked out of the window into the sodden street. There were half a dozen men below hanging about in the doorways, swaying and spitting great gutfuls, and twitching, in cheap leather jackets, like prowling hyenas on the edge of a herd of moving cattle.

'I'm sorry,' I said. 'I didn't imagine it would be like this. I wouldn't have encouraged you to come with me.'

She threw the unemptied ashtray into the bin.

'I'm going to sleep,' she said. 'I don't particularly want to talk about this right now.' She pulled herself into one of the twin beds and turned her face to the wall. She didn't even bother to undress.

I began the job of washing down my suitcase, then set my travel clock for the morning. I didn't want us to miss the train.

'It does mean a lot to me,' I said, 'that you've come with me to meet him. I want you to know that.' I went to kiss her, but she was asleep.

I hung my suit up, hooking it on a picture of the Virgin of Guadalupe. She seemed to be looking at me as if I'd made the most enormous mistake.

3

When I woke it was still very early. The dawn sky was grey and full of foreboding and I could hear a goods train rattling towards us on the rails that ran along the centre of the street outside. As the train got to beneath our shattered window the driver treated us to an almighty blast of its whistle. Then it began to rain.

Lucinda shrieked. It was seven o'clock. Our train didn't depart until ten. She looked up at me as I fussed about packing.

'Every bone in my body aches,' she said, staring up at me as I hovered with my shoes. 'This bloody bed's tried to kill me. The springs are sticking through the mattress. I'd have been better off on the floor. I'd have been better in the street – they'd have knifed me quicker.' She closed her eyes again, rolled over and got twanged by another sharp spring. She screamed and banged her fist down on the bedclothes, muttering my name as a curse.

'Look, I'll tell you what,' I said as gently as I could. 'Why don't I take a spin down to the railway station, sort out the tickets and come back with a taxi? You can take your time, get some coffee or something. I'll have the driver wait.'

She opened her eyes briefly and nodded.

I took myself out of the hotel and into the continuing torrential rain that came off the canopy in great straight lines and poured from the beaten palm trees. They were the only indication that this place was supposed to be hot and sunny at this time of year. As I'd promised Lucinda it would be.

I looked for a cab to take me across town to the railway station. The guidebook recommended that we should get there at least an hour early for the Pullman.

A few old buses with their destinations painted on the

windscreen in whitewash thundered through doing their best to drown me in mud again, last night's mud having dried on my suit like the scales of a reptile. There were no cabs to be seen.

After I'd walked almost a mile with a sodden map falling to pieces in my hands, the cabs finally got themselves out onto the street. I flagged one down and went, at an exorbitant rate, the other mile to the station. Outside the station was a steam engine, from pioneer days, rusting on a bit of scrub where a row of tarpaulin-covered stands were busily serving breakfast, doing a brisk trade in tortillas.

Lucinda will love this, I tried to convince myself – it's real local colour. Even if that colour was mainly brown and grey. The people milling around were the most miserable I had ever seen. I guessed they were hoping for work as porters.

I was directed to a booth where I could make my reservation. The woman behind the glass of this practically redundant office had decorated her booth with pictures of her fat little children, something of a status symbol round here, I guessed. There were pictures of flowers torn from magazines, too, and small religious plastic ornaments, the type of thing you might see swinging from the dashboard of a Greek taxi in Finsbury Park.

The woman looked pretty severe, with her black hair swept back, and little sufferance of non-Spanish speakers attempting to travel by a Mexican train.

Before I knew it I was speaking Spanish, only a quick burst admittedly, and rehearsed beforehand, but just enough to get her attention. This produced a large piece of paper with a whole load of rather advanced-level Spanish on it, the crest of the National Rail Company, and the official stamp and seat reservations in first-class. But it wasn't a ticket. The tickets themselves are much more modest affairs and bought from a man behind a grille on the other side of the station.

Beside the ticket booth the schedule was posted in white plastic letters on a black pegboard for the two trains a day that the station dealt with, one going to Guadalajara and one coming from it. The grille opened onto a dank bare office with nothing but piles of tickets and a safe. I didn't imagine that there was much love lost between this man and the woman in the decorated reservations booth. I imagined that from time to time heated feuds would break out between them, throwing the issuing of tickets into total confusion, and indeed, it was at this point that I stepped, not for the last time, into a Mexican cleft stick.

I'd been informed by the guidebook that the Pullman left at ten o'clock. When I checked with the Mexican Government Tourist Office in Los Angeles they told me it left at eleven o'clock.

It didn't. The train left at nine o'clock.

This caused untold confusion. A confusion that deepened when the clerk revealed that the price of the ticket was six times greater than advertised. He couldn't take dollars either, he couldn't take travellers' cheques, and he couldn't take credit cards. The only thing he could legally accept, he said, was pesos, in fresh crispy notes pressed into his palm, and I didn't have enough after the taxi ride. It was impossible without them. If he accepted dollars then the whole rail system would collapse, the ceiling of his booth would cave in and he would lose his job. Only the banks could give me pesos.

I asked if there was a bank nearby.

'Sí, señor,' said the clerk, enjoying his position behind the grille.

'And it will definitely give me pesos?'

'Sí, señor, when it opens.'

'When does it open?'

'At nine o'clock, señor.'

'But that's the time the train leaves.'

'Sí, señor.'

'Will the train leave on time? Could you hold it just a couple of minutes?' I didn't think this was an unreasonable request. I looked to be the only person getting on. But it caused the most apocalyptic outbreak of woe. If he delayed it his wife would starve and his children would have to be sold to Americans who had been turned down for legal adoption. At least that was what I imagined to be the gist of it. The man's objections were all being conducted in excitable Spanish that had an element of Latin American and included unpronounceable Indian words like: *tlacochahuaya* and *cempoaltepetl*. When I said that I thought his timetable 'absolutely takes the biscuit' the situation became almost irretrievable.

It was becoming apparent why Mexicans, on the whole, do not travel by train. Neither do foreigners: the bulk of the passengers, it seems, are men who work for the railway, and people wishing to transport large numbers of potatoes.

I was beginning to realise that I was going to have to return to the hotel and explain that we may have to enjoy Mexicali for another twenty-four hours. The prospect filled me with dread. I looked at the train sitting in the station humming away to itself, unboardable, and felt the absolute frustration of not being able to begin what I now knew was going to be a long, long journey. I reminded myself what my mission was.

I began the walk to the bank, miserably. Then I saw a sudden vision on the road: a Holiday Inn Crown Plaza Hotel, set in a beautiful garden, with a rainbow in an arc above it. I put my hand on my travellers' cheques and walked in. I breathed in the air-conditioning of the foyer. It filled me with the promise of a proper bathroom with soaps in click-shut plastic boxes, shampoo in little bottles, and plastic shower caps. Tonight we could have cocktails, dinner, and sleep in a bed together. In the bathroom there would be a little sewing kit and I could mend the turn-ups to my trousers. I cheered up.

I walked up to the reception desk and rang the bell a couple of times before a young guy in a crisp salmon-coloured suit emerged. I asked if they had a room. He was standard, corporate-hotel issue, with short back and sides and lightly tanned skin. He took some time to scan the blank computer screen in front of him before saying, 'Yes, I think we may be able to accommodate you tonight, sir.'

The foyer had pink leather armchairs scattered around. They were like marshmallows, and they looked as if they'd never been sat in.

There were two parakeets clinging by their beaks to the very top of their cage as if they wanted to fly up to the glass droplet chandelier above and destroy it. They were set there as ornaments themselves, and they seemed to know it. They tempered their natural inclinations to flap and shriek in deference to the unearthly hush of the foyer. An elderly man, European looking, and possibly the only other guest in the hotel, was poking his fountain pen through the bars of their cage. I watched him for a while as he tried to amuse the birds. The thumb of his right hand was missing. He wore a smart suit with a crisp collar. I wondered how he'd tied his tie so perfectly without the use of a thumb.

Everywhere, seeping insidiously out of hidden speakers in the ceiling, was piped music. Like looped mediocrity it hung in the air of the restaurant and the restrooms. This was, I thought, the frontier town striving for respectability. Trying to make itself a city like anywhere else, clean and smart with a lot of smoked glass. A place for business. But, while Holiday Inns are the same the world over, this one seemed particularly ridiculous. It was trying too hard. Nevertheless it would certainly do me for the night, and it might just get me back into Lucinda's good books. She'd think she was in Hampshire or somewhere, perhaps.

They called me a cab and changed me some dollars for pesos and I went to get Lucinda. She sat in silence all the way and when we arrived at the hotel she entirely ignored it, furious that I'd 'made us miss the train'.

We went up to the room. I looked Mexicali up in my guidebook, determined to plan an interesting day for us. It simply said, 'There is nothing in Mexicali that recommends it to the traveller. Do not stay here unless you have to . . .' I snapped the book shut in case Lucinda should ask me what it said and searched around the room with my eyes for the minibar. She had a fat paperback, a legal thriller, which she stuck her nose resolutely into, and lay on the bed with it all afternoon. Every time she looked up I made sure that I was smiling and engrossed in my own interesting project: I had decided to keep a journal of our journey. It was getting off to a poor start, though.

As the sun began to set I took myself down for a tour of the hotel. Lucinda was still aching from the night before and wanted, she said, just to have a long bath. I'd offered to assist in her convalescence but she seemed to think that a walk in the fresh air might do me more good. The first crickets of the evening had begun to chirp and rasp. As I approached the hotel pool the lights were suddenly switched on and the water, which had looked very grey from the bathroom window, was suddenly transformed into an other-worldly ultramarine. Either I had triggered the illuminations automatically, or I was being watched by one of the staff. It was rather unnerving. There was something truly strange about this hotel, as if it was fraudulent, and had been built as an elaborate trap.

Exotic birds were swooping and diving into the water. I stood and watched them for a while. I thought at first that they were skimming the surface of the water for fun, for the sheer pleasure of its coolness. Then I realised that they were snatching up the small insects and tropical bugs that had drowned in it during the day, treating it as a sort of running buffet. I was hungry again too. I went to the house phone and called Lucinda. I felt uneasy on my own.

'Why don't you come down for a cocktail and then we'll have dinner?' I suggested. 'It'll be fun. It's all lit up.'

'I've already called room service for a salad,' she said. 'I'm going to have that and turn in. I've taken the bed by the window. I hope you don't mind.' She put the phone down.

I took a seat on the patio by the pool looking up at the smooth green trunks of the Royal Palms, and ordered a beer. The waiter had arrived the moment I'd sat down.

A few moments later he returned, marching towards me holding my beer aloft on a silver tray. I got the feeling that this had been the first time in a while that he'd been able to perform this duty. He was holding my beer as far away from himself as possible. He placed it delicately on the glass table top in front of me and when I thanked him in Spanish he turned to me and a great smile lit up his face.

'You are British!' he said.

'Yes.'

'You are from merry England?'

I smiled, a vision of Drake and the *Golden Hind* passing through my mind.

'Yes, from merry England.'

'I too am British. A British through and through.' He said it in a broad Latin American accent. 'I am born in British Honduras. Now it's called bloody Belize.'

'Oh, good,' I said. 'Very good.' He was a short, round man of about forty, and he'd lost a button from the middle of his white tunic.

'It is a very wonderful thing to be,' he said. I didn't want to be rude so I just vaguely nodded my head.

'In nineteen seventy-two, I was working at the hotel in Uxmal, in Yucatan, where the great pyramids are, and I had the best birthday present any British person can have.'

He pulled over a chair and sat down.

'Really?'

'Yes, really.' He beamed at me wildly and I wondered if he was going to order a beer for himself as well.

'For my birthday. Twenty-second February, nineteen seventy-two. When I was twenty-one, the Queen Elizabeth came to stay at the hotel to see the Sound and Light Show.'

'And it was your birthday?'

'Yes, it was. The hotel was all shut up. No guests, no nothing allowed, just the Queen Elizabeth and her bodyguards and the Prince Edinburgh, and me. The Queen Elizabeth was in room forty-one, and the Prince Edinburgh in room forty-four.' I took a sip of my beer, and made a pinch at the macadamia nuts.

'The Prince Edinburgh, he has to walk behind her, he cannot walk beside her, only behind. That is the law. Also he had to stay in room forty-four.' He laughed again. 'Myself, and the other waiters, we say to each other, "Also, he must have to make love behind her."'

I laughed, which pleased him a great deal. We were buddies now.

'And because it is my birthday,' he continued, 'and I am born in British Honduras one of the men with her calls for me and I go to his room and he gives me a present from the Queen Elizabeth. A great big bottle of London Beefeater Gin.'

'Oh, that was good,' I said.

'No, not good. Because I am an alcoholic.' He looked suddenly sad.

'Oh dear,' I said.

'I like boozing and boozing all day and night. More and more booze. Now I live in a clinic. I serve it, I don't drink it. I hold my nose away from it.'

'Very wise.'

'But still it was a present from the Royal Queen.'

'Yes, very nice of her.'

'Yes, and then, the next morning the Queen Elizabeth sends for the manager and the waiters to shake hands with her before she leaves.'

'Very civil.'

'Then she gives out presents to everyone. She gives the manager a gold tie pin, and then she gives me a gold tie pin also and it has her name on it "ER", in real gold. Two presents for me so I am very grateful to her.'

'Yes I'm sure I would be.'

'Yes, but I have been drinking London Beefeater Gin all night and so I throw out my arms wide, like this, and then I kiss the Queen Elizabeth on the mouth, very passionately. I am a great passionate kisser of ladies, but I am, this time, how would you say it?'

'Pissed?'

'Oh yes, very much rat-arse booze-pissed to my bloody eyeballs.'

I smiled for a moment and looked again at the lazy birds swooping over the pool. Maybe I was going to like Mexico. Maybe I was even going to enjoy the unnatural life of hotels.

'Can I ask how Her Majesty reacted?'

He swayed his head slowly from side to side.

'She is very well educated, very polite. That is why she is the Queen Elizabeth. She looked at me and then she shook my hand again, until I began to fall over and then the man that had given me the bloody London Beefeater Gin took me out of the room with my arm up here.' He held his arm up behind his back.

'Oh dear. And did the manager fire you?'

'Oh no, the manager didn't fire me. He was rat-arse booze-pissed too.' He picked up his silver tray solemnly and stood. 'Will you be eating with us in the dining room tonight, sir?' he asked.

'The dining room? Yes, yes I will.'

'Very good, sir,' he said gravely and turned on his shiny shoes. He had terribly small feet. As he went to walk away he turned back and whispered, 'I will make sure that you have the very best table.'

'Thank you.'

'But don't get rat-arsed. It is a very, very bad thing.'

'I'll try not to,' I whispered. God, I thought to myself, I love this country. Even when it's bad, and your lover isn't speaking, there's always something around the corner to surprise you. I breathed in the hot air, enjoying the feeling of being away. I was in my father's country.

I sipped my beer and wondered if that was a gag the Queen's bodyguards regularly pull in hotels, seeing how many of the staff they can get blotto to liven things up.

At eight o'clock, having changed into a jacket and tie, I walked into the dining room. Lucinda was already asleep. I'd changed, of course, solely for the benefit of the waiter. I knew he'd expect it. I couldn't let him down.

The dining room was a vast white hall with the reflection of the overhead fans spinning in every piece of silver cutlery. The room could take about a hundred diners but I was their only guest tonight. The staff stood around, lined up against a far wall. I wondered what they would have done if I hadn't been there. I suspect that they would still have stood there in their crisp white uniforms until the night had ended. They were pleased to see me. The hotel had obviously just been built. It was unused and virgin-like with its smell of paint and freshly laid carpet. I felt as if I was a trial run for the staff.

While I waited for my meal, pretending to be thinking about something important, I sipped at a glass of wine. Out of the corner of my eye I could see the Honduran waiter. Every time I took another sip his head swayed slowly from side to side. I felt sure that he'd be over at any moment advising me not to drink on an empty stomach.

I inspected the silver, weighing the heavy fork in my hand. Then I put it down again. It looked as if I was playing with the cutlery.

Finally my meal arrived and my waiter was most attentive. We were old friends now. When my candle burned halfway down he came mob-handed with three waiters to change it. One to take the old candle away, one to place a new one in the candlestick, and him to light it with a flourish. I began to dread what would happen if I dropped my fork.

A little later there was a sudden clatter and commotion as four waiters struggled to open the doors of the dining room. There was

31 •

another diner. It seemed almost shocking. I looked up. It was the elderly man I'd seen in the foyer irritating the parakeets with his fountain pen.

He positioned himself at a table at the far end of the dining room and fussed with his napkin, sitting bolt upright and turning to the waiters with sharp nods, and gazing around at the decor of the room. Anything but look in my direction. He'd dressed for dinner too. I sipped at my wine and played with the chilli peppers I'd pushed to the side of my plate.

The man was in his early sixties. An agile-looking man with a shock of white hair swept back from his forehead.

I coughed, and, like an echo, he coughed too. The presence of another person seemed to change the atmosphere of the room entirely.

I heard the scrape of his chair as he pulled himself back from his table and stood. He walked the length of the room until he arrived in front of me. He laid his strange hand on my table cloth.

'*Bon soir*,' he said.

'Good evening,' I replied. There was something rather creepy and unnerving about him. His eyes were grey, almost dead, and he looked lost. He was French.

'This is ridiculous,' he said. 'May I join you?'

'Yes, of course,' I said, and stood to shake his hand. It was an odd sensation, shaking a hand without a thumb, and our hands slipped apart.

'We are obviously their only guests tonight.'

'We're probably the only guests in the entire hotel,' I said.

'Most probably. People don't come to Mexicali.'

'I can see why.'

He laughed loudly.

The waiters smiled as he sat down. They looked pleased to see their guests having such a good time in their hotel.

I thought we looked like two shipwrecked sailors observing a Christmas Day that we'd notched up on a bamboo pole, toasting absent friends with coconut hooch.

Over dinner I asked him what his business was. He went silent and looked at the table, rather ominously.

'I'm an engineer,' he said.

'Interesting.'

'Mmm . . .'

I looked at the man and guessed that he would be about the same age as my father, perhaps a little older. I began to wonder if this would be the way I would meet my father finally, unexpectedly like this in a hotel dining room. How our conversation would get started and what, if anything, we'd have to say to each other. Perhaps it would be as stilted and as formal as this. My heart sank a little.

There was a sudden thud as the lid of the piano went up and a pianist in black tie set about playing a piece of Chopin. He added a certain amount of his own to the composition and considerably accelerated it as soon as we ordered our brandies. The murdering of Chopin brought smiles to our faces. We took the drinks out onto the patio by the pool and the head waiter brought over the visitors' book for us to sign. He seemed to have regarded the evening as a great success.

The rain had stopped a couple of hours before and the night was humid. The creatures in the undergrowth of the garden had got quite a chorus going. The crickets were like a class of schoolchildren playing on notched rulers. We listened to the calls of the smaller birds as they roosted, and the bursts of outrage from the larger parrots. There was the wind section of the tropical orchestra too: the tree frogs on piccolos, with the giant toads on bassoon. The noise was quite deafening, as loud as any city at night. I thought about my father again. Maybe we'd sit like this one night soon, under the stars, demolishing a bottle of brandy long into the night. I had a warming feeling inside. It was a wonderful prospect.

The Frenchman had travelled up from Chiapas, the southern-most state of Mexico, for a business meeting in the morning. He had quite a capacity for brandy. He'd insisted that the waiter leave the bottle and he very quickly cleared a third of it.

As he'd dismissed my Honduran waiter with a wave of his hand, I'd felt slightly guilty as I watched the man shuffle sadly back to the bar. I felt I'd betrayed him somehow, not just because I was drinking, but because, having happened across a fellow European, he seemed to feel he couldn't speak to me anymore.

The Frenchman and I chatted away for an hour or so. He was enjoying the resonance of his own voice, as it bounced against the pillars of the hotel. As an engineer, a builder of large structures, I suppose, he naturally enjoyed long sentences and big ideas that suspended themselves, like bridges, above the white water below.

'Chiapas', I said, 'is right down in the south isn't it?'

'Yes, bordering Guatemala. I have been down there five years working in the rain forest. If you make it that far down you should visit me. You would like San Cristóbal de Las Casas. It is like a city that has slept for a hundred years.'

I had read about the place; a city on the southern tip of Mexico straddling the pan-American highway, the road to South America. It was inhabited mostly by Indians and was the frontier with the great rain forests to the south.

'What exactly are you working on down there?'

'A road,' he said, flatly. 'Roads are tedious things to build – they don't have the poetry of, say, a bridge or a dam. It is just slash, slash, slash, for mile on mile.' He looked up at me and smiled thinly. 'But that, I'm afraid, is my expertise. Clearing my small portion of the forest. A glorious end to a long career.'

I cleared my throat. He seemed to want to justify himself to me. I didn't know what to say.

Suddenly I shuddered. What if when I met my father he was a crushing disappointment? An eco-villain just like this man? It would floor me. I hadn't really braced myself for this. I hadn't thought about anything like that at all.

'But, then, it's the way of man to clear the jungle, isn't it?' he said, making a swing for the bottle of brandy.

'I don't know,' I replied, coldly.

'It's his nature. Of all the achievements of mankind the clearing of the forests is the greatest, because it's the first. The second is to keep them clear. That we call civilisation. If God had really meant for us to live in the Garden of Eden he wouldn't have banished us from it and set us to toil the ground.' He held the bottle of brandy close to his face and stared for a moment at the label. 'This stuff is disgusting,' he said. 'It's like gasoline.' He called to the Honduran waiter for a different brand.

He laughed to himself. 'I build the roads that take the heavy plant deeper and deeper into the forest. I would like to retire, throw in such a thankless task, but so many men retire and after a couple of months of jigsaws and gardening they drop down dead in their greenhouses – once they've nothing to destroy, nothing to fight with. So I just have to continue practising my profession, or else I destroy myself. A dilemma, don't you think?'

I said nothing.

'And you, what brings you to Mexico?' he said, changing the subject.

I looked out into the garden and fixed my eyes on a dark palm.

'I've come to find my father,' I said, and gulped at my brandy.

4

I hadn't considered that my father wouldn't want to meet me. I hadn't thought that maybe he'd got a completely new life now on the other side of the world and that maybe my turning up might be something of an embarrassment to him. But it was too late for that now – Lucinda and I were on the train.

The train had its name painted on the side of the carriages. The name was almost as long as the train itself: *El Ferrocarriles Nationales Tren del Pacifico*. It was a grand name but let down, somewhat, by the train itself. There were no sleeping cars at all; there was no dining car either. The word Pullman (as used in the guidebook) was a gross exaggeration. The fact that we had first-class tickets merely meant that we were able to sit down and not have to stand all the way.

The thought of an oak-panelled Pullman had been the thing that had most appealed to Lucinda. I think she'd imagined it would be something like the *Orient Express*.

It wasn't. She was now quietly resolute. We weren't speaking this morning in any case. I'd come back to the room last night drunk and in the attempt to remove my trousers had fallen over. Then I'd tried to creep into bed with her and she'd knocked me deftly to the floor. As well as this I'd been bitten horribly by mosquitoes as I'd sat drinking with the Frenchman, and my scratching was driving her to distraction.

After an hour, at an eternally slow pace, the *del Pacifico* had travelled no more than twenty miles with nothing but flat mud between us and the little finger of the Sierra Juarez.

The carriage was a bit scruffy at the edges but was designed for coolness. The window frames and overhead racks were made of polished steel and the frames had venetian blinds sandwiched between two panes of glass, which you could winch up and down by a ratchet.

I winched mine straight up, much to the surprise of the Mexicans, and revealed a shattered pane that framed the mountains in a spiralling spider's web of sparkling glass.

In the ceiling there were great fans like ships' propellers, silent and motionless behind heavy grilles.

The antimacassars on the seat backs were filthy and most of the ties had been worn away, and the once white linen was studded with thick black hairs. But the seats themselves were as comfortable as old family sofas, and they reclined to a reckless degree.

There was a cast-iron claw for an ashtray in the armrest and shutters at the front of the carriage, which indicated that pretty soon they would be opening a bar on board.

I lit up a Marlboro and licked my lips. I liked its beat-up shabbiness and knocked-off edges.

When we entered the desert the venetian blinds started rattling in their glass sandwiches. The armrests began vibrating, and the drinks trolley, leading its steward down the aisle, set itself up as a sort of *avant-garde* percussion ensemble, joined by the lavatory doors, which burst into a spontaneous round of applause.

The fans in the ceiling at last began to turn. They had their own particular hum and wayward motion as if they were patiently working themselves loose from the ceiling, ready to take off the trolley steward's head.

As if it was because there was nothing else in this absolute flat waste, the steward wired up a tape cassette, with a bit of flex inserted into the overhead light socket, and entertained himself with some passionate Mexican songs.

I lay back into the seat and thought about the journey ahead.

Until just a few months before, I had known next to nothing about my father. His name was never mentioned in our house. All I knew was that my parents had been divorced just a few months after my birth, and, because of that, I'd always felt somehow responsible.

There wasn't a single photograph of my father in the house. The first dozen pages of our family album had been torn out by my mother. Whenever I was allowed to get the album down, from where it was kept on the top shelf of my mother's wardrobe, it was the torn pages that fascinated me the most. I would run my finger along the ruffled edges and try to imagine what awful images those pages must have contained to have warranted such a violent act. The tearing of pages from books, I knew from school, was one of the greatest and most inexcusable of crimes. Consequently as a young child, I formed a fearsome picture of my father in my mind. A man whose name couldn't even be spoken, a man who wasn't even allowed to have a face.

Other boys' fathers became a fascination to me and I viewed them as odd appendages to the domestic set-up, never quite fitting in with the natural running of things. They always seemed to have a special chair in the front room, and a chairman-of-the-board place setting at the dinner table. They had piles of 'papers' that mustn't be disturbed, and they got involved with clubs and enthusiasms that were regarded by their families as being like ancient mystical rites. They took up amateur photography at vast expense. They were as strange to me as the Wild Men of Borneo.

The experience of meeting Lucinda's family had impressed me greatly and I suppose, in some way, I wanted a history too.

Sometimes, as a boy, I'd be invited to stay for tea at a friend's house. I'd generally force such invitations by looking forlorn and hungry. But as soon as The Father got in from work I knew the countdown would begin and I'd soon be ejected from the house at the approach of the great man's dinner brought triumphantly from the oven and laid on the table as an offering. All eyes were on him as he took his first taste, and no one could relax until he uttered his benediction: 'nice drop of beef.'

Not having one of these great men of my own, I felt, marked me out from other kids in an England where divorce was not quite yet the norm in the families of every classroom full of children. I often wished my father had died because then, when people asked me where he was, I'd get sympathy, not just that quizzical look I got as people presumed I must have been the cause of the divorce. When other kids asked me where my father was I would always reply, 'He's in Heaven.'

'Is he dead?' they'd ask.

'No,' I'd say, 'He's God.' I'd been somewhat confused as a child by the daily prayer, 'Our Father who art in heaven'. For a whole term, when I was about seven, I harboured the notion that I very probably was Jesus, returned to earth for His second coming. It worried me when my mother lost her temper and threw furniture around – it wasn't how I thought the Virgin Mary should behave.

I was twenty years old before my mother finally made another mention of my father, and, when she did, she did it so casually that it took me completely by surprise.

We were watching television together one night and something on the news had set me roaring with laughter. My mother suddenly sat bolt upright and turned to me.

'Oh, that laugh of yours,' she said, 'you sound just like your father.'

She then told me a story about a time he was on leave from his ship, when they were first engaged. He'd suddenly announced after Sunday lunch that he had to report back to Portsmouth and he set off for Waterloo station. Two nights later she was listening to a comedy programme on Radio Four with her brother. Suddenly my uncle Sid looked up and said, 'Hang on a minute, that laugh in the audience – sounds just like your Ronald.'

'It *is* my Ronald,' said Mum.

She said she sat down and wrote to him: 'Dear Ronald, you know you said you only had a two-day pass this leave? Well I reckon it was at least four days because you were in the Variety Theatre, Scunthorpe, on the Tuesday.' He wrote back: 'How the bloody hell did you know that?'

As she finished the story she turned to me and said, 'And you know what? You've got the exact same laugh.'

I was shaken to the quick.

5

The cabin steward began dragging a large cardboard box up the aisle. Out of the box came lunch. Lunch in the desert in a polystyrene tray.

It was a kind of battered chicken, and there was a version of macaroni cheese with pork luncheon meat.

'Well that's a surprise isn't it, lunch?' I said cheerfully.

Lucinda looked into her polystyrene tray in disbelief. 'More of a shock, I'd say'. She slammed the lid shut again.

When I looked up from unwrapping my cutlery we were in Gustavo Sotello, a small town where about twenty more people boarded the train, all with bags and children, and the men were wearing huge white hats. The rattling of the train in the desert was replaced by the chattering of people looking at chits and fussing over their seat reservations. People who have been waiting for an hour in the sun want no more of it. As the train filled with people so it went darker as they began attacking the ratchets of the venetian blinds.

The nature of the *del Pacifico* had changed.

The women were going through endless bags and the men were standing back from it all, gripping onto the luggage racks to give everyone the benefit of their armpits.

The police came on board and poked at the baggage in the racks. They seemed to have a system. First they'd look at the passenger, then up at the rack, then back to the passenger. It seemed to depend on the result of this second look – whether the passenger *looked* like his luggage or not – as to whether their bag warranted a poke. People were visibly worried about the presence of the police. I reminded myself that this is a country where uniformed authority is ever-present, except for when it's needed, and that everyone stayed on the right side of the police. If you didn't they'd exact their *mordida*, or 'little bite' as the bribes are called.

They were poking the bags to see if they made a noise. If you had, say, a couple of hens in your baggage – something that the national railroad is known to frown on – then a damn good poke would probably reveal it.

'I suppose', said Lucinda, 'you'll now get us both arrested and we'll spend the night in jail.' She seemed genuinely resigned, and possibly relieved, by the prospect.

'Aren't you enjoying the ride at all?' I replied. She chewed on a custard cream that she'd sneaked out of her box.

We'd been going for only half an hour or so when a woman, all wrapped up in a brightly coloured blanket, crouched down in the aisle beside us.

'Señor! Señor!' she hissed at me and I looked down to where she was unwrapping something from brown paper.

'You want to buy this? You want to buy this?' she said. Then she landed an armadillo on my lap. I started and grabbed it, thrusting it back to her. Underneath its belly felt warm and hairy.

'No, no thank you, no thank you,' I said, looking around me for the guard.

'Good God,' said Lucinda, 'it's alive.'

'You want to buy my armadillo?'

'No, no. That's very sweet of you to offer, but no, I wouldn't know what to do with one,' I said. The armadillo looked up at me and sniffed. The woman smiled.

'You cook it, eat it tonight.'

'Thank you, but we've brought sandwiches, but thanks all the same,' said Lucinda. The woman shuffled off as Lucinda glowered at me as if it was my fault that I'd let the creature land on me.

'Go and sit across the aisle,' said Lucinda. 'You'll have got fleas as well now, I expect.' I didn't move.

As the desert came to an end it gave way to plains of cattle herds and *charros* sitting on their pale chestnut horses.

At four in the afternoon the train pulled into Benjamin Hill and was immediately surrounded by people shouting at us: *'Tortillas! Tortillas!'*

The women were selling their home-cooked chicken, the men their fearsome-looking *burritos* – pancakes rolled up with God knows what inside – and the old men and the children had cardboard trays of bubble gum, *chiclets*.

I got the impression that the entire economy of Benjamin Hill revolved around the two trains that stopped there daily. All the young men and boys were on the platform too. The eight- to ten-year-olds boarded the train and ran up and down the aisles shouting what sounded like 'Hello! Hello! Hello' – but of course they were actually shouting *'jello'* – ice. They carried saucepans, or plastic washing-up bowls, and in them they had ice lollies that had been frozen in small plastic bags with bits of twigs stuck in for sticks. I admired their enterprise. What the older boys were doing was unclear – they just seemed to jig around on the platform kicking each other up the arse. Lucinda looked on in a state of increasing misery.

The tortilla sellers paraded up and down the platform, shouting through the windows and blocking the steps from the train.

Lucinda was hungry but she wouldn't consider anything that the tortilla sellers had to offer. On the station was a small concrete shack with benches that advertised itself as a restaurant.

'Look at those!' she suddenly said, with her first burst of enthusiasm all day. Hung in the window of the restaurant was a mighty hand of bananas.

'Do you want them?' I asked. She nodded earnestly. I jumped up. 'I'll see if I can get them,' I said boldly.

I got out of my seat and went to speak to the conductor who was sitting in his own spot, four seats he had roped off with washing line, at the front of the carriage.

'How long are we stopping in Benjamin Hill?' I asked.

'Favor?'

'Benjamin Hill, how long?'

'Que?'

I began pointing to the station.

'Ben-ha-meen-ill,' said the conductor, pointing to the large sign that said the same in peeling sun-cracked paint directly beside the train.

'*Sí,*' I said and pointed to my watch and mimed the movement of the train by pumping my fists out in front of me. Now the conductor looked really confused. Was the man asking if there were strange wild animals in these parts? The bar steward came to the rescue and garbled the time in Spanish. I was now confused. Everyone in the carriage had begun poking one another to watch the comedy of the foreigner on the train. Lucinda buried her head in her book.

Then the bar steward reached into his pocket and pulled out an old strapless watch that had been worn smooth in his trousers. He indicated fifteen minutes on the face.

As I got down from the train I sensed a definite shift in the attitude of the tortilla sellers. Here, they could see, was a big fish landing in their lap, rich and juicy and gasping at the gills, tired with the slow progress of the great train, weighed down by his wallet, ripe for fleecing.

I stood on the train steps, looking from one to another. They stopped shouting at the Mexicans through the windows, and stopped parading up and down the platform, and surrounded me, all yelling together, '*Tortillas! Tortillas! Tortillas!*'

But my mind was set. A woman thrust her grey cardboard plate of dry flat food into my belly.

'*Tortillas!*' she yelled.

'No, bananas,' I muttered.

To get through this pressing crowd I'd have to be firm. These people wouldn't take no for an answer. I stiffened my body and tried to look as haughty as a new schoolteacher on his first day. I pulled the collar of my shirt closer to my neck. I stuck my nose in the air. I looked like a cat sniffing a fish being gutted on a chopping board.

They stared after me still shouting. There is no one more superior in the world than the man who doesn't want to buy the only thing you have to sell. I felt bad about it, but I knew that if I didn't come back with those bananas then everything would finally be over between Lucinda and me. I walked into the small chaotic restaurant and pointed to the bananas. The transaction was complicated, of course, by the hunger in my eyes and the impression it gave that I was willing to part with all my money for them. They were the most expensive bananas

I have ever bought. Finally I marched back onto the platform with the bananas.

The bloody train had gone.

I cursed the conductor and the bar steward. My suitcase, my travellers' cheques, and of course Lucinda, were all hurtling away down the track. I could see her as she leant out of the window, screaming and waving her arms wildly.

There wouldn't be another train for twenty-four hours, and I didn't have enough money for a hotel. This was a disaster. I could imagine what she was thinking right now and shuddered.

There was nothing else to be done, so I dashed through the crowd of tortilla sellers and leapt onto the track. The train was about five hundred yards down the line. I shouted, but the train moved steadily on.

The tortilla sellers turned to watch, whistling like parrots, and they fanned out along the platform to watch the show.

I began running, clutching my hand of bananas, so that they flapped and banged against my sweating chest, while the platform shouted, 'Run, *gringo*, run.'

I was determined to get back on that train but I ran with a certain kind of desperation. People seemed to come from everywhere to watch, some waving me on as I passed, some making graphic gestures, and a few of the lads abandoned their arse-kicking on the platform to have a go at mine.

Every time one of the bananas broke off from my flapping bunch, and went spinning down to the track, there were whistles from the people on the station and a cheer.

The rear of the train had an open platform, not big, but with a half-metal bar door to it, and, if I could jump, I could possibly grab on and haul myself up. It was the only thing I could do.

I got to within fifty yards of the train when it started to pick up speed. It was hard running on the track – not all the gaps between sleepers were filled – and there was disgusting, suspicious, black stuff too, which I leapt straight into.

I was likely to sprain an ankle, knock out my front teeth, break my ribs, lose everything on the train, and still have to spend the night in Benjamin Hill, lying in agony on a mud floor until the Swiss Air ambulance arrived. That was the way it looked to be panning out. I could still hear Lucinda's shouts and hysterical screams.

My heart was thumping, and I groaned, as the train stretched away from me. The whole trip was falling to pieces around me and I began to resign myself to disaster. Then one of the teenagers jeering from the trackside managed to kick me up the arse, and it served to spur me on. I made a final, desperate burst. The train, for some reason, wasn't going as fast now. The metal bar at its rear was burning hot when I grabbed onto it, and with an absolute act of will, while the trackside spectators booed derisively, I hauled myself up and fell headlong into the back of the train, astonishing the passengers, who pulled their aisle-playing children out of my frantic, tumbling, way.

But I still had two bananas left. I felt exultant. I stood on the rear platform of the train and turned to the station, lifting up the two bananas to them in a well-known English gesture. When I got to see my father this would be one of the stories I'd use to break the ice. And we'd laugh.

I felt I was a true hero and walked stridently back to my seat, turning to everyone on my way, laughing and half offering my hand for congratulation. I was laughing slightly hysterically. There was now a nervous edge to my inherited guffaw. Lucinda was standing in the aisle with the most peculiarly wild expression on her face, and her hair sticking out at angles where she had been tearing at it.

I dropped down into my seat and expelled all the air from my lungs. She sat down silently beside me.

'I got your bananas,' I said. She looked down at the two squishy yellow objects gripped in my hands.

Then, in a few yards, the train stopped and began moving slowly backwards into the station.

At Benjamin Hill, every day at this time, the train switches tracks to wait for the coaches from the Nogales train, further north. Our carriage slid backwards and stopped level with the platform once again. The tortilla sellers were in fits of laughter. It had been a good show from the *gringo* today. I had been quite an entertainment.

My heroic expression was gone now, as the *del Pacifico* hummed in the station with a contented burr having made a total fool of me. Lucinda returned to her book, and as she read she let out little groans.

The tortilla sellers and the kids hung around for quite a while, coming up to the window to taunt me, imitating the whistle of the train and sticking their chewed bubble gum onto my pane.

Very slowly I peeled a banana and chewed it, with an expression something like a camel eating sand. The other passengers were avoiding my eye.

Then there was a sudden blast from the engine's whistle, a great clatter which shook the carriage, and the engine, now uncoupled, pulled away from us, never to be seen again. We sat on the train as the sun went down. The tortilla sellers and the kids got bored and ambled away. Walking into the darkening narrow streets. No other trains arrived or departed; the business of the station at Benjamin Hill was done for the day; the restaurant closed and the lights dimmed. It seemed fairly certain that we would not be going any further today.

People remained calmly silent over the next hours, rustling in their seats, resigned to the torpor of their national railroad. Then the lights failed. The bar steward came out of the luggage store with a torch, opened up the shuttered bar and took out his pullover. Then he locked the bar and left the train. Never had I seen such an abject waste of a perfectly good cupboard.

The train was now without any crew, lights, refreshments, overhead fans, lavatory paper, or indeed an engine.

Dark figures of men, like those we'd seen at the frontier, started to collect around the train in the siding, moving slowly and menacingly, peering in at the windows silently, crossing and recrossing the redundant track.

With the absence of the sun, the menacing moon stole back its sovereign state. Something happens to Mexico when night descends. It's as if the day were only a show of brightness and beauty veiling the dark monster beneath.

The siding was beside a cantina, the roughest sort of bar, where women are banned and the men drink all their wages in one go. They are hard, bare drinking places where the men are real *hombres* away from women and children and alone with a chosen true company of liquor and dogs, trading cocks for fighting, demanding pesos with knives.

I could see the clientele of the cantina swaying in their drunkenness on the porch and falling towards the crewless train, with all its doors open to the night.

Finally, Lucinda spoke.

'Why don't you go and get us something to drink? I need to get seriously drunk,' she said. I looked at her and smiled.

'I'll watch the luggage,' I said. 'Why don't you pop over to the cantina?' At this point we almost laughed together, but Lucinda managed to fight back the laughter and began to sob instead.

6

Just before dawn, and without ceremony, the *del Pacifico* slipped clandestinely out of the siding where we had spent the most miserable of nights. I was still uncomfortably awake, but looking forward, today, to reaching our destination: Mazatlán, and the Hotel Belmar. I watched the crew as they returned and marched up the aisle checking off our luggage on bits of tatty paper. They looked remarkably fresh and I wondered where they'd spent the night. There must have been a nice little *posada* in the town.

It was impossible to see what sort of country the train was heading ignominiously into. There were no lights anywhere. There was just a dark flatness bathed in a dull light leaking from the crescent of a moon that hung in the sky like a blade. At least we had a moon back again.

At Benjamin Hill a new engine and the passenger carriages from Nogales had been added so that the *del Pacifico* was now a considerable length of train.

As the light came up I saw that there were two young people sitting a few seats in front of us. They looked to be about our age and were obviously refugees from the over-crowded Nogales train. I stood in the gap between the carriages, hovering before risking the *caballeros* – the gents' – and stretching my aching limbs. The young couple were sleeping quite languidly – what light there was seemed to have sought them out to lie on their perfect skin. They formed a picture so striking, with their limbs draped around each other, that they looked like figures composed in a Victorian painting. They were a good-looking couple and they looked happy with their journey, even as they slept, and, worse still, happy with each other. I was immediately, and intensely, jealous of them.

After the disaster of our unscheduled stop, and the awful night, I knew I was now in the most terrible trouble with Lucinda. I was about to be confined to a doghouse from which I could see no hope of release. All I could do was to put my chin on my paws and look doleful. I returned to my seat and met Lucinda's glare.

I took myself to sit across the aisle.

I kept myself busy, again, by thinking about the journey. It had been an odd course of events that had set me off to find my father. The whole thing had kicked off in a dull kind of way really. Then it had built.

My father had had a brother called Roderick. I'd never met him. Until I was about eight years old he had always sent me something at Christmas. Nothing extravagant: a book token or a postal order for two pounds. The value had always remained the same whatever inflation did. He was my uncle, after all, and I'd always presumed he did what he did out of a sense of duty. The previous November he had died. No one was more shocked than my mother when, on his death, he left me five thousand pounds. I'd always been told that he was mean and dull, and not worth meeting.

He was childless and unmarried and had saved all his life, and built up a respectable accountancy firm. I suppose he didn't really have that many people to leave his money to. He wasn't an adventurous sort and had remained all his life in the Lincolnshire town of Scunthorpe. I'd missed his funeral by the time I'd heard he'd left me the five grand, but I managed to persuade my mother that the least I could do was to attend the memorial service that was given for him in the week before Christmas by the Scunthorpe Chamber of Commerce.

Afterwards I was invited by his housekeeper, Mrs Higson, back to his house for some insufferably cheap sweet sherry. During the canapés and pleasantries – no one seemed to have really known him – Mrs Higson invited me upstairs. She had been charged with the task of sorting out his things. There wasn't anybody else to do it.

'I wondered if you wanted any of this,' she said, putting a small cardboard box into my hands.

'There's no one else'll be interested, and as he left you all that money I daresay he was fond of you and would want you to have his personals.' There seemed to be a sour note, bitterness, in her voice, so I didn't let on that I'd never met him, although she must have known this.

'Thank you,' I said. We stood for a few moments.

'You might want to go through it all before you decide. Your uncle was a bit of a hoarder. The boxes of bits and pieces I've had to go through you can't believe. Every cupboard's stuffed. I don't think he ever so much as threw away a sardine-tin key. He's left the house to the church so they want it cleared. I don't know what I should shy and what I shouldn't.' She sighed deeply and I sat down on the end of Roderick's bed and looked into the box.

It was full of letters. Letters from the town hall, and letters to the town hall. The business of an Alderman. I sat for some time reading through them as I listened to the slurping of sherry and the crunching of cream crackers from the parlour below.

Then I came to a bundle of letters tied together, all written on hotel notepaper with addresses in Mexico. Coming amid all the dull municipal correspondence they were rather startling.

I read them, one after another. It soon became apparent that the letters were from my father to his brother, full of his exploits in Mexico. At first they touched me with sadness because I felt that my uncle Roderick had so obviously been living vicariously through his younger brother's adventures. Then my father's voice began to come alive, and I found that disturbing. The letters were chatty and informal, but with no date at the top. Sometimes they just began, 'Hey Rod!' and signed off 'R'.

I bundled them up and took them with me, leaving everything else behind for Mrs Higson and the Church of England to deal with.

Over Christmas at Mum's the conversation frequently alighted on the money that Roderick had left me, and what I was going to do with it. I knew I couldn't tell my mother about the letters that I'd found and, more, certainly, what I intended doing with the money. I had already decided to go to Mexico with it, and take Lucinda. I felt Roderick had left me a double inheritance. I didn't know why he'd done it, but it seemed only right that

I should visit some of the addresses that my father had written to him from. I felt certain that I would find him.

That was all I had to lead me to my father and I felt there was a certain rightness to it. I had the feeling that I wouldn't have been left that money, that Mrs Higson wouldn't have given me the box, if the time wasn't right for me to meet my father. It wasn't a logical feeling, I know, but it was one that had overwhelmed me. But I kept my news a secret from my mother.

It was evening again, and quite late, when we eventually pulled into Mazatlán – the town where my father had been writing most of his letters from. I woke Lucinda up.

'We're here,' I said, 'We're finally in Mazatlán.'

'It can't get any worse, I suppose,' she said. The tropical night was heavy in the air. We were by the sea. We would be happy here, I hoped.

When we got off the train I showed the taxi driver the address of the Hotel Belmar printed at the top of a piece of disintegrating letter paper, my father's handwriting neatly laid out beneath. The letter spoke of some kind of business deal with a guy called Harry Koch and small talk about a woman that he knew here whom he called 'Princess'. The letters from the Hotel Belmar built up a lively picture of the place; a bar full of characters; business deals; Harry, and of course, the Princess.

As we arrived at the hotel it was, in some ways, enough for me that it actually existed.

I smiled at Lucinda. Lucinda looked up at the building.

The Hotel Belmar was a strange old place, with tiles and arches, quite grand, I suppose, but it had seen better days. And they'd been quite a long time ago. Lucinda looked around with a refined expression of disdain. Of the hotel's one hundred and fifty rooms only a few were in use, twenty or so. The others had been allowed to fall into such disrepair that their stucco ceilings and window frames had collapsed. The rooms were off high-tiled corridors with faded posters of long-dead matadors from Valencia and Madrid, their fleeting glory preserved in great woodworm-ravaged frames.

There was a long ramp of a corridor leading from the front desk. It was ornately tiled and stretched into the darkness of the vast hotel. There was a flight of backstairs dating from the days when the hotel had room service and bellboys and it was the finest hotel in Mazatlán, sitting here sedately on the line of the Tropic of Cancer.

Even the marble-faced clock above the reception desk had lost its spindly hour hand and it stared out from the wall suggesting that time here had been suspended back in the 1940s. All the corporate smoothness of the hotel in Mexicali dissolved instantly. I rather liked the place. Lucinda tapped the reception desk impatiently with her passport. Well, I thought to myself, I've seen her father's house – now she's seeing mine. Mine is much more exotic.

I tried to picture my father in this place and wondered whether he had been attracted by its faded beauty or whether the letters from here had been written a long time before. Perhaps he was still here. I didn't know. I felt an electricity in the air even as the dimming lights of the reception area dulled with the alternating current.

I began to rehearse in my mind the way I would walk into the dining room in the morning, find him at breakfast, and say—? I really didn't know what I would say. I had been toying, after my doubts at dinner with the Frenchman, with the idea of getting to know him first, and then judging the moment when I would break the sensational news that I was his son come looking for him in Mexico.

I smiled again at Lucinda and hoped that, perhaps, she might just make some small gesture: touch my hand, or kiss my neck, or say something unprovoked and supportive.

'My God, we don't have to stay here tonight do we?' was all she said.

'But it's my father's hotel . . .'

A man shuffled out after Lucinda had begun shouting. He was about eighty. He looked up at us for a moment and then plonked himself down in a chair behind the desk, exhausted. We checked in, which seemed to surprise the old man greatly, I asked if my father was registered.

'I would not be knowing this, señor,' he said. 'I am very, very new in this hotel.'

I smiled that the newest thing here was an eighty-year-old man with a comic book tucked under his arm. I asked for the register to be checked, but they hadn't bothered with a register for years.

We took a room on the fourth floor with a balcony that looked onto the small beach where the surf pounded the sand and the exotic shells that rattled against each other like discs of mother-of-pearl hung from wind chimes. It sounded reassuring.

There was no one about but a few shaggy old pelicans resting on the rocks in the moonlight. My legs were still shaky from the train. It was as if I'd been on a long voyage and had just stepped onto the dockside. We both felt the same, I guessed.

The room, like the reception desk, was clad in dark wood panelling, ranchero style. The beds were large and hard with a thin sheet and a loose purple coverlet. The pillowcases were a grubby yellow and stuffed with a cushion, the swirling pattern showing through the thin linen.

The electrics looked something like an experiment. There was enough naked flex pouring from the bedside lamp to set up a small telephone exchange, and for some inexplicable reason when you shut the bathroom door the light went off as you approached the lavatory.

Above the bed was a fan set in the low ceiling and made from beaten sheet metal. There was a dark stain running around the room at the level of the vicious-looking blades. I guessed that it had sliced up a lot of flies in its time and had flung their minced little corpses at the wall. To me this was Mexico as I'd imagined it to be and I was happy. I expected this kind of thing. I would have wanted nothing less. I laughed uncontrollably for a few moments. I looked up from the bed at Lucinda. She was pacing the room.

'So what do you think?' I said, probably foolishly. She walked silently out onto the terrace, and then she came back into the room.

'The sea is beautiful,' she said, 'but the hotel is unbelievable. Just look at this. It's just . . . it's just . . . I'm speechless. I'm not sleeping on those sheets. I'm going to sit up in a chair.' She sat down.

'Would you like me to unpack for you, darling?' I said, hoping to lure her over to the bed I was lying on.

'I don't want you to do anything for me. Nothing at all, thank you.'

'I think I'll just take a look around then,' I said. I wanted to drink in the atmosphere of my father's house.

The hotel was quiet, it was late, the bar had closed. I walked the unlit corridors of the old part of the building. There is no grandeur as potent as faded grandeur, I thought. At the end of a long tiled corridor was an archway, with a room at the end with its door off the hinges. I could see that it had once been the housekeeper's room. When they had a housekeeper. It still held a store of elaborate lace bedspreads and tablecloths standing in dust-covered piles and an old steam press was gleaming in the moonlight from a broken window.

The place had such atmosphere and an indelible dankness that pervaded everything. The stage was set, I thought.

My first night in bed at the Hotel Belmar was an odd one. The pillow seemed to be stuffed with nothing but air, and the thin sheet lay on me like the page of a newspaper. The fan made a noise like the blades of a lawnmower hitting stones.

When I woke there was the ringing of a church bell, and the sound of workmen outside erecting stages for Mardi Gras.

I collected my thoughts and walked out onto the balcony.

It was a stunningly beautiful day. The sea was silver where it crashed against the rocks of the point and a few children, on their way to school, were playing on the beach and screaming as they dared the waves to wet their shoes.

The little bay of old Mazatlán was rather as you would imagine Marseilles to have been between the wars. I took my daylight bearings. There were just two hotels, this and the Hotel Siesta. The Hotel Freeman next door stood derelict, but it still had an advertisement in stand-out art deco letters on the side reading 'Cocktails in Our Sky Room'. I pictured the place back in the fifties, filled with American men in loud shirts downing 'screwdrivers' after a day's marlin fishing.

It was quiet this morning, even though the town was preparing for Mardi Gras. Shirtless men were pulling the tired branches from the palm trees and cutting the hedge along the centre of the sea road, the *malecón*, making their town the best it could possibly be for their visitors, fellow Mexicans from the surrounding towns. They looked like proud, happy and rather conservative people. They drank their coffee at the restaurant below, read the papers and bid each other polite good mornings.

I liked the place: it had real resonance, and the solidity of a fishing town that had known its trade for four hundred years. A couple of miles further up the coast was the modern resort, with its all-inclusive hotels, but in the quiet of this bay you would never have guessed it. After Mexicali and Benjamin Hill, it was a haven. It said something about my father, too, that he had chosen this place, and of the quality of life he must expect.

I walked back into the room to put on my shoes for breakfast. There were sounds coming from the room next door. Gasping noises, and little screams.

I finished polishing my shoes with the small bathroom towel and went down to reception. Lucinda was still in the chair pretending to be asleep.

It was later than I thought. Ten o'clock. There was a young Mexican guy on the desk and it was as if the old timer had been rejuvenated at dawn.

'Excuse me,' I said. 'Am I too late to grab some breakfast?'

I motioned towards a long corridor, lined with old men sitting in rocking chairs, rustling newspapers, at the end of which I guessed was the dining room.

'Oh, I am sorry, señor. You are far too late for breakfast.' I looked at my watch.

'Our dining room collapsed twenty years ago after Mardi Gras.'

'Oh dear. Sorry to hear that. Where *can* I get breakfast?' I asked. 'Where does *everyone* take breakfast?'

'In the restaurant next door. The Fonda Santa Clara,' he told me.

The breakfast on offer was an odd combination of eggs floating in a hot chilli sauce. It certainly gave a kick to the day. I looked around the restaurant. There were half a dozen elderly Mexicans, and a handful of old Americans who were already drinking beer. I looked from table to table and made a couple of trips to the loo to look at them all close up. It was unlikely, I thought, that my father was among them. I hoped he wasn't. I was disappointed, but undaunted. It was late in the day for the tropics and my father would have breakfasted early, I thought.

There was something that had puzzled me about the letters that my father had sent his brother. They were inconsequential enough in themselves – just pleasantries and small talk about the weather – but at times it was almost as if he was writing them in code. Sometimes he'd just make a pair of brackets with a dash between, as if he'd like to say something more but felt that he couldn't. The addresses, when there were addresses, were invariably prefixed with a 'c/o', and the name following would be enclosed in quotation marks.

'C/o "F. Madagan",' for example.

I hadn't really paid any attention to it when I'd first read them – I was too excited by my find. But now I began to think that maybe he was a man in the habit of checking into hotels under false names. It was the only explanation I could think of, although it seemed very bizarre.

When I went back to the Belmar I checked with the man on the front desk. When I said my father's name he seemed to know it. But there was, of course, no register to check. I went back to my room.

As I put the key into my door I heard a shout from along the corridor.

'Hey, *amigo*, you here too?' It was the American couple that I'd seen on the train.

'Ah, yes, weren't you on the *del Pacifico*?' I said.

'Too damn right we were, derailed out of Nogales,' said the young man. 'Guess that's what held you guys up.'

'We were going to Guadalajara,' said the girl, 'but we thought, what the hell, get off by the sea, we'd had enough.'

We introduced ourselves. They were Todd and Jody.

'So, you on vacation?' said Todd. 'You got an accent, you're European?'

'No English,' I said.

'England? You're a long ways from home.'

'Yeah.'

We smiled at each other. Keys in hand.

'You were in the next carriage to us, and we thought we would come and speak with you,' said Jody.

'Well now I'm in the next room,' I said. Todd put his arm round Jody's shoulder and smoothed it with his hand. Lovers on holiday always want to meet other people, to keep the conversation going, I thought. I smiled at them broadly.

'And you're travelling on your own?' said Jody.

'No, no, my girlfriend Lucinda's along too.'

'Oh, right,' said Todd. 'We got the impression—'

'Yes, I expect you did,' I said, trying to draw the conversation to a close. They stood with their keys in their hands smiling. It was odd, introducing myself to people I'd heard tumbling on their bed only half an hour before.

'Well, maybe catch you later?' said Jody.

'Sure,' I said. Todd nodded. Maybe I could torture Lucinda with them, I thought, and they'd bore her so much that she'd find me interesting.

'Well, we're off to check out the beach. See you around,' he said.

I went into the room and brushed my teeth. Lucinda appeared in the bathroom doorway.

'Just look at the disgusting state of that hand towel,' she said. 'It looks like someone's cleaned their shoes with it.' I nodded and explained that I was going to do a bit of research about my father and maybe she wanted to go in search of breakfast. I didn't have the guts to tell her there was no dining room in the hotel and recommended the restaurant next door. Why didn't I meet her on the beach after her breakfast in an hour?

I went downstairs in the lift. It was a wood-panelled contraption not much bigger than a phone box, and it never quite made it all the way to the ground so that you had to jump the last eighteen inches.

In the hotel bar there were half a dozen old men sitting at a long black bar top silently drinking their way through the selection of hard liquors that were ranged before an old oxidised mirror.

The only attempt at decoration was three ancient sombreros caked in dust and cigarette smoke hanging from nails behind the bar.

The barman was younger than his clients, and had a finely groomed moustache, a crisp white shirt and perfectly greased hair. He was in sharp contrast to the shabby array of men. All of them were in their late sixties. I joined them on a high stool with a thick, shiny, cowhide seat battered by years of bums. I ordered the local beer, *'Pacifico'*, so that I wouldn't look out of place.

I looked down the line of men. They were all serious drinkers and they studied their glasses of dark liquid. A few stools away from me was an old salty seadog of a man. Every now and then he'd laugh out loud as if he had just remembered some ridiculous episode from his past. He had short cropped hair, ex-service style, and the brightest blue eyes sunk into his wrinkled face. He was drinking Pernod and ice and looked just like Popeye.

He was a very short man but it looked like the shrinkage of age. It gave him an excess of flesh on his face and his arms that was left over from when he was bigger, so that there were rich folds around his eyes and chin. He had a neck like a turtle's.

When he laughed again he turned to me and winked. It was as if he thought I had remembered the same thing at the same time too. I laughed for him. The man slowly got himself down from the bar stool and walked towards me. He dropped his fleshy hand on my shoulder for balance, and went behind the bar to spit in a small silver bucket. He returned to his seat and laughed again. There was a very attractive sort of twinkle to him. He looked like a seasoned old traveller still living a full life in his memories, somewhere deep inside a disjointed brain.

I leant towards him when he laughed again and held him with my eyes.

'Excuse me,' I said. 'Can I ask you, are you English by any chance?' He got off his stool again, wandered round to the back of the bar, spat in the bucket and said, 'You know what? The carnival doesn't start for another three days.'

I smiled. The accent was American.

'I thought the carnival was today,' he said, 'but it's not for another three days.'

'We will all just have to wait,' I said.

'Another three days,' he said sadly, and spat again. He came to stand by me.

'Do you live in this hotel?' I asked.

'I live here,' he said. 'I've lived here ten years – no, not ten years, seventeen years is it? How long have I lived here?'

'I don't know. I just arrived last night.'

'You live in the hotel?'

'No, I've just checked in.'

'It's okay. They let you have all your own things. They'll let you move in some of your own furniture if you ask them. Where are you from in the States?'

'England,' I said, now speaking up, realising he was hard of hearing.

'I went to England,' he said, and silently remembered it, and then laughed out loud. 'I went there when I invaded Normandy.'

'Well we're all very grateful to you,' I said.

He raised his glass of Pernod in a toast. 'But France is terrible. It's all bombed out. Not worth seeing now. Just a load of burned out jeeps.'

'My father knows this hotel. Perhaps you knew him. Ronald Morgan. Do you know him?'

'Ron Morgan?'

'Yes, Ron Morgan.'

'Ron Morgan,' he said again. 'Was he in Normandy?'

'He was in the navy, but he would have been too young for Normandy.'

'We was all too young. I was eighteen. It was a hell of a thing. He was in Normandy?'

'No, I don't think so.'

'He was killed in Normandy?'

'No.'

'That's sad,' said the old man. The years were obviously a confusion to him now.

'You've retired down here in Mexico?' I asked.

'It was a good time though,' he said. I supposed he was still talking about Normandy. It was obviously the single most impressive event in his life. The most impressive event, I suppose, in a whole generation's lives. Now it was the only thing his drink-addled old brain could recall. He stared back at his Pernod.

I hoped that my father hadn't been a member of this silent drinking club. It was hardly heroic. I patted the old man on the back and left the bar.

7

I walked down to the beach to where Lucinda was sunbathing with the American couple. As I arrived she looked up.

'I saw you in the bar as I came out,' she said. 'I see you found your father.' I thought that was unfair but I tried not to let her see it.

'Did you manage to get breakfast?' I asked.

'Of course I managed. It's hardly an Olympic event. Actually, it was rather good. Wonderful eggs.'

I was surprised – she was almost cheerful.

After an hour, greyish clouds came in from the sea, so we went back to our rooms.

'I really like Todd and Jody,' she said. 'They've invited us to dinner tonight. I've said we'll go.'

'I think they're trouble,' I muttered.

Lucinda laughed again. 'How can they be?' I shook my head. 'You know why they've come to Mexico?' she said. 'They've got the most brilliant idea.'

She seemed to be entirely mesmerised with our American neighbours. At least, I thought to myself, they've cheered her up.

So we went to dinner with them that evening. I wasn't particularly interested in their brilliant idea and I sat quietly looking out of the restaurant towards the beach. Work had resumed on the stages and temporary restaurants for Mardi Gras.

A debate was taking place around one of the stages where a member of the carnival committee was insisting that they take it down again. His objection seemed to be that they had inadvertently built it up around a lamppost and this would undoubtedly limit the scope of the *ballet folkloria*. How would the men be able to strut like bulls, and the women swish their dresses? The workmen were angry. It had been hot work putting it up – why take it down again now just to move it all a few feet?

The man from the committee lost his temper. The reputation of the town was at stake. He jumped up onto the stage and began making some exaggerated dance steps to demonstrate his point. Then he climbed down, got a mallet, and knocked out the corner strut. Slowly the workmen took up mallets, muttering among themselves, and took swipes at the stage as if it was its own fault it was erected in the wrong place. The whole thing collapsed very suddenly and the men leapt back. Some of the vital struts had splintered. It would never be ready in time now and the man from the committee wandered off down the centre of the street shaking his head in disgust. The workmen adjourned to the nearest bar.

'What do you think of the Hotel Belmar? Isn't it just amazing?' Jody asked Lucinda.

'Yeah,' she said enthusiastically, 'I love it. Much better than staying in one of these corporate hotels.' I couldn't believe my ears. At first I thought that she'd had a change of heart. Then I decided that she probably just didn't want to lose face in front of her new 'friends'. She seemed so happy to have exchanged my company for theirs.

At dinner, they were both wearing expensive clothes and I wanted to find out where their money had come from. I didn't have to ask, of course: they told me even before the main course arrived. For twenty-two-year-olds they were pretty well fixed, and they'd made all the money themselves. At the age of fifteen Todd had begun writing computer games. *Mega Star Wizard Fights The Universe* kind of stuff. He'd spent most of his time from the age of nine fighting electronic goblins and wielding laser swords in countless arcades. He haunted all the electronic caves downtown. He didn't quite express it like that, but that was what all his cyberbabble sounded like to me, as I pretended I was interested.

A few months before he'd sold up the games company he'd started with a friend for what he described as an 'unspecified sum'. Half a million bucks.

It was sickening how much money can be made in America when you hit the lowest common denominator so exactly.

Eventually I had to ask them what they were doing in Mexico. They suddenly became very excited.

'We've taken the big decision,' said Jody. 'We've thrown everything up – our jobs, our house – and we're going to live here. We're going for the Millennium Dream.'

'Blimey,' I said, 'The Millennium Dream?' They laughed.

'Too right it's blimey, mate,' said Todd doing a cod British accent.

'We just decided to get radical with our lifestyles. Like, there's no job security in the world anymore, so we just decided not even to try and chase it. Careers don't exist anymore.'

'And who wants to become part of a corporation,' said Todd, 'even if it's your own corporation? God, imagine being trapped inside a job you made for yourself? People are commodities. The boom's over. Now we're going with the Flop.' He was very excited.

'We're going to live in a hut on a beautiful beach,' said Jody. 'We've got the perfect business plan to do it. 'That's why we took the train. Planes are too fast. We wanted to slow down, smell the desert instead of just aviation fuel. So we're going to just travel about for a bit till we find our perfect place.'

'It sounds idyllic,' I said. 'And you certainly picked the right train to slow down on.'

'Yes, amazing scenery,' said Lucinda.

'The twentieth century is over,' declared Todd, dramatically, flashing his eyes and grabbing a handful of chillies. 'It ended in the mid-eighties. People didn't realise it at the time.' He stubbed out a cigarette. 'Once you've realised that, the rest is simple.'

We slammed down another round of tequila. I could picture them sitting in a hut by a white sandy beach connected to the world by their laptops. Surfing and surfing. Not that I understood anything about the information superhighway – I was still on the information gravel path.

I could see the lure of a dream like this. The half a million bucks would help enormously, of course.

'We're not giving up work,' said Jody, 'just our fixed economic base.'

'We'll just work the Net,' said Todd.

All they needed to make money was a telephone line into which they could plug their modems. Failing that a radio mast. They'd work only when they felt like it. They saw themselves as the New Lotus Eaters.

'But if you find your paradise, won't you get bored with it?' I asked. 'Isn't dreaming of it far better than actually getting it, and waking up there every morning?'

'That's the kind of crap they tell you at school to stop you from going searching for it. Any case, how could we get more bored than we are with the corporate misery of America?' said Jody. 'We don't want to get sucked into that. We could see it ahead of us.'

I wished them luck. Lucinda was entirely starry eyed. She thought they were real heroes of the modern age.

I went for a pee.

Eventually they asked us what we were doing in the country and Lucinda told them that I'd come to search for my father. I wished she hadn't – I wanted to give them the impression that I was just as footloose as they were.

'Really?' said Jody, looking suddenly serious. 'Everyone comes to Mexico for a reason, that's for sure.'

I smiled at her. I was getting drunk.

As we walked back to the hotel Lucinda proposed the idea that all four of us should travel together. Todd and Jody greeted the idea with enthusiasm. My heart sank.

I decided to make another stab at talking to the guys in the bar. Todd's hand was playing at his crotch and he said he wanted to turn in, so Jody and he jumped up into the lift. Lucinda didn't seem to want to join me in the bar without them, and jumped up into the lift as well.

I went into the bar where the same men were still drinking and playing games of dominoes for money. The long-suffering barman was chopping limes and wrapping them in clingfilm for the morning. He looked up, seemingly quite pleased to see me.

'*Pacifico, señor?*' He said.

'*Sí.*'

The old man I talked to earlier didn't appear to recognise me at all so I sat down near a table where two men were leaning back in their chairs not speaking after a game of dominoes. I got myself into conversation with them.

'So what brought you down to Mexico?' I asked.

'Why not?' said the fatter guy. 'I got it made down here. Beautiful beach, charming señoritas . . .' I wondered how much of these pleasures he was able to enjoy drunk the entire time.

'Anyway the damn wife ran out on me so when I got to retire I was my own man. Get my pension transferred down here to the bank, so I can sit and damn well drink myself to death. When I first came down I thought it would take two years. I've been ten years already. I blame the Mexican beer. It's got nothing in it that kills.' Then he thumped his hand on his chest. 'Trouble is, I'm built like an ox. I'm built like a buffalo. Look at those muscles,' he said, squeezing the flab of his arm. 'You arm-wrestle?'

'No, I'm afraid no, not often,' I said.

'Best thing, you can knock your drinks over.'

'You like it in this bar?' I asked.

'Like it? We're like a club, ain't we Hyram?' he said to the man across the table, still silent after his thrashing at dominoes.

'What's that?' he said reluctantly.

'I said we're like a damn club.'

'What club's that?'

'Oh forget it.'

'My father drinks in here you know,' I said casually, 'from time to time.'

'Is that so?'

'Maybe you know him, Ronald Morgan.'

'Morgan?' said the fat man. 'Welsh?'

'I don't think so.'

He took a solid gulp of beer straight from the bottle.

'Was he a big guy this father of yours?'

'I don't really know. I was rather small when he went.'

He turned to the other guy at the table.

'Hey, Hyram, you remember a . . . what's his name?'

'Ronald Morgan,' I said

'Ronald Morgan?' said the fat man. 'Drank in this bar. You remember him Hyram?'

'Ronald Morgan,' repeated the man in the button-down shirt, knocking dominoes onto the floor. It looked to be an awfully complicated process for him to get his brain started up. His eyes flipped from side to side, and he blinked heavily as he searched through faces from the past like slides revolving in a carousel.

'Ronald Morgan,' I repeated.

The mental effort being demanded of him seemed almost cruel in a man this inebriated.

'Ronald Morgan,' he said again, with a little more recognition. I'd never heard my father's name spoken, let alone repeated, so many times in my life. There was a peculiar thrill to it.

'Yeah, Ronald Morgan,' I said boldly and proudly.

'Well, yeah, you remember Ronnie,' said Hyram. 'He used to drink with us all the time. Speaking of which,' he said, looking forlornly at his empty beer bottle, 'this table looks like it's gone dry. Your father would never have let that happen kid. Whose round?'

Hyram had perked up considerably at the thought of another drink.

'Let me,' I said, without hesitation. I took their orders, beers with large spirit chasers, and went to the bar. When I came back with them on the tray I laid them on the table and they were snatched up like rations under bombardment.

'Now let me think,' said Hyram. 'When did we last see him, was he here for the last Mardi Gras?'

'Difficult to say,' said the fat man. 'We got a bit drunk at the last Mardi Gras.'

'He was a big guy,' said Hyram.

'Oh yeah he was a big, big, big guy. He had shoulders like a tree. He use to wear a hat most times.'

'Yep, a real big hat.'

'He drank . . . now what did he drink? Modelo Negro.'

'Oh yeah, Modelo Negro, the black model – that's a strong beer.'

'You remember Mardi Gras?' said Hyram snorting a laugh. 'You remember what he did?'

'Sure, sure . . .'

'He damn well jumped up onto one of the big floats in the parade. It was all kind of made from giant snakes and skulls and stuff, and he climbed right up to the top and kissed the beauty queen from Mexico City smack on the lips. And he never spilled a drop of beer . . .' The two men laughed. I was wide-eyed with excitement. The image of my father in a big hat climbing the float was thrilling.

'He had quite a laugh too. Didn't he?' I volunteered.

'Oh yeah, he could laugh all right. We laughed a lot with your father, kid. Let's have a toast to him, why not?'

'Why not?' I said.

'Damn,' said Hyram. 'We're all fresh out of drink again. What does this stuff do here, evaporate?' Everyone laughed.

'I blame the heat you know,' said the fat man. 'A drink don't last no time in a glass.'

'Too bad we can't toast,' said Hyram.

'Of course we can,' I said. 'Let me.'

'And of course Joe there knew your father. Joe, come over here and meet this kid. We're just about to toast his father. Ronnie, you remember Ronnie.'

'Ronnie?' said Joe, leaving his empty beer bottle and staggering over, dragging his chair on the tiles.

I was excited. It was like a riotous family gathering and these were my wayward uncles.

'What do you want, Joe?' he asked. 'The kid's buying.'

'That's decent of you, kid, let me think. Now if we're toasting Ronnie it ought to be something apt. I guess a mescal with a beer to wash the damn stuff down.'

I came back with the enlarged round.

'To your father,' said Hyram raising his quivering glass of Dom Pedro brandy in front of his face so that his features became condensed in the bowl, like the snout of a goblin, 'a fine *hombre*.'

'A fine *hombre*!' I echoed, my cheeks flushed, my heart beating solidly as I took a handsome swig from my bottle of Modelo Negro.

'You know who used to stay in this hotel all the time?' said Hyram. 'John Wayne. You know, the film actor John Wayne?'

'Sure, sure, and he used to stay here?'

'All the time. He liked it'.

'I suppose he must have done.'

'You know what? Your father and him were real buddies.'

I was stunned. 'Really?'

'Oh yeah. They used to shoot at cans together in the hotel garden.'

'And you know something?' said the fat man.

'No.'

'He was a better shot.'

'And the boy looks like him, doesn't he Joe?' said Hyram.

'Oh yeah, he looks like him.'

'Even drinks the same damn beer,' said Hyram.

'Same laugh,' I said, 'same beer.'

'Yep,' said Hyram.

I signalled to the barman for the same round again.

'Let's line 'em up,' I said, wanting to stay with these men all night drinking this way. I went over to the bar to pick up the tray.

The barman looked at me seriously for a moment.

'Señor,' he said, 'I can't help but hear the conversation at your table.'

'Yes?'

'You are buying too many drinks for these men.'

'It's a celebration,' I said.

'Forgive me, señor, but no. They did not know your father. They want you to buy drinks, that is all. They are mean men at the end of the day, waiting for a stranger to keep them drinking when their pockets are empty and so are their bottles.'

'I'm sorry,' I said, 'but my father did stay in this hotel. And he liked to drink, and they do seem to have known him, really.'

'And what would men like these remember?' he said. I looked back to the table where the men were smiling towards me like expectant beggars. It hurt. I had been taken for a ride.

What hurt more was trying to dismantle the mental image of my father as the big man climbing the float, kissing the beauty queen from Mexico City, shooting cans with John Wayne. Shit, I'd enjoyed the notion of it while it lasted, without imagining for a moment how ridiculous it all was.

'You mean my father never drank in this bar? His name was Ronald Morgan.'

'To be honest, señor, I wouldn't know. I pay little attention. It's the only way in this job.'

'But you don't get many Englishmen in here.'

'No that is true.'

I was clutching at straws as all the progress made slipped away from me. 'You don't remember an Englishman?'

'Señor, with respect, American, Canadian, English, when you're a barman in a place like this they are all *gringos*.'

'Yes I understand,' I said, sadly.

'Señor, don't let them take you for any more drinks. These drinks I shall add to their cheque in the morning for taking such an advantage.'

'Thank you,' I said.

Of all the men in the bar, this was the only honourable one. There was a look of sympathy in the barman's eyes, which suggested that, once, he too had been taken for everything. That was why he was keeping bar.

'I think I'd best go to bed,' I said.

'*Buenas noches, señor.*'

'*Buenas noches,*' I said.

That night I dreamt of my father, the image of John Wayne, in a low-cut dress and tiara, riding on top of a float waving, and of myself climbing up to kiss him while the crowd cheered and pelted us with bottles of Modelo Negro.

8

I woke in a bitter mood and didn't come downstairs until mid-morning as a protest against the bastards in the bar. Lucinda was already up and out. From the balcony I could see her down on the beach with Todd and Jody. I wore a hangdog expression of disappointment. I felt like emptying her suitcase over the rail into the street. Now that she'd found herself some new friends I felt that a *rapprochement* would be hard to ring out of her.

I threw myself on the bed. I thought of school in England, and of sitting for long afternoons in the music room. It was a room of uniformly dull decoration, depressing light, and the insidious smell of rosin from the store cupboard where the violins were hung up like sleeping bats. But I liked it there. There was a cello covered in chalk dust in the corner that had never been played. One afternoon it had managed to snap one of its strings entirely of its own volition. That was how I was feeling now. I felt like packing my things and leaving Lucinda, heading on out into the great hot country.

I closed my eyes. The cello string, when it had broken, had given out a vicious-sounding twang and a cloud of chalk dust, and had woken the class from our sluggish scribbling of meaningless dots on badly ruled staves. Then Snelson, the music master, had looked up and stared for a moment at the wayward cello. Then he stood and pushed back his chair.

He walked to the front of the class, and said gravely, 'Gentlemen, I'm in the wrong job.'

He picked up his pipe and pouch and walked out of the room. We never saw him again.

I wondered now what had prompted my father's departure.

I wondered why so many men of my father's generation had simply upped and left. Almost every week another family would leave our street, emigrating to Melbourne, or Vancouver, or Durban.

I wondered now, this morning, if Snelson had ended up not as I'd imagined – paddling up the Amazon river – but teaching scratchy violin to small boys in Bournemouth.

Because of the journey I was on, I found myself thinking about my childhood a great deal. I suppose you begin to do that when you get to around twenty-two. You've just about got enough of a life behind you to warrant a review.

I went downstairs to get some coffee. As I was standing in the reception area, my head thumping from last night's Modello Negra, the young guy on the reception desk called to me.

'Señor,' he said, 'Ramon the bartender has spoken to me. What was your father's name?'

For a moment I couldn't remember it.

'Ronald Morgan,' I said.

'There was an Englishman here a while ago. He stayed for quite some time. I think this is maybe the man you are looking for. There was, if I remember, some sort of a scandal with the Princess.'

'Princess?' I said.

The desk clerk smiled and laughed. 'The Russian woman that lives here. I wouldn't think it was much of a scandal, the Princess likes to blow these things up. She's Russian.'

I thought, of course, of the mention my father had made to a princess in his Mazatlán letters. I hadn't imagined for a moment that such a woman could possibly be resident in an hotel like this, fading and crumbling, as it was. I'd been so excited by the letters that I'd wanted to believe, I suppose, that he meant a *real* princess.

'How grand!' I said. 'I had no idea you attracted such an exclusive clientele.'

He smiled.

'In this hotel, señor,' said the desk clerk, 'she is a princess, and all the old men in the bar are war heroes and the old night porter fought with Pancho Villa. It's the atmosphere of this hotel. I'm sure you have noticed,' he said.

I laughed. 'There are an awful lot of Russian princesses in the world,' I said.

'We have been fortunate only to have the one. I don't think you will have seen her – she lives in the old part of the hotel.'

I expressed some surprise that people still lived in the older part.

'It is only her. She would not move out to the new wing when most of it collapsed. She barricaded her door with her closet until we gave in. She would not move because the ceilings in the new rooms were too low for a princess, she said.'

'She knows you all call her the Princess?'

He laughed. 'She insists upon it.'

'She sounds a bit of a character.'

'Ah, yes, she is completely mad. When she leaves the hotel she goes out from the back gate behind the pool and through the garden.'

Ah yes, I thought, the garden where my father shot cans with John Wayne. I flinched at my drunken stupidity.

'The old garden and the manager's house were sold many years ago to the doctor, but still she goes out by it. Every year the doctor writes to us to complain; we write to her, she ignores our letters.'

'Sounds like quite a little war.'

'Oh yes, señor, every Sunday she used to pick the doctor's flowers. That is why there are no flowers in the garden. To stop her the doctor has planted cactus. The sort that only flower once every twenty-five years!' He laughed. 'We say in the hotel that she won't die until they flower and she picks them.'

'How can I get to talk to her?'

'Oh my god, señor, it isn't easy. You have to write to her requesting an interview. We put your letter in her pigeon hole. Maybe she will read it, eventually. Maybe she will write back to you saying you can go up to her room.'

'It sounds like I'm going to have to be a bit devious,' I said.

'You'll have to be as devious as she is.'

I took some letter paper down to the beach to write my request. As the pelicans swooped down from their perches on the abandoned fishing boats, catching a fish every time, I searched for words.

It seemed particularly surreal to me to be sitting on the beach, in shorts, beginning a letter with 'Your Royal Highness . . .'

Jody and Todd came gleaming together out of the surf and walked up the beach towards me. Lucinda was behind them. She was actually smiling to see me, or at least smiling anyway.

'Hi there, how you doing today?' said Jody.

'Fine, fine. Nice day,' I said, looking up at the perfect blue sky with just a couple of white clouds scattered against it here and there. It was good to feel such strong sun on my face and I was feeling quite elated about the Russian woman. Whether she was a princess or not, she was the first tangible contact with my father.

'You're writing a letter?' said Todd with a talent for the obvious, shaking his hair so that spots of water blotted my page.

'Well I'm trying.'

'I'd write home,' he said, 'but the folks don't have e-mail – they just have snail-mail.' They squatted down beside me, Todd fingering the shingle out of his trunks. 'You're writing home?' he said.

'No, no,' I said. 'I'm writing to this woman who lives in the hotel who may have known my father.'

'Oh, neat,' said Jody. 'So you've got a lead?'

'I hope so, but it's a bit complicated.' Lucinda raised her eyebrows. She didn't seem to believe anything I said these days.

I explained that there had been some sort of a scandal, probably not much of a scandal because the woman was mad and claimed to be a Russian princess. But I was sure that it had involved my father. Jody and Todd were enraptured.

'Shit, man,' said Todd. 'Shit, a princess?'

'Well we don't know about that,' I said. I wasn't, whatever happened, going to be taken in a second time. Not after the old bastards in the bar.

I still hadn't finished my letter when I joined them for lunch at the Fonda Santa Clara. I couldn't think of a convincing enough reason to ask to see the Princess. I obviously couldn't just come straight out with it. When I got to meet her I'd have to build up to it gently.

'I think it's a real adventure you're on,' said Jody, and she touched my hand in a gesture of support.

'It's like you're searching for your roots or something. It's pretty elemental,' she said. 'God, if I didn't know where my dad was I'd have to go find him straight away.'

'I suppose it is quite elemental,' I said, trying to sound interesting.

'And you've written a letter to her?'

I explained the difficulty. If I said why I wanted to see her she might not want to see me. She was a difficult old bird. I had to think of something clever, some kind of ploy. Some reason other than my father to want to go up to her rooms. It was all too important to me to screw it up.

'Sure,' said Jody. 'It's just like when you need to get an interview with someone and they don't want to talk. You could always say it's about something else and then just try and stir it round. Just the kind of thing we covered in my term at journo school.'

'Journo school?'

'Sure,' she said. 'I was thinking of becoming a journalist and went to summer school.' She thought seriously for a moment and then looked up wide-eyed.

'You got some more letter paper with you?'

'Yes.'

'Pass it here. I have a brilliant idea.'

I watched Jody as she scribbled. She passed me her version of my letter.

'But how does this get me anywhere?' I asked.

'Don't you see? The letter's from me. I'm just an American journalist who happens to be staying at the hotel on vacation. I've heard wonderful things about her in the town. What an interesting person she sounds. I wonder if there might be an article in it. Perhaps we should meet casually for tea . . .'

'And where do I come in?' I asked.

'Oh,' she said nonchalantly, 'I take you along as my photographer.'

'And what are you doing "casually" on holiday with your photographer?'

'Well obviously I'm screwing you.'

Both Todd and Lucinda looked somewhat startled.

'It sounds like a very good plan actually,' I said, 'but I haven't got a camera.'

'You can borrow Todd's.'

Todd looked up. 'Well, sure, yeah, sure. I'd have to show you how to use it. Like, it's a pretty sophisticated piece of equipment.'

'I'm sure it is,' I said.

The mad woman did reply – she replied the next day.

'The Princess Ivana Shenka is pleased to accept your invitation to an interview at tea. Please be at my suite, 205, at 3.00 p.m. tomorrow. Do bring buns or pastries,' said her note.

'Well we'd better get some buns,' said Jody.

After lunch the next day, in an excitable state, Jody and I went to the market to buy the pastries. The market stank fearsomely of salted fish and animal entrails, and from the quiet conservatism of the old town streets we were plunged headlong into the atmosphere of a Third World marketplace.

Back in Jody's room we laid out the pastries, a selection of what they call *pan dulce*. Eight pieces in all. Sweet-covered croissants filled with apple and lemon curd. Soft iced buns. Lattice pastries filled with crushed sugared almonds and pecans. Fine little rolls with a shining dark glaze.

'Well I sure hope these will do for a princess,' said Jody, and she bent over to smell them to make sure that none of the acrid aroma of the animal entrails lingered on them. She was taking the escapade very seriously and I was grateful for that. But I was nervous about it. While it sounded quite a good ploy, it was very devious, and not something that I was convinced I could pull off with any grace.

'I'm sure they'll be very acceptable,' I said, fiddling with my equipment. 'She's obviously a woman who likes her little fancies.'

We laid the *pan dulce* on a pewter tray borrowed from the barman and set off up the ramp to the old part of the hotel like a bizarre re-enactment of the now defunct room service. I couldn't help but feel that our procession was a little surreal as I held the tray and turned to this young woman I'd met only days before.

'It's wonderful, it's just wonderful,' said Jody, looking up at the crumbling plasterwork and the high fractured doorways.

'It's *so* Mexico,' she said. I sighed with its beauty too. I smiled at her, a thank you for her support.

We knocked on the door and a small and deliberately frail voice from inside the room said, 'Hello?'

'Hello,' we replied through the wood of the door.

'It is open,' said the voice, which was, perhaps, faintly middle European. We opened the door and walked in. The door creaked and some plaster landed on the pewter tray.

'Ah!' said the Princess. 'You have brought *pan dulce*! You should not have troubled. It is so kind of you. So extraordinarily kind. I am lost for words. You are kind Americans. Kind Americans coming to an old lady. It is wonderful, so wonderful of you to come.' She was most obviously not lost for words. I smiled uneasily. Jody giggled nervously. She shouted her sentences so loudly that we were in serious danger of denture spray.

The room stank of old voluminous underwear, and cabbage. She was a small woman for such volume and she wore a black frock coat with tattered embroidered scribbles of an indeterminate design in red silk hanging from it in threads. I wondered if it was her best. Her hair was lumped on top of her head something like a skein of reused wool. Around her throat was a necklace of a heavy kind, a sort of battered metal which lay on the folds of her flesh like a barbed-wire fence. I thought of the guillotine.

Her hands looked as if she'd been kneading dough and her welcoming smile stretched between a pair of heavy earrings that were too weighty for her lobes. They forced her head into a queer attitude, something I can only describe as that of a frog looking up out of water.

'It's really great of you to meet us. I'm Jody Wannerkrutt, *Pittsburg Tribune*,' said Jody, with consummate confidence.

'Enchanted,' said the Princess waving her awesome ring-adorned hand in the air and allowing a pause for Jody to make a furtive, unrehearsed curtsy.

'And this is Dwight, my photographer,' said Jody. Where the bloody hell did she get *that* name from? I thought.

I stepped forward and made a short German sort of bow,

narrowly avoiding clicking my heels. The old bird adored it. I was feeling guilty and decidedly fraudulent already. This, I thought, had been a very bad idea.

'Do, do, sit down,' she said. The charade was almost too much. Who was indulging whose fantasy here this afternoon?

We sat down. The chairs were incredibly small with quasi-Louis Quinze backs made from a rough sort of redwood that had been badly varnished. It looked as if she had torn a page from a picture book on Versailles and given it to a local joiner to copy.

Although the chairs may have been a fancy, the walls of the high-ceilinged room were decorated in the grand style. Someone had once spent money on frames, a long time ago, admittedly, but there was definitely something of a cachet about them. Contained in the flaking gilt were prints of some of the great art works of the world: Leonardo's *St Anne*, Botticelli's *The Birth of Venus* and in the grandest and most monstrous frame of all was Goya's *The Family of Charles IV*.

Of all the pictures it was the Goya that seemed to be the most potent in this room, poor, disintegrating, worm-eaten, paper print though it was. It was practically now in monochrome – only the blues and the greys, the last colours ever to leave an old print, were remaining.

'So you are on vacation here in frightful Mexico?' said the Princess.

'Yes,' said Jody, 'from Pittsburg.'

'Ah Pittsburg,' said the Princess. 'To me it is a most beautiful name. It reminds me of my Russia and of St Petersburg, glittering by the sea, crowned with palaces, blessed with crispy air. I do not speak too fast for you?'

'No you're fine.'

'You will be able to write down everything I say for your newspaper?'

'Sure,' said Jody. 'When we begin the interview I'll use my micro-recorder.' We seemed to be committed to the thing now.

'You will record me?' said the Princess astonished.

'If you don't object?'

'Object? It would be wonderful, wonderful. I have never been recorded. Should I speak louder?'

'No, no, it'll pick you up just fine I'm sure,' said Jody.

'Will there be very much equipment when you record me? Will I have to be attached to something?'

'No, no, just this,' said Jody, pulling out a small electronic box of matt-grey plastic. She placed it on the table.

'It's miraculous,' said the Princess. 'You Americans bring such wonderful things from Japan.' She seemed to make this last comment to prove that she knew a thing or two about the modern world. She knew where micro-recorders and Sony Walkmans came from. She read magazines.

I looked down to the table to admire the miracle machine myself. I looked up sharply at Jody. She looked away from me. It wasn't a tape recorder at all. It was an electric razor. She was proposing to conduct this interview with a Remington Lady Shave. I shook my head. I could barely believe that I'd got myself into this situation. Yet I'd begun to trust Jody, and enjoy her company.

I began to twitch. This whole thing was bound to turn into a fiasco. I hoped I wouldn't have to make it worse by speaking myself. Jody had rehearsed me briefly in the use of an American accent, just in case, but it seemed to wander between states at will. All I could hope was that Jody wouldn't go so far in this charade as to switch the shaver on.

The Princess turned to me, bearing her fearsome decayed teeth.

'And are you going to take my photograph for your wonderful newspaper?' she said to me.

'Ah . . .'

'Yes, yes we will,' said Jody.

'I think I should be against the light, *chiaroscuro*,' she said, 'in the manner of the Italians.'

I felt dreadful about leading this old woman up the garden path and tried to satisfy myself that at least she was having fun.

'I have had my picture taken for a newspaper before,' she said proudly. 'The *Guadalajara News*. A paper for retired Americans, an esteemed publication. But it was a great disappointment to me. In the background of the photograph a disgusting man had his hand here.' She thrust her withering hand to her private parts. 'It was a distraction, I felt,' she said. She reached for another *pan dulce*.

It was going to be impossible to get this woman onto the main subject, I thought, and I stood there in abject misery.

'I do hope that your article will in some small way advance my sad cause,' she said. There was a spot of lemon curd on her chin. Even Jody seemed to be feeling uneasy now.

'Your English is very good, your Highness,' she said. 'Where did you learn it?'

'In bed,' she said.

'Oh, right,' said Jody, startled by her frankness. 'You must have had a very interesting life.'

'Yes,' she said. 'Record me.'

Jody made all the actions of switching on the Lady Shave and the Princess adjusted her hair as if she expected the clever machine to capture her appearance as well. We waited. She took a deep breath and then spoke.

'I was eight years old, and in a pale crimson dress, playing in the orchard of our summer dacha when I had my first lover. He was a count of seventy-two. In a high-wing collar and a shooting stick which he jabbed into the ground next to my little rope swing . . .' She reached out again towards the diminishing tray of *pan dulce*, Jody and I stood stunned and slightly mesmerised. It was obvious to Jody that the normal line of questioning, taught at journalism summer school, would have to go straight out of the window here. It was also obvious to me that her mind was filled at this moment more with imaginings than with historical fact. She was too young to have been in pre-revolutionary Russia. I looked at Jody and smiled for a moment. She smiled back – she didn't believe a word of it either.

'May I ask?' said the Princess, now with pecan nuts about her mouth. 'Has the interview begun?'

'Oh, yes, yes,' said Jody.

I listened as she talked about her childhood in St Petersburg, which would already have been renamed Petrograd, or even Leningrad, by then. She gave the impression that her family had clung onto a life of dances and salons long after her father had gone into the labour camp in the Steppes. It all had the air of something picked up from magazines and movies. The more interesting story would have been why she was still here in Mexican exile two years after she could have legitimately gone home to an ostensibly democratic state. Perhaps she didn't know.

Her face was sandwiched between a top knot of yarnlike hair and the shrapnel necklace. She obviously thought that she was something of a diva, but she looked more like an ageing English piano teacher. The sort that murders the *Moonlight Sonata* every night before bed.

Once, perhaps, she had been a fine and handsome woman, but the sun had got to her skin, and she'd let herself go. I couldn't imagine that she'd been my father's lover.

Jody asked her why she had chosen Mexico for her exile.

'My plan was to go to America and live in a condominium,' she said, 'and so I came here to Mazatlán, clandestinely, to wait to cross the border.' Her eyes flared with the drama of it. We nodded.

'And when this article is read by the good people of Saint Pittsburgh they will say "let her come!" no?' she said.

Even though she seemed to dream most of her life, her dream to live in America was real.

'This country does not know how to graciously receive royalty. Sometimes I think of the Emperor Maximilian and his young beautiful wife, sent here by the French, and I weep. The hairy bastards shot him.' The old dry wood in her chair back creaked sharply and flakes of croissant flew into the air. She reached for another. This time one with icing. Her bony hand gripped it like the head of a baby being forced to the breast.

'But in my heart,' she said, bringing her iced bun up level with her cleavage so that crumbs tumbled in, 'I know the time is coming when Russia will live again now the awful bloody revolution is over.'

Both Jody and I were suddenly moved by the sadness of her dreams.

'How many years have you lived in the Hotel Belmar?' asked Jody softly.

'Too many years,' she said. 'Too, too many years in this hole inside a hole in hell.'

Then she began to make great sweeping gestures in the air

as if she was about to go berserk. I think we both felt that we were going to lose her. After her few moments of lucidness, her jewellery had begun to rattle and it looked as if she was about to descend into a mental maelstrom. The whole thing was leaving a sour taste in my mouth. The more I watched the woman bung down buns, the sicker I felt. There was an overwhelming sense of abuse, gluttony and decay.

'In my article,' said Jody, trying to pull it back, 'I'd like to paint a picture for my readers of your life here in the hotel. The hardships a princess must face in a Mexican exile.'

'Ah the hardships of exile!' she replied. 'The heat, the dust, the burning sun, the battle with the banks, the lateness of the laundry. I long for snow, pure driving snow . . .'

'And the people you have met here over the years, those that you have shared this exile with, have none of them been supportive, none of them reminded you of Europe?' said Jody. Ah ha! I thought.

'Common people,' she replied. 'Drunken Canadians and dying Americans who pee-pee on the sawdust of the floor.'

'Hasn't there been anyone who would know your station?' she asked. I was impressed.

'No, not one,' she replied dramatically, chewing her iced bun as if it had suddenly turned into a painful memory.

I became suddenly agitated and wanted to leave. I'd had too much sun on my head that day and it had given me a throbbing, sickly, headache. I felt woozy and was finding it hard to think straight. The stench of the offal in the market returned. I could smell the sticky sweetness of the rabbits' guts again and I began to sway.

'Don't you remember an Englishman who lived here,' I said, 'called Ronald Morgan?' I wanted to draw the whole nauseous charade to an end.

The Princess's face froze like pack-ice.

In the heavy obdurate silence my eye was caught by the smallest of lizards – a newborn gecko – flashing across the wall from behind a flap of flaking plaster. It stopped suddenly against the wall like a rubber-suction-tipped arrow from a child's bow.

Motionless.

I looked back at the Princess. She was staring into space in a slight state of shock. Her mouth was open as if she was hoping to catch a fly, like the lizard, now that the *pan dulce* was all gone.

'Perhaps this would be a good moment to take our photograph?' said Jody, brightly, trying to recover the whole thing.

'A photograph?' said the Princess slowly.

'Sure,' said Jody. 'Nobody in America reads an article unless there's a photograph.'

'Of course, of course,' said the old woman, instantly brightening, and she began swiping at the crumbs of the *pan dulce* on her frock. 'Should I be in front of the window – to show Mexico behind me – or should I be before one of the paintings? The da Vinci or the Goya perhaps?'

'Well,' said Jody, pointedly turning to me, 'you're the photographer, what do you think?'

'The street outside is too bright,' I said. 'The Goya, I think.'

'Ah yes', said the woman, standing to adjust the whalebones in her corset, and puckering her lips and pinching her cheeks into a blotchy pinkness, 'my distant cousins.' She cocked her chin into the air. 'You see the likeness?'

I positioned the camera and took pictures as well as I could while she posed. She looked like an old actress dressed as a fairy godmother for publicity shots of a provincial pantomime.

'You don't need a tripod or lights?' she asked.

'Not these days,' I said.

'The camera is very small.'

'It's Japanese,' I said, 'It's bigger inside.'

9

At seven o'clock in the evening a couple of days later a maroon was fired from the roof of the hotel. Mazatlán was filled with visitors from all the surrounding towns. They arrived on horses and mules and sitting in the backs of trucks on top of thousands of fresh green limes that, like themselves, were heading for the bars.

They were excited, thumping their horns and throwing confetti into each other's eyes. The men were in their best white hats and the women in splendid floral frocks. As they lined the *malecón* they looked like a great moving herbaceous border.

Mardi Gras was their last blast of eating and drinking before the abstinence of Lent and the build-up to Easter when they would have to go to church every day. The air was heavy with excitement and I was looking forward to seeing something of mad noisy Mexico.

The street below was noisy with fire crackers. I thought about our equivalent festival in Britain: Pancake Tuesday. It didn't have quite the same ring to it. How I'd managed to get excited about it as a child I didn't know. Perhaps it was because my mother would always screw up the flipping of the pancake and it would invariably stick for a few delicious moments to the fluorescent strip light on the kitchen ceiling, and then drop with a great slap onto the lino.

I stood, sipping a margarita from a toothmug, looking over the balcony. I could see Lucinda taking up her place in a makeshift restaurant from where she was going to watch the parade. Behind her there was a sign nailed to the bar banning handguns on the premises. It seemed rather apt.

I heard sounds of movement from Jody's and Todd's room. I stood up and walked to the low dividing wall between the terraces and called.

Jody came out.

She was wearing a bathrobe and her hair was in a towel. Water glistened on her face and caught the lights from the street, sparkling in a rainbow effect.

'I've made a jug of margarita, just wondered if you wanted to watch the parade from here and share it,' I said, 'as it's party night.'

'Well sure, we'd love to join you. Just give us a second and we'll be over.'

A few moments later, still glistening wet and wearing a silk sarong, Jody leapt over the dividing wall. I handed her a margarita.

'No Todd?'

'Oh, he's having one of his everlasting showers. He doesn't like the people that've checked into the room next to us so he's trying to use up all the hot water in the hotel.'

She sat down in the leather-upholstered throne-like chair next to me. If Lucinda looks up from the restaurant now I shall wave, I thought, and maybe she will be jealous. She'll see how successful my jug of margarita was. Not just another excuse to get outrageously pissed.

Beneath us the Paseo Olas Atlas was alive with people, and the anticipation was growing as they looked up to where the parade would begin.

Jody and I looked at each other and smiled. She had forgiven me for screwing up the interview with the Princess. She wasn't the sort of person who bothered herself with recriminations.

'Isn't this living?' she said, excited.

'Well, yes,' I said, 'I suppose it is.'

She looked at me in my jacket and tie, and laughed. I knew why. She guessed that in some respects I was playing the part of the Englishman, the cold fish caught up in all this heat, stranded on the beach gasping. I'd just thought it would be fun to dress up for Mardi Gras. It was a good setting for it too, in our ridiculous baroque chairs. She seemed to like it enormously.

In the distance the lights of the front of the parade were

bearing down on the *malecon*. A shining truck was hauling a wild creation in fibreglass. We watched as the elaborate seashell in glittering turquoise approached, with young boys in gold lycra shorts waving tridents, and attending a beauty queen thirty foot up on the wavering edifice.

'You know,' said Jody, 'that kinda reminds me of the house that Todd and I just finished building back home.'

I looked again at the seashell and the floodlights and laughed.

'We had to have this security system installed. You know the kind of thing: anyone steps onto your property in the night and *bam*! All these floodlights come on like you're trying to escape from a Nazi prison camp or something. It used to scare the hell out of the dog when it went out to pee.'

'You built a house? And you just threw it all up and came down to Mexico?'

'Yeah, looks like we did.'

I shook my head.

'I don't know that I'd have the courage to do that,' I said.

'Courage doesn't come into it. It would have killed us anyway. We'd have started spending our weekends repainting the weatherboard, and sooner or later Todd would have found an excuse to fall off the roof. That's what people with their own homes do.'

We looked down to the beach. The pelicans, affronted by the sudden noise of the crowd, had retreated disconsolately to the fishing boats anchored in the bay. They sat there sulking, shaggy against the reflection of the lights. The drums of the salsa band at the head of the parade filled the air.

'So you two have been together for a while?'

'Yeah, I guess. I met him the week before I was due to get married. The guy I was marrying was a mechanic in a bike store, all muscles and grease and hair that smelled of gas. But I thought I was pregnant. What I was really, of course, was paranoid. I've always done well in class. People back home, well, they don't like their women too clever. Like when they're in films and things, you know, the clever woman is always the one with the glasses and her hair tied up. Never the one with the dyed hair and the big jugs. So rather than tie up my hair, I guess, I thought a bit of grease and muscle would make me one of the girls again. Also, he had a huge Thomas Jefferson.'

I offered her a bowl of crisps but she brushed it aside and reached for the jug of margarita.

'Then along came Todd, a week before the wedding. My mom goes crazy and Todd and I go surfing.'

The first float came level with us. It was the home beauty queen, from Mazatlán, waving sedately and acknowledging the cheers and wolf whistles of the townsfolk. Then suddenly the beauty queen looked up, directly at me, and blew a kiss. For a moment I tingled. I remembered the story of how my father had supposedly climbed the float to kiss Miss Mexico City with a beer bottle in his hand. I raised my toothmug.

The beauty queen passed and Jody laughed. Then she touched my arm and blew me a kiss as well.

'Aren't you hot in that jacket?' she said.

'I'll survive,' I said. 'It's all that's left of the British Empire.'

I told her how I'd had to go with my mother to all sorts of dos. Family weddings and the like. In the absence of my father I was her escort, hanging on her arm, as we promenaded the room. I'd be dressed in a stiff little bowtie looking like a puppet announcer from the BBC. I told her about the time I'd found a black felt pen at a wedding and had given myself a neat little moustache in the toilets. I would have been eight at the time and I'd thought that the moustache would make me look older, and terribly distinguished, and my mother would be pleased. Instead she slapped me round the back of the legs for making a fool of her. We'd already toured the ballroom twice before she had noticed it.

Jody's home state was California, but they'd built their house just outside Pittsburgh. I was surprised.

'Yeah,' said Jody. 'That was something of an upheaval too. But that's where Todd comes from, where his business was until he sold it. I was getting too stressed out in San Francisco anyhow.'

Then she told me about a February morning in San Francisco two years before. It was the morning of a minor earthquake when a piece of freeway intersection had collapsed on a small car. The driver of the car was an old high school friend of Jody's and she was killed. A beam of concrete had taken her head clean off. Jody shuddered as she spoke about it and she shivered, as though a clammy coldness had spread through her body. I put my arm lightly around her shoulder for a moment.

She told me how again and again in her waking dreams she saw that little car being crushed.

'But in my dream it's not my friend in the car,' she said. 'It's me.'

The death of her friend had bemused and disturbed her greatly. If a heavy truck passed her condo and the floor shook she was seized by panic, she said. Her fear of another quake had become almost obsessional. It was the illogical nature of it. Of the world itself being so fundamentally unstable. It gave her a distrust of the ground on which she stood, of the condo she lived in, of the streets and the freeway. She couldn't get it out of her mind. Everyone in San Francisco knew, she said, that one day the Big One would come, but they seemed somehow to manage with the idea. She couldn't. It had already come too close. 'My life is unstable enough without it,' she said.

She told me how countless people had written in to the newspapers to say that four seconds before the earthquake struck their pets had gone crazy and had hidden under tables.

I tried to picture the scene. Dogs tethered outside K-Mart stores straining on their leads; strays on waste tips hunting in packs suddenly freezing; guard dogs running the length of their chains; chihuahuas at coffee mornings disgracing their mistresses; the mutts in the dog catcher's van trying to warn the driver. Then there were the parakeets shrieking and flapping in their cages, bending the bars, beating their beaks on their mirrors, overturning their water baths.

'Everyone I knew bought little dogs.'

I tried to take it seriously. 'Presumably', I said 'because little dogs are nearer to the ground.' Then she confessed that this was why she'd bought her Yorkshire terrier. I asked her why the dog didn't make her feel any better.

'Because every time I came in the house it went berserk, hid under the table and barked its head off.'

We held each other with our eyes, before laughing again. I was beginning to like her enormously.

Todd arrived on the balcony, his hair perfectly coiffed. I was disappointed. I would have liked my conversation with Jody to go on for longer.

He was in a white silk shirt that flapped loosely around him.

Jody's expression changed as her eyes left mine. She reached up her hand to him and stroked the silk of his shirt with her palm. I looked out into the street again, trying to see Lucinda through the crowd.

Then Todd looked out.

'This is the parade?' he said, pouring himself a margarita. There were only two chairs so he straddled his legs over the terrace wall. The Mexican family on the next terrace turned to look at him and the teenage daughters began to blush and giggle in high-pitched voices. He smiled at them and the young girls began hiding behind their hands. He looked out into the parade, a cigarette between his teeth.

Then the crowd erupted in cheers as the grandest float of the parade arrived. On top was the pride of Mexico, the reigning Miss World, a girl from Mexico City. Her face was on all the carnival posters; on all the beer promotions, and on the life-size cardboard cutouts in the photo processing shops.

Miss World's float was, quite inexplicably, a great fibreglass Hindu temple surmounted by a purple elephant. She sat on top of its curling trunk with little girls, hopeful no doubt of such future glory themselves, clinging to its ears. It was like a medieval morality painting.

'It's quite a thing then, this Mardi Gras,' said Todd.

'Quite obviously,' I said.

'It's been wonderful,' said Jody. 'We haven't been able to keep our eyes off them.' She was a little drunk, I thought, and overcompensating for the way we had been looking at each other. I detected a thrilling sense of guilt in her voice.

The crowd were going wild. The flashbulbs of their cameras were blinding and all the men and boys were calling to Miss World for her to look in their direction.

As she came level with our terrace she looked directly at Todd, showing all her perfectly corrected teeth. She smiled at him broadly. Todd returned the compliment.

As Miss World passed, Jody looked down on her wryly.

'By the end of the parade,' she said, 'that face is really going to ache.'

Then the door to the room opened and Lucinda walked in. She came out onto the terrace.

'Hi,' I said. 'Enjoying the carnival?'

'Sure,' she said, 'sure. Daddy took me to the one in Rio. Now that's something.'

I shook my head. Why can nothing ever please her? Why is nothing ever right?

I looked along the row of balconies, sooner than meet her eyes. At the end of our floor was a solitary figure, standing and waving to the crowd. It was the Princess. No one was waving back of course – she seemed to be in a fantasy all of her own. On the balcony of the Winter Palace perhaps. But at least she was enjoying herself, making the best of it. That this wizened old woman was accepting the adoration directed towards the reigning Miss World was, I thought, a triumph of the human spirit.

When the last of the parade had passed, with a hundred men in sombreros playing guitars, the serious drinking began. I'd seen the beer arriving by the truckload for days. Every restaurant was stacked up so that you could barely get to a table. Even the old dining room of the Hotel Belmar had sprung again, probably unwisely, into a temporary life of white plastic tables and chairs, with boxes of beer stacked between great slabs of ice.

I looked towards the Princess again. I had unfinished business there. I tried to catch her eye so that I could raise my glass to her.

'Would you excuse me?' I said to everyone, picking up the jug. 'I'm just going along the corridor to give that daft old bird a drink.'

'This is not my room, you know,' the Princess took pains to say when I walked in. 'My rooms are in the grander more exclusive part of the hotel, and of course I am only a temporary guest.'

I liked the way she said 'rooms'. She must have included the lavatory.

'This accommodation,' she continued, 'is loaned to me by the management from which to view the fiesta. From here I can witness it all privately.'

'Yes,' I said, 'I realised that. I have been to your rooms in the grander more exclusive part. I am the young man that came to see you for tea and to take your photograph. I wondered if you might like to join me in a margarita?'

'They're extremely alcoholic,' she said, imperiously.

'I'm afraid they are.'

She held out a plastic mug that she'd been using to drink coffee from a thermos. She slopped the remaining coffee over the balcony into the street.

'Don't spare the horses,' she said. She motioned for me to sit down on one of the ancient cracked-leather chairs. She looked like an old Venetian doge in drag.

We watched the dancing in the street for a moment and then she said, 'Tell me, are you the young man that came to photograph me?'

'Yes,' I admitted, 'I am. I wanted to talk to you about a personal matter, and ended up getting talked into a ridiculous charade. I thought I owed it to you to explain.'

Her eyes lit up. 'Ah! Intrigue!' she said. 'All the time I am in Mexico people have tried to gain access to me. Secret service men I suspect. I knew they were the KGB. I made love to several of them. Are you KGB?'

'No,' I said, 'I'm nothing at the moment. I've just left university,' I said, 'but it's true that I did come to visit you under false pretences.'

Her eyes sparkled and she gave a shriek of excitement. I hoped a bit of mystery would focus her mind. She wasn't exactly mad. She had merely indulged in a life that wasn't truly hers.

'I'm actually from England, and I'm here looking for my father, who I've never met.' I said, 'and I think you know a great secret about him.'

I said this as dramatically as I could, hoping to engage her.

'You do?' she said, extending her drained plastic beaker to my jug.

'His name was Ronald Morgan.'

'Ah, yes,' she said, 'you spoke his name when you came to photograph me and now I look in your eyes as I did then and I think, ah yes, they are the same eyes, and your face, and the way your jaw is here . . .' She stroked her hand across my chin.

'Charming, devious . . .' she said. I shuddered as the flesh of her hand touched my face.

'So you did know him? He was at this hotel?'

'He drove me almost mad,' she said.

She stared into space for a moment as a rocket was fired by hand by a dark figure on the beach. As it burst into spirals she shook her head and looked at me directly as if so much of the past had rushed back. She looked for a moment as if it had overwhelmed her in a great crash of tide.

'Ah, he was a handsome rogue, a devil!' she said, looking down to where the figure on the beach was throwing another rocket into the dark sky. Her head wobbled for a few moments as she focused on him.

'Do you like fireworks?' she said.

'Yes,' I said. 'We only let them off on one day of the year in England, and then only for the most obscure of reasons.'

'Oh, I'm sorry to hear that. I love them, so I couldn't ever live in England.' I was charmed by her. It wouldn't do any good if I rushed her. 'Sometimes at Mardi Gras they fire them on the beach and they go out of control and hit the hotel. We run from the balconies. It's fun, no?'

'Yes, it's fun,' I said laughing.

'It reminds me, of course, of the revolution. I wasn't there, you understand. I am far too young. But I have seen it on newsreels and it is just like being there, except for the music they put on it of course – there would not have been an orchestra.'

'No, I suppose there wouldn't. Tell me, when was my father last at the Belmar?' We watched another burst of pacific gunpowder showering over the sea.

'One day he was here and the next gone. His bill was left unpaid at the front desk. They didn't tell you this at reception?'

'No mention of it.'

'It surprises me they didn't make you pay it. They charge me through the teeth for my laundry and still they steal my drawers for souvenirs.'

'But he just disappeared?'

She looked at her empty beaker sadly. 'Yes, just disappeared,' she said. I topped up her glass.

'But why?' A wayward rocket careered into the roof of the hotel. I was losing her. 'Why did he suddenly disappear from this hotel?' I asked, a little more insistently.

She looked out to sea. 'I don't know. It was unexpected. I thought that he would take me to America. The afternoon he left I screamed from the balconies but he didn't even look back. I knew from my stars, you see, that we were destined to have become lovers.'

I smiled to myself. Another rocket hit the cornice of the hotel and plaster showered into the street below.

'And he left town?'

'Yes. Vamoose. You are not the first to come looking.'

'Who else has been looking?'

'When I interviewed them I received the impression that they were the CIA. Their trousers are so much better cut than the KGB, don't you think?'

'Where did he go?'

She looked down to the beach where a man was throwing another rocket out across the bay. 'Where do those burned-out rockets go after all their big fizz and sparkle? You never see where they fall to the ground do you?'

I found myself staring into the throng of people in the street as if my father might be among them, returned for Mardi Gras, weaving anonymously through the crowd.

The Princess was exhausted now after such an extended outburst of cogency. Her eyes were circling in their sockets in sad confusion.

'You have no idea where he might have gone?' I asked.

'Who? Who has gone?' she said.

10

The next morning we tried to get breakfast at the Fonda Santa Clara but it was closed. No one had turned up for work.

The plants in the centre of the road that had been so meticulously clipped and pruned looked as if a herd of bison had passed by. The terracotta planters which lined the *paseo* were smashed. There was soil and broken roots across the pavement. The remains of restaurant chairs were everywhere, like dismembered limbs. The shutters of the shops were pulled down, and where there were no shutters the shop fronts had been stove in.

There was the smell of beer mixed with urine everywhere. The ground was scattered with spent shell cases from where the men had been drunkenly firing their pistols into the air. The street dancing had gone on until dawn.

The lobby of the hotel, to which we returned, stank of sudden sickness. The floor was awash, and the lift had finally given up the ghost.

'We can't stay here. We can't stay in this town,' said Lucinda, sitting disconsolately on the end of the bed in our room.

I smiled.

'No,' I said, 'and we don't have to.' She looked up at me as if there was a chance I was about to concede defeat. She smiled at me briefly.

'You mean you want to go?' she said.

'I think we should pack up and get on our way right now.'

I had woken that morning with a revelation. I'd been running those letters of my father's through my mind again and again. Every time another gunshot woke me, I thought about them some more.

I pulled a selection of them out of my bag and laid them on the bed.

'Lou,' I said, 'just have a look at these letters.'

She got up wearily and stared down at them, a blank expression on her face.

'I don't know, what's so special?'

'Look at the one that's written from here.'

'Yeah?'

'It's got the address as "R. Morgan, Hotel Belmar", right?'

'Yes?'

'But all the others have *care of* such and such a person, and no mention of his own name at all. That's why I wanted to come to Mazatlán first, because the address had his name and so I presumed this was where he was most likely to be. At his real address.'

'Well, it would follow.'

'No, not at all. From what the Princess told me last night I think he must be a rather secretive person by nature. Doesn't always want to be tracked down.'

Lucinda sighed. She was bored with it now, and lay back down on her bed. The rare moment of her support was over.

'Just tell me where you want us to go,' she said.

I looked over the letters again.

'The Princess said that a couple of guys had come here looking for him. And that he'd suddenly bolted. That's intriguing, don't you think?'

'Fascinating,' said Lucinda and she sighed. 'You mean you actually believed what that old biddie told you?'

I shrugged my shoulders.

'Who knows? Look at these letters from Guadalajara and the one from Veracruz. They've both got the name Harry Koch on them – care of Harry Koch.'

'What kind of a name is that?' said Lucinda. 'It's a ridiculous name.'

'Exactly. I don't think it's a real name either. I think it's assumed. I think he only used his real name here because it's such an out-of-the-way kind of place. Either that or after he left here he started using the name Harry Koch. What do *you* think?'

'Jay, I really don't know. I think maybe you're just letting your imagination run away with you. I think you've had too much sun on your head. And I think we ought to make a decision about where we're going. I'm ready to move.'

I spread out the map of Mexico on the bed.

'Well it's Veracruz or Guadalajara, I reckon,' I said. I flicked open the guidebook. 'You want to hear about them?'

'If I must.'

I scanned the page, already having decided that I wanted to go to Guadalajara. There were more letters from there and the ink looked crisper and more recent.

'"Guadalajara is Mexico's most sophisticated city, with the finest shops and the most congenial atmosphere and climate,"' I read. 'Or there's Veracruz. "It consists of flat lowlands that are characterised by terrible heat, swamps and several noisome oil refineries." Which do you fancy?'

Lucinda looked up at me slowly.

11

We were on our way by early evening.

I decided to sit at the front of the bus so that I could keep an eye on things, although I have no idea what I thought I could possibly achieve by this. I sat there because I thought it would give me a better view. It did. A view of hair-raising bends, sudden potholes and, just outside a lorry park, the remains of a horrifying crash. The blue flashes of the ambulances illuminated the scattered and crushed parts of a bus identical to ours. I hoped Lucinda was asleep.

We had decided to take the overnight bus to Guadalajara. It was a slow and tortuous journey. The driver stopped at every tortilla stand en route where he'd get off for ten minutes to eat *tortas*, big Mexican sandwiches filled with burnt chicken and avocado. I went with him and while he ate beside the bus I smoked a cigarette as if it was my last. I almost suggested to him that the firing squads of the revolution were more humane than the bus company. At least the revolutionaries issued you with a blindfold.

His dashboard had an impressive array of saints precariously sellotaped to it. There was St George, popular here, and I commended the saint for choosing to travel by horse. The driver's St Martin had a quizzical expression and his Virgin of Guadalupe rattled recklessly about in a silver plastic shrine, clinging on for dear life. But, instead of inspiring confidence, the saints – some of whom were in the throes of being horribly martyred – underlined the very real possibility that at any moment our luggage would be strewn across the road, and us with it. The journey was made more bizarre when he stopped the bus and cranked down a battered screen to show a shaky video of *Wayne's World* dubbed into Spanish.

Jody had been keen to come with us and had talked Todd into it as well. I suspected that the real reason they tagged along was simply because they had no plans of their own. They hadn't even bought a guide book. They were just happy to be travelling further south.

I didn't really know anything about Guadalajara other than the song of the same name, and the fact that the English football team were pretty peeved when their fixtures were moved there from Mexico City during the World Cup.

When we arrived it looked a very bland and dirty place, deadly dull in the grey light of dawn. We stood and looked about us for a few moments, desperate for coffee. Things did not bode well. Jody and I were trying to remain bright and confident, but now the usual scowl on Lucinda's face was matched by an equally dark one on Todd's. Todd was claiming he'd been brought here on false pretences – no one had told him that it was a hundred and fifty miles to the beach.

'Chill out,' said Jody. 'It'll be great. We can take in some culture. It's a real historic city.'

Todd's face dropped further. 'Culture?' he said in abject fear.

'Museums,' muttered Lucinda. 'That should keep you happy, Jay,' she said sarcastically.

Jody and I had chosen the hotel together, to halve the blame. We took rooms next to each other.

The room was a far cry from the Belmar. The hotel had recently been restored and had been declared a national monument. The ceiling was high and timbered, the floor was made of large terracotta tiles. The window had a great swathe of chintz and calico, layered like a baptismal gown. I undid the fine baroque catch and opened the window onto the small iron balcony. It revealed a quaint ledge with a view directly onto the sixteenth-century Palacio del Gobierno. The Governor's palace. To the side was the Plaza del Constitución with a vast Mexican flag the size of a tennis court. The flag was lifting itself heavily into the breeze. It was as if one of the great squares of Moscow had taken leave of its depression and run away to a new home in the sun.

I could just see the spires of the cathedral, bright yellow, like ice-cream cones plonked upside down on top. A carriage with a fine horse passed beneath me. The air, on the edge of the great central plateau was so clear and good to breathe that I felt as if I had been taken back to a former age. The city had a feel of sophistication, and of old-world grandeur. I liked it. There's not a city in the world that can give you a good first impression if you arrive in the greyness of dawn at its bus terminus.

Lucinda was unpacking and I smiled at her.

'For goodness, sake don't smoke on the toilet while you're here,' said Lucinda. My God, she had a brilliant way of breaking the spell of the moment.

'What the hell are you talking about now?' I said bitterly.

'Don't you remember last year? It was here they let a whole load of petrol leak into the sewers and there was that explosion. Hundreds killed. It was on *Newsnight*.'

'Oh, right,' I said. 'I won't smoke on the lavatory then. I'll smoke in bed instead.'

'We don't want a bloody fire either.'

'Well I don't have much else to occupy me in bed do I?'

'Do we have to row? It's seven o'clock in the morning.'

'Yeah, I suppose that's a record even for us at the moment.'

'A record? What do you mean? We never row. That's your trouble; if you had the guts to have a damn good row with me we wouldn't get ourselves into this kind of mess. Rows are sometimes necessary, you know. They clear the air. Every time we're on the verge of one you wriggle out of it. It's a real weakness of yours you know.'

'I'm sorry,' I said. She looked at me and sighed.

'There you go again.'

'What do you think of the hotel?' I ventured.

'It's okay,' she said begrudgingly. 'Quite grand really. Nice room. What's the view like?'

'Historical,' I said. Why didn't she bloody well look for herself?

'I can probably get some laundry done here.'

'Yes, I expect so.'

'There'll be room service too,' she said brightening.

I went into the lavatory, sat down and lit a cigarette.

'I can't go on,' I said. 'I'm ending it all.'

There was no response from Lucinda. I looked down to the floor. Water was leaking in a stream around my trousers. The lavatory was something of a national monument too. I pulled the handle but the damn thing wouldn't flush. I went back into the room.

'I'm sorry,' I said. 'I failed to explode.'

'Are you as tired as me?'

'Yes,' I said, 'I think I am. I shouldn't have sat at the front. I feel as if I drove the bus here myself.'

'Look,' she said, smiling weakly, 'why don't we both have a sleep and wake up and start again?'

'That's a bit radical isn't it?'

'We're living in each other's pockets right now.'

'I'd hardly say we were that close.'

'Oh, stop it. You know what I mean. We're not used to . . . well, being with each other all the time.'

I got a hint of what was worrying her on this trip. When we got back home we were planning to live together. She was getting cold feet about it.

She tried a smile. 'I've had the grumps, I know. I've been a bit of a bitch, but you can be so infuriating sometimes. You probably don't realise. Everything comes off half-cock with you.'

'I told you it wasn't necessarily going to be a dream holiday.'

'I know, I know,' she said, coming over to me and putting her arms on my shoulders. 'And I really want this to work for you. I want to meet your father as well, you know.' I frowned. 'You're tired. You're exhausted in fact,' she said and took my head into her hands, put her breasts into my face and gently lowered me onto the bed.

'Get some rest, sleep,' she said, and walked slowly backwards away from me, and lay down on the other bed, looking up at the ceiling.

Though the coverlet looked luxurious, the bed frame creaked like a fishing boat and there was an awkward dip in the mattress that seemed to have been made by a succession of extraordinarily fat but very short guests. It was impossible to get comfortable in any position but one that was disturbingly foetal. I closed my eyes and curled up tighter but I couldn't sleep.

I lay there for a while and got up again. Lucinda was already sleeping soundly. I pulled the telephone directory out of the bedside cabinet. I flicked through the pages. I ran my finger down the extravagant names.

Moreno, Vera Amanda.

Moreno, Vilchis Genaro.

Then I got a shock.

Morgan, Roberto Jesus.

I could barely believe that the Guadalajara phone book had a Morgan in it at all. But if an Englishman Mexicanised his name it would be unlikely for him to choose 'Jesus' as a middle name. Then it occurred to me to look up Harry Koch.

There was no Harry Koch in the book.

I lay back on the bed, exasperated.

When the four of us congregated in the hotel restaurant for lunch I was looking quite dejected.

'I don't know what you're so down about,' said Jody. 'You're bound to run into him at some stage. Which part of Guadalajara did you say he lived in?'

'Chapala,' I said. 'Apparently it's on the lake.'

'Well, there's probably not much of an ex-pat population down there. You should just go down and ask around.'

'In my book it says it's got the largest American ex-pat community in the world. There's thirty thousand foreigners retired down there because it's on the same latitude as Hawaii but the houses are cheaper.'

'Oh, right.'

'I think I might take a spin round the shops,' said Lucinda. 'Who's coming?'

'Sure,' said Todd.

'Why don't you call information? You got the address,' said Jody.

'I've tried the phones, they're impossible. I can't get anywhere with them. I couldn't even get through to Roberto Jesus.'

'Roberto Jesus?'

'We've got the same surname. I tried him before I came down.'

'Well, do you want me to have a go?' said Jody.

'If you think you can.'

'Sure, my Spanish is all coming back to me since I've been down here.'

'You speak the language?'

'I took it at high school. It's California's second language. You just have to get your confidence back, that's all. I feel confident.'

Todd and Lucinda went shopping. Jody and I went up to my room.

She spent about twenty minutes haggling with the operator. She tried several different ones. Then she tried different tactics. She told one operator that she had just found out that she was terminally ill and had to speak to her father. They had to give her the number. She told one she'd found his winning lottery ticket. She told another she was having his baby.

I admired the way she stuck at it. Once Jody had got onto a thing, she didn't let it go.

Just as I lay down on the bed again, in exasperation, I saw that she was scribbling down a number, and making the operator repeat it.

She handed me the paper. On it was a telephone number for Harry Koch.

I couldn't believe it. I jumped up and kissed her, and we stood for a few moments smiling into each other's eyes.

'You're brilliant,' I said. 'You know what we've got to do now? We've got to call.'

Then I sat down, suddenly nervous. I could see the next moments panning out in front of me. I imagined the sound of the phone on Lake Chapala ringing, the click of the receiver, and the sound of my father's voice for the first time.

'Well do it! Call!' said Jody.

'I can't,' I said. 'I can't. What if he won't see me? What if he wants nothing to do with me. What if he slams the phone down?'

'Well, you can't second-guess what he's going to do. You've just got to take hold of the moment, Jay.'

'What if I said I was someone else?'

'Like who? A double-glazing salesman or something?' I shook my head. I really didn't know what to do. 'You've got to call, you've just got to come out with it straight. It's kinda now or never.'

I sat back down on the bed.

'I'm not ready,' I said. 'I'm not ready for this. I'll call tomorrow.'

'What good will that do? What'll be different about calling tomorrow? I'm going to dial the number.'

'No, wait . . .'

Jody dialled the number. I cleared my throat. She held the receiver out to me.

'It's ringing,' she said.

I held the phone to my ear. I could hear the strange, alien, burring of its ringing at the other end. Maybe, in the midday heat it was taking him a while to get to the phone. Maybe he was out. I hoped he was.

I was shaking.

Then the receiver was picked up. I heard the sound of breath down the line. Then a female voice said, *'hola.'*

'Señor 'Arry Koch, por favor,' I said, in imitation of the way Jody had pronounced it to the operator.

What came back was a whole string of Spanish and I couldn't understand a word of it. I tried English, but there was no response.

'I think I must have the housekeeper,' I said, thrusting the phone back to Jody.

Jody began speaking to her. As she listened to the woman's response she turned to me and nodded.

'He's out of town right now,' she said. She spoke to the woman again.

'Cuando regresara, posado mañana, sí?' She turned to me again, asking the woman to hold. 'He's back tomorrow afternoon, you want to go over there?'

'Sure!'

Jody finished off the call.

I sat in silence for a few moments.

'Who the hell did you say I was? Who did you say was coming over?'

Jody looked at me seriously. Then she looked back at the telephone as if it would give her a clue.

'Well, I didn't,' she said. 'She seemed to be expecting you to call, I think.'

'What?'

'I got the impression, I guess, that she was expecting someone anyway. She must have thought I was your secretary or something.'

We puzzled over it as we took a walk across the square.

'What time's my appointment?'

'Three o'clock.'

'Well, I'm going to have to face it aren't I?'

'Yep.'

'God knows who she thought I was, but it can't possibly be me. Surely I'm the last person he's expecting.'

That evening we all went for dinner in the Plazuela de Los Mariachis. We were immediately surrounded by smartly dressed waiters, all keen to pounce on any prospective diners now that the season had ended.

The square is the home of mariachi music: the wandering groups of men with trumpets, four-string guitars and violins, who play at your table. It was the sort of place that you really need to be in a holiday mood for, or you begin to pull the whole evening apart like an old jumper.

Very soon we had our own over-cheerful waiter flourishing menus and guiding us towards the more expensive dishes.

As he returned to his restaurant with our orders, neatly returning his notepad to his crisp shirt pocket, I watched as he passed through a decrepit doorway. Inside I could see the bubbling squalor of a decaying kitchen, where the women battled with variable-pressure gas to produce the chicken supremes.

At the corner of the square a dozen mariachi bands had gathered, sitting around the filthy fountain. Their uniforms differed only slightly: overtight trousers with strips of silver or gold brocade. They had matador-style jackets and large hard felt sombreros turned up at the back, outrageously embroidered.

Hanging around on the corner and unable to enjoy the privilege of a perch on the fountain were a posse of photographers. They had ancient Instamatic cameras and they hovered, looking like freelance photographers the world over. They were hungry-eyed and thin as pigeons, with terrible trousers. They looked shabby next to the splendid mariachis, and they looked at us miserably, as if it was our fault that there weren't more punters around this evening.

We looked down at the table as our sad, dried-up chicken arrived and was placed before us with a balletic flourish.

'Oh, God,' said Lucinda. 'Another helping of the chickens from hell.'

At the end of dinner Todd clicked his fingers and called the mariachis over. Our table was instantly surrounded by gleaming trumpets and manmade fibre smelling of sweat in the hot night. My heart sank. Everyone was looking at us. The photographers came over.

As they began to play a passionate love song, Todd put his arm around Jody and she laid her hand on his leg. She kissed him lightly.

I turned slowly to look at Lucinda, feeling that I ought to do the same, and she stared at me for a few painful moments. I sat on my hands and Lucinda watched the musicians, feigning interest like a school governor having to listen to the first-year string ensemble at an end-of-term concert.

As the music swirled around us Todd put his face next to Jody's for a photograph. Though the music was loud and exuberant I looked into the musicians' eyes and saw the deadness there. It was born, I supposed, of repetition and having to hang around every day in the company of other guys all dressed up in the same ridiculous outfit. The tight trousers couldn't be too much fun in this heat, either.

Todd and Jody were now flanked by the handsome young trumpeters, and they looked into each other's eyes. I turned to look at the ageing violinist between Lucinda and me, scraping away at his fiddle. The back of his sombrero rose high up on the back of his head as if the other band members were in the habit of whacking him from behind when he fell asleep.

When I turned back to the table Todd and Jody were kissing. I tried to avoid catching Lucinda's eye. A pain started in my belly where the chicken supreme had reached. It felt as if I'd eaten the bones and that all the fractured shards were crossed like swords in my intestines. As if they were marking the scene of a battle on a map.

I hadn't been much company all evening. I was somewhere else. I was very nervous indeed about what I might find the next day.

My father had been mysterious enough during my childhood, but now he had taken on almost mythical proportions in my mind. I knew that I would always remember this evening, sitting amid the grandeur of that decaying square. But I was entirely detached from it. They all seemed to have realised that there was no real advice they could give me. The situation I'd face the next day was unprecedented, and so no one mentioned it.

The mariachis were still playing and I watched the old violinist, wondering how old and degenerate my father might be by now. There were stains on the violinist's brocade jacket, pigeon shit mostly, and some red wine. His eyes were cloudy with cataracts and at the end of his solo he rubbed his chin, where for years his instrument had irritated him. During the bar rests he cleared his throat, and when he thought no one was watching he spat on the flagstones.

The passionate love song they'd been playing ended with a sweeping crescendo and the people in the square clapped. Todd paid his fifty pesos and they sauntered off – all, that is, except the old violin player, who didn't hurry himself. He stayed beside me and pulled his violin up to his ear. I listened. He was playing a single phrase of Mozart over and over again to himself.

'Do you want us all to come to Lake Chapala with you tomorrow?' said Jody.

'No,' I said, 'I think I'll go by myself. I think maybe it's one of those trips you make by yourself.'

12

I travelled the forty-two kilometres to Lake Chapala on a beat-up yellow bus. The only air-conditioning was a small battery-operated fan taped to the dashboard. The driver had fixed up a rather fetching set of small kitchen units in which his saints stood.

I stood all the way with one hand gripping a rail, which covered my palm with grease. It was incredibly hot, in the hundreds, and the petrol fumes and the sweat, mixed with the smell of burning rubber from the shanty town shacks on the outskirts of Guadalajara, accumulated in the packed bus and seeped into my pores and my clothes.

I was a couple of hours early for my meeting and I decided to walk around town to collect my thoughts. I walked down to the water to freshen up in the lake shore breeze. There was absolutely no sign in the town of the American presence. It was just like any other small town in Jalisco. The women sat by the roadside peeling *nopales*, the prickly pear cactus, which they diced for salsa, and sold. Old men sat in the shade of the hat shops where the white panamas and stetsons were hung out across the pavement from awnings.

In the church, a life-size image of Christ lay in an elaborate glass casket. It had a slot in the top and He was surrounded by crinkled peso notes.

Along the waterfront a few people sold baskets and quixotic papier mâché figures in a half-hearted way. Not a great deal could have really changed, I thought, since D.H. Lawrence lived here.

The lake was absolutely flat and grey. Its islands were veiled in a hazy mist and the blue mountains of the farther shore were indistinct and broody, like a distant view of industrial waste. At the edge of the lake a false lapping tide made the swamp weeds and the willows rise and fall in a timeless, lacklustre motion.

The lake was so vast, but lifeless, largely polluted now by the effluent of prospering Guadalajara. The last of the Chapala whitefish died years ago.

There was just the occasional boat with a static figure at the tiller meandering aimlessly across the water. It was as if the lake had once been a great sea, but, like the Americans, it had come inland to retire.

I walked back into town. A few rats scuttled around the dried-out lido on the tree-shaded promenade. It was incredibly quiet.

The flat deadness of the lake pervaded the town. Few cars moved. Every now and again bands of riderless horses cantered in sudden and reckless abandon across the main street. Then they would stop again, just as suddenly, and pull themselves back to the deathly tempo of the town.

I still had an hour to kill so I looked for D.H. Lawrence's house. I asked about, but nobody in the town had ever heard of him. Eventually I found it, not far from the waterfront. The house was easily given away by the primitive and rather botched carvings of naked men and serpents on the front door. But the Americans who owned it and ran some kind of Lawrence-love-in motel wouldn't let me in unless I went back to Guadalajara and made a reservation by telephone. I thought of stripping off and wrestling them naked. I decided instead on coffee in the restaurant. The restaurant where Lawrence had two young children arrested for begging on his very last day living here.

I pictured the skinny bearded man from Nottingham, sitting where I was now, eyeing the people suspiciously, and the people looking back at him, the ghostly white spectre of the Priest of Love, wondering if he wanted to buy a new hat.

I watched the young people promenading casually along the shore front as I wrote an entry in my journal. It was a day I wanted to record.

I liked the pace of the place in many ways, and I liked the gentle Jaliscan features of the townsfolk. It wasn't just a lack of hurry here: there was the overwhelming feeling that action itself was pointless, undignified, inhuman. The slow pace of Mexico was beginning to get into me. I liked it. It had a soothing effect which I appreciated, I was so nervous about my meeting.

I wrote for half an hour and then I paid my bill and left.

The house was perched on a hillside at the top of a sharp rise. All the houses in the neighbourhood seemed to have been constructed according to the whim of the owners. There were small bungalows with archways that were far too grand for them. There were driveways with multicoloured gravel chips. The gardens were those most favoured by retired people: paving slabs with plantings of cacti. Low-maintenance arrangements.

When I came to the house I stood for a few moments. It was a sprawling bungalow set on several levels of the hillside. It had a fine roof of terracotta tiles and a satellite dish, gleaming white in the sun. I took a deep breath, smoothed down my hair and rang the bell.

The housekeeper opened the door. She was an elderly woman with dark heavy eyebrows. She looked me up and down for a moment, her expression fixed and blank. Then she showed me in and walked silently in front of me through a hallway lined with framed pictures of ships. The living room was dominated by a TV playing a ball game to itself. There was a purple leather three-piece suite with wooden ranch-style arms supporting silver drinks coasters.

The housekeeper slid open the smoked-glass picture window that led out to the poolside patio. He was there, lying on a candystripe lounger with his dark suntanned belly flopped over his shorts. He was wearing flip-flops. Two dark plastic discs were laid across his eyes to protect them as he sunned himself. He had a kidney-shaped swimming pool. He was in his sixties, slightly older than I had expected.

I hovered nervously as the housekeeper muttered something into his ear and he looked up, the black plastic discs popping from his eyes. He snatched them up from his belly and turned to look at me.

'Who the fuck are you?' he said.

'I telephoned. I telephoned yesterday and you said to come over at three o'clock. It's three o'clock.'

He looked furious.

'Never did,' he said. His accent was almost English but with some mid-Atlantic to it as well. He looked out across his kidney-shaped pool and exhaled a great draft of wheezing air.

'Juanita here said for you to come over. I wasn't here,' he said. 'I wouldn't have said for you to come over, whoever you are. I only heard about it when I got back from Guad.'

I supposed this was why Juanita, the housekeeper, was in such a sulk with me.

'I'm sorry,' I said. 'I didn't realise that I wasn't exactly expected.'

'Well, no, you're not exactly expected. I'm expecting my accountant, but you don't look like an accountant to me.'

'Can't I just take a few moments of your time? I've come from England.'

'Listen, kid, moments of my time are kinda precious, so no, you just can't take moments of my time.'

Suddenly my eyes fell on the drinks table next to his lounger. Lying there, glinting in the sun for all to see, was a handgun.

'How the hell did you get my phone number anyway?'

'I got it from the operator.'

He turned to look at me with anger burning in his eyes. 'You can't have done, I'm ex-directory.'

'Um, well they did.'

He flashed me another furious look and then dashed a small dish of macadamia nuts to the tiles. I thought he was going to reach for the gun.

'Fuck the phone company in this damned country,' he said. 'Can't they get anything right?'

'I suppose not.' I said. He became silent. He was snatching about for his black plastic eye shields. I searched for words. I had to say something before he threw me out.

'I'm looking for someone.'

'Well that's just too damn bad, isn't it? Why don't you look him up in the book?'

'Please, you've got to speak to me.'

'Is that so?'

'I just came down from Mazatlán,' I said, trying to ease into it. 'I was at the Hotel Belmar.'

He looked me up and down. I moved slightly closer to him, just a foot or so, to let him see that I wasn't frightened of the gun. I was practically rigid with fear.

'The Hotel Belmar?' he said. 'What are you trying to say to me? Didn't I pay my bar bill or something?'

I smiled.

'It's a bit of a long story.'

'Well, when you've finished it wake me up.' He closed his eyes and replaced the black discs.

'I have some letters with your name and address on them . . .' He didn't move. 'My uncle Roderick kind of left them to me . . .' I looked across the surface of the pool and then back at him to see if there was any change of expression. There wasn't.

'I'm the son of a guy who came here to Mexico . . . He left England, I think – I'm not sure – either just before I was born, or just after. That was twenty-two years ago.'

He stretched his hand out towards the table beside him and found a glass. It was empty.

'Juanita!' be bellowed. '*Mas limonada!*' Then he slowly took the discs from his eyes and turned to look at me.

'Come over here,' he said, 'and sit down.'

I climbed onto a second candystriped lounger beside him. I was more nervous now and I couldn't crank the headrest up and so I was forced to prop myself up uncomfortably on my elbows, having put the book I had been using for my journal down on the tiles beside the lounger.

'Look at me,' he said. He stared into my face and I felt as if I was undergoing a medical examination. 'Mm,' he muttered reflectively, but there was a shift in his voice. Just a couple of notches down on the scale of aggression, but I was grateful for it nevertheless.

'I see,' he said, 'that you got a brown fleck in your left eye.'

I looked at him quizzically. I knew I had a brown fleck, like a freckle, in the blue of my left eye.

'Juanita!' he bellowed. '*Mas limonada!*' He looked at me seriously, as if he was now suddenly interested in what I had to tell him.

'That's uncanny,' he said. He stared at me a little more. 'You ever parted your hair on the right?'

'No?'

'Part it. Part it on the right.'

I fumbled with my hair. 'You recognise my face don't you?'

'I never saw you before in my life. Who the hell are you? What are these letters with my address?'

'I think,' I said slowly, 'that I may be your son.'

Juanita arrived with a jug of lemonade and a glass for me. As she filled my glass great lumps of ice dropped into the tumbler and splashed my shirt-front with lemonade.

As she walked away he began to laugh quietly to himself. 'And what leads you to that conclusion?'

'Your real name is Ronald Morgan, isn't it?'

He laughed again. 'So let me get this straight. You've travelled over from England, right?'

'Yes.'

'And you say you've got some letters in which my name features, and you got my number from the operator?'

'That's about the level of it.'

'Don't add up to much does it?'

'No,' I said. 'I suppose it doesn't.'

'And these letters, you have them with you?'

'Er, no, I left them in Guadalajara.'

'Oh that was smart. And you have the only copy of these letters?' he asked.

'Copy?' I said. 'Yeah, I suppose so. I don't think there'd be any copies – they're all handwritten.'

He smiled at me, and called for a bottle of vermouth.

'Listen, son, I'm going to put you out of your misery,' he said. 'Ronald Morgan was my business partner for a while. That's all there is to tell.'

I was relieved. If this man *had* been my father I didn't think there would have been too much of a future for the relationship.

'You know,' he said, 'I'd never have had your father down as a letter-writing man. Generally, in business, we kept things pretty close to our chest. Moved around a fair bit.'

A sudden coldness passed over me. I hadn't asked the most critical question, but, until now, I hadn't had the opportunity to do so.

'He's still alive?' I asked.

'Sure, sure, kid. He's still alive. I haven't heard anything otherwise.' I laughed excitedly. 'My God,' said Koch.

'That laugh?' I said, and smiled. 'I know. My mother told me. I've got his laugh.'

'Did you say you stayed at the Belmar in Mazatlán?'

'Yeah, I loved it.'

'Loved it? It's a dump, full of drunks. We got out of there pretty fast.' He was warming up, the vermouth was helping.

'I know,' I said.

'My God, you've been digging around, boy,' said Koch. 'You want to watch that. You can dig up worms as well as treasure, you know? The Princess, is she still alive?'

'Yeah, I saw her three days ago. What happened with her?'

'Nothing much. She had a thing about your dad. She tried to get us to smuggle her into the States. We should never have let her know we were in the live export business.'

'You do believe I'm his son, don't you?' I said.

'Sure,' he said. 'You've done a pretty reckless sort of thing coming out here like this. The sort of thing your father would just go and do.'

'How did you get to know him?'

'Korea,' he said.

'Korea?' I muttered. 'A business deal?'

'Well no, son. Korea was a *war*!' Then he laughed again. 'Well, as wars go, I guess you could call it business. But at the time we thought it was going to go nuclear. We thought it was the beginning of the Third World War.'

'You both served in Korea?'

'At the end of it. We were just kids. I'd been loaned, courtesy of the US Navy, to the Brits during the clear-up, when it was over. Nobody clears up better than you Brits. We were real pals.'

I stared at him silently for a few moments. The impression he'd given me at first, that they were just casual business acquaintances, just wasn't true. If they'd met in the Korean War then he'd known my father long before I was even born. Before he'd even married my mother. I was excited by the fact that they'd had such a life-long bond, and I felt that I could see something of it in his eyes as he looked at me.

'You're an American?' I asked.

'Yeah, I guess so. Never lived there much. I got naturalised British in the sixties. Now I ain't anything really.' He looked at me seriously again and gave a short laugh. 'You know, kid, it's uncanny.' He shook his head. At first I didn't realise what he meant. Then it dawned on me: I must have looked exactly as my father had done, my face must have been just the same as when they'd fought together. I smiled.

'Were you in intelligence?' I asked.

Koch laughed. 'Well I suppose so,' he said, 'though we were the kinda dumb end of things. You ever heard of the Special Boat Section?'

'Certainly I have,' I said, 'It's the naval equivalent of the SAS.'

'Well, that's not the way round the navy see it, but you got the general level.'

'What was your mission?' I asked, excited.

Koch laughed and looked up into the sun. He seemed to be quite enjoying himself now. Even quite enjoying my company.

'Oh, just paperwork mainly. We were dealing with paperwork.' He was getting into his stride. 'We just had to get away certain military documents of a sensitive nature that the army had mistakenly left behind in the north for the commies when we pulled out.'

I gasped. He seemed pleased with my reaction.

'You were quite some guys then,' I said.

'It was a job,' said Koch, in the way that all military men describe their exploits for effect. He could see I was full of admiration. I pulled myself back for a moment. Was I being strung along with another set of fantastic imaginings?

I looked at him hard. I did believe him.

'Then, twenty years later, we meet up in Mexico. Unbelievable,' he said. I nodded. He went silent, his eyes cold as steel. 'Look, kid,' he said, laying his hand on my shoulder. 'Did you ever really know your father?'

'No,' I said. 'I never met him.'

'So why the hell do you want to find him now?'

'Well,' I said, 'I've got his jawline; I've got his laugh; I've even got his damned fleck in my left eye, haven't I?'

'Kid, I gotta tell you,' he said, suddenly seriously. 'It ain't enough. In all the years I knew him he hardly mentioned you.'

I didn't believe him.

'But he did mention me?'

'Not much. He said he had a wife and son in England once.'

'Did he tell you why he left, what made him leave England?'

Koch went silent and stared at the pool for a moment. 'He had to leave,' he said. 'He felt it was for the best.'

'Why? What happened?'

Koch sighed heavily. 'He was still working for the security services. It was still the height of the cold war, or at least one of its heights,' he said. 'Ours is not the safest of occupations and so I guess he thought you'd all be a little better off without him.'

'You mean he was in danger, so he left to keep us safe?' My face began to tingle with excitement as I realised that he'd abandoned us for the most noble of reasons. 'I suppose my birth must have brought things to a head, and he knew he had to go,' I said.

'Something like that,' muttered Koch.

'You're not telling me everything,' I said.

'Well, I wouldn't want you to get a false impression of his motives.'

'Meaning?'

'Look, son, you've found out what you wanted to know. Why don't we just leave it at that? Did you ever get a birthday card? Or so much as a dime from him?'

'Not even a ten-pence-piece at Christmas,' I said.

'Well maybe you should read something into that.'

'But it would have been a security risk.'

Koch smiled and shook his head.

'Yeah, sure. But maybe you should come to the conclusion that he'd made a new life for himself to which you just weren't a part.'

'I know that,' I said determinedly.

'Once you've been out on active service, you know, home life in the suburbs can sometimes seem a little bit dull. You just sit there, staring at the TV, or whatever, and you look across at your wife knitting bootees, and you want to be back out there again.'

'Yes, I can understand that.'

'No, no, you couldn't understand that, boy. After so much excitement as a young man, boredom is, well, kind of even more boring.'

'But he left for our own good, to protect us.'

Koch shook his head again. 'Who knows? He also left, you've got to remember, because he was bored out of his brains. Women sometimes change when they have a kid, and I guess your mother bored him shitless in the first place. If you ask me he just took his chance. So why don't you just enjoy your holiday in this beautiful sunshine, sunbathe and screw, do what kids are supposed to do down here and then go home?'

He genuinely seemed to mean it.

'I just feel that I've got to meet him. I can't explain it, but I think most people would know why. I'd just like to see what he's like. I don't know why. I haven't thought about anything else for a while. I've got to do it.'

'Kid, I don't want to be harsh on you, but that sounds kinda pathetic to me.'

'It'd be enough,' I said.

'Look, let me put it another way. Maybe you got this picture in your mind of a certain kind of guy. Maybe you've built him up already. But you know, kid, it beats me how a bright boy like you can wanna see a guy who's never done anything but shit on him. Hell, he hasn't even taken the time out to do that, and you think he's some kind of hero. Shit, if you met him you might think he's just another dull old guy rattling on about his war.'

'Well that's just a risk I have to take.'

'Ain't a risk you've had to take until now, so why start?'

I stood up and moved to stand in front of him. 'Do you know where's he's living now? Please tell me if you do. Just give me the address and let me make my own mind up.'

Harry sat up on his lounger looking troubled. Then he got up and walked to the edge of his pool. 'Look, I don't know,' he said. 'Your father and me, neither of us is the keeping-in-touch kind. Maybe he'll call me sometime. When he does I'll tell him you called by. Give me your address in England. Maybe he'll want to get in touch. Maybe he has feelings like you, who knows?'

I looked at him sadly. 'You want me to give up and go home?'

'Sure I do. This is a big country. Where are you headed next? Mexico City?'

'Well, as a matter of fact, yes.'

'Shit, kid,' he said, shaking his head. 'Mexico City is the biggest damn city in the whole damn world, and you're looking for a man you've never met. You gonna check everybody's left eye?'

'It's not much of a plan, I know,' I said. 'That's why I hoped you could help me.'

He shook his head and looked towards his house.

'Well, I guess if anyone can find a person it's their own blood. Look, son, I'm going to wish you the best of luck.'

'I was hoping for a little more than that.'

He shook his head again. 'Okay, okay, I give up. I'm going to help you. Wait there.' He walked towards his house and disappeared inside. I sat down and waited. He came back out with a letter in his hands. 'Here,' he said, 'a souvenir of him for you. I had a house down by the port in Veracruz until recently. Your father often used to stay.'

'Uh huh?'

'Well, I gave this place as a forwarding address for my mail.'

'Uh huh?'

'Uh huh. I guess your father, at some time, must have given out that address too. This letter arrived for him about, oh, three months ago. I guess you may as well have it.' I seized on the letter. It was from England.

I put my thumb under the flap and flicked it open. The handwriting was small, and miserable, and written with a failing blue biro. Every now and then a sentence would begin in a strong blue ink, which tapered out, as if the writer had shaken the biro at this point. It was from my uncle Roderick. It was more recent than all the other letters I had in my box, I reckoned. It was dated, as Harry had said, just three months before. I looked up and smiled at Harry with gratitude. He touched my hand twice to show his affection.

Dear Brother,

Thanks for yours of the last. Hope you're keeping well after your snake bite. Sounds nasty, wouldn't fancy it myself one bit, though I must say, I had a nasty run in with the hedge trimmer myself on Tuesday last. Came over queer in the front garden. Lucky not to lose a finger.

Hope the weather's good, I suppose it always is there. Sometimes I think I could do with a bit of old Johnny Sun myself. But I don't know as I could stomach Mexico, but a fortnight on the Costa Bravo I wouldn't sneeze at. Fred and Dilly – you probably won't remember them – lashed out on a four day break in the Algarve. Brought me back a bottle of something I'm frightened to open.

Well, I hope this letter reaches you before you set off on your wanderings again, though if the Mexican post is anything as bad as what we've got here now the phone's gone privatised I don't suppose you will. Anyway, hope you do. Where is this Huatulco place anyway? I've looked on my map but I can't find it for the life of me. Can't be much of a place can it? But then, I've only got my National Pictorial.

But anyway, it's good to hear about Karina. She could be just the sort of thing to get you settled, though I must say, from your description of her she does sound a bit grand. Maybe though she's been what you've been looking for all these years eh? Well, I'll sign off now. I'm a bit chesty of late and I think I'll turn in with my book. I'm halfway through Monty's memoirs and I think it might be getting to the good bit. Send us your new address when you get to Huatulco, wherever it is.

Your loving brother, Rodders.

Rodders had a comic little signature but I was rather touched and moved by the letter. It was obvious that he absolutely idolised his brother. I was rather saddened for a moment, realising that he must have died shortly after writing it.

'Well,' said Harry, 'what are you going to do?'

'I'm going to go to Huatulco,' I said. 'He says he's moving to Huatulco. I'm definitely going to go. Where the hell is it?'

He laughed.

'It's a way down the coast in Oaxaca,' he said. 'You could get a bus but it'd take days. Oaxaca's got some of the worst roads in Mexico. It's all mountains.'

'How many days?'

'Four? Pretty hair-raising too. You wouldn't get me on one of them roads. They got gunmen that hold up the buses too. I'd forget it if I was you.'

This was worrying. If a man who'd gone behind enemy lines in a war wouldn't do it, how was I going to persuade Lucinda? But I was determined to go.

'Can I fly?' I said.

Harry thought for a moment. 'Yeah, you know I think you can. They just opened up a Sheraton and a Club Med down there. They must have an airport of some sorts. They're trying to make it the new Acapulco. You'd have to go via Mexico City, of course.' That sounded just fine. 'Now get the hell out of here,' he said. 'I have a girl come up from the village today to give me aromatherapy.'

'Is it any good?' I asked.

He laughed at my innocence. 'At my age, everything's good.'

I shook his hand and he gripped mine. 'I can't thank you enough.'

'Don't thank me,' he said. 'You might not actually have cause to. Just promise me you'll be careful. Very careful.'

'Sure.'

He looked suddenly troubled. 'And I'm sorry if I gave you a hard time when you came over,' he said. 'I was pretty thrown when you arrived. I was expecting a girl . . . well, to be perfectly frank with you, a call girl from Guadalajara. I could only think that the call Juanita took yesterday was from this guy, a pimp I met in a bar.'

'Oh,' I said. 'I can see why you were surprised when I turned up.'

'Yeah, I thought that there'd been a fundamental misunderstanding.'

I smiled. I glanced down at his gun, still glinting beside his glass of vermouth. He followed my eye.

'Yeah, well, sorry about that too. It's a habit I guess. Hope it didn't worry you too much. With the kind of line of work I've been in you get to make a few enemies along the way.'

'That's why you've got the firearm?' I asked.

'Well it don't hurt you to keep one by you out here. Some of the local boys think us pensioner folks are easy game. But not old Harry here. I could hold out against the marines.'

'I'm sure you could.' I smiled. I liked him and I was touched that he'd apologised for frightening me.

With an hour to kill before the bus back to Guadalajara I took a walk along the waterfront again. A nasty squall was blowing up in the centre of the lake. I watched as a boatman set out from the small island in the middle, fighting with the tiller. I watched as he turned back to the safety of the island. If I took Harry's advice, I'd do the same.

13

After speaking to Harry I thought about a telephone conversation I'd had with the British Embassy in Mexico City. I'd called, from England, as soon as I'd found the letters, to see if they had any record of him.

They had put me through to a guy named Gregor in the consular section. At first he'd been decidedly uninterested, but now, as I mulled over that call again, I realised that he'd shown a real change of tack as soon as I had given him my father's name. So I decided to drop in at the embassy on the way to Huatulco. We had to change at Mexico City anyway. This time we flew.

The Mexicans themselves call their capital 'El Monstruo', the monster. The moment we stepped from the pressurised cabin of the plane my lungs seized up in the thin foul air. To breathe the air in Mexico City is the equivalent of smoking forty high-tar a day. The birds have begun dying on the wing.

I sat on my Delsey suitcase while Todd went off, unimpressed, to queue for a taxi chit. We got into a *collectivo*, a shared taxi, with a priest, and waited half an hour for a driver. Just as with airports everywhere the place was populated by an army of priests and nuns. They seem to be forever scurrying about the world with their small brown suitcases and their sturdy black shoes, I thought.

The priest was American, and had added a baseball cap as a final worldly flourish to his clerical garb. He sat between Lucinda and me on the back seat, forcing our elbows into the awkward alcoves left by the stolen ashtrays. Jody was sitting on Todd's lap in the front with the driver, a cracked windscreen, and the faithful Virgin of Guadalupe. They were excited because they wanted to see the capital's nightclubs, and because the next day we would be flying down to the Oaxacan coast. We'd read up about the place and it sounded very good indeed. It may even be the place where they'd set up their laptops.

Lucinda was happy too, encouraged, most probably, by the facilities afforded by the Club Med. She was planning on doing some water sports. All I could think about was the task in hand, and I wondered what this woman, Karina, would be like. I might be something of a shock for her.

As we hit the main traffic flow the view was frightening. Vehicles were hurtling at us from every direction. There seemed to be no difference between lanes, and the other cars were fearsomely close. Everyone was going at breakneck speed. It was like a game of snooker where all the balls are played at once. They veered towards us like kamikaze out of the sun. They had wheels exposed to a naked degree where the protruding bodywork had been ripped off the VWs. Bonnets, boots and even doors were missing. Exhausts were held on with smouldering string. Sardined passengers were clinging, like me, to the undersides of their seats.

Some of the cars had no seats at all, so they could get more people in. Exhaust pipes lay mangled in fantastic shapes on the road and the cars pumped their fumes into the heat in great clouds. They drove like refugees before an invading army, playing their horns as if the engine was driven by nothing more than volume. It was a dance with motorised death. Everywhere was Hitler's legacy: dismembered VWs powered unnaturally from behind like flying bombs. Everywhere the Virgin of Guadalupe clung to the dashboards, being put to her ultimate test.

'Amazing city,' said the priest. 'Kinda vibrant, don't you think?'

'Yes, it's vibrant,' I agreed. Lucinda was starting to look a little ill.

'Grows in size every year at the same rate as the entire population of San Francisco.'

We suddenly lurched towards an elaborately carved façade. As we swerved towards the heavy stone I glimpsed the inner courtyard of a bank behind. The tellers were staked up in tiers, behind brass rails like people in boxes at the opera. Working away furiously as the pesos crashed around them. Then they were gone again, just the expression of panic on their faces left on the retina like a snapshot.

A street market came from nowhere, just safe of the main drag, the stallholders taking the chance that no one's brakes would fail on this bend and scatter all the cheap dresses and music cassettes.

Todd was thoroughly enjoying himself and imitating rock guitar breaks as a sort of soundtrack to it all.

The driver spat out of the window. From the state of the floor of the cab I guessed he only did this out of deference to the priest.

Todd was now slapping his thigh in time to the ghetto blasts of music that penetrated the cab every time we had a close shave with another vehicle.

I took out my guidebook and flicked to a street plan of the city. On the map we were an inch away from the hotel. An inch that held, perhaps, ten thousand cars backed bumper to bumper – those that had bumpers. I closed my eyes, feeling faint and wanting to shut it all out.

Finally we reached the Hotel Fleming. Jody and I had chosen this hotel simply because of its English name. It was something in this vast tangled street plan to cling to. It was cheap, too. I hoped that it had been named in honour of Sir Alexander and not because the rooms produced penicillin on the walls. Also, it was only two inches away on the map from the British Embassy, where I was intending to go at the first opportunity.

I let them all settle into the Hotel Fleming and I went out into the heat again.

The British Embassy stood in a broad street with a fine front garden of palms and geraniums. The Union Jack flew from the top of the colonial building. I stood and stared at the flag for a while as it fluttered in the heat. I'd never quite realised before just how psychedelic a piece of design it is, with its reds and blues at crazy angles, until I saw it flying amid scorching heat and palm trees. It broke the air as if it had been designed in the sixties for a fun-loving empire administered by rock stars. For a flag of compromise it sure as hell has a kick to it.

I walked up to the door of the consulate at the side. The Mexican guards spoke no English and, until I waved my passport and shouted 'God save the Queen', they were reluctant to let me in.

There was a queue of five or six people, and after signing a visitors' book, on the insistence of the guard, I joined them in the small wallpapered waiting room. There were four Mexicans who were there for the tiresome business of visas and work permits. They looked as if they'd been waiting for several years. There was a middle-aged playboy clutching his expired British passport on his lap.

I registered the fact that I was here to see the consul.

It was like a reception room in any nice Georgian reproduction house in the Surrey commuter belt, with white panelled doors, brass handles and wainscotting. There were lace curtains and heavy beige drapes blocking out the street, and Mexico, entirely. There were out-of-date copies of *The Times* and the *Telegraph*, all rubber-stamped with the command, 'Not to be removed from the British Embassy'.

There was a notice on the wall detailing the new quarantine arrangements at Dover and Heathrow.

Dominating the room was a large portrait of the Queen in a gold-leaf frame surmounted by a carved Imperial crown. The Queen looked a fresh young woman of twenty-five, all in pastel blue, holding a little posy of wispy white flowers. She was smiling broadly as if she was responding to a joke from a foreign potentate that she hadn't quite understood. Underneath her, in small print, an inscription ran, 'Her Majesty the Queen, reproduced by kind permission of the Institution of Civil Engineers'.

It was all, I felt, a vain attempt at being a little part of Britain.

At two-thirty the consular section closed and still no one had spoken to me, except for the guard who had a fondness for my Marlboro cigarettes. Together we had filled the diplomatic-service-issue crystal ashtray.

Finally a bellowing voice with a horse-and-hounds county accent cut through the fug.

'Oh, you're still sitting there?' said the middle-aged English woman appearing at the grille with an armful of papers. She was in full sail. 'We're absolutely up to our eyes in it today, I'm afraid, what with this rather untimely royal visit landing on us. Prince Charles of all people. You really can't imagine.'

'No, I'm sure not,' I said, smiling expectantly. She had that full head of flaxen hair and garish mascara that you expect to see only on women in the wind section of a philharmonic orchestra.

'Just give me the tiniest moment to plough through this little lot,' she said, slapping her sheets of paper against her pleat-skirted thigh. 'You're the chappy here to see the consul, am I right?'

'Yes, that's right,' I said, 'to see the consul.' She pulled a Kleenex tissue from a box and mopped her forehead.

'Added to everything,' she said, 'the overhead fans are failing on us lock stock and barrel.'

I imagined she'd been here, in her grade-two diplomatic posting, indispensable to the consul, for twenty years, running the place along the same lines as a girls' private school on the south coast.

I'd expected to be shown through to the consul's oak-panelled study but he appeared behind her, on the other side of the grille, working away with what looked like a dental instrument at the bowl of his pipe. She turned to him and froze, not daring to interrupt the delicate operation.

He was one of those large-framed, big-boned, Englishmen. The product of too much starch as a boy. His string vest was visible through the blue polyester of his shirt. He was the sort of 'far-back' chap that only really still exists in the City, or the law, or in the diplomatic corps. All of them forty years behind the rest of us in their speech patterns, like a Pathé newsreel.

'Well, hullo, there,' he said, offering his hand through the grille to be shaken. 'I'm the consul for my sins. Sorry to keep you waiting. Had one of these royal visits landed on us. All we need at this time.'

The woman and he were obviously absolutely thrilled by the prospect of the royal visit.

'Yes, I'm sure it is all you need,' I said, 'what with the new quarantine regulations at Dover.'

The consul looked across the waiting room to the poster of the rabid dog baring its gnashers.

'Yes, yes,' he said, slightly bemused, 'that as well.'

'It just never ends,' said the woman.

'So what can we do for you?'

'I phoned you a month ago from England,' I explained, 'trying to trace my father, and you said that if ever I was in the vicinity of Mexico City I should drop in. Well here I am.'

He looked genuinely surprised. 'Good gracious,' he said. 'Good show,' and re-lit his pipe. It smelt awful.

'I suppose you would have been dealt with by our Mr Gregor?'

'Yes, we spoke on the telephone.'

'Lucky devil's back home on leave right now. Would we by chance have something like a file on this anywhere, Cynthia?'

'Oh yes, most definitely, Consul, if there was an exchange of letters.'

'Oh yes,' I said, slipping into the consular vernacular, 'there was an exchange of letters.'

'I'll have a little rummage,' said Cynthia. The consul smiled. He seemed pleased with the consummate efficiency of his office in the presence of a fellow countryman.

'So how long are you in the country for?' he asked.

'I'm not sure. As long as it takes I suppose.'

'Oh, excellent idea. What did they give you then? A ninety-day visa?'

'Well actually, no, I don't have a visa at all.'

'Oh Lordy!' he said, looking up at the ceiling. 'Not planning on crossing any Mexican state borders are you?'

'Well, yes, I might, I've crossed three already.'

'Oh Lordy! You'll have to watch that. These buggers play a neat little game with the old tourist visas. They board the buses at the state line and bloody well fine you on the spot.'

'Is that so? I didn't realise.'

'Well, of course, it's not a fine in any shade that we'd recognise it back home. The justice system here is particularly concise. More of an income-support network for the police.'

'It can get awkward can it?' I said. (My God, I'd become so horribly English.)

'Oh yes, it can get awfully awkwardish. Generally depending on how many children or mistresses the officer concerned has to support.'

I suspected that this was one of the consul's favourite little speeches to British tourists.

'So what does your father do here in Mexico? He's an ex-pat is he?'

'I'm not entirely sure,' I said. 'He's been here quite some time. Something of an unknown quantity to me.'

'Bit of a dark horse eh?' he said twinkling with wardroom innuendo.

'Well,' I said, trying to stop this line of enquiry stone dead, 'I don't know about that.'

'You flew direct from UK to Mexico DF? Did you?'

'Well, no, there were no direct flights when I wanted one and I thought I'd take a spin through the northern part of the country first.'

It was hardly a 'spin', I reminded myself. I was speaking like a minor public school master in his first job, being interviewed by the headmaster.

'I can well imagine,' said the consul, sighing with the weariness of it all, 'there never are any direct UKs. The few that there are, are an absolute godsend.'

'I'm sure they must be.'

'Heaven knows what hell holes our diplomatic bag ends up in sometimes.'

The indispensable Cynthia appeared with another wodge of papers.

'Do we have a surname?' she asked.

'Ah, yes, yes, it's Morgan. My father's name is Ronald Morgan.'

'Morgan, Morgan, Morgan,' muttered Cynthia. I thought I detected a sudden flicker of recognition on her face, as if she'd heard the name before. I looked at her hard but her diplomatic smile was fixed on her face.

'Yes, here we are,' she said, and handed a letter to the consul. He scanned it and handed it back to her.

'Yes, yes, you're quite right, our Mr Gregor suggested you pop in here if you're ever in the vicinity.'

'And here I am,' I said brightly. Back at square one.

'I see from his note that you live in Brighton?' he said.

'Yes.'

He turned to Cynthia with a twinkle in his eye again. 'Now don't tell me. Cynthia, Brighton?'

Cynthia pursed her lips for a moment, concentrating hard. 'Don't press me but I think it's, yes, O-two-one?'

'Good heavens no!' said the consul, triumphantly, 'that's Birmingham. Brighton is O-two-seven-three.' He turned to me. 'Correct me if I'm wrong.'

'You mean the dialling code?'

'Yes, O-two-seven-three.'

'Yes, that's right. Soon to become O-*one*-two-seven-three,' I said.

'Well, absolutely,' said the consul. 'Excellent idea.'

'Oh, jolly well done, Dickie,' said Cynthia, adding a quick 'Consul' to correct herself of her familiarity in front of the national.

'We like to keep our finger in,' he said smiling. 'Maria, our Mexican girl on the switchboard drives us to absolute distraction with the UK dialling codes. You'll find while you're here that the Mexican operators are obsessed with them. You can't imagine. You give them a perfectly good code and all they want to know is what town it is. It's O-seven-three-two, I said to her this morning. What's it matter to you if it's Southend-on-Sea or Weston-bally-super-Mare? Then of course she can't find the damn town in the bally book. Why she thinks we'd be plying her with fictitious dialling codes heaven alone knows.'

'Terrible carry on,' I said.

'Of course Brighton is where they bombed the Grand Hotel and Margaret only survived it because she was in the *en-suite* at the time. I hear the IRA landed a couple of firebombs on Manchester at Christmas,' he said.

'Yes, I saw it on the news. They tried to burn down Mothercare and the Arndale Shopping Centre.'

Cynthia tutted. 'Oh is it really necessary?' she said, outraged.

'Quite a few office workers injured if I recall,' said the consul. Home news seemed to be another one of their little games, like the dialling codes.

'My God,' said Cynthia, 'you'd expect to feel safe as an office worker in Manchester. You wouldn't imagine that firebombs were on the cards.'

'Well, certainly not,' said the consul. Cynthia shook her head in disgust. 'And rotten at Christmas time too,' she said.

'Well,' said the consul, drawing a veil over the atrocities, 'I wonder where our Mr Gregor was up to with his enquiries. Cynthia, was there a little something scribbled in the margin? A name of some sorts wasn't it? Carol or something?'

'Karina,' said Cynthia. 'Karina.' She pronounced it again in a most obvious way. The consul turned to me smiling, 'Well there we are, that's something. Karina. I take it that's your mother's name is it?'

'No, no,' I said. 'I've no idea who that could be.'

The consul smiled in that wardroom way again. 'Oh, I see,' he said. 'Your parents are not together, as it were, in the eyes of the Church of England?'

'Well no they're not.'

Cynthia looked at the letter again, and then shuffled the file, and looked at another piece of paper.

Then she looked up, smiled at me, and flashed the consul a quizzical little look.

'It's just possible there may be an addendum on file,' she said. The tone of her voice was now slightly wary and cold.

'Ah, jolly good, an addendum! We're getting somewhere. I don't suppose your father registered his residency with us here?'

'I'm afraid I don't know,' I said.

'It's just that it does help enormously if people think to do so. I mean, there really is very little we can do to help our fellow countrymen if they don't even let us know they're in the bloody country. Our hands are somewhat tied. But I suppose that would have been the first thing our Mr Gregor would have checked.'

'I would have thought most definitely,' said Cynthia, rather nervously. 'I'll just pop and have a look in his case file. It's such a shame Mr Gregor himself isn't here, being away on leave.' She flared her eyes again at the consul, but once again he didn't seem to be picking up on whatever it was she was trying to signal to him.

'Righty-ho,' said the consul. 'Well let's keep our fingers crossed it turns something up.'

Cynthia scuttled back into the office beyond.

'Anything would be a help,' I said, trying to keep a casual air in my voice. Something was on that file, I could tell, that Cynthia didn't want me to know. Something that even the consul was blissfully unaware of.

The fan above the consul shuddered and began to wind down.

'Well that's bloody rich,' he said, looking up. 'The damned wiring in this place is a knotted maze. Electrically the whole bloody country is booby-trapped. Do take my advice, while you're here avoid all electrical wires, naked or otherwise. They'll blow you to kingdom come and back again as soon as look at you.'

I got the impression that he was glad of someone to talk to this afternoon. It was all part of his earnest desire to keep his finger in.

'The light switches in the embassy', he continued, 'are an absolute liability. We'd be better off with gas lamps, or candles. Not that the gas is to be trusted as far as you can throw it, either. We'd be better off sitting in the dark.' The consul shook his head in exasperation. 'Last Tuesday, I think it was, I was sitting in my night study working late on our royal visit, battling away with the seating plan as you can imagine. And there was one of those little lizardy things – what do you call 'em? Bally gecko, that's it. He was stuck to the wall by his feet. Catching flies by the light bulb. Quite a pretty little chap he was too. And out of the blue there was a short sharp electrical bang. He was killed instantly.'

'Dreadful,' I said.

'Yes, shame, because they do tend to keep the mosquitoes down to manageable proportions.' He shook his head at the tragedy of it.

'Dickie?' said Cynthia's voice from an inner office that was just visible through a louvred partition.

'Yes, Cynthia?'

'A quick word?'

'Righty-ho. Do excuse me a tick,' he said and walked into the office to join her.

I craned my head around the grille. The slowing shadows of the failing fans swept like bristled brooms across the paper-strewn desk tops.

They were talking in hushed voices. I could make out only sudden grunts, but I did hear my father's name pronounced in a decidedly pointed way. I was concentrating so intently on the timbre of their voices that when a drip of water, escaping from a pipe above the false ceiling, splashed across the counter, I jumped. My heart began beating faster.

I could see Cynthia's elbow as she performed the motion of replacing the file in a cabinet, and I heard a key turn to lock it.

They returned, walking with broad, bland smiles towards me. They stood for a few moments, as if searching for words. Smiling at me, not knowing what to say. I smiled back. We stood stupidly for a while.

'Well, a bit of false hope, I'm afraid,' said the consul.

'Yes, a crushing disappointment, I'm sure,' said Cynthia, with a slight quiver in her voice, and rather too swiftly as well, I thought.

'You don't have any little trails of your own to follow, I suppose?' said the consul. I thought for a moment.

'No, no leads at all I'm afraid.'

'Well, I'll tell you what,' said the consul, reaching for a slice of consular letterhead, 'why don't you give us a bell here and let us know how you're getting along, and if anything turns up at this end we'll be only too happy to pass it on to you. I'm sure if we all pull together, we'll get it cracked.'

'Well, that's very kind of you,' I said, 'very kind indeed, especially when you've got so much on at the moment.'

'Oh, no trouble. If we can't help out our own countrymen from time to time . . . well, that's what we're here for, I suppose,' said Dickie.

There is something, I thought, about the manner of English pleasantries that covers a multitude of dissemblance.

'So your stay in Mex is somewhat open-ended?'

'Yes, I suppose it is.'

'Probably be a good idea, don't you think, Cynthia, if we got this chap together with our Mr Gregor?'

'Yes, yes, excellent thought. Should be back the day after tomorrow.'

'Excellent, excellent. Be a jolly good idea if you, as a Brit, registered your residency here with us you know. Especially as you're not up to par on the old visa front.'

'Yes,' I said, 'I suppose it would.'

'Cynthia, my dear, can we lay our hands on one of those infernal forms?'

'Oh, I'm absolutely sure we can, Consul,' she said, spinning on her flat-soled shoes.

The consul filled in the form for me and then stopped and looked up with his fountain pen poised in front of his face.

'What address should we give?' he said. They were suddenly very interested in me.

'Ah, it's the Hotel . . . Fleming,' I said. There seemed no reason not to tell them.

'Just pass me over your passport and we can have the whole thing knocked out in a jiffy,' said the consul.

I handed over my passport.

Cynthia whisked my passport through to the back. I fancied I heard the whir of a photocopying machine. Then she returned and gave it back to me with a nervous little smile.

I left rather puzzled by it all, the spectre of the mysterious Mr Gregor looming over me. I remembered Harry Koch's comment that my father had always given them a wide berth. I wondered why.

14

First thing the next morning we got out of Mexico City. I was a bit twitchy.

'Did you see that guy sitting in reception when we checked out?' I asked Lucinda.

'No.'

'Reading a paper, just sitting there. He looked British. I fancy he was from the embassy.'

Lucinda snorted a laugh. 'You're losing your marbles,' she said.

It was a two-hour flight to Huatulco. The airport there was just a single strip of tarmac set in the driest country I'd ever seen. The airport building was a thatched hut. Our Boeing looked strange and intrusive in the dry wasteland. The air was so hot it made us dizzy and the tarmac quivered with mirage waters.

There were no taxis to be had – only lines of mini buses that shuttled groups of holidaymakers, with tour company chits, to their all-inclusive accommodation.

We bribed one of the drivers and hitched a lift with some hearty mid-Westerners. We drove for half an hour up the coast and checked in to a hotel owned by a frozen-food company.

That evening, just before sunset, Lucinda and I were having a drink in the beach bar, waiting for Todd and Jody to come and join us for dinner.

A young woman pulled up a barstool next to mine and ordered a mai tai. It was cocktail of the day. She had ultra-blonde features and spoke with a broad Texan accent. It was only about a minute before she turned to Lucinda and me and said 'Hi!'

Lucinda looked at her leopardskin bikini and turned away to look out to sea.

'You just arrived?' said the Texan woman. I said that we had. 'What are you here for?' I didn't know how to respond. 'Here for the diving? Yeah?'

'No, no,' I said, 'I don't dive.'

She looked shocked. 'You don't dive?'

Under her barstool she'd dropped a pair of flippers and they lay there like the feet of some slain god of the deep. Her aqualung was slung beside her.

'No, I never have,' I said. 'I'm scared of heights.' She looked confused. I explained that diving's only the same thing in reverse. If you have a problem with heights, it has to have its obverse fear: depths. That's why I don't dive.

She said that she couldn't relate to this at all. Everyone came here to dive, from all over the States, she said. It was the latest place on the diving map. She asked me if I was crazy, and I told her that I came from a long line of mental ridiculousness.

A man had taken up a position on the other side of the circular bar. As I looked up I felt sure that he was staring at me. He was wearing a crisp fawn shirt and light trousers. He didn't really look like a holidaymaker. He stared down into a glass of mineral water and slowly sipped it. His nose was slightly crooked as if it had been broken in a fight, and his teeth looked capped. He made me feel uneasy. I knew he had been staring at me.

'Hey Greg!' yelled the Texan girl across the beach to a man divesting himself of weights and rubber pipes, 'Come over here and meet these crazy couple!'

The other people in the beach bar turned to look at us. Were we crazy Britishers or what! Were we the fun couple just arrived for the party-party! The man in the fawn shirt was looking at me again. I shuffled on my bar stool.

Lucinda closed her eyes in pain as the man with all the diving equipment came over to us.

'Look what you've done now,' she muttered bitterly. The girl got up to smother her man with kisses in a semi-pornographic display, and then she led him over.

'I was looking forward to some peace down here,' said

Lucinda, and she pulled her paperback out of her beach bag and stuck her head into it.

'Hi there, crazy guy! The name's Greg.' He was a forty-year-old blond muscleman with a hearty handshake and a dripping rubber suit.

'Well, hello,' I said. 'Jay.'

'Well, how'ya doin'? And who's the little lady?'

Lucinda slowly looked up from behind the lurid cover of her thriller. She cleared her throat.

'Lucinda Parker-Harrington,' she said.

He stretched out his hand. 'Greg Brandon the third. It's great to meet you,' he said.

'I'm sure it is,' Lucinda mumbled.

Greg was full of himself. He lived to dive. It didn't matter how much money his company made for him, he said, the high of profits was nowhere near the high of diving. He was a styrofoam millionaire. His company made polystyrene for hi-fi manufacturers. He told us about its intricacies in some detail. It was so boring, I felt he was slowly turning our heads into some of his styrofoam.

'Look, I'm sorry,' said Lucinda, 'but I think we're at the wrong bar. We're waiting for some friends and I think maybe they're at the other bar over there. Hate to have to drag ourselves away, but I think we must.' As she said this I saw the man with the mineral water and the busted nose get up and begin walking over towards us.

'Oh, sure, sure,' said Greg. 'Well, we'll see you around. It's been real interesting talking with you. Maybe we'll catch some dinner or something huh? They got an all-you-can-eat here tonight.'

'Mmm, maybe,' said Lucinda.

'Well, cheerio,' I said.

'Hey man! "Cheerio". I just love that. That's terrific. Cheerio!' he yelled.

'Well done,' I said to Lucinda, as we got onto the beach.

'Why didn't you do something about it?' she said. 'They've obviously bored everyone else in the hotel to death. That's why people like that leap on the new arrivals.'

'Yes, I suppose so.'

'And you, like a schmuck, drop us right in it. Sometimes I think you actually enjoy talking to boring dorks like that. It's sad, it's truly sad.'

'Excuse me there,' said a voice from behind us. We turned around to see the man with the fawn-coloured shirt, catching us up.

'I couldn't help overhearing your conversation,' he said, smiling. 'You're British aren't you?'

'Yes,' said Lucinda.

'Weren't they just dreadful?'

'Appalling,' said Lucinda. 'Where are you from?'

'Oh, just outside Chester, originally, but now I live down south: Surrey.'

'Oh, really? I'm Hampshire,' she said, brightly.

They shook hands.

'Don't get a lot of English down here, I wouldn't think,' she said.

'No, no. You've just arrived?' he asked.

Lucinda nodded. 'We got in this morning. You here for the water sports as well?'

'Yes, yes, just checked in.'

Despite the rather rough impression that the broken nose gave him he was obviously an educated man, with an Oxbridge accent. He seemed very keen to get to know us.

'Are you here on your own?' Lucinda asked him.

'Yes.'

'Well we must organise an expedition,' she said enthusiastically. 'This is Jay, by the way, and I'm Lucinda.'

'Well, hello. I'm Sam, Sam Fergusson.'

'You just flew in as well?' I asked.

'Yes, yes.'

'Oh, we must have been on the same flight this morning,' I said.

'Yes, I expect so,' he replied.

It was well out of season in Huatulco now. There had been only about eight of us on the plane, and he hadn't been one of them.

'Well, we'd better be getting on,' I said. 'I'm sure we'll run into you later.'

We walked across the beach. Once again Lucinda and I weren't speaking and I didn't know how much more of it I could take. It was wearing me down.

'You were incredibly rude to that guy,' said Lucinda, finally.

'No I wasn't.'

'You were. He only wanted to talk. He's on his own.'

'He looked a bit shifty to me.'

We saw Todd and Jody walking down the beach towards us. The sun was going down and people were out with their cameras to photograph the sunset.

They looked quite happy and settled as we strolled into the hotel's terrace bar for our customary early-evening shot of tequila, dashed over ice with lime juice.

The hotel staff had begun lighting *flambeaux* all along the beach and were hanging lanterns from the palm trees. The trestle tables were being set up for the all-you-can-eat, and a man began playing a marimba. With the remains of the sunset still dimly in the sky and the gentle rushing of the surf to listen to, we fell peacefully silent. Without really realising it, I was biting my thumbnail.

'What's the matter with you?' said Lucinda.

'I'm not sure,' I said. 'I don't feel easy. Excuse me for a minute. I'll be back.'

I walked into the lobby. There was a young woman at the end of the desk in charge of 'guest services'.

'Can I help you, sir?' she said.

'Yes,' I said. 'I'm expecting a friend to join me here from Britain. He should have been arriving this morning. I'm worried that he might have missed his connection. Do you have an airport timetable?'

'I do,' she said, 'but it's not a busy time of year. There's just the one flight in at eleven in the morning, and then it returns to Mexico City after lunch.'

'There aren't any direct flights from Britain?'

'No.'

'I wonder if he's already checked in and I've missed him. Could you check for me?'

'Certainly, his name?'

'Fergusson, Sam Fergusson.'

She scrolled up a list of names on her desk-top computer.

'Yes, he's here,' she said. 'He checked in a little while ago. Do you want to call his room?'

'No, no, that'll be fine. He's probably resting,' I said.

I walked slowly out of the lobby, deep in thought. He hadn't been on the morning plane. He'd chartered a light aircraft – that seemed the most plausible explanation, I thought. He flew directly from Mexico City as soon as the embassy had established where I was heading. I knew I'd been right about the guy I'd seen sitting in reception. I'd have to tell Lucinda. I started to frame a way of putting it.

When I got back to the terrace bar he was sitting there with them, next to her, helping himself to our jug of margarita and laughing and joking.

I sat down in silence.

'Sam's going to join us for dinner. We're all going into town,' said Lucinda, brightly. 'It's going to be murderous here.'

'Oh, right, good,' I said.

Jody looked at me quizzically.

'Is something the matter, Jay?' she asked.

'No, no, everything's fine. Bit tired. It was an early start.' Jody poured me a drink.

We called two cabs and went into town. For now, I thought, I'm just going to have to go along with it.

A large white cruise ship had anchored in the bay and was illuminated from stem to stern. The cruise passengers were coming ashore in launches to tour the town and buy up the souvenirs. The local speciality souvenir was bullfrogs in different poses, drinking at a bar, playing cards or kicking a football with their webbed feet.

'They're cute,' said Sam Fergusson, 'and so realistic.'

'That's because they *are* real,' I said. 'They are real frogs. The local boys catch them and kill them. Then they put a drinking straw up their arses, blow them up and dry them in the sun.'

'How the hell do you know that?' said Lucinda, cross again that I was being rather cool to him.

'It's in the guidebook,' I said.

She smiled at Jody, giving her one of those looks that say, 'he's jealous'.

The evening was not panning out terribly well. I really didn't want this guy around me – there was something overbearing about him.

We ate dinner at a small restaurant in the main square. Right at the beginning of the meal I'd signalled to the others that I didn't want my father discussed. Fergusson had asked me why we'd decided on Mexico.

'No real reason,' I'd said, pointedly. 'Just thought it would make a change.'

The others looked at me knowingly, guessing that I was probably getting fed up with the whole business and my lack of success.

When we left the restaurant I encouraged Lucinda to get in the first cab with Todd and Sam. Lucinda readily complied, presuming that I was in a bate with her. I got into the second cab with Jody.

'What's going on?' Jody asked as we pulled out of the square.

'I don't trust that guy. I think he's from the British Embassy. There's something not on the level about him.'

'I know what you mean,' she said. 'He's trying too hard. He didn't really give us any choice about him joining us for dinner. And we didn't really find out too much about him did we? I mean he said he was a schoolteacher for God's sake. Didn't strike me much like one.'

'He's creepy,'

'How do you reckon he got his busted nose?'

'By poking it into other people's business,' I said.

The next day Jody agreed to come with me for a long walk around town. Todd and Lucinda were happy to hang-out on the beach. Their tans were at a crucial stage now, they were 'between factors', Lucinda having come down from 10 to 8, and Todd from 6 to 4. These things, apparently, have to be timed very precisely, much like frying a perfect egg. Personally, I was just sick of the sweet nauseous smell of coconut oil. Everything smelled of it now, our towels, our clothes, even the bed sheets and the curtains in our room.

Jody and I decided to ask about town for Karina. We visited the restaurants in the marina where the yachties sipped camparis and the men wore ridiculous little captains' hats. The women were dressed in loose-fitting designer nautical outfits from the houses of Yves Saint-Laurent and Pierre Cardin. We asked the restaurateurs if they knew of her. They didn't. I was hesitant about inquiring after my father because of the presence of that man Sam Fergusson, who was no doubt lounging on the beach with Lucinda.

I enjoyed weaving through the white tables of the marina with Jody. The water sparkled and the glare of the shiny white yachts reflected in our sunglasses. We looked quite a couple, I thought.

We stopped anyone that looked as if they might be a local dignitary of some sort, or a foreign resident. But always we drew the same blank faces, or a shake of the head.

Sometimes the Mexicans, who always want to please, would scratch their heads and mumble for a few moments before finally having to disappoint us. It was a very small town, I couldn't believe that no one had ever heard of this woman.

Finally in desperation almost, we called into the small tourist office on the quay.

The young woman behind the desk looked quite confused by our question. Like other towns they had tried to implement an 'open house' scheme where tourists can visit a 'real Mexican family in their own home'. It was supposed to provide an opportunity for cultural exchange but it had died on its feet here. At first this is what she thought we were asking about.

When we explained ourselves again she looked deeply sad. I suspected that we'd been her only customers all day and she was keen to assist.

She suggested that we went to the main square in the evening when the town comes out for its *paseo*. The evening walk where traditionally the men walk round the main square anti-clockwise while the woman parade round the other way.

We shook our heads.

'The only other thing I can suggest,' she said, 'is that you talk to the nightclub owners. Maybe she is a member of a nightclub?'

I was filling with despair. 'I don't think so,' I said.

Suddenly the girl brightened up as an idea struck her. She grabbed my arm.

'I know, señor!' she said. 'You should go and speak to the Frenchwoman who owns the new nightclub. It is a very smart place, just opened. She invited everyone in the town for a party there before she opened. It was a big thing here in Huatulco. A free party. Everybody, *everybody* went. No tourists, just us!'

Jody and I smiled at each other. The girl couldn't hide her pleasure at being invited to a party where there were no tourists.

She directed us to where the French woman lived, a villa on the *malecón*, facing the sea.

It was now late afternoon and we walked towards the house. As we got near we could see the woman sitting in her garden.

She was about forty-five to fifty and was wearing a smart cocktail dress. She was sitting by her pool with a drink. It looked as if she was working away at a ledger, company books perhaps. She smoked and tapped away at a pocket calculator. Her features were decidedly European and she had blonde hair. The garden was filled with oleanders and bougainvillaea and the air was heavy with their scent.

We walked slowly to the railings of her arched gateway.

'Hello?' I shouted.

She looked up briefly, raised her glass to us and smiled. Then she went back to her books.

'Excuse me,' I called. 'May I have a word with you?'

She smiled again and pushed her ledger aside. 'Certainly. Come in, come in.' We walked gingerly across the terracotta tiles to where she was sitting. 'Pull up a chair,' she said. 'Isn't it a lovely afternoon? I only got back yesterday. It's freezing in Europe. What can I do for you?'

'Well, I'm looking for someone – well, two people actually – and I wondered if you might be able to help.'

'Oh, really? I thought you'd come to see me about the Paradiso.'

'Paradiso?'

'My nightclub. I'm sorry, I presumed you were looking to join or something?'

'Well I'm sure we'd love to,' said Jody.

'Sure,' I said.

'So who is it you want to get in touch with?'

I took a deep breath.

'Karina.' She smiled thinly. 'And Ronald Morgan if possible,' I added.

'Oh, right,' she said. 'And you are?'

'Er, this is Jody, and I'm Jay.'

'Hello, I'm Nicole,' she said.

'Karina?' she repeated, slowly.

'You know her?'

'Sure,' she said. 'At least I think I must do. Both those names, I know both those names. God, I know the name Karina, that's for sure, but I can't quite place it now. Are they friends of yours?'

'Yes,' I said. 'Sort of friends – relatives.'

'Oh, right, I see,' she said cheerily. 'Look, I've got a big lunch party tomorrow, quite a few of the locals coming over. I like to keep them sweet, if you know what I mean. Why don't you come over at about twelve. You can ask around. Would that help at all?'

'Oh yes,' I said. 'That's really kind of you. It'd help enormously.'

'It's a small town, a new town,' she said. 'I'm sure we can sort you out. They live here do they, your relatives?'

'Yes, yes.'

'You've no address for them?'

'No. We weren't expecting to be coming down here so didn't bother, and they're kind of long-lost relatives, if you know what I mean.'

'Sure,' she said, smiling. 'Well let's hope you get to meet up with them. Maybe you'll all come over to the Paradiso Club.'

'Of course,' I said.

15

The next morning Jody and I announced as something of a *fait accompli* that we were both going off to a lunch appointment. Todd didn't give a toss. The thought of lunch with the locals terrified him. With Lucinda, however, it was a bad move politically. I was heaping more coals on my head and I was probably thrusting her further into the arms of the insidious Sam Fergusson. When I'd explained to her my doubts about his claim to be a lonely tourist she just laughed in my face, called me paranoid, and stormed out onto the balcony. A basking iguana scattered on the lawn outside.

Jody and I arrived promptly for lunch.

'You're early!' said Nicole, pouring us a drink. 'For twelve o'clock read about half past one in Mexico,' she said laughing.

We sat down by the pool.

I was determined to find out what my father could possibly be doing in a strange new town like this. There really wasn't anything here but the hotels, Nicole's new nightclub and the small port and marina. I asked her to tell me something about the place. It might give some clues about his business.

As a resort, Huatulco was only five years old. The story went, said Nicole, that one day in the 1980s, the Mexican president had been sailing past its deserted bays in his yacht. He was holidaying with his mistress, who just happened to be the Minister of Tourism. 'I'll give you this place,' he's reported to have said to her, 'and you can build a new Acapulco.' It had been something of a shock to the villagers.

When the airstrip was built, she told us, the Colombians had immediately seized on it as a place to fly their cocaine into. It then travelled by boat up the Pacific coast, or overland, to the USA. Eight months before, a plane had landed from Colombia loaded with tons of cocaine. When the sacks, which were disguised as agricultural fertiliser, were unloaded they disappeared from the airport. There was a tangible tension in the town as the Colombian hoods went frantic. Nicole laughed then as she approached the punchline. The whole lot had been mistakenly taken to the town's football pitch and spread on the grass.

I sipped at my drink, and glanced at Jody. She opened her eyes wide to me. We were both thinking the same thing, about Huatulco's 'other industry'.

'It's quite comic, really,' said Nicole. 'Last month our two gallant local policemen – we only have the two – managed to capture a whole load of marijuana on the beach. They were so excited about managing to pull off a bust for once that they decided to burn the whole lot on the beach as an example. Halfway through the big bonfire the wind changed. I can tell you, there were a lot of very stoned and dazed middle-aged holidaymakers staggering off the beach that night. The kids seemed to come from everywhere. The police were totally out of their brains.'

She told us that this part of Mexico had always been genuine 'bandit' country. Until recently they had been attacking tour buses; fearing for the tourist dollar the State Governor had sent in troops. They dressed in plain clothes and filled a bus. When the bandits attacked they broke out their guns and shot the lot of them dead.

'It's a particularly Mexican kind of justice,' said Nicole.

'Concise,' I said, quoting the consul.

'Yes, extremely. You have to remember that this is a country working so hard to become part of the First World, it will summarily execute, run people into jail, and offer its arse to a string band for the sake of the North American Free Trade Agreement.'

'You're not keen on the country, yet you live here?' said Jody.

'Of course I'm keen on the country. It is God's own country – it's beautiful. The people are wonderful. You're saying that the American government doesn't discreetly put the odd bullet in the occasional head? Or that we French don't courageously attack Greenpeace vessels in foreign ports under cover of darkness?'

We nodded in agreement.

Lunch was fun. There were a dozen of us sitting around a long table. Nicole had brought in some of her nightclub staff to serve the drinks and she sat at the head of the table like a benign countess.

The local bank manager was there, with his wife, and they seemed rather overawed by the whole thing. There were the owners of some of the beach bars, the manager from one of the hotels. A couple of her neighbours. There was also Enrico.

The moment Enrico had walked through the gate Nicole had grabbed my arm.

'Now I've got it, now I remember,' she said. 'Enrico, it's him you should speak to. It's from Enrico I heard the name Karina.'

While we were sitting over lunch I watched her get up, on her way to the kitchen. She stopped momentarily behind Enrico's chair, crouched down on her haunches and begun whispering in his ear. Then he flashed me a look. A deeply serious look.

I sat back in my chair and relaxed. It's done, I thought: it is sorted. Nicole is a nightclub entrepreneur, an expert in facilitating introductions. All I had to do was to wait until the formal lunch had ended and we all made our way to sit by the pool.

I touched Jody's arm.

'I think we're there,' I said. 'We're going to meet Karina.'

She looked at me and shook her head.

'How do you know that? We've not even mentioned your dad or her.'

I giggled. The sun and the wine had lulled me into a happily bleary state.

'I've really enjoyed this lunch,' said Jody. 'It's so great. You can't get anything like this by just going to a place on holiday. You kinda have to be there for a reason first.'

We kissed, lightly.

Lunch was over and people were getting up from the table.

Enrico owned and ran the diving shop at the marina. He was

an extremely handsome young man, well educated, and his once-black hair had been bleached a vibrant bronze by the effect of the sun and the salt. When he didn't have tourists to take diving out on the reefs he would go down with his spear gun to shoot fish for the big hotels.

After lunch he sat by the pool for quite a while, sitting thoughtfully on the edge of a stone banquette. We still hadn't spoken after Nicole had whispered in his ear.

I was bold with drink and went over and sat next to him. He stared at me hard for a moment.

'Enrico,' I said. 'I wonder if we could have a word?'

He narrowed his gaze.

'We need to talk,' he said.

We walked to the far side of the pool and sat in a bower of oleanders and hibiscus.

'Why are you here?' he asked.

'Didn't Nicole tell you?'

'She said a little.'

'All right. I didn't tell her exactly why I'm here. I'm actually looking for Ronald Morgan, who is my father. I've got absolutely nowhere so far, except that he's got a mistress, or a new wife, and she's called Karina, and she lives in Huatulco. Nicole thought you'd brought them to her nightclub.'

Enrico began to laugh.

'Oh, my God,' he said. 'I couldn't think who the hell you could have been coming here looking for Karina.'

He laughed again. I was quite sober all of a sudden.

'Okay,' he said, 'you want to meet Karina. Is that what you want to do?'

'Yes.'

'You want to meet her this afternoon?'

'Yes.'

'Okay, then, go and drink a load of black coffee.'

'And you'll take me to meet Karina?'

'Yes, I'll take you.'

'Tell me about her,' I said.

'Sure,' he said, but there's something you ought to know first.'

His face took on a slightly wicked smile.

16

I was genuinely terrified. We had agreed that Enrico would pick us up at our hotel at four o'clock that afternoon. Jody suggested that it would be a good idea to bring Todd along, too, and I agreed. Lucinda was keen as well. Maybe it would change things.

At half past four we got into Enrico's fibreglass boat and sailed out of the marina. The boat listed because of the weight of his diving equipment. We sped past the rocks for half an hour. Then he anchored. Above us were fearsomely craggy cliffs. The sun was already getting low in the sky.

Todd looked up.

'What's that cross for up on the rock?' he asked.

'Oh, that,' said Enrico. 'A diver died here, in the undercurrent, a couple of months back. That's why no one will dive here. The local people think this stretch of water is cursed and no one will bring the tourists up here. Are you ready?'

'As ever I will be,' I said.

Enrico pushed me backwards over the side of the boat and into the sea. I was kitted out with weights and an aqualung. I performed a sort of ungainly backward somersault off the side of the boat and plunged into the water in a cascade of bubbles. I was upside down for some time before I bobbed back up to the surface, flapping away furiously with my flippers. I looked up at Lucinda, in her bikini, in the boat. She wasn't coming down. For all her talk of water sports there was nothing that would induce her to join us. Diving wasn't her idea of sport, she said.

'I think you're mad – you'll never do it,' she said to me encouragingly, as I flapped about in the water.

Enrico had taught us about atmospheres, equalising our pressure, and how to avoid the bends and bursting our eardrums, in our hotel pool. Now I was in the water I'd forgotten it all. Even in the splash pool it had frightened the wits out of me.

I began to descend in the water. I could sense Jody and Todd, and finally Enrico descending after me. Apparently it's always best for the novice to go first, Enrico had told me, but I think that he suspected that if I didn't I'd panic and jump back into the boat when I saw the others disappearing.

We made our way to the nylon anchor cord and began hauling ourselves down by it. As I looked back up at the surface of the sea it looked like a field of crinkled baking foil. I was taking in great lungfuls of gas from the tank.

Then the sharp pain hit my ears as I arrived at the first equalisation stage. At ten metres the atmospheric pressure is double that which the human body is built for. And your body lets you know it.

I squeezed my nose and pumped my brains into my ears hoping that they would pop. I wasn't very good at it at all – my right ear resolutely refused to do what I'd managed with the left. It was as if they were arguing with each other on either side of my head. I was intensely aware of being a physical creature – intelligence, calculation, sensitivity had nothing to do with it.

Down there it was a strange world of changing colours, and absolute silence, except for the sound of my bodily functions. Functions that I'd never noticed before, my thudding heartbeat (which I'd felt before but never actually heard), my heaving lungs, the sound of blood rushing around my ears. I was terribly uncomfortable, and in a state of suspended panic.

In deep water the light is refracted, at a bizarre kind of tilt, so that nothing appears to be the colour that it is. One's flesh becomes lilac, fingernails look like spiky splintered shards, one's skin seems to be crumbling and falling away. It was decidedly troubling. One's diving partners look like magnified extras from *The Living Dead*. I began drawing hard on my air tank – to a dangerous degree, as it turned out, filling my lungs with so much air that I could shoot up to the surface again at any moment, which would give me the bends, I remembered. And there wasn't a decompression chamber for two hundred miles.

As we descended further the light faded and the water grew colder in sudden rushes. We were diving deeper than the ordinary tourist or novice diver would, and we may as well have been in the North Sea. It seemed an interminably long passage down, and since, from this depth, it would take us six minutes to rise again safely, we would have only enough gas in our tanks for a short time down there. I was conscious of not holding things up because of the trouble I was having with my right ear.

Breathing air, at this depth, when there is tremendous pressure all around you, is an uncannily bizarre sensation. The gas makes you slightly heady too and you begin to believe that you are actually breathing water. This is a very dangerous notion indeed, because you become tempted to actually do so.

I relaxed my mouthpiece. I'd been biting on it so hard that I'd almost bitten through the rubber.

I took in a mouthful of salt water. My God, it hurt my throat, and seemed to rip into my lungs like acid. It gave me such a fright that I began drawing too heavily on the gas. Then I suddenly broke free of the anchor chain and shot upwards, in a swirl of bubbles, at an alarming rate. My chest felt as if it would explode. Enrico came chasing after me and caught me by the flipper, hauling me back down again. I looked down. I could see the others far down below me. It was like looking down a lift shaft. I suddenly felt as if I was very high up, instead of very deep down. I just didn't seem able to sink. I steadied myself for a few moments, equalised my pressure and carried on down.

We passed through a narrow fissure of rock where sponges grew. I was nervous of the sponges. In their natural habitat, which Enrico had warned us was not the bathroom, they are not soap-loving friends at all. If you brush against them when they are alive they will fire deadly paralysing spines into your flesh, like a volley from an army of bowmen.

Finally we arrived on the dark seabed and switched on our lamps. It was odd but strangely satisfying to be standing on the seabed, upright. Todd was signalling and pointing. He had almost landed on a manta ray and seemed to be delighted by it. He watched as it flipped up and swam around him, like a spacecraft.

I took a little time to watch the fish that lived down here. We were down with the ugly ones, those consigned by God to the depths of creation. There were rays and flatfish with their eyes beaten to one side like a barroom drunk's, and those with scaly ill-fitting skins like old men's charity overcoats. There were the unspeakable molluscs and the devil fish that throw their stomachs up from the bends when they are trawled by fishermen, those unidentified monsters that draw a crowd on the quay. It was the part of creation that must have surprised its creator, a nether world, a world that God himself never meant us to see, until we invented the aqualung.

It was a treacherous element, but strangely there was a beauty in its soulfulness. It was the pathos of the place: a world that didn't even seem to find itself familiar. The creatures that were consigned to live there were constantly startled by happening across each other. If a fish can be said to look horrified, then some of these did.

We swam along the seabed for a while and then Enrico mouthed the word 'Karina!' We stopped and looked, and there, quite terrifyingly, rising before us was my father's ship.

She had lain there for only a week but in the angry tides she was already breaking up. Debris from the ship was scattered all around. Wiry pipe plants had already begun to root on her decks, plants that drift and whose roots hook around any projection.

Enrico had told me at Nicole's that he was the only person who knew the exact location. He'd come across her while spearing fish a couple of days before. Since the death of the other diver no one would go down here. I didn't blame them.

The ship was a ghastly sight that struck me with a range of deep emotions. We were all shocked to a degree. There was the folly of building such things and setting them upon the sea; the feeling of being in the presence of a mighty grave; the continuing violence of its destruction. It was something from our own world lost in another.

Enrico guided me to a large cylinder lying beside the wreck and rubbed it with his hand so that the small plants and sand fell away. He revealed the maker's nameplate on one of the ship's boilers. It gave me a chill to read it by lamplight.

KARINA – VERACRUZ

I watched as Todd swam through the broken side of the hull, Enrico following him. I wanted to see inside too, but I was nervous of what I might find: plastic bags filled with white powder, perhaps. I swam in through the rip in the metal. The rusting metal was strangely purple, like my flesh, as it came under the beam of my torch.

Then without warning a sudden rush of current propelled me forward, and sucked me down what was probably a stairwell. I struck my head on a great piece of iron. My knee had been gashed against a broken, twisted stair rail. Then the tide carried me back up again and my air pipe was whipped out of my mouth and jammed itself between two spikes of rusting metal. I reached my hand in to grab back the pipe, but the water tore me against it. I could see the blood streaming from my hand. The salt stung it immediately. I wanted to cry out but daren't open my mouth. My head smashed against a large square rock. I seemed to see strange drawings in front of my eyes. Were they on the stone? There was nothing I could do to battle against the current. I was beginning to pass out. Again the side of my head smashed against a square white rock.

The weirdest of sensations overwhelmed me. Whether it was a huge rush of adrenalin or not I don't know. It was like the feeling people describe when they've had a road accident, everything seeming to happen in slow motion. I knew that if I panicked I would be drowned for sure, but somehow I had no compulsion to panic at all. Maybe I was heady from the gas. I simply began to drift in the water, and within my own body.

I was blacking out. Suddenly I was conscious that there was air in my mouth again. Enrico was passing me his air pipe. I took soothing gulps as he held me in his arms. I felt the sensation of rising in the water. I must have lost consciousness – apparently you do under these circumstances – because, although it must have taken some time for us to ascend, it was only seconds, it seemed, before I saw the blazing glare of light playing on the surface above. I stared up into it as if it was heaven and the angels were descending on a ladder. Enrico pushed me up into the boat.

I lay in the back by the tiller, muttering. There was blood across my face and down my legs. I looked up into Lucinda's shocked eyes. Then I heard Jody screaming.

'Where's Todd? Where's Todd?' she was shouting, leaning over the side of the boat. Enrico leapt back into the water. We all leant over the side of the boat staring at the silent sea. I was coughing and retching. The bubbles from Enrico's aqualung dispersed. The boat rocked languidly. There was a deathly silence. My heart was thumping. I'd been a danger to the party, and because of me Todd had drowned.

The minutes stretched out.

Then up plopped Todd, Enrico just seconds behind him.

'Wow, man, amazing,' said Todd brightly, and flipped into the boat. 'Any beer in the coolbox?'

We sat eating dinner with Enrico in the marina. We'd both suffered some damage to our ears, from when I'd suddenly begun shooting to the surface. He gave me a small bottle of pure alcohol which I had to tip into my ear.

'That's an orifice you've never tried before,' said Lucinda, unsympathetically. She thought the whole expedition, on my part, was bound to go this way from the start.

I was silent. The image of that awful ship lying in its ghostly state, in that angry tide, was impressed deep on my mind.

'What do you know about the *Karina*, Enrico?' I asked him.

'Well, she was often anchored off here for a few weeks at a time. Then she'd sail off for a month or so. I used to look forward to seeing her dock. We're a very quiet little port here, just a few local fishing boats. The rest are all visiting pleasure craft. I could never think why she came in here. It was almost as if she was lying low.'

'How long had she been here this time?'

'Three weeks I think. They were taking on supplies, I guess, or waiting for their cargo. There was just a skeleton crew on board, three or four. You never saw them on deck. I don't think they even went into the bars to drink. Unheard of for sailors. Then suddenly she slipped out of the bay without warning. They didn't get far though. She must have gone down like a stone, in the early hours of the morning.'

'Went aground on the rocks?' I asked.

'Well, there aren't rocks to go aground on there, really,' he said. 'As you saw, it's a pretty deep channel.'

'Has it happened before? Do you get a lot of ships go down here?'

'Well, no, none that I know of.'

'Did the crew survive?'

'They must have done. There's no sign of anyone down there, and the current would have brought any bodies up into the bay. They just seemed to disappear into thin air.'

'But surely people must know something? I mean, it was a fairly major event around here, I would imagine. What did the local newspaper have to say about it?'

'Nothing,' said Enrico. 'Our newspaper only has good news in it. How much sunnier it was here last week than in Acapulco, how many tourists rode on the big banana.'

'You mean there was no interest from anyone? No newspapers, no police investigation?'

'Nothing. One night she was there, anchored off shore – the next morning she was gone. There was talk, of course, but until I came across her when I was spearing I'd presumed she'd just sailed out into the night.'

'There must have been debris washed up on the beaches, though?'

'I'm sure there was but it wouldn't have stayed on the beach long. People find a use for everything around here. People are out early combing the beach for every bit of wood, every tin can.'

'Seems pretty obvious to me why she went down,' said Todd, pouring himself another glass of wine. 'Didn't you see all those rocks stuffed inside her? And the hole ripped out of her side? Man, she was scuttled.'

We all stared at Todd.

'My God,' said Jody. 'Do you think he's right, Enrico?'

'It's an explanation. I've not really been inside her too much but I noticed those rocks too today. I'd just seen them when you lost your air pipe,' he said. 'The night she went down some people said they heard an enormous bang, like something blew on the ship.'

'An explosion?'

'Who knows?' he said.

'Or a bomb,' said Todd.

There was a bright moon in the sky as I sat on the terrace of our hotel room, nursing my aching ear. I was gazing across the beach. I could see Jody, in silhouette, in a short evening frock, walking barefoot through the surf.

Lucinda was sitting at the little dresser in our room, writing up her journal. I couldn't bare to think what she was writing about me today. I'd long since given up on mine – in fact I'd lost it.

'I think I'll take a walk along the beach,' I said.

'Whatever you want to do,' she said. 'I just want to finish this.'

I dashed down the concrete ramp that stood in the place of stairs. Then I slowed my pace, wiping away the sweat around my neck as I strolled onto the beach.

'So where's Todd?' I said. 'Having one of his record-breaking showers?'

'Yes,' said Jody. 'We've got a terrible Texan couple next to us.'

'I wanted to talk to you for a few moments alone,' I said.

'I think I know what you want to say.' We looked at each other for a moment. She took my arm and led me on along the beach.

I looked down at the fine sand and the small crushed pieces of shell and coral being rushed up around our feet.

'I feel a little at a loss, and rather confused,' I said.

'Uh huh.'

'I have a lot of things going through my mind. It's exhausting.'

'I know,' she said.

'I just feel that I can talk to you. I think we've become friends, haven't we?'

She kissed me lightly on the cheek.

'Yes,' she said, 'I think we've become friends.'

'Do you think that Todd was right, that my father's ship was scuttled? That there may have been a bomb? Lucinda won't listen to any of this any more. She thinks I'm overdramatising.'

She smiled at me. 'Who knows? What are you going to do now?'

I shook my head. We had begun walking back down the beach. There was a picture in my mind of the sunken *Karina* that made my father even more distant now and the task of finding him more hopeless.

'I want to travel on further. I have to know what this is all about: I must find out if he's still alive, or if he died in that ship.'

'Sure you do,' she said. 'I want to come with you.'

'You don't have to, you know. I don't know where I'm going.'

'But you always end up in such interesting places,' she said, smiling, and trying to cheer me up. 'We've got no agenda, it's great to just drift. And in any case, you make me laugh.'

'I make you laugh?' I said, incredulously. And at this point we almost kissed. We stood staring at each other.

'That guy was in reception tonight. It was as if he was waiting for us,' she said.

'You mean that Fergusson bloke?'

'Uh huh. I think you're right. I think you're absolutely right. He asked me what we were doing for dinner tonight. He looked a bit desperate.'

I was lying on the bed the next afternoon when I suddenly thought of Gregor. The 'our Mr Gregor' that I'd heard of at the British Embassy. By now he would be back from leave, I thought, and I was debating in my mind the idea of calling him. Even though I distrusted them I didn't see that I had any option. It had even crossed my mind that Gregor and Sam Fergusson might even be the same man.

I picked up the phone and called the embassy.

I got through to Maria on the switchboard, and, as the consul had said, she was pretty damned awkward. I phoned three times before I got through to Mr Gregor.

'Hello, there,' he said curtly. I explained that I'd phoned him and that I'd dropped by the embassy as he'd suggested, and that I was still in Mexico.

'You should have let us know when you were pitching up,' he said. 'What exactly can I do to help?'

'Morgan,' I said. 'My father's name is Morgan and I believe you were making some enquiries on my behalf.'

There was the smallest catch in his voice.

'Just give me a moment,' he said. 'I'll see if I can hunt out the case file. Don't go away.'

It seemed to be a very short time indeed before he found the file. If only all government offices could be quite this efficient. I thought.

'Yes, yes, yes,' he said, as if playing for time. 'How exactly can I help you?'

'Well, I wondered if you'd got any further with it.'

'Ah, yes, just a moment.' He paused again. 'You've not had any luck yourself, then?'

'Um, no, none whatsoever. It's like looking for a needle in a haystack.'

'I suppose it is. Where have you been looking?'

I was uneasy about answering. 'Acapulco,' I said, as the first place that dropped into my mind.

'Big place,' said Gregor.

'Yes!' I said. I'd guessed it must be.

'And what led you down there?' he asked.

I hesitated. I should have known he would ask me. 'Well, I wanted to see the beach and . . . Acapulco struck me as the sort of place that ex-pats might be drawn to.'

'Well,' he said, unconvinced, 'all I can tell you is that it's my belief that he's in Oaxaca or Puerto Vallarta. Have you been there at all?'

I thought as fast as I could.

'Where's Puerto Vallarta?' I asked.

'Um, Jalisco, on the coast.'

'What makes you think that he might be there?'

'Oh we have our little ways of finding these things out, Mr Morgan. He seems to have applied at some stage for an export licence.'

'Oh right, right,' I said. It seemed eminently plausible.

'And you think it'd be worth my while going there?'

'Yes, I should imagine so. If nothing else you'll certainly enjoy the place. Probably Mexico's best resort, surrounded by tropical jungle. Very livable sort of place.'

'Right,' I said. 'I'll certainly think about going down there. When exactly was this export licence granted? Recently?'

'Oh yes, this year,' he said. 'Might I suggest a hotel to you? You'd do worse than to try Los Arcos. Decent sort of hotel and not too fearsomely priced.'

After I put the telephone down I felt a little perplexed. He had sounded so reasonable. I puzzled about it for the rest of the afternoon, and read up on Puerto Vallarta.

We had an early dinner again, just Lucinda and I this time, trying to patch things up between us. We didn't really get anywhere. When we got back to the room she showered and went to bed.

I telephoned Harry Koch. He'd been playing on my mind too. He was gruff at first. I suspected he'd been drinking. And then, just as when I went out to see him, he gradually warmed up.

'I met up with *Karina* here in Huatulco,' I said.

There was silence for a moment.

'You did?'

'You seem surprised,' I said. You old bastard, I was thinking.

'Well, yeah, I guess I *am* surprised,' he said.

'Why didn't you tell me she was a ship? Surely you knew.'

He went silent again. 'Well yes kid,' he said eventually. 'I did know that but I thought she'd be gone by the time you got there. Thought it might make you think.'

'You're a motherfucker,' I said. 'What was I supposed to do, stand on the edge of the quay waving his ship goodbye?'

I heard him laugh down the phone, a wheezing, cackling laugh. I could hear the clunks of the ice in his drink as he brought it to his mouth, it clonked against the receiver.

'Calm down. So the *Karina* was still in dock?'

'No she fucking wasn't. She was at the bottom of the sea.'

There was complete silence on the phone line. 'She's been sunk,' I said.

I heard a wheeze of air.

'What?' he said, at last.

'The ship's in pieces breaking up at the bottom of the sea. Don't tell me you didn't know that.'

There was silence again.

'Well, no. I didn't know that. When did this happen?'

'I don't know, a week ago?'

'Shit,' he said. I heard him pull the phone away from his mouth and then I heard a howl, echoing around his room, and the sound of something like an ashtray being thrown against the wall.

I waited, hanging on the line.

'You didn't know she'd gone down . . . ?'

'Damn it, damn them . . .'

'Surely you must know when a ship's been sunk.' I said. 'It's hardly the sort of thing that goes unnoticed.'

'No, no . . .' he muttered, 'This isn't England. A ship can sink silently here if someone wants it to.'

So Enrico had been quite right about the entire event going unremarked, covered up almost.

'Let me think for a moment,' said Harry.

The man was in a confusion.

'Look,' he said. He sounded shaky. 'Tell me how it sank.'

'She was either scuttled by the crew or there was an explosion. Can I come and see you again?' I said.

'For sure as hell no.' He sounded genuinely scared.

'What was on board? Drugs? Was it drugs?'

Harry laughed derisively. 'Drugs? No, your father would never be bothered with anything like that. That's a business where there's too many people taking a cut. Drugs . . .' He laughed.

I told him about my call to the British Embassy.

'Mmm . . .' he mumbled ruminatively, 'They're devious bastards, all of them. Don't matter what embassy it is where, they're not out here as tour reps. They've always got some other reason for whatever they do. Don't you trust them an inch. Puerto Vallarta has always been one of your father's bolt holes. They must know that somehow. God knows how.'

'They said I should stay at the Hotel Los Arcos.'

'Did they? Cheeky bastards,' he said. 'Sure they did.'

'Why?'

'We used to use it as a business address, that's what. We paid the guy on the front desk and used it for various deals, you know what I mean? It was sold to us as a confidential service.' He went silent for a moment. 'You got me thinking now, kid,' he said.

'About what?'

'Well, I'll be level with you: it sounds to me that the embassy would really like to have a talk with your father. There's obviously an invitation outstanding to the ambassador's tea party. You should watch it. You never know. It seems to me that they'd quite like you to find him. Then all they've got to do is follow you up his path. Keep your eyes open.'

'It all sounds too weird for me.'

'Oh come on,' he said. 'You've done great so far. You got this far, that's good.'

I was touched, moved even. The old man seemed almost proud of me. This was the first real encouragement I'd had, and I felt as if I was finally beginning to break through the barrier of secrecy and silence that surrounded my father.

'So where do I go now?'

'Well, I'm kinda nervous to tell you that. You know, calls are so easy to pump into these days. If anyone's tapping in by now, we've already been too foolish. Do I sound paranoid?'

'All of a sudden, yeah. I thought it was only me.'

'I'll call you at exactly eleven o'clock in the morning and we'll speak. I'm a little bit drunk anyway. Right now you should go to bed.'

He put the phone down on me.

I got into bed next to Lucinda. She was asleep. She could sleep through anything and I envied her for it.

It was a hot night and she'd pulled the sheet away from her body. There was just the gleam of the moon lancing through the blinds, and the defused light turned her body into the fine soft features of a daguerreotype, like a Victorian pornographic postcard with just enough drapery to cover her vanity. I pushed my face into the fold between her shoulderblades. Even uncon- scious, her skin flinched, and her body tensed. I lay for some time, squeezing my eyes tightly shut to block out the moonlight, trying to erase the image of the *Karina*, rolling and breaking on the seabed.

Before my eyes a drama was being played out in the dark waters of the bay: blackened divers, detonators strapped to their bodies, swimming out noiselessly in the black water; then the blast, and the orange screaming fire ripping into the hull as the crew woke in panic. The execution of the men as they leapt into the water from the deck, garotted silently and dragged to the depths; or their bodies loaded into a rubber inflatable for their distant disposal.

Then the phone rang.

I picked it up.

'Listen quickly,' said the voice. 'Go to Puerto Vallarta . . .'

It was Harry, sounding remarkably sober.

'. . . Ask for Isobel in the town. She's an Indian rights activist. Deals in art. That's all I know of Ron's life there. That's where his bolt hole is. You'll be fine. Any trouble, call me. Best of luck, kid. Get there before the boys from the embassy do.'

The phone went dead.

18

We travelled throughout the next afternoon and the night. At dawn, amid a universal chorus of chickens and cockerels we crossed the Río Cuale as it trickled over boulders to the sea, and the bus took us into Puerto Vallarta.

Lucinda shook me awake. It was a bright dawn. All the town's streets were cobbled and it was surrounded by the exuberance of tropical jungle. Because of the cobbles the cars had to take a leisurely pace. It gave an air of peace and wellbeing to the place. The townspeople were breakfasting on the pavements at the *jugos* fruit-drink bars.

'It's beautiful!' said Lucinda. I agreed. We woke up Todd and Jody.

'Are we in the jungle?' he asked, wiping the sleep from his eyes.

'We're in the jungle,' said Jody. He smiled stupidly, as the busy shop fronts and the hotels passed by the window. Jody kissed him.

'At last,' said Lucinda, 'you've brought us somewhere half decent.'

We checked into the oddly named Posada de Roger. We had a system now. We carried each other's luggage naturally, as if it were our own. Counting the pieces out of the bus and into the lobby. We had rooms next to each other's. We spent the first couple of hours showering and sleeping off the rigours of our long bus journey.

I woke at lunchtime and opened the louvred windows and looked out into the street. There was no siesta here. There was the steady roll of rubber tyres on the cobbles. The buildings rose, piled high on top of one another as they stretched up into the foothills of the Picacho de Palo Marias mountains. There was dense, green vegetation everywhere between the restaurants and rich apartment buildings. Posses of North American tourists rode around in hired jeeps. I felt as if I'd woken up from an exhausting nightmare, and I hoped that maybe there would be a few hours of respite here.

After the shock of the dive and the revelations of the *Karina*, I sensed that they were all trying to be sympathetic to me. Even Lucinda. I think they'd had some kind of meeting and decided to go easy on me. My father's ship was sunk. Maybe he was killed in it. Maybe I was emotionally drained.

I didn't believe he was dead for a moment. No bodies had been recovered, I repeated to myself.

Our room was simple with a cool stone floor, and all the furniture and fittings were elaborately carved. The only drawback to the room was the door to the bathroom, which was, like most doorways in the country, constructed in the belief that people don't grow any taller than five foot five. But, despite giving myself another crack on the head when I went for a pee, I liked the place. I was determined to.

The town had such a peace and a charm that for a while I was lulled out of my nervousness and my increasing sense of impending doom.

We went downstairs to the homely little bar where Juan Carlos, the barman, was presiding over a party of newly arrived Canadians. I was introduced to Roger, after whom the place was named. Roger was the hotel cat, a stately ten-year-old tortoiseshell sitting erect on the bar beside the olives. He only roused himself to take the occasional swipe at an errant fly with his paw. If the fly couldn't summon the courage to die upon his talons, then he left it to the overhead fan.

We went to explore. I was extremely happy to have Lucinda coming along with me. She listened as I rattled on about the town. She even seemed interested.

Despite the developed hotels up the coast, the old town was still a leisurely place with simple homes, and sweatshops, sandwiched between folk-art galleries and stylish restaurants.

Lucinda and I smiled at each other.

'I really, really like it here,' she said. She was positively enthusiastic. 'I really hope you find your father here and we can stay.'

'What is it?' I asked. 'You're being nice to me.'

She shrugged her shoulders, and changed the topic.

'You know that creep, that Sam guy?'

'Uh huh? Sam Fergusson?'

'He tried it on in the cab the other night, the snivelling shit.'

'He tried it on with you?'

'No, not with me. With Todd.'

'Oh, I see,' I said smiling.

'I think he thought he might get all of us into some almighty gang-bang.'

'Well, as you said, he was just a lonely tourist.'

We passed a house. There were two monkeys, on chains, sitting in the window. As we stopped to admire them one of the monkeys reached through the wrought ironwork, looked at me for a moment, and spat in my face.

Lucinda sank down onto her haunches laughing.

'Why me?' I muttered.

The streets were lined with vendors of every commodity – food mostly, cooked at stands where the local people sat on benches.

There were news stands everywhere, the front covers of the magazines shouting out with gruesome colour photos of murder victims and car crashes. The Mexicans love the blood and guts of life, and have a morbid obsession with death. Maybe reading about such horrors makes them feel better about their own lot.

We'd had our first decent, civilised day in the country, but when Lucinda finally gave in to the heat and went back for a siesta I went for a walk on my own. Actually I went on a bar crawl. I needed to get drunk to stop all the whirring about in my head.

It made it even worse, of course.

19

We all spent that evening getting outrageously pissed in the hotel – or in my case continuing the process – and watching a movie on the bar TV. The movie was called *Death Weekend* but it had been dubbed into Spanish as *Tragico Fin del Semana* – 'A Tragic End to the Week'. I was rather taken with the title.

'You know,' said Jody, laying a drunken arm around my shoulder, 'I'm really glad we came here. We love it.' They were talking excitedly about renting one of the apartments that sat above the town on the lush hillsides. Maybe *this* would be the place to set up their laptops.

The next morning I felt very ill and stayed in bed. I kept slipping in and out of a miserable sleep. Every time I became conscious I let out little whimpers and groans of remorse.

Suddenly the door cracked open and Lucinda and Jody burst in on me.

'Get up. We've found her,' said Jody, excited.

'What?'

Lucinda walked over and threw me my trousers. 'We've been up and out and found Harry Koch's Indian rights activist.'

'What?'

'Isobel' they said, 'The Indian rights activist that your father's kinda friendly with. His *bolt hole*.'

'We're taking you to meet her.'

'Now?'

'Yes, now,' said Lucinda. 'We're getting the eleven o'clock *panga* to Yelapa.'

I rubbed my eyes, got out of bed, took hold of my shirt by the cuff and dragged it, with my trousers, into the bathroom. 'What the bloody hell's a *panga*?' I said.

'It's just a little boat that takes us a short way down the coast.'

I looked back from the bathroom door and shook my head. 'A boat?' I said, feebly.

Lucinda threw some things into a bag and dragged me downstairs for some coffee in the bar, while Jody went to get Todd from the pool. I gazed around uneasily at the scene of last night's crimes by the tequila company.

'How the hell did you find her?' I asked, after the coffee had begun its work. 'It was a bit quick wasn't it?'

Jody told me that it really had been very simple. This part of the old town was full of Indian craft shops, and so they'd taken a tour of them, asking around. Everyone knew Isobel, and finally they'd got an address. She'd been dealing here in Huichol art for the last twenty years. She was practically the sole supplier to the tourist shops. She was the only one the Indians trusted. The bad news was that she didn't live in Puerto Vallarta. She lived in a small village two hours' boat ride down the coast, faster if you went by the little local *panga*. The village had no electricity, no TV, no mains water and no roads. It was entirely inaccessible by any way other than the sea. There was no road there and the jungle surrounding it was impenetrable. Jody's eyes were sparkling as she told me about it. She was very excited about seeing the place. I rubbed my head. 'I need another coffee,' I said.

'No time,' said Jody. 'Come on – we'll miss the boat.' She pulled at the collar of my shirt until I stood up. The three of them led me towards the door.

'Can't we just phone, and go tomorrow?' I mumbled.

'I told you, there's no phones, no electricity, no cars. It's paradise.'

I looked back at Roger, lying on the bar top, shading his eyes with a paw. I was quite envious of him.

'They will have paracetamol, though?' I asked.

We arrived for the *panga* at the jetty on the Playa de Los Muertos. The name seemed apt: it means Beach of the Dead. A terrible massacre had taken place here during the War for Independence.

The trick with a *panga* is to sit well back. They're small fibreglass fastboats and anyone sitting to the fore gets soaked and bounced up and down as it hits the waves. Sometimes people are bodily thrown out of the boat altogether. The service is run by a collective from the village of Yelapa, where we were going, and the boatmen, perhaps bored by their twice-daily nip along the coast, vie with each other to deliver the greenest-looking tourists. I was sitting, of course, in the very front seat. One of the boatmen sat behind me, on a can of petrol, smoking a cigarette.

The view of the coastline was remarkable. There were two great natural arches, Los Arcos, where the pelicans nest and have their shaggy fortress. The coastline became entirely tropical, punctuated only by the small beaches of La Borca, and Las Animas, the Beach of the Spirits. They were ravishingly idyllic from the boat, with just the occasional thatched house set on a deserted beach.

Then, as the *panga* approached a rocky point, the sea turned torrid with foam as it pounded against the rocks and blow-holes of the jagged cliffs. Just here a large fish, a barracuda perhaps, lunged up and snapped at the boat. Its mouth was exactly the size of my head. I was leaning close to the water trying to decide whether this would be an ideal moment to throw up.

We were all soaked, and already our noses and foreheads were getting burned by the combination of sun and sea spray. My backside was bruised and sore from where I had been continually propelled out of my seat at every wave and then crashed back down as the boat descended into great ultramarine troughs beyond.

Lucinda was shrieking with laughter, and taking photographs of us.

We curved into the bay of Yelapa. Before us was a stretch of white sand about half a mile long, with simple beach bars, a lagoon, and small quasi-Polynesian huts scattered like potpourri on the jungle hillsides. The four other passengers, all locals carrying kerosene and chickens tied with string, were set off at a ramshackle concrete jetty which had been built to land the tourists. I got up to follow them.

'No,' said Lucinda, 'we've arranged with the boatman to take us on over to the Point, and let us off at Isobel's Rocks.'

'My God,' I said, 'rocks?'

We crossed the bay. The boatman showing off even more now that he could be seen by his friends on the beach.

The boatman turned to us with little confidence as we approached the promontory of lethal barnacle-spiked rocks.

'Is too rough today,' he said. 'Too many big wave for landing.' I looked up, beyond the rocks, to where a kind of staircase, made of unevenly spaced boulders, towered up the sharp incline of rock face. It was practically sheer for about a hundred feet. I could see a rambling hut, a *palapa*, at the top.

'Come on,' said Todd, excited by yet another physical challenge involving a lot of water, 'we can make it if we jump.'

'What about my boat?' said the captain. I was growing to like him.

'Don't get too close – we can jump it,' said Lucinda.

He smiled at her admiringly, and then, unfortunately, he agreed that, if we could throw up our bags, judge the wave, and jump, then we could possibly just make it. Though, from the look on his face, he didn't really seem to believe that we could be lucky four times over.

Todd climbed to the front of the boat, humming a guitar riff.

'When I'm up,' he said, 'throw the bags and I'll catch 'em.'

He stood on the prow as the wave lifted, eyeing the rock like a moving target. The wave descended again, and stripped the rock to reveal the treacherous shelves beneath. Suddenly he leapt, with the wave only halfway up, and the momentum carried him with it and he sprang up onto the rock.

'Okay, throw me the bags,' he said triumphantly.

As I threw my bag up I felt a rush of nervousness as I committed myself to this foolhardy act. At the same time I cursed myself for my lack of courage. I despised Todd as he stood there gleaming and smiling on the safety of the rock. Jody looked at me. 'Do you want to go next?' she asked.

'No, no, ladies first,' I said. Jody used the same trick as Todd, the half-risen wave, and sprang up onto the rock. Lucinda went next, and although she landed a little awkwardly seemed well pleased with her efforts.

I sat rocking in the boat, looking winsomely at the boatman trying to see if there were any clues on his face as to when the next decent wave might be forthcoming. Then I jumped up onto the prow and leapt off just as the wave was descending.

Thank God for rubber-soled shoes. I stood on the rocks smiling inanely, having just succeeded, I knew, in the world's first fear-powered jump.

We all waved goodbye to the *panga* – I, perhaps, more enthusiastically than the other three. The boatman laughed and hit the outboard, shaking his head at the crazy *Norte Americanos*.

The ascent of the cliff had awful overtones, for me, of our descent to the wreck. I felt like a poor sailor, who'd survived a shipwreck, but was about to be killed by the coast.

I was some minutes later than the others arriving at the top. They'd already walked towards the house. From a small plateau at the top a rock way led a little further up to a beautiful garden of ginger plants and trees subdued from the jungle. In the centre of the garden was a thatch-covered house. It had a plaster floor with shells and pieces of broken pottery set into it. The *palapa* – as these constructions are called – looked as if it had been there for some time. It was stuffed with fading books and Indian craft works.

In the garden, exotic yellow-winged birds were about the business of building their own little thatch structures in the overhanging trees, and noisily reporting their progress to their mates. Lush green banana plants were in full bloom, their lavish, almost sexual, podlike flowers hanging in the bright midday sunshine. There was no one about.

We stood for a few moments watching the birds as they leapt into the air flashing their bright yellow underwings. Locals called them 'kiss-me' birds, because of the calls they make. The air was filled with the sound of them calling to each other: 'Kiss me, kiss me, kiss me.'

The house was deserted. We walked in. I flopped down onto a hard wooden bench, covered with a bit of foam rubber.

'Well,' I said, looking up at the others, 'she isn't bloody in, is she?' I shook my head and stared at the floor. There were ants everywhere. Lucinda began to laugh, and I looked up again and glared at her.

'Guess I'll go and take a look around outside,' Todd said.

I looked around the room at the riot of objects. There were carvings, masks, bowls made from gourds and studded with bright glass beads. There was an old oven, lashed up to a bottle of gas which must have been hauled up the rock face with considerable effort. It was an odd sight. I walked over to an old tin coffee pot that was still warm on the stove. We decided to sit and wait for the owner of the house. I poked about the shelves, looking at the books crammed onto the vine-strangled shelves. *The Home Doctor* was ominously well thumbed. Flowers were pressed between the pages of the old books so that they had taken on the dry veiny quality of the paper. I pulled out a book: *Snakes & Scorpions: How to Treat Yourself*. I shuddered slightly. There were a great many feminist works, too, most of the beat literature of the fifties, and loads of stuff on psychedelic art.

Todd came back into the room from his exploration of the estate.

'It's amazing,' he announced. 'There's this sun deck kinda place, overhanging the sea. It's like a pirate ship.'

'It's just beautiful here, isn't it?' said Jody. She walked over to him and kissed him. They looked out across the bay together.

'You thinking what I'm thinking?' said Jody.

'Sure, I am,' said Todd. 'This is it. This is really it.'

Jody turned to me. 'I just can't believe it, Jay. You know, like, thanks. Thanks, you've led us just where we wanted to be.' I raised my eyebrows. 'Look, down there, Todd,' she said, squeezing his waist. 'There's a couple of guys surfing.'

'Shit, I gotta get a board.'

'And those little bars and restaurants, it's just perfect. You see there's a lagoon behind the beach?'

'It's the most beautiful place I've ever seen,' said Lucinda, almost sadly. Two young boys rode along the beach bareback on half-breed palominos.

'It's so long since I've ridden,' said Jody, wistfully. 'You reckon they'd let me ride?'

'Sure they will, honey,' said Todd.

'So what time's the boat back?' I asked.

They stared at me in disbelief.

*　　*　　*

An hour later we heard voices from the path and saw two women who looked to be in their late fifties approaching with a dog. One, who had short cropped hair, held an egg carrier, and the other, with her hair piled high, was shouting at the young dog. As they bounded up the boulder-made path to the *palapa* I wondered what on earth had brought these women to live in a hut in the Mexican jungle.

'Hi there,' shouted the woman with the piled-up hair. 'You just arrived by the rocks?'

'Yes,' said Jody, walking over to her. 'We're looking for Isobel.'

'Well, you've found her. You've come to buy masks?'

'No, not exactly, we wanted to talk to you,' I said.

'Well, sure. We got time, Jean,' she said, 'why don't you put some of that shit coffee on. You want a cup of coffee?'

'Sure,' we said. They staggered in and dropped their provisions. 'It's made of nuts, not beans,' said Isobel. 'You'd think we'd know better than to buy cheap coffee from a dropout on the beach. But I can't live without coffee.'

'It can't be any worse than the stuff you get in all the restaurants,' said Jody.

'I wouldn't bet on it,' said Jean. They were both Americans. Jean smiled at us and went to do battle with the stove.

'Sit yourselves down and relax,' said Isobel. 'You're probably sore after the *panga*.'

She pronounced it *'ponga'*.

But the moment we sat down all hell broke loose as a couple of cats began a fierce duel on the thatched roof.

'Oh damn those two!' yelled Isobel. 'You know, they're mother and daughter. You wouldn't believe the way they fight. They fight like cats.' The cats hissed and spat. Jean looked up from the stove. 'Everyone says how peaceful it is here,' she said. 'I wish someone would tell those two.' She ground the nuts in a mechanical grinder.

There was a terrible screech from the roof and a thin ginger-patched cat fell off and landed in the hibiscus bush.

'Quick!' yelled Isobel to Jean, 'the machete!' Jean reached calmly under the sink and pulled out a long rusting machete with string wrapped around its line to provide grip. She threw it to Isobel. Isobel caught it and stood in the middle of the room wildly swiping it at the ceiling.

'It's a queen, it's definitely another queen,' she growled. Her eyes grew steely and intent as she chased around the room after the huge buzzing bee that had been disturbed from its home in the thatch by the cat fight. With both hands on the hilt she hit the queen bee a broadside with the blade and propelled it, stunned, out into the undergrowth, where the patchy ginger cat was limping away with as much dignity as it could muster. The dog got into its basket and buried its head.

Isobel pulled up a wicker chair and sat down, dropping the machete to the floor beside her. I was looking, I suppose, apprehensive.

Jean looked up from the coffee pot. 'They nest,' she said. 'You get a queen nesting in your roof and you got a bee problem.'

'So what can I tell you folks?' Isobel said as Jean brought the coffee over in rough clay mugs that had been fired in the sun.

We screwed up our faces as we drank.

'Yeah,' said Isobel, looking into her coffee mug, 'reckon you could run a generator on it.'

'I'm looking for my father,' I said.

'Uh huh?' said Isobel.

'I understand he stays here sometimes and I wondered if he was here now?'

'Oh right?'

'Ronald Morgan.'

Isobel picked up the machete and tossed it back to Jean.

'You hear that, Jean? This is Morgan's boy. He's nothing like him is he?'

Jean smiled at me.

'You know him well?' I asked.

'Sure we know him. Known him years. We deal in Huichol art. He comes by every now and then and stocks up. He likes those jaguar heads. Go for a fortune in the States these days.' Isobel got up and went to pick out a carved wooden head from a display on a shelf. 'These,' she said. 'Of course, this is just the basic carving. What the Huichol do is cover them with beeswax and stud it with glass beads. They fetch pretty high prices like that.'

I held the carved head in my hands. It was of a light soft wood and the carving was highly stylised. It was like a Brancussi, but it had sharp fangs.

'Could work out a decent price for you,' said Isobel.

'They've not come here to buy,' said Jean. 'They've come to find his father.'

'Sure, sure,' said Isobel replacing the jaguar head on the shelf.

'How much are they?' I asked.

'To you, fifty dollars,' said Isobel quick as a flash. I said that maybe I'd take one before I left. I wanted it desperately.

'He's not here at the moment, but you're welcome to wait,' she said. He often stayed over in the *palapa* just behind this one further up the mountain, but he didn't mix much in the village. Tended to avoid the Americans who lived here.

'But he could be here again tomorrow,' she said. 'The fun about living here is that you never know when someone's going to tumble off the *panga* onto the rocks. If they don't pitch themselves into the sea first that is.'

I realised then that her invitation to 'wait' was based on jungle time. It didn't necessarily mean they expected him to bowl through the door in an hour or so.

When we finished our coffee, Isobel said that she needed to do some jobs in the garden. The papayas had ripened and she wanted to get them into the house before something else ate them. I went with her and we carried on with our conversation. The others took a walk down to the beach.

'Of course, he used to have an export business with that old son of a bitch Harry, but I think something must have happened. Some sort of falling out between them. It doesn't surprise me. Koch was a cantankerous old twister from what I hear. Your father, on the other hand, is an absolute charmer. He could charm the fruit off the trees.' She cut off a papaya and dropped it into the basket that I was holding for her as an illustration of the fact. She suspected, though, that my father had maybe secured his own line of supply with the Huichol. They'd finally seemed to accept him. He'd started to deal with other tribes too.

The Huichol are shy people, she told me. 'It can take years for them to trust anyone. They were never conquered by the Spanish and the present government've given up on them. They still live in their old way, cut off from the rest of Mexico, and the world, in their villages high up in the Sierra Madre Occidental. You can try taking a light aircraft up into the mountains, but if they don't know you when you arrive you just got to stay on the airstrip. They'll simply ignore you and you'll have to sit there without food or shelter until the next plane arrives, whenever that is. It takes a special kind of person to win their trust.'

'And my father's that kind of person?' I asked.

She suddenly stopped cutting her papayas and turned to look at me seriously.

'You don't know him, do you?'

'No,' I said, 'we've never met.'

'Oh shit,' she said. 'I didn't realise that. Is he expecting you here?'

'No.'

'But he knows you're coming to see him?'

'Well, no.'

'Oh!' she said, chuckling a little. 'This ought to be fun. What makes you think he's coming to pay us a visit?'

'Harry said he was.'

'Well, as I said, you're welcome to wait. There's a few jobs need doing around the place. You and your friends won't mind helping out, huh?'

I smiled. 'I'm sure not.'

I asked her more about the Indians they dealt with. Maybe he was up in the mountains with them and wouldn't come here at all.

'No,' she said, 'there's drought on right now. They'll be down here selling their works.' In the months before the rain comes, she told me, they set off from their villages in groups of two or three with red cardboard suitcases filled with their artwork to sell. They're poor salesmen, though. The tourists on the beaches like to barter with them, and that embarrasses them. They can't understand why rich holidaymakers only want to argue with them, so they prefer to deal with people like my father and her.

We walked back to the house. Jean was drawing.

'I daresay', said Isobel, 'we'll have some Huichol call by in the next few days. Half expected them today. They'll know where your father is. They always do.'

'They just turn up,' said Jean.

'They usually bring me stuff and then spend the night here sleeping on the floor.'

'After we've cooked them dinner, darned their socks, and they've drunk us out of tea.'

'They're a beautiful, childlike, trusting people,' said Isobel.

'They're a pain in the ass,' said Jean.

I bet these women, like the cats, have the most fantastic fights, I thought. They were wonderful and you couldn't help but take to them instantly.

I could see the others from the rock. They were at a beach bar drinking beers. Jean offered to show me the way down.

'You mind if I join you for some lunch?' she said, 'haven't gone out for lunch in ages.'

'Sure, great,' I said. We invited Isobel but she wasn't interested in restaurants. She had work to do, writing something for an exhibition catalogue of Huichol art she was organising.

As we walked down the path that led towards the village, Jean began telling me about Yelapa.

The tourist season lasts for two and a half hours each day from October to February, when the battered old *Serape* hauls itself like an ancient cross-Channel ferry into the bay from Puerto Vallarta. The tourists are shuttled ashore in *panga* relays to the hotel jetty.

It was a mile along a narrow ridge to the village itself. The village had been there, where the river forms a lagoon behind the beach, since the beginning of the century. There were about a hundred houses, a small priestless church, and half a dozen very basic shops. The village had no roads at all: the houses and the tracks were all arranged around large boulders that looked as if they had been sent down the river in a huge, and catastrophic, flood. The chickens and the dogs ran freely.

The women were outside cooking tortillas over open fires. The young boys and men came trotting past on tough noble-headed mules. Everyone said 'hola', and the little girls came up with flower blooms. I was surprised that a place like this could still exist so close to the boom town of Puerto Vallarta.

'I know,' said Jean. 'It's a miracle. If we weren't cut off by the jungle there'd be hotels here too.'

We joined the others at the beach bar. The tourist boat was just pulling in, but for the moment the beach was white and deserted. Around the lagoon, which was at low water, the thatched huts rose up on stilts and behind them more huts rose up above the rocks.

We sighed with the beauty of it.

'You're so lucky to live here,' said Jody.

'You get used to it after a while,' said Jean smiling. 'But it was tough at first. We didn't even have a toilet then.'

We sat watching the tourists arrive from the *Serape*, about fifty in all. The attractions here have all been ingeniously devised by the villagers and because the visitors are here for only a couple of hours each day there's an uncharacteristic urgency to the restaurant trade, Jean told us.

Outside every restaurant the waiters stood in neat uniforms by the surf edge. They had menus under their arms and were holding plates of food – jumbo shrimp, or red snapper, complete with vegetables – covered with clingfilm or polythene as examples of what was on offer. Each restaurant was butted right up against the next and as the visitors walked along the beach the same catchphrases were repeated: 'You want good lunch, you sit here!' 'No, señor, you want good lunch, you sit here!'

So the visitors stood, in confused little groups, asking themselves the eternal tourist's question, 'Do we have lunch here, or do we have lunch there?'

Now that they were captive at a table staring at the huts and palm trees, and mesmerised by the bobbing of the boats in the bay, it was open season. The children arrived with sleepy orange and black iguanas that had been fed on peyote leaves or aspirin to keep them docile while they were slung around their shoulders.

'Picture, picture, picture!' screamed the children. So the visitors paid to take photos of each other squirming with reptilian discomfort as the lizard was wrapped around them. Some of the older visitors, with their wrinkled faces and their gaudy tropical print shirts and shorts, are almost indistinguishable from the iguanas they are photographed with, said Jean.

'When lunch is nearly over the men from the village'll arrive with their horses,' she said, 'offering to take people up to see the waterfall.

'The waterfall's famous. They've all been shown photographs of it by the tour reps that lure them onto the *Serape*. But it's three hours up river by horse. Thing is, they don't know that, they don't know either that there's another much smaller and shabbier one just behind the village, and that's where they're headed. They don't take into account that it's the dry season either. When they get there, there'll be no water falling at all. But when the restaurant up there is full they send a young boy up the rock to open a sluice gate that's stored the trickle that comes off the mountain in the night. The waterfall's switched on. There's this almighty clatter of twigs and leaves, and rocks.'

Meanwhile, back on the beach, she told us, the village women will have arrived. They are led by Juanita and her daughters, all laden with plastic washing-up bowls filled with pie. Juanita was one of the most respected people in the village because it was she who brought back the secret from America of how the women, too, could make money from the visitors. She had worked for a while as a cook for a family in California. More than anything else this family loved lemon meringue pie. They showed her how to make it and almost every day they asked her to cook one. When she came back home she spoke to the women of the village.

'What *Norte Americanos* really want,' she said, 'is not to ride our husbands' horses. What *Americanos* really want is lemon meringue pie.'

So they bake their pies and pack them into washing-up bowls. As the visitors sit, chewing through a resilient brochette, Juanita approaches.

'You want a piece of pie.' It is not a question, it is a statement of fact. And, even though these people are sitting eating their lunch at the time, they do all buy the pie.

Then it's the turn of the last and the lowest of the village. The packs of dogs will turn up to try their luck. The skinny creatures gather round with big brown pitiful eyes, gently pulling at the heartstrings.

They like lemon meringue pie too.

We were impressed. The economics of the village were absolutely concise and effective. Everyone had their place in it. There was no unemployment.

At the end of lunch, when the dogs were sitting balefully around us, I looked up at everyone and smiled.

'Well,' I said, 'Isobel and Jean have invited us to stay for a bit. You want to?'

Back at the house on the rock we began sorting out the arrangements.

'It'll be good to have some life around, won't it Jean?' said Isobel. 'We're sick of canasta.'

'Whenever do we play canasta?' said Jean.

'Well there you are, it's because we're sick of it.'

'We don't want to be any bother to you,' I said. 'We were planing to book into an hotel.'

'There's only the one place that calls itself a hotel, down on the beach. It's just a set of huts with padlocks.'

'They can stay in the spare *palapa* up the rock,' said Isobel. She turned to us. 'What shall we say, fifteen dollars each?'

'That hasn't been lived in for ten years!' said Jean.

'We'll find the broom!' declared Isobel, excited by the project. Maybe we'd stay a while, she suggested, and at fifteen dollars . . .

'Let me show you Annie's place up the rock,' said Isobel bounding up.

We began climbing a mud pathway at the back of the *palapa*. Halfway up was the lavatory. It had a small makeshift bamboo roof on it and an old pedal bin for the paper, and the entire structure was overgrown with a vine in flaming orange blossom. The vine had entered the cistern and put down roots into it. The porcelain toilet bowl must have been another bizarre sight as they hauled it up the rock face. As it sat there with the silver sea sparkling behind it, and the flowers all around, it looked perfectly ridiculous. Isobel had rescued the vine from the jungle 'to make friends with the john and make it feel at home.'

At the top of this section of the mountainside was the wooden deck that Todd had said looked like the forecastle of a pirate ship. There was another expanse of plaster flooring, this time stained blue, a herb garden in wooden troughs and what had once been a makeshift kitchen, open to the elements, except for a piece of thatch suspended from the palm tree around which it was constructed. The only finished element to the place was a handsome kumquat tree with its fruit full and fat and pulling on the branches.

'Oh dear,' said Isobel. 'It's a while since I looked at this place as somewhere to live.'

'Or even spend the night,' said Jean.

Isobel turned to Todd with beady eyes. 'You any good with your hands?' she asked.

'Sure,' he said, 'I'm brilliant. Where do I start?'

'Well I guess we'll need a roof and some walls.'

We set about making the place habitable for the night. Todd was in his element. While we hung ropes from the palm tree to support a wooden board that was to serve as a double bed, Todd took charge of the machete to build a wall from palm fronds.

Jean was working away with the broom. 'Isobel just loves building houses,' she said.

'Well,' said Isobel, turning to Lucinda and me, 'I'd better take you up to your accommodation. I take it you're together, yeah?'

'Our accommodation?'

'Yeah, sure. I guess you want to stay at the place your father always uses, don't you?'

I was slightly startled. 'Well, yes,' I said. 'The same bed?' I looked at Lucinda.

'Sure,' she said.

We walked further into the jungle, scrabbling up a little path. Then there was a clearing. It wasn't a house, it wasn't even a hut. It looked like Napoleon's campaign tent. It was like a small marquee with a striped canvas roof, the sort of thing you might see at the Chelsea Flower Show. It had an en-suite shower: a hose pipe that ran down the hill from the rain tank above, hooked up to a tree. The marquee had a plaster floor, and a mosquito net hung above the bed. There were no walls. Beside it there was an area for sunbathing with a hammock slung up.

'It's sweet,' said Lucinda. I was speechless. It wasn't at all what I'd expected.

'I'll show you the john,' said Isobel and she led us a little deeper into the undergrowth. The lavatory was a hole in the ground covered by a deflating football.

Isobel turned to Lucinda, 'When you shit,' she said, 'you chuck a handful of wood shavings from the sack down after. But if you're going to pee, pee in the trees.'

'Right, have you got that Jay?' said Lucinda.

'Yes, I've got that,' I said. Life in the Jaliscan jungle had made Isobel a most direct and practical woman, I could see that. I was not at all sure that we would be able to adapt quite so well. But we went back down to help the others, our own accommodation deemed to be sorted.

'Isn't this place so perfect?' said Jody.

'Mm . . .' I muttered. 'And we've been lucky enough to get rooms next to each other again.' I tried to smile. She laughed and kissed me on the forehead as I bent over an old biscuit tin, washing out the rust so that it could be used as a sink in their 'kitchen'.

'If we play our cards right,' she said, whispering so that Isobel couldn't hear, 'we might be able to stay here a while.' I said nothing. 'Oh come on Jay, it's going to be great. And I bet your father comes bounding up that rock.'

20

That first evening in Yelapa we lit a fire in the ginger garden and cooked dinner over it. The yellow birds were still calling, 'Kiss me, kiss me, kiss me' overhead, and the cicadas were playing on their ratchets in the undergrowth. Sunburnt and exhausted we each enjoyed the flicker of the orange flames on the others' faces as we chatted about our lives.

Isobel warned us about scorpions. We were never to go barefoot in a place like this at night. We were always to hang our boots up on a tree: scorpions love to take a nap in the moist warmth of an insole – it was absolutely their favourite place to be. Isobel had been stung nineteen times and the last time her life had only been saved by Jean performing an impromptu tracheotomy on her with a biro. She proudly showed us the scar. They were astonishing women. I could see that Jody and Lucinda were full of admiration for them. Though they looked younger, we discovered that they were both in their sixties.

When it was time for bed they lent us torches and we took ourselves back up the path, all the way searching the ground for scorpions, and turning our torches towards any rustling in the bushes. We kissed Jody and Todd good night.

We got into bed. Like Todd's and Jody's bed, it was a board hung from the roof by ropes and it swayed terribly, and the sheets had an eerie jungle dampness about them. I'd tied our shoes to the roof supports by their laces, while balancing precariously on the bed. I tucked my torch between my legs just in case anything made a jump at me from out of the jungle darkness. The air around felt solid with its impenetrable blackness. There was no moon. I couldn't understand how Lucinda was coping with it so well, especially after the way she had reacted to some of the hotel rooms we'd stayed in. Her attitude since we'd arrived in Puerto Vallarta was so radically different, I couldn't fathom it at all.

The deep oddness of the situation dawned on me. We were in a jungle, in my father's bed, and I had a torch between my legs.

We lay for some time, chatting about Isobel and Jean, speculating on their past lives, but all the time I had one ear on the jungle beyond the inky blackness. There were sudden noises. The type of noises that make you start. Slithering sounds, snake hisses, snapping twigs, snorting creatures, and sudden thuds of falling fruits and branches from trees that were rotten with beetles and termites, crashing to the jungle floor.

'What the hell was that now?' I kept finding myself saying.

'Oh do shut up,' said Lucinda. 'What the hell do you expect from the jungle, piped music?'

I realised that you can look at a jungle in two ways. Either as a place of abundant exotic creations, virile with fabulous blooms and fruits and orchids, or as a place of insidious darkness. A place of insistent and manic decay. It's the difference between the day and the night. Constant rotting, destruction by insect, rain and heat. The darkness and the noise invaded me. I had the awful sense of my father's body lying here sweating through the night, just as I was. This was my first taste of a jungle and I felt as if I'd been dropped into it ill prepared. I'd rather have fussed about in an outward bound shop for the morning, getting supplies and proper clothing. Perhaps not a safari suit exactly, but at least some insect repellant and something to ward off large snakes. Of course, I reminded myself, Lucinda had spent a great deal of her childhood in Kenya when her father worked for ICI. She was hardened to it.

Lucinda suddenly switched on her torch. 'It's too hot,' she said. 'Aren't you too hot?' I said that I was. 'Do you mind if I go and sleep in that hammock? It's bound to be cooler.'

'If you must,' I said. She made her way down to it with her torch, and when she switched it off she disappeared into the night, leaving me swinging away alone. I was determined to sleep soundly just to spite her.

If it hadn't been such a strenuous day I don't think I could have got to sleep at all, but miraculously I did, breathing in the sweet smell of the night-scented blooms.

In the early hours of the morning I felt a licking at my ear. The bloody dog's got in the bed, I thought, but then a shock ran through my body as I remembered there were no walls and that it could be anything. What had got in under the mosquito net? It nipped my ear and I reached for the torch between my legs and switched it on. As the interior of the netted bed was illuminated I saw a creature the like of which I'd never encountered before, and it was staring me in the face. It was about four foot long and it looked like a fox wearing sunglasses, except that it had a long snout and nose, which it could swivel around. It growled with a husky kind of hiss and it smelt most peculiar. It looked as if *it* was wondering what *I* was, too.

'Lucinda . . .' I whispered. 'Lucinda . . . ?' She was sleeping soundly.

It was most obviously not a domestic animal, nor even related to one. It had fine teeth which it bared for my benefit. I wanted to call out, but whatever I do, I thought, *I* can panic if I like, but the animal mustn't. We began to stare each other out. After a while it retreated a little and stood heavily on my knees. It had a black and white ring-striped tail which flailed around in the air. For ten minutes our eyes were connected and I began to realise that the creature had as little idea what to do about the situation as I did. It would have desperately liked to get away; I was surely far too big to eat, and my sunburned face poking up out of the purple blanket probably didn't look too appetising either. Maybe I bit too – it didn't look sure. It began looking for an exit, but the illumination of the torch made the interior of the mosquito net look impenetrable against the dense blackness outside.

I willed it to leave quietly, like a man trying to stand down a bar fight without losing face. It was as if we were drunkards after an unintentional insult; a joke taken the wrong way. If I switched the torch off maybe it'd make a bolt through the net, but I didn't fancy being bitten in a panic in the dark.

We stayed there, in this stalemate, for what seemed about twenty minutes. Then my patience snapped and I shouted at it.

'I don't know what you are, but get out of my bed!' The animal listened, and whimpered. Then suddenly it panicked and jumped back. Its back leg got stuck between the edge of the foam-rubber mattress and the net. It got itself into something of a tangle and tumbled out of the bed onto the floor. I watched as it tried to recover its dignity, by biting at my pack of Marlboros, and then it fled into the darkness.

When I woke in the morning the light was bright, and the rock was silent. I pulled back the mosquito net and gazed out across the bay. I sighed. It was a beautiful day and I had survived the night. It was a tremendous feeling.

I lay for a while watching the surf breaking and a band of fishermen hauling their catch out of a boat, laughing and throwing fish about. I jumped out of bed and looked around for my shoes. Lucinda was gone, probably on the beach.

I went down to the main house. It was empty. There was just a note lying by the oven which read, 'Help yourselves to coffee. Gone to get fish.'

I sat at the old wooden table drinking the odd-tasting coffee trying to convince myself that it was better than nothing.

There was a shout from the path and an elderly man, wearing just shorts and a white floppy hat, was approaching. I stood up to get a good look at him. He had soft flabby features. His face had the skin of an old woman rather than a man. If he hadn't been naked above the waist I would have thought he was a very old woman. He walked in without introducing himself, and stopped in front of me.

'D'you pull tics?' he asked.

'I'm sorry?'

'Tics. Do you pull them?' He raised his arm to show me a red patch just below the whitened hair of his armpit where he had been scratching. I was startled.

'This is Casa Isobel,' he said, insistently. 'They told me you pull tics.'

'I've only just arrived,' I said.

'It's just it's a real small tic and I just can't reach it. It's playing house in a real out-of-the-way kind of spot.'

'Oh, right, I see,' I said. 'Problem is, I bite my finger nails. Maybe there's some tweezers around somewhere.'

'The big ones I burn off with a cigarette,' he continued, 'but with the little ones you just end up burning yourself worse than the damn tic.'

'I imagine you would.'

'But it's the small bastards that are the dangerous ones. There's been a whole outbreak of lime disease. It slowly cripples you neurologically, and it's these damn little bastards that are the carriers.'

'Right, I can appreciate your concern, then,' I said.

There was a first-aid box on the kitchen shelf, so I spent my first morning in paradise tweezing out an infectious parasite from the nether regions of an ageing adventurer. The tic was a resilient little blood-filled bastard. And the armpit was pretty formidable too.

He left without thanking me, which I thought was poor. I spent a while reading medical books from the vine-strangled shelf, and scratching myself, telling myself that the coffee was growing on me.

Then I heard more shouting, this time from the rocks below. I went up to the deck to look over. There was a *panga* at the landing rocks. A man with blond hair and a ponytail, wearing a tie-dyed shirt, was shouting at a woman in the boat.

'Come on, honey, you can do it!' he yelled. But she sat there, a young woman, her body crouched nervously in the boat. She looked so small and fragile set against the rocks. She was neatly dressed in an unusually stylish new-age print frock, holding a clutch bag embroidered with peonies. Behind her was a collection of travelling cases, one of them with a tennis racquet in a press attached. He just had a backpack. She was resolutely refusing to get out of the boat. I was captured by the drama. She could have been me, yesterday. This must happen every morning.

'Come on, honey,' called the man. 'All you gotta do is get out of the boat and climb aboard the rock. It won't be any worse than when we got you in the boat in the first place.' He was obviously getting angry.

'Oh yeah?' she yelled, in a broad Bronx accent. 'At least there was a jetty.'

'Look, Terra, we're all supporting you, we're all sympathetic, we're all sending signals.'

'Well get my signal, *honey*. I ain't getting out until there's a ramp! You said this was a really neat place.'

'It is, honey, it is. Just do as the boatman says and wait till the wave gets up and step onto the rock like you would on the escalator in the mall. It's just like getting on your pony.'

'This ain't no pony. These are fucking rocks.'

'Come on beautiful, you gotta get out of the boat, we're here.'

'Well I ain't,' she said. 'I'm *outa* here.'

'Look,' he said, with a finality in his voice, 'you didn't like the boat ride. Do you really want to have to go all the way back again in that boat?'

This seemed to jog a nerve. There was a sudden look of inevitable disaster in her face.

'Come on, honey, come on darling, we're all with you spiritually.'

Then she threw up her cases, deliberately aiming, I thought, at the man. I quite liked the look of this woman already, her attitude. She flattened down her dress and gritted her teeth. She took a deep breath, and, with a gait like a gazelle's, she leapt from the boat. I closed my eyes as the *panga* veered backwards from the rock and she crashed headlong into the sea.

I began scrabbling down the rockside to help. The boatman had already leapt into the water to pull her bobbing head up above the waves. When I got down there they had pulled her up onto the rock. Her dress had been ripped and her shins scratched. It took some time to get her up to the main house. She was spitting salt water and cursing us all.

We laid her down on the foam-rubber sofa to recuperate. The first-aid box was still on the wooden table and I handed the man a bottle of iodine for the scratches.

I made more coffee and as I handed her the cup she looked up at me, as if I was the proprietor of the place.

'I was expecting a hotel,' she said. And then she smiled weakly at her own folly. 'I brought my tennis racquet.'

The man introduced himself. He was called Newman.

'Pleased to meet you, Newman,' I said.

'No, not *New*man,' he said, correcting me, 'New *Man*. I changed my name five years ago from Newman to New Man. I nodded my head as if this had been a truly terrific idea.

He was a businessman but he'd got into new-age philosophy after joining a stress therapy group. They had come to rent the *palapa* on the adjoining property to 'get in touch with ourselves'. I made them breakfast of cornflakes and goat's milk, with sugar from which I'd picked the ants (from Terra's that is – I left his in).

Todd and Jody arrived. They'd been lying in the shade of their palm tree. They'd had an idyllic night's rest. I introduced them.

'How did you sleep?' Jody asked me. 'You had a good morning so far?'

I smiled. 'Sure,' I said. 'It's been like *Jungle Drama Hospital.*'

Newman was staring at the cereal packet on the table. 'You know,' he said, 'when I was young I used to cover up the cereal packet. Put it in a paper bag, because, you know, I found myself reading the back of it the whole time. I worked it out. I must have trashed whole months of my life reading about my breakfast every morning, the ingredients, the offers, the sendaways, and I just got to a place where I needed to reclaim that time.'

Terra flashed me the briefest glance and her eyes went up to the ceiling. I put my fist up to cover my mouth.

Then Jody looked across at me, smiling, and nodded towards Todd. He was reading the back of the cereal packet.

That afternoon I showed Lucinda a picture of a coatimundi in one of Isobel's books. It's a sort of rabid Mexican raccoon with a swivelling nose. She shook her head at me.

'Why do you have to make these things up?' she said.

21

John and Lawander were two guys in their forties from Santa
Cruz in California. They'd lived together since they were twenty-
one. Lawander was of Puerto Rican extraction, Jean told me,
and had been a stunningly beautiful boy, and was still 'one of
the prettiest things in Yelapa'. John was strong and muscular
with Kirk Douglas features. We'd seen him from the rock
taking his daily swim, heading far out beyond the rocks into
the bay. He swam in a determined line for an hour or more,
way out to sea.

On our third night in Yelapa, Jean suggested that we go and
pay them a visit in their *palapa*.

'Ah, Jean!' called John, as we came up their path. 'You've
come down from your rock!' He handed the shovel he was
holding to Lawander and opened the gate to us.

'Oh God!' said Lawander, not knowing what to do with the
shovel. 'You would visit us just at this moment! You have just
picked the most appalling moment to arrive . . .'

'Has something happened?' asked Jean.

'Has something happened!' said Lawander. 'Of *course* something's happened. We've had another death. And just when we
were getting the garden and our approach so blissfully lovely.
Now this has to happen.'

'Oh, my God what?' said Jean.

Lawander stabbed fitfully at the herbage with the shovel.

'A possum's gone and died in the hibiscus,' he said. Then
he held the tip of his nose between his thumb and forefinger.
'Now instead of the welcoming scent of blooms on our garden
approach, we have a cloud of dead rodent stench.'

We laughed and were introduced to them as interesting young people who'd just arrived to stay with Jean and Isobel. I'd never seen a possum before, another of the jungle's furry mysteries, so I asked to be shown it in the hibiscus.

'Ah, you must be the boy we've heard so much about,' said Lawander, 'the one that sleeps with raccoons. Really, young man, do you have no taste at all?'

I said that I was indeed that same boy, and agreed that I had no taste whatsoever. The story had got round the ex-pat community of the village and John and Lawander had found it particularly amusing.

'What a way to lose your jungle virginity,' he said. It had never happened to anyone before. Lawander pulled back a swathe of hibiscus with the blade of the shovel, turning his head away.

I stared at the possum. It was like a very large rat, about the size of a loaf of bread, with a fat snakelike tail, and a surprised look on its face. Its teeth were protruding and its mouth was open as if it had choked on the brilliance of the hibiscus blooms.

Todd looked at the shovel. It was a fine shovel.

'And you're having a funeral for it?' he asked.

'No, not exactly,' said John, smiling broadly at Todd. 'We were planning to lay the shovel across that boulder and catapult the possum over the cliff.'

We were led into their *palapa*. Although there were only two walls to speak of, the rest of it being open to the jungle, it really was the neatest, most spotlessly clean hut in any jungle anywhere. They'd re-whitewashed the mud walls on arrival. They had hung up David Hockney prints of boys in swimming pools. They had a coffee table on which copies of *The Advocate* and *Homes and Gardens* were neatly piled.

They served us drinks, martinis or beer, and we settled into their puff-cushioned rattan chairs.

'We just couldn't resist staying here,' said Jody. 'After our first night we just went back to Puerto Vallarta and got all our luggage.'

'I know,' said John. 'We came out for a two-week vacation ten years ago. Now we spend four months of the year here.'

They were international antiques dealers who had made a *life decision*. They wanted to make only enough money so that they could spend time down here living with the plants and the jungle, swimming and sunning themselves on their deck.

Jean was smiling. This was exactly why she had brought us here. She had a real sympathy for Todd's and Jody's dream of leaving it all behind, and she knew that John and Lawander could help them.

They began to talk about how they would love to stay here if only they could find a way of modem-linking their laptops to the rest of the world.

'Ah,' said John, 'I think we should take them up the hill to meet the Adams boy.'

'I think so,' Lawander agreed.

John explained that the Adams boy was a member of a very old, and very rich, American family, and that he owned a fabulous *palapa* further up the hillside, just outside the village. He was now in his late twenties and lived a fairly wild, if reclusive, life. He rarely came down to the village and didn't mix with anyone. John had known his uncle in the States, so occasionally they were invited up to the house.

'And his *palapa* has everything,' said Lawander, 'solar panels and a generator, a satellite dish. He's even got a laser CD player. He's got his own little cinema up there!'

'The reason we think you ought to meet him is because he's desperate to get in on this Internet thing,' said John. 'He's planning to put up a radio mast.'

'My God,' said Jody. She turned to Todd and kissed him.

'We take it you'd like to meet the Adams boy?' said Lawander.

'Sure,' said Todd. 'It looks like we could get it cracked. When can we go up and see him?'

'Well,' said John, 'I guess any time really. He doesn't keep regular hours, and he doesn't come down here.'

'And since nobody else has a telephone in Yelapa,' said Lawander, 'we can't exactly just call him up. We'll just have to march up his track banging tin trays.'

'Tomorrow afternoon?' said John.

'Sure.'

We staggered back to the rock, along the narrow cliff track, our torch batteries failing, picking out only faint orange spots on the boulders.

We climbed up behind the flame-vine-strangled lavatory to the house that Todd had been building. We all wanted to see it. Jean came behind us, with Isobel, who'd woken on our arrival, carrying oil lamps to illuminate it.

'My God,' said Jody, 'what's happened to our kumquat tree?' We stood swaying and looking up at the tree. It had been stripped of all its leaves, every single one, but the kumquat fruits remained, dangling from the spindly twig ends like decorations left on an abandoned Christmas tree.

'That's a truly weird thing,' said Todd.

'What kind of person,' said Lucinda pondering it, 'would steal all the leaves but leave the kumquats?'

'It's a real shame too,' said Isobel. 'It was the only green tree we had left.'

'Not anymore,' said Jean. 'Now it's just twiggy brown.'

'And kinda orange,' said Todd.

'Weird,' we agreed.

We had been smoking joints.

I began to giggle happily, and, I suppose, I began to relax. I was truly glad that Jody and Todd had found their place, and that their quest to set up their laptops in paradise had come a step nearer to fruition. I was just a little sad for myself that I seemed no closer, really, to a resolution. But I didn't begrudge them their happiness. Jean put her fingers through my hair and smiled at me.

'Look!' screamed Todd, breaking us out of our somnolence, pointing to the blue plaster of the sun deck.

There was something moving towards us. It was the biggest snake I'd ever seen, at least forty foot long, and three feet wide.

It was a massive army of ants. They were marching through the *palapa*, hundreds of thousands of them, were marching across the floor and over the window ledge, and into the jungle beyond, all carrying bits of kumquat leaf.

'Leafcutter ants!' said Jean, giving them the sign of the cross. Todd and I went down on our knees and studied the remarkable creatures. Fat, round and red, and remarkably determined, they held out portions of kumquat leaf high above their heads, pieces much bigger than themselves. They were marching, marching, marching, with a single purpose. It looked like an ant demonstration that would bring down the ant government.

'You know what we're going to have to do?' said Isobel, pulling us all back down to earth. 'We're going to have to rig up a hammock.'

We got a hammock up from the main house. 'There's no way to beat these bastards if they want to come through your house – you just have to rise above it.'

Slinging the hammock was an entertainment in itself, and getting into it hilarious, which put several thousand of the ants in danger.

We swung there in the hammock, it seemed, for hours, often in silence listening to the exaggerated sounds of the night creatures calling and crunching, staging ambushes on one another on the other side of the thick dark night. At times Jody combed my hair with her hand and Isobel hummed a tune that searched hopelessly for its end. We lay there, something like a heap of contented snakes.

Gradually the oil lamps burned down and one by one figures rose without speaking and dissolved into the thick darkness like wood spirits returning to their arboreal forms.

The real world of sunken ships and devious dealings and disintegrating love affairs seemed a million miles away.

22

They came back late, and very drunk and excited. The Adams boy's house had been a good mile and a half out of the village. It couldn't even be seen from the track. It was perched high up, they said, hidden behind casuarina and kapok trees. They'd hit it off with 'Stevo', as they now called him, straight away. They were going to help him set up his computer station, and help him with the erection of the radio mast that he was just putting up. They were going to buy a plot of land from Isobel, and they were going to run a line from the mast to their *palapa*. They were going to get new terminals brought by boat from Puerto Vallarta. They were going to set up their dream of computer-working in paradise.

I sat for a moment and imagined what the approach to the perfect bay would look like from the sea when it was dominated by a towering steel radio mast, with red and white flashing lights twitching on it after dark. I didn't like to point out that the very reason why they had loved the place was because of the absence of such things. It saddened me, and I realised I was growing to like the place, and feel almost protective of it. I didn't dare voice my feelings for fear that I'd be even further isolated, and left out of everything.

Their project was succeeding as mine was failing, and Lucinda had, as was her wont, aligned herself with the winning team. I'd stayed behind in the hut while she'd gone up to meet the Adams boy with them. It presented me with a dilemma. I no longer believed that my father was ever going to turn up here. If he was going to go to ground, and I could see that Yelapa was an ideal place for it, he would have been here by now. I wanted to get on but I felt certain that if I was to propose a trip to Veracruz then Lucinda would finally abandon me. I would be travelling alone. It would be the end of my relationship with her, and I was finding it a very difficult decision to make. Many people had come to Yelapa and just hit a plateau. It lured you with its natural beauty, and drained you of your will. I was no exception.

Over the next couple of days Lucinda left me alone more and more. Every afternoon she set off with Todd and Jody to help build the radio mast.

On the third day I could see that something was happening to her. Each time she came back from the Adams boy's house she looked more wild. She was generally quite stoned as well. How they could all smoke so much hash and wire up something so precarious as a radio mast amazed me. Jody seemed to be doing all the work. Todd and Lucinda had taken to wearing hibiscus flowers behind their ears. Todd had made himself a pair of chamois leather shorts. Lucinda was wearing practically nothing at all.

They'd collected shells from the beach which they'd strung into necklaces, and had made themselves headdresses from feathers. At first it had just been a bit of fun. Jean had taken to calling Todd 'Jungle Boy', but after a while they wore little more than shells and flowers.

Lucinda had been obsessed with the laundry throughout our journey. When we'd first got to Yelapa she'd paid a local woman to wash our clothes in the river. I'd walked through the village one afternoon to see all my underwear flying on washing lines, decorating the centre of the village as if for a fiesta. Now she didn't seem to bother washing, or wearing, her clothes at all. Quite the reverse, in fact: she'd bought a pony-hide short skirt that smelt appalling, and had just wrapped a piece of flowery silk around her breasts. All the Americans found it great fun, but I found it deeply worrying. I dreaded to think what Lucinda's father would say if he ever saw the holiday snaps. She did make me a necklace of small pink seashells, but I felt an absolute fool wearing it. The more they exhorted me to 'loosen up' the more wired I became.

At the end of the second week Stevo had to go into Puerto

Vallarta to meet his accountant. They all sat around the *palapa* looking slightly lost without him.

I tried to fill the gap by attempting to sound enthusiastic about their project up on the hill. But every time I spoke I sounded like the kid at school who's always trying to buy his way into friendships with sweets, or swapping his most expensive toys for a handful of cracked marbles.

The next evening Todd came back from the beach excited.

'Look what I've scored!' he said. 'It's the stuff Stevo was telling us about!' He produced a plastic bag with about two pounds of rough brown powder. It looked like dried manure. Isobel and Jean confirmed that it was peyote, from the hallucinatory dried cactus that the Huichol Indians use in their religious ceremonies.

Everyone was terribly impressed. Todd decided that we should all take some straight away.

I looked up from my cup of tea. Isobel and Jean said they'd had all the hallucinations they needed in the sixties, but if we could take the bitter taste of it then we were welcome to go ahead.

Todd divided it up into four equal portions. I really wasn't keen, but I was desperate not to be left out.

It was the foulest-tasting stuff I've ever put in my mouth. It was like eating dirt with powdered bleach in it and my saliva glands worked away as if they were in shock. A sort of foaming mud formed around our mouths. It wasn't a matter of just a few spoonfuls either. You had to eat a whole soup bowl full. I heaved against it, but I carried on, encouraged by the beads of sweat forming on Todd's forehead. He was looking more uneasy than I'd ever seen him and I was pleased about that. Of all of us, Lucinda seemed to be having the least trouble with it.

It took about twenty minutes for us all to eat our portions. Then I began to feel very ill. I looked up and saw that everyone's face had gone deathly white.

'It might be best to take a walk – it sometimes helps,' said Isobel. 'Gets it round your system faster.'

'Yeah, right,' said Todd, slowly.

'You should go and lie on the beach,' said Jean, trying to get us out of the house, I thought. I was thoroughly miserable.

We staggered out into the ginger garden. Jody turned to me

and held on to my shoulder for support. 'Do you feel as bad as I do?' she said.

'Not too bad really,' I said, trying not to let her detect the urge to retch in my voice. Then suddenly I lurched uncontrollably towards the foliage. I collapsed headlong into the jungle and lay there for a few moments. The others lay down in the undergrowth as well, and it was deathly quiet. My ears were ringing.

Why have I done this? I asked myself. It was pathetic. I'd simply wanted to be part of it all again, to join in and not be left on the sidelines. Now I would do anything to be on the sidelines. Now the bloody jungle had got us all by the scruff of the neck.

After a while we managed to get up and walk to the beach. We felt marginally better walking.

'How long before we hallucinate?' asked Todd.

'Isobel said forty-five minutes,' said Jody.

'It seems hours already,' muttered Lucinda.

The moon was hanging in the trees on top of the mountain and silver clouds were passing across it like the reflection of the foaming surf in the bay below. We stood staring at it for a while. It seemed to be moving through the sky at an incredible rate.

When we got to the beach we all partially passed out, lying on our backs in the sand. I watched Beany, one of the hippy beach bums, shuffling along. I'd despised him for his dereliction the moment I had seen him. He lived by begging scraps of food from tourists at the beach bars and finishing off all the warm dregs from their beer bottles when the *Serape* sailed out again. He'd roll up discarded roaches from the ashtrays into smouldering joints. He smelt bad and it was impossible to enjoy lunch downwind of him. He had no clothes at all. He wore a sleeping bag that he'd cut the bottom out of for his feet, so that he could stand up in it and walk. It made him look like some sort of mutant caterpillar. When he was sufficiently drunk and stoned he would simply topple over and go to sleep where he fell. He was already in bed after all. He had managed to reduce the daily round to the absolute minimum. He was the ultimate example of what can happen to boy from a good family when he makes a visit to paradise.

Right now I didn't think there was too much difference between Beany and what we had become tonight. I could hear Todd pawing a hole in the sand, and I heard him throwing up into it. Jody staggered off to the sea and threw up in the surf. Lucinda was on her haunches retching.

We lay in this wretched state for at least an hour. Then things began to clear and, as I felt less sick, so my eyes began to sharpen and I had the sensation that I could see in the dark. I could zoom in on an object, a rock or a piece of driftwood, and when I altered my gaze I could take the object with it. I found I could move sizable rocks across the sand. I focused on a baby being rocked in a hammock above one of the beach bars, and managed to levitate it into the air and back down onto its father's chest again. When I'd got a little more practised I raised the baby, when it began to cry, high above the roof and left it there some time, floating in the air. Then I catapulted it into the sea where it splashed about like a cherub that had fallen out of heaven.

When the moon had gone behind the mountain we all felt strong enough to take a walk along the beach.

'So you reckon that was the hallucinations then?' said Todd. 'All I saw was the sand moving. What a rip-off. I wanted to see monsters and stuff. I thought your body would be all crawled over by snakes.'

We walked further. We agreed that we were all feeling remarkably lucid. The effect must be over.

'Hey!, hey!' shouted Todd as one of the beach dogs ran by. 'Did you see that dog? Amazing!'

'What?'

'You didn't see the dog? He had, like, stars coming out of his paws!'

Jody and I laughed.

'Oh God, you've started,' she said. 'It's starting on you.'

'Took longer than forty-five minutes,' I said.

'This is Mexico,' said Lucinda.

'No,' said Todd, 'it really did, there were real sparks coming out of the dog's feet.'

Further down the beach the dog turned around and came racing back. As he passed we watched open-mouthed. There were sparks, like little stars, coming out of his paws and cascading behind him for two feet.

'The local kids have tied fireworks to his paws,' said Jody. We laughed. But there definitely were sparks. We found a stick and threw it and a shower of sparks flew up from where it landed and the dog was baring its teeth and snapping at them. His fangs were illuminated with a sharp violent whiteness.

'But how can we all be having the same hallucination?' asked Jody.

The dog came by again and showered us all with stars. Todd began kicking sand high into the air and found that he could do it too. Jody and I kicked at the sand and sent showers of tracer fire towards him. Todd did a handstand and white sparks flicked between his fingers. He threw himself into the sand, then looked up at us.

'Pretty cool, huh?'

The next morning I was having breakfast with Jean and I told her about our collective hallucination.

'I know,' she said, laughing. 'We saw it too.'

'What do you mean? How could you have done?' I asked.

'We were sitting at the top of the rock and we could see you all down on the beach. We'd seen the stars coming in from the sea earlier.' She laughed again. 'They're amoebas,' she said. 'Tiny little phosphorescent sea creatures that get washed up this time of year and bury themselves in the sand.'

'Little buggers,' I said, laughing. I went bounding up the hill to tell Lucinda. After I'd said what Jean had told me she just stood there for a moment, staring at me coldly.

'Why do you have to take the magic out of everything?' she said. She picked up her cigarettes. 'Stevo's back,' she said. 'We're going up to his place.'

I watched her as she walked away down the track, laughing with the other two.

That afternoon I decided to take myself off on a long rambling walk to work out what I had to do next.

I set off to see what was around the point and took a route up the hill, scrabbling up the dry palm fronds that were now everywhere. After an hour or so I came to a banana plantation.

It was among the banana plants that I lost my way from the track, simply, I suppose, because there were so many tracks to choose from running between the lines of plants. I'd gone over the first ridge of the hill as well and could neither see nor hear the sea anymore. When at times I could hear it, it was invariably being bounced off a high rock, and so the echo set me off in entirely the wrong direction. There was something about bananas that always seemed to lead me into trouble. I still found it painful to remember the episode on the train at Benjamin Hill.

In my mind I could see night coming down and the scorpions coming out and I began to get genuinely fearful. I called out a couple of times but all I heard was my own voice coming back at me from the flat-faced rocks.

Every now and then there'd be a mighty rustling in the undergrowth and something would go charging off, but I never saw whatever it was. Occasionally I came across the thick black rubber pipes that brought the water down to the village from rain-catching tanks higher up in the mountains. These pipes, I knew, could be several miles long. I thought of climbing a tree to try to get some sort of overview, but I seemed to be in an entire grove of kapok. While these trees are harvested for the soft downy fluff that bursts out of their pods for stuffing pillows and soft toys, the trees themselves are vicious. They have thick white trunks studded with evil spines all the way up. Much more hurtful than grapefruit or hawthorn, the spikes are three or four inches long and they point out horizontally. I was getting scratched and stung. Insects were buzzing about my head and flying into my face. Blood had begun to trickle down my legs.

I walked for two hours and then I thought I heard music. I cupped my hand to my ear and listened. It wasn't the marimba player from Gloria's restaurant, nor was it the tinny sound of the local radio station on a transistor radio. I followed the sound. It was rock music from a formidable sound system.

I scrambled down over some boulders that were exposed to the sun and burning hot, and then started my way through another expanse of kapok, interspersed with casuarinas.

I stopped as I saw a house through a narrow avenue that had been cleared through the trees. It was the largest place I'd seen in

Yelapa. It was entirely alone, and set on several levels, with the jungle growing into it and bursting out with cascades of coloured blooms across its terraces. As I got to within about twenty yards of the house I saw that it was entirely surrounded by a high wire fence that was impassable. It was like the compound of a fanatical doomsday cult. I began to follow the route of the perimeter. Then I heard voices, and groaning, mixing with the rock music.

The grounds of the *palapa* had a pool with a wooden deck running around it and umbrellas set at angles for shade. I had no doubt in my mind whose house I'd come across. It was, after all, the only one this far back in the jungle. They'd all be surprised to see me. I was quite interested to meet this Stevo who had absorbed all their time and thoughts. I was about to shout but as I opened my mouth the air dried in my throat.

I could see a bare backside moving slowly up and down by the poolside, below the window. I watched as its owner reached down and pulled his naked companion to him. I heard Lucinda's shrieking laughter and then she fell silent as they kissed, violently, the sweat gleaming on their bodies. I could see then that the bare backside was Todd's. Another head came into view a few feet beyond, hidden in a mess of rock-star hair. This would be Stevo, the Adams boy, I realised. I stood transfixed, gripping onto the wire fence so that it hurt my hands. Riding on top of him was Jody, waving her arms about wildly like someone on the back of a motorbike on a dirt-track. Then I watched as Todd smoothed his hand over Lucinda's back, as they pulled themselves up onto their haunches. They groaned and gasped for breath.

I stepped as quietly as I could back into the trees, almost impaling myself on the kapok. Perhaps I did impale myself – I wouldn't have noticed, I felt so numb. I could barely breathe.

I wanted to howl, or charge at them suddenly out of the trees like an irate primate in the wild. Instead, I negotiated my way silently around the perimeter fence, every now and then glancing back to see their bodies writhing through the kapok and casuarina trees. Finally I found the track at the front of the house.

It was a long walk back down that track to the lagoon, and I was feeling stunned, and sick. No wonder, I thought, that they hadn't encouraged me to join them at the grand *palapa*. I felt excluded and, more than that, betrayed.

I must have sat on the beach, after wading through the mud of the lagoon, for an hour or more, watching the pelicans diving, my eyes filling with tears.

It still wasn't dark, but the sun was low in the trees. I felt a light tap on my shoulder and slowly turned around. It was John and Lawander, out for their early-evening walk.

'You're keen!' said Lawander.

'I'm sorry?'

'For the waxing. Tonight's the waxing. You're here for the hippy full-moon party?'

'No, no, I've been for a walk,' I said.

Seeing, I think, that I was looking sad, and being sensitive to these things, they invited me over to one of the beach bars for a beer. I wandered over with them, moving like an automaton. I had nothing else to do.

'Everyone goes slightly crazy at full moon. Even the animals, so watch out for your raccoon tonight.'

'I will,' I said, trying to smile. I wanted to tell them that the animals had already gone wild. I was in a mild state of shock. I was trying to decide if I could blame them at all for what I'd witnessed at Casa Stevo, for introducing them to the house, but I couldn't really. I simply needed to lash out.

'It should be quite a good do, actually,' said John, 'because it's the biggest full moon you'll ever see. Right now the moon is closer to the earth in its orbit than it has been for a hundred years.'

'We're all expecting to get quite affected,' said Lawander, dramatically, 'God knows what we'll do!'

I gave out a short cynical laugh.

'Oh dear me,' said Lawander. 'I can see you've had quite enough of the local hippes. Are they driving you mad?'

I nodded, and then turned my head sharply towards the sea so that they didn't notice that tears were beginning to form in the corners of my eyes. If they got so much as the smallest foothold I knew that the floodgates would open and I would suddenly collapse onto the sand. If I had to explain why, it would only make the whole thing more real, and I didn't want that. I preferred to leave what I had seen as a blurred image of a bundle of naked bodies, like a nest of wriggling snakes, like an old pornographic movie in a foreign language.

I looked towards the hippies, piling up a vast stack of driftwood a little further up the beach. I tried to concentrate my mind on the present.

'That bonfire looks a bit precarious to me,' I said. 'Why on earth have the stupid bastards built it on a slope?'

'Oh,' said Lawander, 'it has to be built in exactly the right place, at a point equidistant to the sea, the lagoon, and the rock. In that way the fire focuses the cosmic energies of the full moon. But that aside,' said Lawander, 'it's a pretty good place to bake potatoes for when you get the munchies.'

'If we don't all get busted by the *Federales*, or whoever they are,' said John.

'Apparently a bunch of heavy-looking guys arrived on the afternoon *panga*,' said Lawander.

I looked up.

'So we'll expect to see you all down here later?' said John.

I shook my head. 'I really don't know,' I said. 'I don't know what the plans are.'

I didn't feel like going back up to the rock to see any of them, if they were there. I thought that maybe I would just stay on the beach all night, getting soaked up.

John and Lawander excused themselves, laid down their beer bottles, and went home to change for the party.

Evening always descended swiftly on the beach because the sun was prematurely lost behind the mountains and it gave the impression that it actually set somewhere in the jungle itself, a mile or so distant. It added to the strange atmosphere of the place and the dark silhouettes of the houses on stilts pervaded the village with a strange otherworldliness. Tonight I thought it looked like Vietnam. The moon hadn't risen yet and so it very quickly got dark, a dense hot darkness, with just a few slumped figures on the beach unaware that the day had ended. Beany and his mates.

I was sitting staring at the table top, still at the beach bar, when a hand slapped heavily down on it.

'Ah, here you are. Wondered where you were.' I looked up, it was Todd. 'We were thinking of us all going to this waxing thing this evening. The girls are all getting some food ready to put on the fire. Thought I'd come down and see if I can buy some draw. Are you into this waxing thing?'

'Not really,' I said, looking back at the table top. 'I think it's a lot of old shit.'

He called for a beer.

'You look a bit down,' he said.

'You could say that,' I replied, coldly. We sat for some time and the situation seemed truly absurd. I couldn't decide what to do about Todd at all. I remained silent.

A young Mexican guy came and stood by our table.

'Got any smoke?' said Todd.

The guy shook hands with us. 'Yes,' he said, 'I can get you some smoke.'

'Look,' I said, 'I think I'll go back up to the house to see what the girls are up to.' The young Mexican grabbed me by the arm.

'I get you good stuff too,' he said.

'No, thank you.'

He turned back to Todd.

'You give me twenty American dollars and I'll get you good smoke.'

Todd disagreed. 'You get me good smoke and I'll give you twenty dollars then.'

'Okay. For ten dollars more you can do fucky-fucky with the girls up the hill. I take you up there, yes?'

'Ten dollars?' said Todd.

'For fifteen dollars, two.'

'They're up the hill, how far?'

'Not so far, behind the lagoon, fifteen minutes only to the special house. You both come with me? We get smoke there too. I make sure you are safe. A nice two girls each, good time, free drinks, much fucky-fucky . . .'

'No thank you,' I said. 'You can count me out of this.'

The Mexican boy looked at me, confused. Then he smiled. 'You want to screw my brother?' he asked, brightly.

'It's a kind offer,' I said, 'but I really ought to be getting back.'

I stood up, leaving a wodge of crinkled pesos on the table top. My God, somehow I'd even paid for Todd's beer.

23

I never made it back to the house. I couldn't face them. When I returned to the beach the waxing party was in chaos: everyone was running about with lumps of charred wood, their clothes sodden, and the bonfire destroyed. Although they'd worked out the cosmic positioning, equidistant from the mountain, the lagoon and the sea, they hadn't bargained for the high spring tide that the full moon would also bring with it. It had drowned the entire thing.

'It was the most screamingly funny thing you've ever seen,' said Lawander, as I stood back watching the mayhem. 'Everyone's just got nicely on the weed and then the biggest queen of a wave comes crashing in from God knows where. Half of us were so stoned we didn't know what hit us. The dope's gone everywhere, and my baked potatoes are buried without trace!'

'Are the girls here?' I asked.

'Yeah, sure, they're all over there drying off their sarongs,' said Lawander.

'It's all over?'

'Oh no, they're going to reposition the bonfire up the beach and we'll just start all over again.'

The fire was rebuilt and relit further up the beach. I looked at them as they sat around. It was a rather shabby affair, I thought. Several people were lying on their backs St Francis-style receiving the stigmata as they worshipped the moon. As soon as the fire flared so all conversation died away, and people were staring into the flames as if mesmerised.

Jean and Isobel had decided against coming down to the beach.

'There's been a rumour going round that the *Federales* have arrived and are going to stage a drugs raid,' said Jody. Strangers had been seen.

Jody was worried about Todd. She hadn't seen him since he'd come down to the beach earlier to get some draw.

An hour passed. I watched the moon playing on the waves. Then in the distance we saw a figure limping painfully, making its way towards us, every now and then stumbling and falling headlong into the sand. Jody tapped my hand to watch and she pulled herself up. Even in the brightness of the moon we couldn't make out who it was because his head was bowed low and he swayed from side to side. He was coming from the direction of the ramshackle hotel.

Jody grabbed my arm.

'It's Todd, it is, oh my God it's Todd.'

She raced towards him, to where he staggered in the sand a couple of hundred yards off. As Jody grabbed him he seemed to crumple and collapse in her arms. There was blood all over his face. His nose looked to be a little to one side, and he was limp and fainting. I ran toward, them with Lawander.

Todd looked up into Jody's face.

John and Lawander helped him to stagger back to the fire where they could get him into the light and do something about his wounds. The others looked up idly from their stupor and turned back to the glowing fire again. A guy cradling a guitar looked over. 'Who was it, man?' he said, slowly. 'The pigs?'

Todd's eyes glazed over as Jody cleaned his face with splashes of Evian water. The guy with the guitar picked up the bottle of Evian as Jody put it down and drank from it. 'There's *Rurales* everywhere,' he said. 'They're in town to raid us for drugs, maybe *Federales* too.'

'Yeah . . .' said another reveller, and then she laid her head back in the sand.

'Who beat on you? Who hit you?' Jody was asking, frantically.

'I dunno,' said Todd. 'I can't remember.' He looked across at me, a look of confusion in his eyes.

Lawander bent down and smelt his breath. 'We're not going to get much sense out of this boy tonight,' he said. 'He's been drinking that horrible *racilla* hootch with the local boys.'

John and Lawander helped to get Todd back to Isobel's rock. They laid him in bed.

We all sat on the pirate deck for a while.

'Quite frankly,' said Lucinda, 'that was the worst hippy peace festival I've ever been to.' Both Jody and I stared at her, saying nothing.

'But where's he been to? You must know.' Jody asked me again.

'I've no idea,' I said.

The next morning I got up and packed a bag. I went down to the main house for some of the dreadful nut coffee. Jody was sitting at the table talking to Lucinda and Newman. As I walked in he was inviting us all to join him at Gloria's restaurant in the village for lunch that day.

'I don't know it would be wise,' said Jody. 'Todd had a ruck with some of the local guys last night. Well, we guess it was them, so it's probably not a good idea to show our faces in the village today. He's pretty messed up any case.'

'Oh, that's bad,' said Newman. 'That's really unsettling for you. You want maybe we should give him some of our aromas? It's a real soothing treatment.'

'No, that's okay,' said Jody. 'Isobel's already been playing him her nose flute.'

'Oh, right, good, that should rebalance him. So who beat on him?'

'He can't remember. He'd drunk *racilla*.'

'Oh, no. That stuff's real unsettling. You think maybe it was the *Rurales*? I heard there was a whole bunch of *Rurales* came in a fleet of *pangas*.'

'No, no, we don't think so. He still had money in his pocket.'

'Man, what's happening to the world? It never used to be like this. Maybe it's all over here. I heard the waxing was, like, really unsettling too.'

'Yes, I guess it was. We expected to see you there,' said Jody.

'Did you hear how the waxing ended up?' said Newman.

'No, we left when Todd got beat on.'

'Oh, it was real bad. Really, really bad. I heard that everyone got real mellow again, you know, after the tidal wave, and, I guess, Todd's beating. Really starting to get in touch with themselves and everything. The moon was really strong. Then some of the young guys from the village came down and you know what they did?'

'No?'

'They threw firecrackers into the bonfire. It really broke the aura.'

I smiled to myself. I imagined that it must have done.

'Everyone thought it was the *Rurales* shooting,' said Newman.

Jody turned to me. She looked worried. 'You don't think that maybe whoever attacked Todd was something to do with your father, looking for you maybe?'

I raised my eyebrows and considered it. Lucinda looked up. 'Oh for God's sake don't put ideas like that in his head,' she said. 'He's bad enough as it is already.'

'I'm getting the *panga* into Puerto Vallarta in half an hour,' I said. 'There's some things I want to do.'

They all looked up, surprised. They waited for me to explain, but I didn't.

'You're getting supplies, or something?' said Jody.

'Yeah,' I said. 'So if anyone's got any postcards they want sending or anything, let me have them.' I walked up to get my bag.

I waited on the rocks until I saw the *panga* heading out from the beach. I waved and it came over to the rocks. I jumped in.

'When will you be back?' I heard Lucinda shouting from the rock, but I pretended not to hear her.

I didn't even look back as the *panga* sped on its way to Puerto Vallarta.

We arrived at the Beach of the Dead. The sea was filled with heads bobbing in the water like a plague of black flies. The beach was crammed with families from Mexico City. It was Easter week and Puerto Vallarta was full. It was a national holiday, the time when the land was dying for want of rain, the time when the Aztecs and the Maya would throw themselves into an orgy of blood-letting. The priests would tear out the hearts of twenty thousand victims in a single day to ensure the coming rains. Now it's the time when the city folk go to the coast.

I walked up from the beach and outside a church a scaffold had been erected. Swinging from the gallows was an effigy of Judas Iscariot. They'd dressed him up as a sort of yuppy, in a suit and trilby. In the early days of the revolution he was frequently dressed as a landowner, a *hacendado*, and before that as a Spanish colonist. On Saturday they'd pack him with explosives, take him to the piazza and blow him to bits.

I could see why the Mexicans loved Easter so much. It had everything they knew: a band of young revolutionaries, a mule, a secret meal in an upper room, treachery, the rigged trial, and the horrible public execution. It was a contemporary story. Now it was the blood of Christ that cured the parched land and cooled their tempers.

I began walking towards the Posada de Roger. There were people everywhere, but no Americans or Canadians now that the season was over and the resorts were given back to the Mexicans.

I walked up the Avenida Insurgentes past the stands selling *tacos al pastor* and the endless racks of bloodthirsty magazines. I stopped at one of them for a beaker of coconut milk. My eyes were playing idly across the garishly printed covers as I waited to be served. Then something caught my attention. Something in the background of one of the cover shots: a kidney-shaped pool. The headline shouted out in black: ASESINATO EN CHAPALA. I bought it and sat down with it on a bench. I sipped my coconut milk. The murdered man on the cover, lying beside his pool, was unrecognisable. He was drenched in blood, and his body was contorted. He was slightly bloated, I suppose from being quite a while in the sun before he was found. The police must have some sort of reciprocal system with the press for the provision of the most graphic – if badly focused – shots, I thought. I flipped through to find the accompanying article. There were few words – those that there were printed in bold red type. There were more shots: a close-up of the side of his head where a third of the skull had been taken clean away by gunshots and the mashed-up brain glistened in a mushy pinkness like a bowl of trifle spilling on the poolside. Beside the body was a candystriped lounger splattered with blood.

I threw the magazine into the litter bin with my paper beaker. The coconut milk was curdling in my intestines. I began walking away from the stand, walking unevenly. I felt as if I was going to pass out. 'Poor Harry,' I kept repeating, 'poor Harry.'

Another monkey hissed at me through a window and I glared back. It scuttled into the dimness of the cluttered parlour filled with pictures of saints and spat out at me.

I kept walking. I was scared. I had no doubt in my mind that Harry Koch had been brutally murdered and that there was some sort of connection between his death and the sinking of the *Karina*. I remembered the way his revolver had glistened on his poolside drinks table. I could hardly forget it: it had given me such a shock at the time. I'd never been so close to a gun before. Had he been expecting them?

I felt numb, and rather cold, even though the sweat was running down my chest and breaking out through my shirt front. I felt detached from reality.

I walked straight into a *Caseta de Larga Distancia*, a long-distance telephone office, housed in the back of a stationery shop. I gave the number I wanted to the clerk, and waited in the booth for my call to be connected.

I was thinking about England. England at Easter time when all the public parks would be full of daffodils in clumps; trees in their fresh greenness, primroses in the hedgerow; the brash bursts of rhododendrons on the country estates; the smell of bluebells and wild garlic crushed underfoot as people took their first country walks of the year. I thought affectionately of the gentle nature of home; of the English countryside, a natural equivalent of Elizabethan prose style; each delicate spring flower like the emblem of an ancient house.

As a child I'd always loved this time of year when Mum and I would go on our first expeditions. Off to pick sticky bud – the first shoots of the horse chestnut – to put into vases around the house. I remembered my childhood in terms of the seasons, seasons that no longer seem to register at all. May for the bluebells, June the strawberries on a local farm; July the pea-picking, and then, best of all, August and the wild blackberries in the woods. I thought of those trips into the woods with Mum, our fingers stained blue, clutching our Tupperware boxes. Every year Mum snagged her stockings on the briars and small trickles of blood would run down her legs.

Right now my mother's house would be filled with hyacinths and impatiens, in purples and pinks on every windowledge and occasional table. There would be a pot of bulbs beside the telephone on the hall table. A fresh homely scent everywhere, a mixture of flowers and clean sheets.

The telephone rang. I was through to England.

'Hello, hello, who is it?'

'It's me, it's Jay.'

'Oh thank God. I thought I was never going to hear from you. I've been sitting by the phone for weeks, I'm worried out of my mind. I'm a bag of nerves. Thank God you're back from America.'

'No, Mum,' I said. 'I'm not. I'm still here.'

There was silence for a moment, then she said, 'What's happened? Why haven't you come home? You never said you'd be gone this long.'

'Nothing,' I said. 'I just thought I'd call for a chat. See how you were. How are you?'

'So you're still in Los Angeles?'

Her tone was deeply serious. I couldn't lie to her so I didn't say anything for a few moments.

'I'm fine, I'm fine.'

'When are you coming home?'

'I'll be home soon. In the next week.'

'Come home now.'

Just as she sounded more relaxed a Mexican string band turned into the street leading a procession of the Children of Mary. They were letting off fire crackers. They stopped right outside the *larga distancia* to fire them. The sound they made as they smacked against the walls made my head spin. My voice wavered and dried up completely.

Mum went silent.

'Are you sure you're in Los Angeles? I don't think you are. I know you're not.'

I tried to answer but floundered.

'You're in Mexico. You've gone down to Mexico?'

I couldn't answer. She knew I was there, and she obviously knew why I had gone. She knew nothing of the letters that I'd found at Uncle Roderick's. I had kept them a secret from her, but somehow I sensed that she knew where my father had gone, all those years before. I knew that I'd betrayed her, and I regretted it deeply now.

'I've had a visit,' she said, 'from some people from the Foreign Office.' She paused.

'Really?'

'Yes, really,' she said sternly. 'They asked me a couple of questions. They asked if I'd ever stayed in touch with your father after we divorced. Then they asked me if I knew where you were.'

'Oh God,' I said.

'Look, I don't care if you've gone off to get in touch, but I'm worried. I'm worried about you. Why would they come and ask me questions like that?'

'I don't know,' I said. 'I asked them to help. It's just routine.'

'It doesn't sound routine. They were here all afternoon.'

'Everything's fine,' I said. 'Lucinda and I are having a lovely time.'

'After all these years . . .' she said and began to sob.

'Oh don't cry, Mum, don't cry.'

24

I left the *larga distancia* and walked further into town. I felt awful about Mum and I was thinking about Harry Koch, mentally scanning the inside pages of the magazine. Why had they tied his hands behind him with electrical flex? Had they tortured him before they'd murdered him?

Those magazine images paraded in front of me, and as the shock of them settled in I began to feel sick. My face was tingling as if all the blood had withdrawn from the surface of my skin.

There was a shop I'd seen in passing from the bus when we'd first arrived and I was trying to find it. I couldn't help but continually look over my shoulder. It took me half an hour, heavy going in the midday heat, but finally I found it and walked in.

The shop was cool with huge fans spinning silently above and all the walls were lined with dark wood cabinets with glass doors. The proprietor stood up as I walked in, and laid both his hands on the counter, wishing me a good afternoon in English.

'What can I show you, señor?' he said. I looked around me and brought my hand up to my chin thoughtfully.

'Nothing too big,' I said, 'something easily portable. One that'll slip into my jacket or my trousers without too much of a fuss.'

He looked at me quizzically.

'How much do you wish to spend, señor?'

I really didn't know how much revolvers cost so I pulled out my wallet with a flourish, and said, as if I knew about these things, 'What have you got for around the hundred-dollar mark?'

He nodded his head and opened one of the glass cases behind

him. It turned out that you can get a pretty good gun for that kind of money. You can obviously pick the things up for about fifteen to twenty. I was rather shocked.

'This is a very good model,' he said, 'reliable, finely made. What are you shooting?'

'Ducks,' I said. He looked puzzled for a moment.

'With a revolver?' he said. Then he smiled, and laughed. He wanted to make the sale. He didn't care what I wanted to shoot at – he was only asking from a technical point of view: range, accuracy, the speed of the chamber. Wouldn't I be better off with an automatic? The good old Walther PPK?

I picked it up and weighed it in my hand. It was surprisingly heavy for its size. I tutted a little and looked back towards the cabinets. He brought out another three models. I examined them closely and held them up, each in turn, aiming and closing one eye. I finally decided upon the one that had the fanciest engraving on the handle.

'But that gun, señor, is a hundred and twenty dollars,' he said.

I thought for a moment and pulled out my wallet. I counted out the bills and handed them over. The fact that it was so elaborately ornamented somehow made it less of a threat.

I walked into the Posada de Roger to check in. As what had happened to Harry settled in I found myself getting more and more fearful. I'd bought the gun to try to ease my fear, but it hadn't made me feel any safer at all. If anything, it was making me feel worse. I wondered if I was losing the balance of my mind.

'Hello, hello!' said the desk clerk, smiling. 'We see you again!'

'Yes, yes,' I said, 'but my God, what's happened here?'

The clerk shook his head. 'Every hotel in town is full up,' he said. 'We will find you a room, or course, but we have all these young people from Mexico City. They are monsters.'

There were sixteen-year-olds running around everywhere. I could hear them shrieking in the pool, and the bar was full of them drinking and shouting. They must have been a school party on their Easter break.

'And where are your friends?' said the clerk.

'It's just me today,' I said. He gave me my key and I went into the bar. I wanted a drink. I swaggered as I pushed the doors open – it wasn't the bravado of having a newly bought gun, but because I wasn't used to walking with such a heavy object in my pocket.

I walked in and pulled myself up onto a stool. After a few moments Juan Carlos the barman came out from the kitchen. He looked pale and distraught. He shook my hand but he looked troubled.

'Whatever's the matter?' I said.

'These awful children from Mexico City,' he said. 'They are terrible, they're evil.'

'I can imagine,' I said.

'No, I don't think you can. They have tried to kill Roger. They have thrown him off the roof. I've got him now in the kitchen in a blanket. I don't think he's going to live. I think they've killed him. His legs are broken and there's blood coming from his nose.' Juan Carlos was almost in tears. I looked around me at the young kids as they laughed and threw menus about.

'You little shits,' I growled at them. One of them looked up and sneered at me. He made an O with his thumb and forefinger and slowly waggled it at me. I put my hand into my pocket. I glared at him and stood up. Then I turned to Juan Carlos and pulled out a wodge of pesos from my wallet.

'Here,' I said, 'get Roger to a vet. Let me pay. Call a taxi for him.'

Juan Carlos nodded his head and smiled.

'Thank you,' he said, 'thank you.' He pulled down the grille, closing the bar, and went to get the cat. I snarled at the kids. I hadn't even been able to order a drink.

I walked out and went up to my room. It was tucked away right at the top of the hotel. It was much more spartan than the last room I'd had and I suspected it was one of the staff rooms. I was glad: it was small and womblike, and I felt safer at the top of the hotel.

I dropped my bag to the floor and then I slid it under the bed with my foot.

I laid the gun on my bedside table and sat and stared at it. Then

I opened the box of shells and pushed the chamber open. I began sliding the shells in. When I'd filled the chamber I realised that I had no way of knowing whether I'd completed the operation correctly. While there was no doubt that the shells were pointing in the right direction, there was no way of testing the success of it without letting one off. As I'd slid the shells in I'd told myself that it was physically no different from putting new batteries into a TV remote control. But there *was* a difference. My hands shook as I did it.

I sat on the bed with both hands on the gun and aimed it at the door. Then I stood and aimed it at myself in the mirror on the wardrobe door. I quite liked the way I looked with it.

I was in a fantasy world.

I laid the gun down again but I couldn't stop touching it, polishing the length of the barrel with my palm, shining up the handle with my sleeve, admiring the engraving of the eagle gripping a snake in its talons.

Then I put the barrel into my mouth and I felt the cold metal against my tongue. It tasted of gun oil and smelt as if it had been recently fired. It must have been second-hand. I wondered if it had killed anyone. A great shiver went through my body as my tongue lingered on it. I held the barrel with my teeth. The sweat was pouring off my forehead and dripping onto the metal.

I put it back onto the table as if it was about to go off. I didn't intend shooting myself with it at all. It just seemed to beg me to consider it. It wanted to fire.

It was such a powerful thing, full of reckless possibilities. I stared at it. It made me nervous and twitchy, but at the same time I had the strangest of feelings, a feeling of being supremely virile and arrogant. But it didn't necessarily make me feel any more secure. If anything, I felt more vulnerable. I felt that everyone who saw me would know that I had such a thing about my person.

I pulled up the corner of the mattress by the pillow and slid it under. I lay on the bed watching the fan above me revolving, trying to think of nothing. Watching for lizards on the ceiling.

25

In the evening I went to the Hotel Los Arcos. I wandered around its bars and lounges searching all the faces that I saw. It was a fairly smart hotel but the restaurant menu had some of the finest misprints I'd seen and they took my mind off things for a while. Among them was a 'sparrow grass' soup, and 'a sordid ice cream', and I found I could still smile at little things like that.

I had dinner there and afterwards I went to sit in the hotel's cocktail bar. As I was going to a table I walked straight into Cynthia, the indispensable woman from the British Embassy in Mexico City. I had been sure that these people were determined to know my every move. I was convinced, without a shadow of a doubt, after the conversation with my mother.

She was wearing a purple chiffon evening gown and had let her hair down. She looked like someone hosting an awards ceremony.

'My goodness me,' she said, standing momentarily on one leg, while the other hovered nervously about the seam of her stockings, 'what a turnip for the books!'

She was quite drunk. she'd obviously been in the bar all evening.

'How nice to see you again,' I said. 'What brings you to PV?'

'To PV? Oh it's one of our regular little spots. Mexico City is a stinker at this end of the season. You can't imagine the dust. One swallows so much of it in a morning one can barely find the space for lunch. I'm quite sure that appalling things are done to one's lungs by the pollution, and can you get any dry cleaning done? Sometimes I think Her

Majesty can't possibly ever realise how much we stand and serve.'

'I imagine that's why she goes on state visits,' I said, 'to get the feel of it all at grass-roots level.'

'Oh my lawn is long gone,' said Cynthia. 'Hose as much as you like and all you have is a horrid little stretch of scrub. My kitchen garden's been reduced to the Australian outback.'

'And how did your royal visit go?' I enquired.

'A nightmare,' she said. 'We were up to our eyes in it with bally seating plans.' She sighed. Then she hiccoughed.

'Do pardon me,' she said. 'I can't think what dreadful things go into their margaritas. I certainly wouldn't trust the ice in this hotel.' She invited me to join her for a nightcap and we began walking to a distant corner table, as far away as possible from the resident marimba players.

'I simply can't bare the noise those chaps make with their deafening bits of wood,' said Cynthia. 'It really is worse even than their trousers.' She turned to me conspiratorially. 'They will insist on wearing such tight trousers, and of course if you're going to spend every evening thumping away with hammers then the zips are bound to go at some stage. It's not my idea of atmosphere.'

I was actually very glad to see her. As the evening had worn on I'd become increasingly disturbed by the pictures I'd seen on the magazine stand. Over dinner I'd tried to convince myself that it couldn't possibly have been Harry, but it didn't work at all. Whatever I thought of the motives of the British Embassy, they had to be better than those of whoever had been to see Harry. I shivered again as I thought of him.

There was a young Englishman sitting at her table in a stiff white shirt and slacks. He looked like he'd had a difficult time with the drink-loosened Cynthia. His spirits visibly sank as she returned to his table dragging me over.

'Any luck in the direction of your father?' she asked as we crossed the room.

'No, no luck at all.'

'Oh, rotten for you, and having come all this way, too. Let me introduce you to our Mr Gregor.'

'Gregor? Here?' I said. 'That's Gregor?'

'Yes. Isn't that a stroke of luck?'

Gregor was a man of about thirty-five. His hair had just begun to thin and he had dull staring eyes, like those of a dead rabbit hung from a hook outside a high-class butcher's. I was glad to see the man at last. We looked at each other for a moment. He didn't appear to have caught my name.

'How do you do?' he said. 'The name's Giles.' We shook hands and I sat down.

He didn't appear to want to engage in conversation and looked at Cynthia, peeved that she had landed me on him.

'This is the young man who's on a bit of a hunt for his father,' said Cynthia, rather pointedly. 'Morgan isn't it?'

'Oh, right,' said Gregor.

'We spoke on the telephone a little while ago,' I said. He crossed his legs and moved his drink two inches further away from himself across the table. Odd piece of body language I thought – it was as if this had suddenly become business. As he perked up I got the impression that he had been waiting in this bar for me all evening. I couldn't think how we'd missed each other, I'd been trying hard enough myself to get spotted by somebody from the embassy. It was time, I thought, for a summit.

'Yes, yes, of course, you telephoned me,' he said.

I could see straight away that Gregor was an entirely different type of diplomat from Dickie, the consul. He was altogether tougher and more professional. He looked like a man who had his own agenda. There was a hungry look about him. There was no doubt he was here to see me. I couldn't imagine what he would be doing spending a weekend away at the coast with Cynthia if it wasn't business.

Then I realised. Cynthia was here because she could not only identify me, but bump into me casually, as someone who'd met me. As indeed she had done. Gregor couldn't.

'So you took my advice and came on down to PV,' he said. 'Any luck?'

'Well, no, no luck at all I'm afraid.'

'Such a shame,' said Cynthia, slurping at her drink. 'It's rum to end up empty handed.'

'Are you enjoying Mexico anyway?' asked Gregor. 'Seeing anything of the country while you're here?'

'Well, yes, enjoying it enormously. Been doing a bit of walking, rock climbing, that kind of thing.'

'Oh!' said Cynthia, with almost a shriek. Her lipstick was smudged from her last slug at her goldfish-bowl-sized cocktail. 'I simply adore anything at all Outward Bound. I was a Duke of Edinburgh Award Scheme as a girl'.

'I imagine you were,' muttered Gregor under his breath. He looked up and smiled at me, sharing his joke, as if to compensate for his earlier bad humour. He had a small glass of beer that looked as if it had been warm all evening.

He flashed Cynthia a warning glance and she replaced her glass in a clattering swirl on the table top. He looked back to me without speaking. I could sense his brain working away behind those dull eyes. Beneath the thin white linen of his shirt I could see one of his nipples, where the sweat had made it stick. I could see the black hairs spiralling around it and it looked like the hole left by a bullet in a windscreen. I thought about my gun, wondering if he'd noticed it weighing heavily as I walked over. He was smiling broadly at me, winning my confidence. I didn't like it. After his initial coldness it was a little obvious.

As he had done all my life, I felt the person of my father hanging over me like a long dark shadow. I dropped my hand to my side and felt the metal of the gun through my pocket.

Gregor seemed to be sizing me up. When he finally spoke again he surprised me with his candour.

'You visited Harry Koch,' he said.

'Yes, yes,' I said, 'the chap that lives on Lake Chapala.'

'Yes,' said Gregor, slowly.

'Lovely spot,' said Cynthia.

'Lovely for some,' said Gregor, dryly. 'Why did you visit him?'

I looked him in the eyes for a moment, as long and as hard as I could. How could he possibly know that I'd been there?

'Because I felt that he might know where my father was, they were associates or something,' I said, and quickly added, 'in the Korean War.'

Gregor nodded. 'And did he?'

'No, he didn't.'

'When was your visit?'

'Weeks ago now,' I said. 'When I was in Guadalajara.'

'What were you doing in Guadalajara?'

'Oh,' I said, trying to sound as casual as I could, 'I visited the *cabañas*, did a bit of shopping, you know. Why are you so interested Mr Gregor?'

He didn't alter his expression at all, but continued.

'You must have known that Koch lived there?'

'An inkling,' I said.

Gregor breathed heavily, indicating his exasperation.

'Do you know that Harry Koch was shot last week? He's dead. A nasty little murder.'

'Oh, my God, no, I didn't know that,' I said.

I leant back in my chair, seeing the pictures from the magazine again, and the blue of that kidney-shaped pool, and the crimson of his blood, and that terrible flex cutting into the flesh of his wrists behind his back. And all of it in garish ink, cheaply printed, out of focus. He had been as unrecognisable as meat. And worst of all it looked as if someone had taken pleasure in his killing, and had strung the whole thing out in the afternoon sun, in that quiet lakeside town.

Now that I heard it confirmed, in Gregor's matter-of-fact grammar-school accent, the coldness of it made me feel suddenly very sad. Sad for Harry, and sad for myself, too. I felt that a link with my father had been severed. Harry had probably been quite a guy.

I could see Juanita, his housekeeper, staring out of that picture window, sobbing as the police did their work with chalk and photographs. The evidence being removed in a zip-up body bag. I couldn't help but dwell on the lurid details of his violent death.

Gregor could see that I was shocked and troubled by his murder. I began wondering if my visit to him had had anything to do with it. Whether I had unwittingly led the assassins there.

'Who killed him?' I asked.

Gregor raised his eyebrows. 'Your guess', he said, pointedly, 'is as good as mine.'

'How do you know that I visited Harry?' I asked.

Cynthia was now sitting back in her chair, knowing that the conversation had taken too serious a turn for any of her drunken interjections.

'The Mexican authorities contacted us to see if you were registered at the embassy. They wished, shall we say, to eliminate you from their enquiries.'

'Why?'

'You have been keeping a journal on this trip, haven't you?'

'Yes, but . . .'

'. . . But you don't have it any more do you?'

I didn't like his tone, which had turned even more aggressively inquisitorial.

'Er, no, no, I've had to start it again. I lost it.'

'Yes, you did,' said Gregor. 'It was found at Koch's place.'

I thought back. Damn it, yes, I'd left there so excited, and I remembered laying it on the ground when I got awkwardly onto that candystriped lounger. That was where I had left it, damn it, by Koch's pool. He must have kept it.

'And so', I said, 'I'm now a suspect in his murder?'

'Well, we needn't dash to conclusions,' said Gregor. 'I think they're satisfied that you're not. There's no warrant out for your arrest or anything. There's nothing to worry about in that direction. The last date in your journal was far in advance of his murder.' I wondered if the journal had now come into Gregor's hands, and tried to mentally scan its pages. What had I given away in it about my father? I couldn't think, but it couldn't have been much at that stage.

'You wouldn't want to be a suspect,' said Cynthia, brightly, swigging her drink again. 'You wouldn't want to be involved with the Mexican police force, you can't imagine—'

Gregor flashed her another look and she shut up but I sensed that he was enjoying this all enormously. He had me absolutely where he wanted me. His enthusiasm for Harry's murder was disturbing. I looked into his dull staring eyes, with their thin blond lashes, surrounded by the sun-pinkness of his face. He looked like a pig sniffing about in the dirt for scraps. I despised his sense of superiority.

'Are you telling me that my father's suspected?'

'No, no, not at all. We're not a party to the investigation, although, I must say that whenever British nationals are involved we do have a natural interest. Of course.'

I couldn't be doing with any of this nonsense anymore. I was shocked, and I was frightened. I snapped.

'So what are you saying?' I said, and caught a waiter by the sleeve. 'Would you like a drink, Mr Gregor. yours looks awfully flat.'

'Certainly,' he said, smiling superciliously.

'*Dos cervezas, por favor,*' I said to the waiter. I looked at Cynthia.

'And just the smallest margarita,' she said, winking at me. She seemed entirely out of her depth with the whole business. I looked back at Gregor. He was making me angry now.

'What exactly do you want from me, Mr Gregor?' I asked. He rubbed his chin and pulled his shirt from where it was sticking to his body.

'Well,' he said at length, 'we'd obviously like to be assured that you were not a party to the death of Mr Koch, and also we'd like to assure you of your own security.'

I sat back in my chair, polishing off my drink as the next one arrived. What did he mean about my own security? Could they assure it to me on a bus hairing along a mountain track? Assure me like they did Harry?

We stared at each other for a few moments. The man wasn't a fool, I could see that, and I was sure that he knew I was more aware of what was going on than I was telling. Since he'd been so bold as to confront me with the business in hand I thought I may as well be a little more direct myself.

'So why did you come down to Puerto Vallarta?' I asked. 'To find me? Don't tell me for a moment that you're just down here on a break?'

Gregor smiled and turned to look at the marimba players for a moment.

'We're all on the same side, you know,' he said.

'Side?' I repeated. 'I wasn't aware that there were any sides.'

I pushed my drink away. 'So what has my father done that has so offended Her Majesty's Government?' I asked. I was cross, and looked it.

'Try to calm down a little Mr Morgan,' he said, ignoring my question.

'I'm perfectly calm,' I said. 'I've had a difficult couple of days, that's all. I've had a slightly difficult time with my girlfriend.'

His eyes widened, I hoped they might.

'You have a girlfriend with you here?' he said. He'd taken the bait.

'Yes,' I said, casually. 'You may know her, Lucinda Parker-Harrington. She's the daughter of the chairman of the Confederation of British Industry.'

Gregor nodded and began to look decidedly worried at this news. It would obviously complicate things further for him. I wanted to let him know that I wasn't just any old John. I knew important people, people who would ask awkward questions if I wasn't treated decently by his embassy.

I stood up.

'I'm going back to my hotel,' I said. 'It's obvious that you're not going to tell me anything. Goodnight.'

'Look, why don't we meet again, say lunch tomorrow, when you've had a chance to calm down a little? I can see you're a little shocked by the news of your father's friend's death. We can talk some more,' he said.

'Sure,' I said, 'why not?' He reached into his pocket and pulled out a small card.

'Take this,' he said. 'It's got the number of my mobile on it, or you can get me here at the Los Arcos' – he looked at me seriously for a moment – 'should anything arise.'

As I moved away from the table I heard my gun clunk against the wood. I hung my hand by my side. Gregor looked up at me knowingly. The thing was making me look decidedly guilty.

'Call me when you're ready for lunch,' he said.

'And sweet dreams,' said Cynthia. This time we both stared at her.

I walked back to the Roger running the scene with Gregor through my mind again and again. What was likely to 'arise'? I wondered. The men who had murdered Koch?

Back at the Posada de Roger the young Mexicans were still drinking in the bar and tearing up beer mats. There was the smell of adolescent vomit. I walked up to my room. When I switched on the light I felt instantly that there was something altered about the room. The coverlet on the bed looked different, and then I realised what it was: it had been removed and replaced the wrong way up. The flowers on the pattern were now pointing downwards.

It couldn't have been the maid. It was too late in the day for the room to be cleaned, and a maid wouldn't make a mistake like that. I looked under my bed for my bag. It was still there but there were three drag marks in the dust and fluff: one where I'd thrust it under with my foot and two more where it had been pulled out again and then replaced.

I looked through the contents. I'd brought only toiletries and a change of clothes, a couple of postcards and a book. I opened the book. I'd put the postcards between the pages where I'd left off reading as I sat on the rock waiting for the *panga*. But now they were several chapters further back. My God, *The Plumed Serpent* is a tedious enough read without losing one's place as well.

I went downstairs to the bar. I caught Juan Carlos's eye.

'Good evening,' he said wearily.

'Can I have a word with you?'

He looked towards the door, then he motioned toward the kitchen.

'Come through,' he said.

I stood with Juan Carlos in the kitchen. He seemed to know what I was going to say.

'Someone has been in my room,' I said. He looked nervous.

'Yes, I think so,' he whispered.

'Who were they?'

'I don't know,' he said. 'They came about an hour ago and Jose on the front desk gave them your key. I am sorry, Jose doesn't think sometimes. Possibly he was given money, I don't know. They said they were from Immigration.

'They were Mexican?'

'Yes.'

'Saying they were from Immigration because I don't have a tourist visa or something?'

'Maybe. They needed to look in your room. I didn't know about it until Jose came running through.'

'They're that efficient about tourist visas around here?'

Juan Carlos shrugged his shoulders. 'I never heard of it before.'

'So who the hell were they?'

'They were some kind of police, I think. Jose had the impression', he said, 'that they might be back.'

He reached into his pocket and pulled out a set of keys.

'Here,' he said, 'you go to number sixteen, Insurgentes, just across the street. Let yourself in. It is my flat. You are welcome. I will bring your things over when I am finished here.'

'That's very kind of you,' I said. 'What'll you do if they come back?'

'I'll tell them that you have gone out disco dancing. The clubs are open until dawn. They can spend the night touring our overpriced bars.'

I smiled. He was a good man.

Number 16 Insurgentes was above the house with the monkeys in the window. I felt marginally safer, but I didn't dare switch on the light. I sat in darkness, with just the glint of the picture frames on the walls that surrounded the stares of deeply troubled saints. I held on to the gun in my pocket. Every time I heard the monkeys screech and scuttle about downstairs I jumped. I did hope that if Juan Carlos came suddenly through the door I wouldn't accidentally blow his head off.

I watched and listened, shaking sometimes, exhausting myself with fear, thinking about Harry. I thought about Lucinda too. Even though she'd betrayed me I didn't actually want to see her killed on my behalf. I tried to listen, in my mind, to what she would be saying to me now. That I was being hysterical, that I was overreacting. That all of this was a product of my imagination. That it's not uncommon for old rich guys like Harry to be murdered by opportunist thieves.

I sat and pondered the wisdom of going on.

Juan Carlos came back at about three in the morning. They'd had some late arrivals, and they'd wanted to see how long they could keep the bar open. Then there'd been an outbreak from the schoolkids, sneaking from room to room and skinny dipping in the pool.

I was still crouched in the corner when he came in. I'd woken with a start and had my gun between my knees.

He stood in the doorway and stared at me for a moment.

'Would you like some coffee?' he said quietly.

'Yes, thank you. I don't think I'm going to sleep anyway.'

I waited for him to ask me what was going on. Why those men were looking for me, and why I had a gun. But he didn't ask.

I laid my gun on the floor and took the coffee and cradled the cup in my hands.

'Juan Carlos,' I said, 'I think I owe you an explanation. Please don't think I'm on the run or anything.'

'Why would I think that?' he said.

'You seem remarkably cool about coming home and finding a guy in the corner with a gun.'

'I'm worried about Roger,' he said.

'Me too. How is he?'

'The veterinary is going to call in the morning. He's putting up quite a fight.'

I smiled.

'I think those men that came to the hotel may well have been from the government,' I said, 'but it isn't me they're after. I'm here looking for my father, whose ship was sunk under, well, rather peculiar circumstances. I didn't know about any of this when I set out.'

'That's okay,' he said. 'I understand.'

'Well, I wish I did. You know what I think? I think they really believe I know where my father is, and they're trailing me to find him. There's a couple over at the Los Arcos from the British Embassy doing exactly the same. It's like it's some sort of race between the intelligence services, to see who gets to him first.'

He nodded his head sagely. He had that manner that all experienced barmen have, and the talent to listen to the most outlandish things, and never ask questions.

After I had drunk the coffee I must have fallen asleep, suddenly relaxed I suppose, that Juan Carlos had returned. I was physically exhausted.

26

I woke in the morning when the door cracked open again. I had a blanket over me and a cushion behind my head.

Juan Carlos stood in the doorway a little breathless from the stairs. He looked as if he'd just dashed across the street from the hotel. He had.

'They are in the bar,' he said, 'the men from last night. They came first thing this morning and ordered breakfast. I could only just get away. They have been eating breakfast for two hours.'

'They're waiting for me?' I said.

'It's a long time to eat breakfast. I almost felt sorry for them, sitting there in their suits. They asked me for aspirin.'

'Aspirin?'

'It is the children from Mexico City – they are screaming and throwing their breakfasts at each other.'

I was worried, but I could still manage a smile.

'Have you heard anything about Roger?' I asked.

Juan Carlos smiled and flopped into a chair. 'He is going to live,' he said. 'Thank you. He's one hell of a cat.'

The morning had an uneasy feel to it as the clouds came slowly, and hesitantly, across the bay. There was a deadness to them, as if they knew they were full of rain that they couldn't drop but had to carry somewhere further inland, hitting a mountain ridge, rising into colder air.

I decided that I would keep my lunch appointment with Gregor.

I phoned him from Juan Carlos's and he invited me over to the Los Arcos.

'No,' I said, 'I don't want to come to the Los Arcos. Something has, as you would say, arisen. Let's meet somewhere else.'

'Name a place,' he said.

I suggested the tacos stand on the corner of Insurgentes. There would be a lot of people about and I didn't want to venture too far away from the safety of Juan Carlos's apartment.

When I got to the tacos stand Gregor was already sitting there reading a newspaper. I sat down next to him. He was wearing sunglasses. Entirely reasonable in this bright light of course, but under the circumstances he looked faintly ridiculous, like someone waiting for a dead-drop. So I took my dark glasses off and laid them on the bench.

'I can recommend the *tacos al pastor*,' he said, 'but for God's sake watch that yellow chilli sauce – it'll blow your head off. Did you sleep well?'

'Well, no, I didn't actually. I haven't really slept at all.'

'Oh dear. Too hot for you out here? It was humid last night. Starts getting that way at this time of year. We're all just waiting for the rains.'

I breathed in deeply. I couldn't be doing with his smart little pleasantries.

'Something happened last night when I got back to my hotel,' I said, 'and I wondered if you could throw any light on it?'

'Well, I'll certainly give it a shot. Do you want to tell me what happened?'

'Someone got into my room and went through my belongings.'

'Really? You're sure it wasn't just the maid? They've an awful reputation.'

'No, I'm sure it wasn't the maid.'

Gregor was silent for a few moments. 'You're an interesting character.' he said, 'Did they take anything?'

'There was nothing to take. It wasn't a robbery.'

'Then what was it, in your opinion?'

'Someone wishing to track me down I think, on account of my father. What do you know about the sinking of the *Karina*?'

He took a bite of tacos and shook his head.

'The *Karina*?' he said.

'Oh, come on, Gregor, you know all about the *Karina*. It's in your notes at the embassy.'

He was surprised that I knew about this.

'You wrote it in the margin on your notes of our first telephone conversation,' I said, pushing aside the little taco that he was offering me.

Gregor leant back on the bench and smiled broadly.

'My God,' he said and laughed. 'I thought *I* was the one who was supposed to be looking out for your wellbeing. You seem to be looking over my shoulder.'

'Who sank the *Karina*?' I asked.

He looked at me as if he was about to level with me. He also looked fairly pissed off that I seemed to have had access to his private notes. I wasn't about to let him know that Cynthia had blurted it out when I was at the embassy.

'We really don't know, we don't know at all. I suspect it may well have been the Mexican authorities themselves. It's impossible to say.'

'The same people who murdered Harry Koch?'

'It didn't have their style. It was too vicious, too professional, that murder. But I really don't know. Perhaps they wanted us to think it was someone else. The sinking of the ship was somewhat botched up by all accounts.'

'You mean because the crew survived?'

'Yes, they did, I understand.'

At last he was levelling with me. He had no choice, really.

'What was Koch's involvement with the *Karina*?' I asked.

'Oh,' he said casually, 'he owned it.' He said this as if I ought to have already known, so I didn't register any surprise.

'What was its cargo?'

'That I don't know.'

I didn't believe him.

'Was Harry murdered because of that ship?'

'I would imagine so, yes,' he said, smiling at me. 'They probably didn't want him claiming on the insurance and making the whole business a public matter.'

'Is my father likely to be murdered as well?'

'There's a definite possibility,' he said, the smile still on his face.

'What is it you've come down here for, Gregor? What is that you want me to do?'

'Well,' he said brightly, 'I'm glad you're beginning to see this as more of a cooperative venture. There is something you could do that might be a wise move.'

'Yes?'

'We'd all be terribly relieved about the whole situation if you would allow us to arrange a flight back to the UK for Lucinda Parker-Harrington.'

'Nothing would give me greater pleasure,' I said, 'but I don't think she'll go. Perhaps it would be better coming from you.'

'And how may I do that?'

'I'll telephone you in a couple of days and arrange a meeting with her for you.'

'Yes, yes, excellent idea,' he said. He seemed pleased with this achievement. I couldn't believe that this was the only demand he was going to make of me. He really did seem to want to let me go wandering into all sorts of trouble. He didn't care about my 'security' at all. Now I knew that. What he wanted from me really couldn't be amicably agreed over a tacos stand.

'So tell me, who was in my room last night?'

Gregor wiped the sweat from his forehead and took another bite of his lunch.

'Are you going to level with me?' he said.

'I've got nothing to level with you about. I've no idea what's going on. Nobody tells me anything. You're all shit-scared of something.'

He smiled. He didn't believe me.

'How determined are you to find this father of yours?'

I hesitated.

'I'm going off the idea very quickly,' I said. 'Who would want to go through my things? The hotel got the impression that they were Mexican police or something. I think it was the security services and somehow you're having a little game.'

'Yes, I expect so. The security services.'

'You can't expect me to believe that the Mexican Secret Service were going through my toiletry bag last night?' I said.

'Well it's certainly got their kind of touch to it.'

Was he playing me again, like an angler after the old pike in the nether reaches of the pond, merely for sport? My exasperation was intense. I really wanted to clear the whole thing up here and now.

'You must know what they're up to.'

'People like that are very jealous of their intelligence. They have so little of it.'

'It wasn't Sam Fergusson then?' I said, to get a reaction.

His face remained rigidly fixed.

'Sam who?' he said finally.

'The English guy who was sent down to keep an eye on me in Huatulco.'

Gregor smiled and shook his head a little from side to side.

This guy just couldn't be caught. I knew that I was playing a very dangerous game with the man. If I was sensible I should have just played the innocent, but I was incapable of doing so now – I couldn't help it. Everything inside me was building up and I wanted it all to come to a head, whatever the consequences. It was reckless, but the alternatives were so limp, and I knew I'd get nowhere with them. I was heady with the drama of it all, and in many respects, I suppose, I'd begun to act out some sort of fantasy, like those I had as a child about my father.

My God, I wished he'd drop all the front. I had almost begun to trust him earlier. Nothing more was to be gained from this meeting, I could see that. I wanted to go back to Lucinda, to Jody. It was safer in Yelapa, I was sure of that – even with rumours of *Federales*.

'You're not going to tell me what you think was on the ship are you? Or where my father is?'

'If only I knew,' he said.

'Look, Gregor,' I said, getting up from the bench, 'the way I see it is this: a British-owned ship was secretly sunk off the coast of Mexico. No one knows why. The British Embassy are involved with investigations. The owner of the ship, also a British citizen, has just been mysteriously murdered, probably tortured too. If you don't tell me what's going on I'm going to blow this to the British press. I can just see what the *Independent* and *Channel Four News* will make of it. I imagine that would put your office under a certain amount of pressure.'

'Are you blackmailing me, Mr Morgan?'

'Yes, Mr Gregor, I am.'

'That is the most dangerous of games. I'd caution you to consider it thoroughly before embarking on anything we may regard as reckless.'

'I'll consider it thoroughly. I'll speak to you again before I leave PV,' I said. 'I have to go now. I don't want to be shot in the street at a tacos stand.' He nodded.

We shook hands.

27

I picked up my bag from the apartment and made a dash for the early-afternoon *panga*. As I got to the corner of Insurgentes and Constitución I pulled myself up dead. There were the two men, as Juan Carlos had described them, heading towards me. They were young, Mexican, and rather smartly dressed. Crisp expensive suits and short haircuts. The smooth skin of the sons of the rich lands of the north. Why they hadn't dressed themselves as tourists I couldn't fathom. They were too full of themselves and their project. My God, I thought, they're heading here, to Juan Carlos's apartment. Please God they didn't beat him up, or poor little Jose on the front desk. I didn't know what to do.

The only thing I could do was to dive into the nearest shop, which was a supermarket. I grabbed a basket and began throwing things into it, hiding my face in the shelves. I moved as quickly as I could to the back of the shop, grabbing things randomly as I went.

I paid for the goods, thrusting peso notes at the cashier, and dashed out of the shop without my change, getting to the jetty on the Beach of the Dead just as the *panga* was boarding.

When we were out of the bay I stopped panting. I looked in my plastic supermarket bag. I had no idea what I'd bought. Inside were a bag of pinto beans, some beef jerky, a pair of stockings, some peppers, a tin of beefburgers, water purifying pills and a light switch. I shook my head and looked back at Puerto Vallarta and its coastal apartments zipping by. No one was following. I looked forward to Yelapa.

The *panga* captain dropped me at the rocks. I threw my

things up and climbed up into the ginger garden. The yellow underwings of the kiss-me birds were flapping everywhere, gathering grubs for their young. The land looked scorched. The mountainsides were all dried out and a great many of the trees had lost their leaves. The palm fronds shone crisp and silvery in the hot breeze. They were blinding to look at. The whole place – the garden and the jungle – was crying out for rain. As the hot wind blew, the plants seemed to be dancing vainly for moisture. Everything was on the verge of a parched death. The insects were growing irritable and vicious. The pitch of their rasping and buzzing seemed to have gone up an octave.

The herb garden was wilting from a lack of watering. Everything looked hopeless. Even the dog was lying lifelessly on the stone step, with its tongue rolling pinkly, listlessly trying to pant away her body heat. It was too hot for cat fights so the mother and daughter just lay in the shade halfheartedly snarling at each other.

I found Jody with Jean in the main house talking and drinking coffee with Newman and Terra.

They were standing around a strange construction in the middle of the floor. It was made from cardboard boxes stuck together, and Newman had painted it blue with happy sun faces daubed on its sides. Inside it was painted black, and it had a perspex lid. Newman was beaming proudly at his handiwork.

It was some time before they noticed I was there.

'Oh, Jay, you're back,' said Jody, smiling at me. Then they looked back at the cardboard construction.

'I thought you'd all be interested to see it finished,' said Newman.

'Sure, sure, it's really something,' said Jean.

I'd been through so much in the last twenty-four hours that I naturally expected more of a reception. But life was as normal here. As far as they all knew I'd just gone off in a sulk to send postcards. I settled down on the foam-rubber sofa.

'What is it?' I said, finally, trying to rejoin the life of the house.

Newman turned to me enthusiastically.

'It's a solar oven that I've invented,' he said. 'It'll put an end to the villagers burning carbon fuels and destroying the ozone layer.'

I sighed, trying to attract attention to myself, but no one responded. I stared at the back of Jody's neck as she leant over the solar oven. Every twitch of her muscles fascinated me. For a moment I saw her naked again, by Stevo's pool, and imagined myself to have been there with her.

'It'll heat up to three hundred degrees,' said Newman, standing by his oven.

'That's hot,' said Jody.

'And it's all made from recyclables. Things that would have burned off carbons will now act as a centre for the power of the sun.' Newman laughed. 'And it's all just boxes glued together.'

'Never,' I muttered from the back.

'You've got to come this afternoon,' he said. 'I'm giving a demonstration for the whole village at Gloria's restaurant.'

'You think the villagers will come?' asked Jody.

'Oh yeah. Everyone I've spoken to on the beach about it has showed a whole lot of interest. Asking me what kind of glue I use and everything.'

I laughed, and they turned around to look at me.

'Well, I'm impressed,' I said, trying to ingratiate myself. 'What'll you be cooking in it?'

'Well, I've given that some thought and I've decided on beans,' said Newman.

Everyone smiled.

'Nice. What time?' I said.

'Well, when they'll be ready to eat I'm not sure.'

Newman picked the thing up, sensing my foul mood, and walked off a little confused, down the path with his cardboard boxes.

I lay back on the foam rubber, staring up at the thatch. I could picture Newman trying to explain the thing to the villagers. Telling them that the burning of fossil fuels was breaking down the ozone layer. Telling them that with their new cardboard solar ovens they could save the planet. It wouldn't be easy for them to take this from a rich American. They looked to the Americans to bring them ever more advanced technology. Fridges, generators, satellite dishes, like the Adams boy up the hill. They didn't expect bits of cardboard stuck together with glue and painted with happy faces.

Jody walked over to me and stared into my face.

I asked where Lucinda was.

'Todd and her have gone swimming,' she said. I sighed deeply.

I heard Isobel coming up the path and turned to see her. She was limping and supporting herself with a stick. She looked tired and ill.

'What's happened to Isobel?' I asked.

'Damn scorpion got her again,' said Jean, 'right in the arch of the foot.'

Isobel perked up when she saw me and plonked herself down and threw the cane aside.

'Didn't expect you back!' she said cheerily. 'Thought you'd fall off the *panga* and drown.'

I laughed out loud. Isobel had a very particular sense of humour.

Jody was staring at me. She could sense that something had happened.

After another cup of coffee I asked Jody if she'd take a walk with me down to the beach. We walked along the track together. We could see Todd and Lucinda splashing about in the surf.

'You seem different,' she said.

'Yes,' I said, 'I think I am. that's why I wanted to speak to you.'

We stopped and sat on one of the boulders overlooking the bay.

'It's all become suddenly real,' I said. 'What I'd imagined has actually turned out to be true. I don't want to have to tell Lucinda any of this because she'll just tear it all to shreds. But I want to tell you.' I kissed her lightly on the forehead and sat back to examine her reaction. She stared into my eyes, silently.

I told her about Gregor and about the ransacking of my room at the Roger. Then I told her about Harry Koch's murder. She was shocked. She just sat silently and listened. When I had finished telling her everything that had happened to me I began to shake uncontrollably.

'It's the end,' I said. 'I've made my mind up. I've decided to leave Lucinda. I'm going . . .'

Jody looked me in the eyes for a moment, and then a smile broke over her face. She couldn't help herself, she tried to suppress laughter, but couldn't.

'What's funny?' I said.

'The idea that you think you're going to leave Lucinda.'

'You don't think I can?'

'No, it isn't that.'

'Then what?'

'You two left each other a long time ago. There's no leaving left to be done. People change when they leave college. You've simply become incompatible. People do.'

I smiled too. She was right, of course.

'I have to go.'

'Yes.'

I looked at her for a long moment. 'You won't come with me?' I ventured awkwardly.

Jody stared at the sea. 'I don't know,' she said. 'I don't see how I can.'

'You're still wedded to Todd?'

She shrugged her shoulders.

'It's what I know. What I like,' she said. I sighed. 'Have you told Lucinda this?' she asked.

'No, but I will. I thought we'd all have a last dinner together tonight and then I'll go. I'll talk to Lucinda. I feel such a mess.'

There was a scuttling among the rocks and we caught sight of a pair of iguanas wrestling lethargically over territory.

We sat for a while in silence.

'You're happy with the paradise you've found though?' I said.

'Yeah,' said Jody, and I could see she was. 'You didn't notice, did you?'

'Notice what?'

'The radio mast is up. Didn't you see it from the *panga*?'

'No.'

'Well it's there. We're linked. It's a dream come true.'

'I hope it'll be perfect for you here.'

Jody nodded slowly.

She pulled my fingers up to her mouth to kiss, then she suddenly stopped short and looked down at my knuckles.

'What the hell has happened to your hands?' she said.

I looked at them and shuddered, my knuckles had come up in browny yellow bruises. I looked down at the dirt of the path.

'On the night of the waxing party on the beach,' I began, 'there weren't any *Federales*, there weren't any local boys either. It was me who beat up Todd.'

There was silence for a moment. I thought about that night again, how I'd returned to the beach before the bonfire was lit and had seen Todd returning from the 'special house'. He was drunk and stoned and he staggered over to me with his arms out wide. I couldn't believe that he could screw Lucinda in the afternoon and then go up the hill to the tarts. I wondered if Lucinda had been sleeping with him since our very first night in Yelapa, when she had got out of bed and had gone over to the darkness of the hammock.

That night on the beach, as Todd swayed in front of me I felt an overwhelming rush of anger. I just remember the look of shock and horror on his face as I punched him, and a spray of warm blood spurted from his nose almost instantly. He fell to his knees and I pounded him with my fists.

He'd tried to defend himself with a piece of driftwood but I snatched it from him, it wasn't difficult in his state, and beat him about the head with it. He gasped and collapsed into the sand. I kicked him hard in the ribs. Then I stopped myself, stood back from him, trying to breathe. I looked around, except for a few figures slumped beside the unlit bonfire the beach was deserted. I began to walk away, and I could hear him gasping and spitting sand and blood out of his mouth. When I'd got a hundred yards away I turned to see him staggering off, back towards the village, where he must have collapsed unconscious in the undergrowth.

I looked up at Jody, she was just staring at me, a confused look on her face.

'Why?' she said, quietly.

'I took a walk the other afternoon, up through the banana plantation and got lost. I saw you all at Stevo's, making out by the pool.' My face flushed with vengeance again.

Jody reached out and smoothed the back of my hand.

'Well you hit him pretty good,' she said.

I didn't tell her about Todd's visit to the 'special house'. I didn't want to hurt her.

'Is dinner still on for tonight?' I asked.

She looked out across the bay.

'Sure,' she said. 'Sure dinner's on.'

She smiled at me.

I asked Lucinda to take a walk in the ginger garden with me. I told her that I was leaving and that I wouldn't be coming back this time.

She just nodded her head and took my arm.

There was no animosity, and strangely, I think I looked at her face properly for the first time. Her skin didn't glow anymore, like it had done once, and she looked rather ordinary. But at the same time neither was I filled with anger, or jealousy, or vengeance. The relief was enormous.

We turned to each other and kissed.

'We were in love,' she said, 'that's something.'

'Yes, that's something.'

28

Just after sunset Newman and Terra arrived at the main house. They were very excited. The demonstration of the cardboard solar oven had gone exceptionally well.

'It was a real shame you couldn't make it,' said Newman, 'a real shame.'

'Yeah, it was beautiful,' said Terra. 'A most beautiful thing happened. I looked up at the door and there were three Huichol Indians really listening and paying attention and the one that spoke Spanish was relating it all for the others.'

'We've got Huichol in town?' said Jean.

'Yeah, they were at the demonstration.'

'They must have missed their *panga* back,' said Jean. 'They must be stranded.'

Newman and Terra were beaming from ear to ear. It was a real honour for them to have had the presence of Indians. They were held in angelic reverence by the New Agers. They regarded them as truly natural people, in touch with themselves and the soul of the world.

'You know,' said Newman, laughing, 'at first the villagers were real confused about my solar oven. Then I realised that they thought I was trying to sell it to them, so they were kinda sour-faced and ready to beat me down over the price. But then I said, "No, all we're trying to do is sell you an idea."'

'This of course,' said Terra, taking up the narrative, 'was an entirely new concept for them. Like, they couldn't understand that it was free, that ideas are free. So New Man had this real brainwave, like kinda inspired—'

'Yeah,' he said, 'like, they said, "How much do you want for

the idea?" So I thought for a moment and I said, "Two pesos."
Two pesos for the photocopy of the instructions and the ethos.'

'And they were real happy with that,' said Terra.

They stood in the middle of the room gently swaying their
heads from side to side, bathing in their eco-glory.

Lucinda looked across at me and smiled.

I blew her a kiss.

She giggled and held her mouth behind her hand.

'And how many photocopies did you sell?' I asked.

'Er, well, it'll take a while to get the photocopy side of things
together,' said Newman.

He invited us all over to his *palapa* for dinner. He had a lot of
beans left over. Isobel and Jean were glad to accept – stores were
running low – but we wriggled out of it, claiming that we had to
get in touch with ourselves again after the 'unsettling' events of
the last few days.

It was a hot night, the hottest we'd experienced so far, and the
breeze blew its scorching dryness through the open arches of the
house. Todd tuned the transistor radio to the station in PV and
managed to get a boisterous version of Mexican hip-hop. It gave
an odd feel to the hut. It was as if we were an ordinary house
somewhere in the suburbs, cooking up a TV dinner.

'That's turned into a fine black eye, Todd,' I said. He looked
at me sharply for a moment. He could see that I just didn't care
anymore. He had no idea, obviously, that I'd confessed to my
crime. He couldn't have shopped me in any case. He thought
I'd beaten him up for going with the tarts up the hill. He wasn't
about to get himself into trouble on that score.

It took forever for the oil to get hot on the failing pressure of
the gas bottle and it began to grow very dark in the house as the
moon rose above the thatch. We lit the oil lamps and they gave
our faces a dramatic biblical glow like figures in a Caravaggio. The
jungle was bathed in a magical silvery light, almost monochrome,
and the sea looked as if liquid mercury had been poured across it
in patches. We all seemed to acknowledge, tacitly, that it was our
last evening together. I'd put my black jacket on, to give it a sense
of occasion, and was standing cooking up my new provisions.

'What's that noise?' said Jody, suddenly, putting down her colander of chipped potatoes. 'There's someone on the path, I'm sure there is.' Todd turned down the radio and we listened for a moment in silence.

'I can't hear anything,' said Lucinda.

'There it is again, someone breathing heavily, a sort of wheezing sound.'

'Snakes . . .' said Todd.

'No, I'm sure I heard footsteps, rustling in the bushes,' said Jody.

'It'll be the *Rurales*,' said Lucinda.

'No, I'm serious, I definitely heard something,' said Jody. 'Do you think we ought to douse the lamps?'

'It's a bit late now,' I said, thinking that maybe I should go and get my gun from my under my mattress.

Then, emerging suddenly out of the cover of the trees were three figures, dressed all in white, wearing pointed hats. We caught our breath. They froze for a moment as they saw us. Then they came up the steps and stood in the doorway, staring at us silently with blank faces.

We stared back. They were the most unexpected guests and they could see it written on our faces. They were obviously a family, the old Huichol Indian had been the source of the wheezing that Jody had heard on the path. His face was heavily lined and in deep shadow under a broad-brimmed red and white hat. Out of the embroidered hatband dozens of blue and white feathers stood vertically. He couldn't have been more than four foot high. Over his shoulders he wore an elaborately embroidered shawl, and underneath it a white embroidered smock, then white baggy trousers which hovered above his sandles. It was so strange to be looking at an old man dressed up in such finery that it was a complete culture shock. He even had a white embroidered shopping bag hung from a strap over his shoulder.

His wife was similarly dressed but not quite as ornately, her trousers more blanketlike, her smock plainer. Their son could have been no more than eighteen or twenty, the sun-travelled faces of his parents giving the impression that they were much older than they probably were. The young man was desperately handsome – even Todd seemed quite shocked by him. He had a wide smooth face, an almost aquiline nose, and thick dark eyebrows above eyes that were lateral, as those of a Japanese, and just as finely, and precisely, drawn on his face. He wore a less embroidered hat than his father, but with eagle feathers dashed at a jaunty angle from the front. A bright red bandanna was thrown around his soft neck, and at his side he carried a red cardboard suitcase.

He stepped forward and spoke a few words in Spanish, very softly, as if speaking a penance. They looked beautiful and pacific as they stood with their jungle and mountains behind them.

Jody replied, and I caught the gist of it. They were asking for Isobel, asking if they could come in. They had nowhere to go tonight except here. Todd and I stood back as Jody ushered them over to the foam-rubber sofa. They sat down in a line, absolutely silent. Their faces didn't move.

They looked exhausted. I offered them some of the rum punch I'd been throwing together but they shyly shook their heads. When Jody put the kettle on however, they perked up considerably.

I was fascinated to meet them, not only because they, or their kind, had dealt with my father, and they made those fabulous jaguar heads, but also because they were so foreign, so alien to anything I had ever encountered in another culture. I'd read about their religion while sitting on the vine-strangled lavatory.

They had three gods: Fire, Growth and Deer. Every year they sent a party off on a three-hundred-mile pilgrimage to their sacred mountain to collect peyote, which they use to communicate with their gods. During that journey everything in the group is reversed. Men are called women and women are called men. A young boy is respected as an elder, and old men are made to gather wood and play. They say goodbye when they mean hello. They eat no salt, eat only cornbreads, but drink huge amounts of alcohol while starving themselves and taking drugs. It's no wonder they hallucinate and get in touch with their gods.

In recent years they have embraced the more colourful parts of Catholicism as well. They believe that Joseph, the father of

Jesus, won the right to marry the Virgin Mary by winning a violin playing competition. I rather liked that notion.

They sat rigidly on the foam rubber and we stood awkwardly about, not knowing how to communicate or what to do. We gave them tea, which they seemed to like. It was like having a new kitten or budgie in the house: we were prepared for them to quiver and shake, and try them out with different kinds of food.

Fortunately Jean returned early from the beanfeast, having left Isobel behind. She couldn't eat that many beans.

'Oh, shit,' she said to me. 'I see we've got the Huichol in again for a free meal, and I suppose they'll be wanting to stay the night?'

'I think that's about the level of it,' I said. She went over to them and said good evening in their dialect.

'I'll make the coffee,' said Jean.

'They've got tea,' I said.

'Then they'll want coffee next,' said Jean. She knew the routine.

Jody came over and caught me by the arm. 'What are we going to give them to eat?' she said, panicking slightly. 'We can't give them what you've brought from Puerto Vallarta.'

'Why not?' I said.

'Well, Jean for a start, she'll freak.' We both looked down at the big round tin that I'd opened. 'I don't think so,' said Jody, poking her finger at the meat.

Jean crossed over to the radio–cassette player, whispering to us, 'They like music.' She put on a cassette of an Andean pipe player. It was a rather lonely, solitary, sound. It had no effect on them whatsoever: they didn't begin to chant, or pray, or prostrate themselves before the moon. They just sipped their tea, politely ignoring it. It served only to silence us. Then Jean saw what I was proposing to cook out of my tin.

'My God,' she said, 'hamburgers!'

I shrugged my shoulders and smiled.

'I could kill for one of them. Got any spare?' she said.

'There's a whole tinful,' I said. 'A dozen.'

'Where d'you get 'em, PV? In the supermarket?'

'Yeah.'

'Don't reckon I've had a hamburger in five years . . .' she said and looked down longingly into the tin, and, although it has to be said, they were poor-looking specimens, pinky grey and floating in liquor and lard, she was lusting after them.

'You reckon the Huichol'll go for them,' I asked.

'I reckon they might. Who knows?' said Jean. 'But if they don't I will.'

Jody looked rather appalled but Jean and I set to with the cooking, she chopped the onions and I began the fry-up. The Indians couldn't take their eyes off me. Jean elbowed me in the side and said, 'Look at them, they can't believe you.'

'Why?'

'They've never seen a man cooking before.'

I glanced across. The man and the boy were sneaking glances at each other and soundlessly giggling. They seemed to be regarding me as somewhat extraordinary and effeminate: these men in embroidered smocks, carrying shopping bags.

We sat down to dinner, Jody, Todd, Lucinda and I on one side, the Huichol family on the other and Jean at the head of the table. They didn't speak while they ate, but they did constantly look up at me and smile and nod their approval of every bite. Whether this was because it was a miracle to them that a man had cooked it, or whether they thought it was some kind of tribal protocol in their honour, I don't know. Perhaps they just thought that hamburgers were just the best thing there is after a hard day of flogging craft works on the beach, and certainly more appealing than Newman's beans.

It was odd, an odd clash of cultures, that meal. Lucinda was using a knife and fork to eat her burger and that looked as bizarre to the Americans as the Huichol did by dividing all the ingredients up and eating them separately, one at a time. Beginning with the meat and then mopping the oil up with their bun.

Halfway through dinner Jean's tape of Andean pipe music ran out and the radio–cassette player reverted to the local radio station. The moment the new track took over the Huichol looked up and beamed. The young man began tapping a potato chip on his plate. The track was that perennial Mexican favourite, 'We All Live In A Yellow Submarine'. Mexicans love the 'Bee-aht-lez', as they pronounce it. The Huichol knew the song too, and in parts began to sing along. They must have picked it up from the beach bars when they were strolling up and down with their craft works.

When it ended, with us all repeating the words 'submarine, submarine, submarine', I stood up to join in with 'Yesterday'. They also knew a little of this and the old man opened the red cardboard suitcase and got out a pinewood violin with steel strings, which he played on his lap, trying to accompany the radio and me. We were beginning to have quite a wild time with them.

After dinner Jean got out some sheets of blank paper and felt-tip pens so that we could make ourselves understood by drawing pictures. They were interested to know where we'd travelled from, and what the world was like that could produce such bizarre creatures as ourselves. The young man knew a little Spanish, and, with Jean translating, I managed to have something of a conversation with the old man. He asked me where I came from.

'England,' I said.

'Where is that?' he asked. 'Is it as far away as Monterrey?'

'No, it is further than that.'

'Further than Chiapas?' he asked, astonished.

'Yes, it is further even than Chiapas.'

Then the old man smiled and nodded, he knew where we came from.

'It is in America!' he said. 'What state in America is it?'

At this point I reached for the paper and the felt pen and drew a map of Mexico on it, which greatly interested him. He took the pen from me and drew a circle in the middle of it, outlining an area of land far larger than Mexico City. This, he said, was their village. I then began adding other sheets of paper to the map, drawing North America, Canada, and then, on two more sheets, South America. Then I laid three blank sheets between myself and him for the Atlantic. Then we added Africa, Europe, the Middle East, until finally, after China, we reached Japan. The entire table was covered with a map of the world.

'The world is so big,' he said. 'It's nearly as big as this table!'

I made an aeroplane out of a small piece of paper and flew it across the Atlantic to the tiny island that was Britain.

'I come from there,' I said at last. The Huichol shook their heads in disbelief. They were, after all, considerable travellers themselves. The old man looked at the map again. Held me with his eyes for a moment and then spoke.

'How many days' journey is that by bus?' he asked. We concluded that, if one could go by bus, it would be many months, and, if one was on a Mexican bus, probably several years.

Finally he asked me why I had travelled so far. What was I selling that no one wanted to buy? What kind of pilgrimage was I on?

When I explained that I was looking for my father, who had got lost in the world, they seemed to understand. They asked me his name. We told them.

'Ah yes,' said the old man, matter-of-factly, 'Morgan,' and he pointed to one of the jaguar heads on the shelf. The heads that my father had traded with them for. The old man took the felt pen from me and made a dot on the map of Mexico.

'There he is,' he said, and looked up to smile.

'I think he means Chiapas,' said Jean. 'Chiapas?' she asked him.

'Yes,' he said, 'he has gone to see the Lacandonnys.'

29

When the Huichol prepared to leave the next morning they asked if they could have the map of the world and they packed it into their cardboard suitcase. I wondered how they'd ever fit it together again correctly, and I hoped that they wouldn't go back with the impression that the world was so big that it had to rest on a huge wooden dining table. After what they'd made of the teachings of the Catholic church, God knows what they'd make of my map of the world.

The next day I left Yelapa myself, also unable to piece everything together in my mind. I found it a hard place to leave.

The Huichol were most certain about where he was. He knew their language and had, it seemed, confided in them. Jean had quizzed them thoroughly and I felt certain. I had names of villages in the selva, down on the Guatemalan border.

It was twelve hundred miles, as the crow flies, to the mountain city of San Cristóbal de Las Casas. How far it was by road, I couldn't say. The journey, much of it through high winding mountain passes, was like being swallowed into the maw of a giant snake.

After the first ten hours or so, the bus stopped rather suddenly and we pulled into the side of the road. Most people were sleeping, I looked out of the window. We were in the middle of nowhere. When we got under way again I noticed that we had a different driver. Where on earth had he come from? And where had the other driver gone? We were miles from the nearest town – there wasn't so much as a hut or a tacos stand around. It made me nervous: the bus had been silently hijacked, I thought. The next afternoon this new driver, too, disappeared in the middle of nowhere and was replaced by the man that we had set off with. I felt I must be going mad.

My last night in Yelapa had been so civilised. There were lots of assurances that I'd be back, or that they'd all come to visit me if I stayed in San Cristóbal for any length of time. I'd even picked out a hotel in the town that they could call me at now that they'd got their radio mast up. Lucinda was staying on with them. She was a much more natural dropout than either of us could have predicted at the beginning of this journey. I'd left her a letter sealed in an envelope, not to be read until I was gone. It outlined my fears about what my father was involved in, and asked her to be careful, mentioning that Gregor would call and that really she ought to go home.

The bus stopped again and when the driver got out I followed him and lit a cigarette. The driver was undoing his shirt as he walked along the side of the bus, then he unlocked the door to the luggage compartment. He said something to it softly, and then a person's arm came flapping out. The other driver, the one who had disappeared in the middle of nowhere, came out rubbing his eyes. They exchanged a blanket and the second driver climbed in with the luggage. The other guy locked the compartment up and returned to the bus to take over his shift.

At the next stop, I decided, I would make that call to Gregor and let him know where Lucinda was. I had no intention of calling him from San Cristóbal in case he had a way of tracing the call.

Jean had assured me that my father could only be in San Cristóbal, that it was the only place from which to deal with the Lacandon Indians. In that part of Chiapas there was nowhere else to live, and, if there was, no one who would know you.

'It's the southernmost state,' Jean had said, 'and the poorest state in Mexico, and the toughest to get to. If anyone wanted to disappear completely, then that's the place to do it.'

Chiapas had the last surviving rainforest in the continent – it was on the very front line with the great South American forests, and on the border with Guatemala. It was the end of the North American world.

By the third day I'd completed the journey between the beautiful city of Oaxaca and the dull capital of the state of Chiapas: Tuxtla Guitérrez. A city as ugly as its name. I checked myself into a hotel room for the night. I'd had enough of the bus. I had the feeling that I was heading into one of the nethermost parts of the world.

I had made my call to Gregor from Oaxaca. I called Maria on the switchboard at the embassy from a hotel, asking him to call me back. I told him where Lucinda was and, I hoped, left him with the impression that my search had led me to Oaxaca City, throwing him off course by about three hundred miles. I hoped that this would be enough.

Then in Tuxtla, fearing that my bus tickets could be traced, I hired a taxi in the street to take me the last hundred miles to San Cristóbal.

The driver had a rusting machete lying on the seat beside him. He didn't speak any English and so our long, winding journey was conducted in silence. It was as complete a feeling of loneliness as I have ever felt, but I liked the sense of going into the far depth of the country. Even if I didn't find anything in San Cristóbal at least, for the moment, the search was preferable to what I'd left behind in Yelapa.

The road to San Cristóbal de Las Casas, through the mountains of the Sierra Madre de Chiapas, is one of the most fearsome roads in Mexico. Worse even than those in Oaxaca, and, God knows, those are bad.

As soon as we began the climb from Tuxtla Gutiérrez the great clouds of a tropical storm rolled over and we swerved past the little shrines at the roadside that marked the places where other travellers had been killed along the way.

The road and the dark clouds were flashed with sheet lightning. In front of us an overloaded truck gritted itself to the winding road while we played a game of cat-and-mouse trying to get past.

If this ancient vehicle with a load of concrete stalled, our tinlike Corvette would be plunged over. It gave the road a certain character. It worried me that I was getting a kick out of it. At the beginning of this journey it would have terrified me. Now I was willing the driver to do battle with the truck.

As we climbed higher, with the Sumedero canyon beneath us, the landscape began to be filled with pine trees. It was a strange country, mountainous and cold at altitude, but still verdantly tropical in the valleys. The rainy season had already reached Chiapas and it had an altogether much more South American feel to it.

It seemed like days on this endless climb before I saw the lights of San Cristóbal.

It was squeezed between two mountains, like somewhere locked in time. The town had been the capital of Chiapas until a hundred years before, when the government had decided that the local Indians were too insurgent to support a state capital. Until then it had been part of Guatemala. So the seat of government was moved to Tuxtla. San Cristóbal still had a reputation for insurgence.

We took another veering bend and began the descent into San Cristóbal. It was glittering in the Jovel Valley, perfectly preserved. No new building work had really taken place for a hundred years, except for one American hotel, and so it lay here sleeping on the road to South America, on the Pan-American Highway, lost in the mountains. I was in love with it already.

The town had been 'discovered' by backpackers in the sixties on their way to Colombia and Venezuela, as a time-locked jewel in the harsh landscape. Apart from this it had very little contact with the rest of the world, and certainly was entirely ignored by the government in Mexico City. It may as well have been a city in another country, as far as they were concerned. As long as the middle classes, the *Hacendados*, kept their old wealth and the Indians were kept under control, everyone was happy.

Everyone except for the indigenous Indians, of course.

It was a city closer to the end of the last century than to ours.

We pulled up outside the Hotel Santa Clara, the oldest hotel in town, on the corner of the *zócalo* opposite the cathedral. It was the house built by the Conquistador Diego de Mazariegos and its sixteenth-century doorway was emblazoned with the Lions of Castile, still declaring the long-defunct power of colonial Spain. I staggered, mountain-road-weary, out of the cab.

It was ten o'clock at night and I stepped into sheeting rain. I have never experienced rain like it – it was wilful and it lashed the awnings of the hotel, falling straight down out of the sky in vertical stripes. As my suitcase was being unloaded from the car three elderly Indian women dashed across the square towards me. There were few tourists in town.

They were carrying baskets. They had jet-black hair, very long and parted in the middle, and they were wrapped in bright blankets. They were bare-footed in the rain. They wanted me to buy hairgrips, beautiful things of woven brocade, and little clay figures of themselves. They wanted just a few pesos. The mestizo desk clerk from the hotel came out, and with my taxi driver's help they threw the women violently backwards into the gutter.

Then they whisked my luggage into the desolate foyer. I watched the women scuttle across the square. I'd never seen such awful indignity meted out. It was obvious already that this was a divided town, the descendants of the Spanish colonists who were once so powerful, and the Indians whose true forests and land it was.

I turned, frowning, to pay my taxi driver. The sum he now demanded was triple the rate we'd agreed in Tuxtla. I was tired and lost my temper with him. As he reached for the machete from his front seat I growled at him, 'Don't screw me about or you die.' I grabbed the umbrella from the desk clerk and rounded on him with the spike. I was a very angry Englishman. He capitulated immediately and backed off, apologetically, with the agreed rate and no tip. I stormed into the foyer.

'Do you have a room for tonight?' I spat.

'Yes, señor, sir, you can have room, er, room number one.' He pulled out the register and nervously asked if he could see my passport.

'No you bloody can't,' I said. 'It's at the bottom of my bag and I'm sopping wet.' He nodded.

'Please may I have your name, señor?'

'Certainly,' I said sharply, 'It's Mr Kurtz and I want a drink and an egg sandwich.'

When I got into my room, which was four hundred years old, I threw myself onto the bed, and it cracked loudly from every joint. My egg sandwich never did arrive, or, if it did, I think they didn't dare wake me.

In the morning I went for breakfast in the *zócalo* and drank coffee in the bandstand gazing out at the cathedral. At the nearby church of San Antonio, the patron saint of lost causes, I reminded myself, they were letting off fire crackers that thudded and cracked against the pink and ochre stucco of the cathedral like gunshots. The square had a loudspeaker in each corner and they were blasting out Strauss waltzes. A van passed, also with loudspeakers, broadcasting political slogans for the Institutional Revolutionary Party, praising the president. I could hear the parrots that were caged in the courtyard of my hotel shrieking, seemingly as outraged as everyone else.

The parrots were three huge macaws, one of which had lost an eye, and the other two had plucked their breast feathers bare. It felt like a cold winter's day. I picked up a newspaper, left on the table next to me, and tried to decipher the Spanish. We were close to the Guatemalan border, where, I gathered, they'd had three presidents in a week following a *coup d'état*. They had been fighting on that border for years. Everywhere a stultified uneasiness filled the air. Then the bells for morning mass began ringing. It was a sullen sound. The timbre of the bells came from their age, from their metal and their tower, and from the way they echoed between the stucco and the pines. There was an echo of faded Venetian grandeur. The sky was heavy with clouds and the light was failing on the mountains, as the people I breakfasted with looked out from our pergola to the hills. I really did feel as if I'd stepped back in time. Next to me two young men were drinking mescal.

Two little Indian girls approached me with their brocade work but were immediately chased away by the waiter. I looked at the hard mestizo faces of the mescal drinkers. They were in such marked contrast to the soft and placid faces of the Indians.

After breakfast I began climbing the narrow streets of the town and as I got to the church of San Domingo a torrential downpour hit. This was the rain of a rainforest region, not drops, not drizzle, not nails of rain, but shafts of hot water. The street flooded instantly while the ancient trucks battled against the water flowing like a river.

I made a break for the church. It was surrounded by Tzetzil Indians sheltering under the saints' statues in its exterior alcoves and lying under sheets of polythene with their artefacts, cowering in the elaborately carved doorways, looking out blankly into the unrelenting rain. I looked up at the saints, all of them with their heads missing, knocked off in the anti-clerical persecutions that ravaged the church in Chiapas after the revolution. There was not one priest left in the entire state then. The governor had shot the lot.

The Indians took no notice of me as I scuttled through the doorway, drenched. The dark interior of the church, with its gold-leaf wood panelling, had been untended and unrestored for many years, maybe since the Spanish left, certainly for a hundred years. The church was filled with Indians sheltering. Their children were lying in heaps in the aisles and the adults were getting on with their brocade work and chatting and laughing.

Behind the high golden pulpit, in a small side chapel, there were women cradling bundles of white lilies, preparing the church for a first communion.

I sat for a while in the chapel of the Virgin of Solitude. There was an old Indian woman sitting barefoot on the floor arranging candles before an image of Jesus, dead in a casket. She was chatting away in a raised voice, in what I supposed was Tzetzil, one of the surviving Mayan dialects. Then she began a strange kind of Buddhist chant, like a concentrated prayer. I was quite mesmerised by the beauty of it until I realised that she was counting the proceeds from the prayer candles she had sold. I watched as people came up to buy them from her and knelt reverently for a few moments. When they left she snuffed them out and put them back in her box ready to be sold again, clipping off the burnt portion of wax with a little pair of nail scissors. Perhaps I was still in the world I knew after all.

In the nave a young girl, almost round in her baggy Indian blanket, was leading a young boy up to the altar by a piece of string tied round his neck. He was wailing in pain. No one did anything about it – it was just a bit of fun during the storm. She was obviously threatening him with crucifixion.

The church smelt of old wood and rain and that peculiar odour of thick rough tweed drying from a soaking on warm human flesh. There was the decayed smell of centuries of incense that had seeped into everything. It smelt like a bishop's funeral. It was a world away from the grand churches I'd seen in other cities. There wasn't any plastic, no cameras, no sunglasses, to jar with the beauty of the place. There was instead a deep dampness to the air. An all-pervasive dampness so that even the living smelt of something dead, of museums, of something comfortingly old. There was an overwhelming sense of melancholy.

It was another kind of beauty here. A beauty made of familiar saints and architecture, of a familiar culture transported here to slowly transmute in a distant far-off dampness, among a people for whom the religion of Spain was a repression that they had taken on their backs with the rest of their troubles.

I was affected deeply by it all. By the soft and constant ringing of the bells of San Cristóbal, and outside, in the rain, the steam rising from the cauldrons of boiling maize, around which figures were huddled, as poor home-made rockets made red-sparked attempts to pierce the low-lying cloud.

I left the church behind and walked past the old governor's palace, a great white edifice with a colonnade of crumbling pillars, locked in its glory of a hundred years before. This was a whole mountain city that had, like my father, disappeared. As I heard the bare-breasted macaws shrieking from the courtyard of the Santa Clara I felt a sudden and definite certainty.

I would find my father here.

30

San Cristóbal was a bigger town than I'd expected. I spent the whole day touring around trying to think how I could possibly make a connection here. I spent some time in the bookshops buying up anything I could on the Lacandon Indians.

After the morning rains the sun came out again and the streets began to steam as the town heated up. By mid-afternoon the climate was humid and tropical. It was as if we'd gone through two seasons in a single day.

In the evening I went to the theatre. Everyone in the town appeared to be headed there. The ballet folkloria troop from the town was performing, along with a small classical ballet company that was making a tour of the far reaches of the country. I wanted to see what the town's people looked like.

The theatre was rather grand with great marble staircases and long cool-pillared walkways. Most of the men were wearing white hats, some of them carrying little wooden fans. The foyer was impressively classical but it was filled with swooping sparrows and starlings that had shat on the Corinthian columns and the red velvet drapes. There was a layer of muddy brown speckled guano on everything. The ushers who stood on the steps, collecting tickets, had all been shat on too. It descended in snowstorms from the nether reaches of the chandeliers. I could now see the sense of the large white hats that the men were wearing.

I took a seat in a box. The theatre was oval and had five tiers of private boxes, a hundred or more, each with its own double doors. The boxes were set out with velvet-covered dining-room chairs and occasional tables. Each box housed an excited family, waiting to see their offspring perform, fluttering away with their fans.

The guano-striped curtain rose and the orchestra scratched its way through an overture. Everyone applauded wildly. Then a line of five-year-old children, dressed as wood nymphs, danced to a stretch of Tchaikovsky, blinded by the lights. Next, the older children came on and enacted a Mayan ceremonial. The feathers from their headdresses floated into the orchestra pit.

The audience applauded every dance and every lighting change, so that the whole theatre was alive with fluttering fans, like a great hatbox full of moths that had suddenly been disturbed. They were a rather proper-looking sort of people, all dressed up in their finery, with a definite air of civic pride. But, as they watched their children going through the motions of ancient Indian ceremonial, I couldn't help but sense the underlying hypocrisy of the way these same people treated the real *indios* in the square outside: banning them from their restaurants and hotels; treating them as third-class citizens; annexing their land. These were the ancient families of the province, descendants of the conquering Spanish, and they looked fat and satisfied on their inheritance.

Just before the interval the professional company came on. They looked almost surreal in their fluffy white tutus as they made their way through edited highlights of *The Nutcracker*. They looked listless and unimpressed by their provincial audience. They were at the end of their tour and tired now. The sweat dripped from the ballerinas and they plonked around the stage, scowls fixed on their faces. I looked away from the stage, staring along the tiers of boxes. My eyes stopped on a man sitting alone in a box near to the stage. He was in his mid-sixties, with a shock of silver hair and blue eyes, sitting demurely in a white suit. I caught him glancing across at me. There was a sudden twist in my stomach and I shot bolt upright in my chair. His eyes looked through me. He smiled.

My God, I thought, it was the Frenchman I'd had dinner with on that very first night in Mexicali. He'd told me then that he lived in San Cristóbal. I smiled back, and then turned to look back at the stage where the ballet troop were taking their bow.

When I turned to look again he was standing and applauding the dancers politely. It was a strange thing, I thought, to watch a man who spends his time destroying the natural wonders of the rainforest applauding the ballet. *The Nutcracker* as it had been performed this evening must have suited him, because they'd hacked that about a bit as well. But I wondered how, like the townspeople, he could sit there in all conscience and watch the Mayan dances and applaud them too, knowing that their existence, thanks to them, would soon be limited only to theatres such as this.

After the theatre I took another stroll round town. I passed a bar in a small square behind the cathedral and as I looked in something caught my eye. On a shelf behind the wall I saw a carved jaguar head identical to those I'd seen at Isobel's house.

There was a sign above the door, JEFF'S BAMBOO BAR. A rather incongruous name for a bar in San Cristóbal, I thought. I went in.

There were three young South American Indians sitting in the corner playing Andean pipe music, and everywhere candles flickered in wrought-iron candelabra. A dozen punters, all of them obviously travellers, sat around chatting quietly. There was a German-looking boy sitting on his own, eating his way through a basket of dry bread, and, I assumed, writing up his journal. A few people sat out on the balcony that overlooked the square.

I looked at the barman. He was young with long blond hair and he was wearing a lively Guatemalan shirt. He was chopping limes and pressing them into the necks of bottles of Dos Equis. This had to be Jeff, I thought.

I went up to the bar and sat on a barstool. I looked up at the jaguar head. It was elaborately beaded and a much more expensive-looking object than the ones I'd seen in Yelapa.

The young proprietor looked like the sort of Californian dropout you get all over Mexico: someone who'd come down here to tour the pyramids and couldn't get himself together enough to go home and buckle down again. He'd got himself a bar instead. He finished his business with the limes and pushed the beers over to a waitress. He looked up at me.

'Hi, there,' he said. 'New in town?'

'Yeah,' I said. 'Last night, late. How did you guess?'

'Oh, don't worry. I say that to everyone. Everyone's new in town – people don't stay here long. You English?'

'Yeah.'

'Neat. We get mostly Germans in here. They're backpacking the world those guys. I reckon the Germans will be the first people to land a backpack on the moon.'

'You get mostly foreigners in here, do you?'

'Sure, sure. The locals don't come in here. I charge twice the price for the beer. You want a beer?'

'Sure,' I said.

He took my money. He was a natural-born bar owner.

'You must be Jeff,' I said.

'No,' he said, 'I ain't Jeff, but then again, yeah, I guess I am Jeff.'

I took a slug of my beer.

'I bought the bar off a guy named Jeff,' he said, 'and it was cheaper to change my name than the sign on the door. Everybody would call me Jeff anyway, so what the hell? Jeff I am. Suits me fine. I'm on the run from a paternity suit.'

He laughed.

'You don't get many English in then?'

'Why, what do you want to do, toast the Queen?'

'Just curious.'

'We get a couple, locals mostly.'

'Anyone by the name of Morgan, elderly guy, deals in artefacts?' I asked.

He gave me a solid look in the eye and pulled his chopping board back over and set to work on some more limes.

'Who's asking?' he said, suspiciously.

'Oh, it's nothing. He's a distant relative, or something, and I was told to look him up if I came down here.'

'You don't say.' he said, slowly. 'You want a tequila with that beer?'

'Sure,' I said. 'At twice the price?'

'Sure.'

He turned to get the tequila bottle. He put the bottle onto the counter and slowly poured.

'He deals art or something, with the Lacandones.'

'Yeah, is that right?'

'Yes. I thought he'd be pretty well known around here.'

'Well, he's well known all right. Probably a little *too* well known right now.'

I laughed, trying to give him the impression I thought that he'd merely disgraced himself in a bar somewhere. That he was a bit of a local character, nothing more. I slammed my tequila and downed it.

'Why d'you pick my bar to come in and ask?' he said, slowly pouring me another shot of tequila.

'No reason, really,' I said. 'I was just taking a tour of the town and I caught sight of that jaguar there. He deals in them.'

Jeff smiled for the first time.

'Also,' he said, 'he pays bar bills with them. Handsome ain't it?'

'It's handsome.'

'If I were you, though, I wouldn't expect to run across him. From what I hear he's keeping himself pretty exclusive.'

'Why's that?'

'Well, you've got to understand that to the tourist this town is something of a fascination. The indians and stuff. But underneath, you know, there's a certain amount of tension.'

'Really?'

'Sure. For real. There's a lot of different interests around here and they're all kinda pulling at each other. I haven't seen Morgan in here for a couple of months. He pissed off the *hacendados*, the landowners, and that's serious.'

'Yes,' I said, 'I already noticed that the Lacandones are treated really badly. I saw a couple of old women—'

He didn't let me continue.

'They aren't the Lacandones,' he said. 'The Lacandones are a different game altogether. They live way out in the selva, and they've got even bigger problems.'

'How far is way out in the selva? I thought that *this* was where the Lacandones were?'

'Oh no, they don't really come into town. There's not many of them left.'

'Oh. I thought I might like to take a trip out to their villages.'

'Uh huh? You don't really stand a chance of that. Like, even with the Tzetzils, a couple of tourists took a photograph in one of their churches last year and they got clubbed to death. The Lacandones are way out there in the forest. You'd have to go with one of their own. You can't even think about it without a guide. I'd give up on that idea, too, if I was you.'

'Oh dear,' I said. 'That's a disappointment. And I don't even get to see Morgan either.'

'If I was you I wouldn't get involved. I would forget about getting in touch with him. The guys that run this area are heavy, truly heavy.'

'It would have been nice just to have got a message to him to say "hi".'

'Sure.'

He looked at me for the first time sympathetically.

'Something comes to mind,' he said. 'I think he's got this little indian friend who's in town. Now he's a Lacandon, but he's kinda given up the selva completely. He works around as a café artist. Does pencil portraits. Gets kicked out of every bar in town.'

'Do you know his name?'

'Sure, Miguel. His name's Miguel. About five foot eight, classic Indian features. He'll be around someplace.'

I thanked Jeff. It was enough for one day, and, feeling woozy from the tequila, I began my walk back to the Santa Clara. The clerk was sleeping behind the desk, with a candle burning down precariously low. He woke as I walked in.

'Señor,' he said, pulling out a piece of paper from the pigeonholes ranged behind him. 'There has been a telephone message for you.'

'For me?' I said. 'Are you sure?' I had, after all, registered under the assumed, and faintly ridiculous name of Mr Kurtz.

'It can only be you, señor,' he said, staring down at the piece of paper. 'You are the only guest in the hotel who speaks English.' He handed me the piece of paper. All it had written on it was 'ten o'clock'. I shook my head.

'It's not much of a message,' I said.

'It was a young lady. She call you and say she must speak, *muy importante*. She said she will call again tonight at ten o'clock.'

'And has she?'

The desk clerk shrugged his shoulders and began replacing his candle with a fresh one.

'No electricity, señor. There has been an earth tremor.'

I shrugged my shoulders, I hadn't noticed any earth tremor.

'In Oaxaca,' he said. He took the piece of paper from me again and stared at it.

'Maybe she will call again at ten o'clock in the morning.' he said, hopefully.

31

The next morning, just before ten o'clock in fact, Jody called.

'Your Mr Gregor called for Lucinda,' she said. 'He tried to convince her to go back to England. I do hope you're being careful.'

I asked how Lucinda was.

'She's decided to move up to Stevo's compound. Stevo's got guards on the door. He's got these young guys from the village touring round the perimeter fence. They think it's high drama.'

'Good God,' I said.

'Lucinda reckons she'll be safe up there.'

'What the hell has Gregor told her?' I asked.

'I don't know,' said Jody. 'Lucinda's got kinda involved with Stevo and we're sort of *persona non grata* all of a sudden.'

'Fickle cow,' I said.

'Gregor asked me where you'd gone. I answered the phone to him. I said you'd gone to Tampico.'

'Tampico? Why Tampico?'

'I don't know. I panicked.'

I laughed, it seemed so uncharacteristic.

'It doesn't matter,' I said. 'I think I've found a way of getting into the rainforest, into the villages. I'm really excited.'

'For God's sake be careful.'

'I'm fine,' I said. 'I've got a gun.'

Jody laughed. 'I'll call you tomorrow,' she said.

I set off to find Miguel, the Lacandon Indian friend of my father's. I felt certain he would be easy prey. All I had to do was agree to have my portrait drawn. I marched around town bright and confident.

I saw him just a couple of hours later when I was sitting in a small square, having lunch. I watched him as he walked, with a roll of paper under his arm, into a restaurant on the other side.

Within moments there was an outbreak of shouting from the place and I watched while he was thrown out into the street, beer bottles flying after him. He got up, brushed his trousers, uncrumpled his papers and set off across the square to where I was. He ambled around the tables for a bit and then approached a young American girl sitting at the table next to mine. She was obviously a tourist from one of the buses that pass through to the ruins. She was sunburnt down one side of her face where she had been sitting by the window. She was nodding her head and agreeing to let him draw her portrait. He sat down at the table and stared deeply into her eyes. I could see the drawing that he was making. The likeness was immaculate. He seemed to have no fear about rendering the deep and thorough vacancy in the girl's face. The drawing wasn't at all flattering. It was a good drawing. When he had finished the American girl looked at it from several angles and began beating him down over the price. I stared at the beauty of the picture as she began to slowly roll it up in her sweaty hands. As he left her, five US dollars in his hand, I touched him on the arm.

'Would you draw me?' I asked.

'Certainly, señor,' he said, and sat down.

Miguel was about five foot eight and I suppose aged somewhere between eighteen and twenty-five. It was difficult to tell. As he stared into my face, so I stared back into his. He had classic Mayan features, with dark hair and deep dark eyes. He had a soft olive complexion, almost Polynesian. He began to draw and his eyes flicked across my face and translated its features into small points of the pencil on his sheet. As he stared at me I felt as if I was undergoing some sort of psychological X-ray. It was as if his eyes penetrated the flesh and the muscles of my face and looked deep into the skull that lay beneath. It made me uncomfortable. He looked at me as I imagine the Mayan priests would have done before tearing the heart out of one of their sacrificial victims. I shuddered. I wondered if there was anything in my face that he recognised.

Suddenly he yelped and dropped his pencil.

'What is it?' I asked. 'Cramp?'

He pulled his sleeve up.

'An ant bite,' he said. 'Around here the ants are bastards.'

'Please,' I said, 'you don't have to go on with the drawing. Let me pay you. You can finish it tomorrow.'

'No, it is nothing, just a bite.' The mark was beginning to swell where he had rubbed it.

'Let me buy you a beer,' I said.

'Thank you, very kind, señor.' I called a waiter over who agreed reluctantly to serve him with a beer.

When he had finished the drawing he handed it over.

'I think we have met before,' he said. 'Somehow, I know your face.'

'I guess I've got one of those faces,' I said. 'Standard Anglo-Saxon. But I'm new in town.'

'What shall we say for the drawing? Twenty American dollars?' he said.

'Certainly.'

He was surprised that I accepted his price and we sat drinking beers for a while. He wasn't in any hurry to draw any more people now that his arm was hurting and he'd made more money than he'd expected. We talked about the town, the decent places to eat, a little of its history, and then I said that I was keen to hire a guide to show me around for a couple of days. Someone who could take me to the Lacandon selva.

'I know the best guide in San Cristóbal,' he said, 'who can show you the great monuments and the Indian villages in the Lacandon selva.'

'And who's that?'

'It is I, señor,' he said.

We agreed a rate for his services and arranged to meet for breakfast the next day in the same square.

That night I went back to Jeff's Bamboo Bar. I walked in with my head held high and pulled myself up onto a bar stool in front of Jeff. I'd been drinking most of the evening with some Germans I'd met who'd just come up from Venezuela. Worse for drink, I'd got chatty. I turned to Jeff.

'Well,' I said. 'I'm off to see the Lacandon villages in the morning.'

'Is that so?'

'Uh huh. I hired Miguel to take me.'

Jeff raised his eyebrows.

'You know,' he said, slowly, pouring me a tequila, 'I knew from the start you was kinda dumb when you walked in. Didn't I tell you Miguel was a thief?'

'Thief?'

'Sure. The moment he gets you into the jungle he'll roll you for sure. He's a convicted criminal.'

'He seemed perfectly charming to me.'

Jeff laughed.

'Sure. Consider yourself rolled then.'

I downed my tequila. Jeff returned to chopping his limes. I looked into the street. I thought that there were more parrots shrieking, but it was the police blowing on their whistles, making an attempt at controlling the traffic. Without any warning there was a sudden shudder and the whole bar shook. The bottles from behind the bar came crashing to the ground. The jaguar head hit the floor with a great thud. Then the lights went out. I watched as Jeff nonchalantly lit up some candles. I looked over to him.

'Earthquake,' he mouthed.

The punters' drinks were all over the place but Jeff and the waitresses were trying to calm everybody down. You don't let a little thing like an earth tremor interrupt people's enjoyment of spending their money. They'd had quite a few of these shocks lately, Jeff told me. They'd have to order more glasses.

Before I left, Jeff turned to me again and said, 'Don't go into the selva with Miguel. You could be taking on something more than you'd like. He's dangerous. Why do you think everyone throws him out? It's not the drawing – it's the thieving. He's a little *bandido*, man.'

When I went back to the hotel the reception desk was surrounded by candles again.

'Any more messages?' I asked the desk clerk.

'No señor, no telephones, *muchos vibraciónes*!'

'*Sí*,' I said and went to bed.

32

As Miguel sat down at my table for breakfast the next morning, two waiters came storming out of the restaurant. They began to shout at him.

'He's having breakfast with me,' I said sharply, 'so just back off.' The waiters smiled thinly and stepped slowly backwards into the darkness of their restaurant.

'Is it always like this?' I asked Miguel.

'Like what?' he said.

'They don't let, er, Indians near the restaurants?'

Miguel sighed. 'They don't know what they want,' he said. 'They want us to go back to our villages in the forest, but also they want to own land in the forest too, and push us out into the town. Where are we supposed to live?'

We began to eat. The waiters served Miguel grudgingly, as if it was beneath them, while all the time they were sickeningly fawning to me. Miguel entirely ignored it. They couldn't possibly despise him more than he despised them. I thought again about Jeff's warning that he was a thief.

In the centre of the small square was a statue of a revolutionary general around which the Indians squatted, working on their brocades. The general stood there with a haughty expression on his face, a sword raised in his hand, and a pigeon on his head. I asked Miguel who he was.

'He was', he said smiling, 'a very great general and his family paid for that statue to be erected. But they forgot to put his name on it, and since there were so many generals in the revolution no one can remember who he is. That is why we call this the Square of the Forgotten General.'

'It's a great name for a square,' I said. 'Your English is very good. Where did you learn it?' I asked.

'From an English friend of mine. He has taught me everything I know.'

'Is that so?' I said, hoping that he would continue, but he didn't.

We got into the old Dormobile van that Miguel had hired for our trip into the selva. First we had to get to Palenque, a town famous for its Mayan remains set on the edge of the rainforest.

It took all day to get there and so we had to stay overnight in a strange little travellers' hotel that was just a set of cabins with corrugated-iron roofs. Miguel woke me up at just before six the next morning. It had rained all night and I had barely slept because the rain had made the roof roar. We stepped our way through ten inches of floodwater to get to the van. Large frogs were shading themselves under the chassis. Then we got back on the road. I was feeling frail through lack of sleep and I had a dull thudding headache from the amplified rain. I was feeling tetchy, and a little nervous about the day's journey ahead.

The tarmac began to run out bit by bit, until there was nothing left but blood-red mud to drive on. Although I'd got used to it always taking a long time to get anywhere, the distances in this country still felt unnecessarily huge. Miguel tried to cheer me up with the promise of breakfast at a little place he knew in the next town, which was called Damascus.

'We're on the road to Damascus?' I asked.

'I hope so,' he said cheerily.

There can't be any place left in the Bible that isn't the name of somewhere in Mexico, I thought. But I felt uneasy about Damascus.

I needed breakfast. I couldn't wait until we got to the town so we stopped at a small log-built village on the edge of the selva where the great tropical trees of the rainforest had been cleared to provide pasture for a scattering of chickens. I'd tried rehearsing an argument with Miguel that the Indians must surely have to clear some of the rainforest to support themselves. They were only doing what we had done in our countries a thousand years before.

He sighed. 'If only that were true,' he said. 'But it is the colonists from the towns with the promise of free land. They come out here and clear the forest thinking that they'll grow coffee, but coffee doesn't grow here. So the land is laid bare for the sake of a few chickens. The colonists end up just like us Indians, working as near slave labour for the *hacendados*. They can't support their investment. They can't even pay off the debt on their dead coffee plants.'

We had a breakfast of *huevos rancheros* – fried eggs on tortillas. The eggs were floating in such a powerful chilli *salsa* that I thought if I dropped off to sleep again, which was likely, I'd fall headlong into my breakfast and be blinded. It would be more than apt, I thought, on the Damascus road.

We got back into the van. The road was full of potholes and we travelled veering from one side of the road to the other every time Miguel was lucky enough to spot a pothole approaching. But it kept us awake, and by now I'd even come to think of the blood-red mud as a road.

Every time we came into one of the villages, which were only really a section of log cabins set astride the mud track, the road would be filled with people. They were Tzetzil Indians and they'd probably already walked many miles with their loads hanging down their backs, secured from their foreheads by a headband. Sometimes they waved at us, sometimes they merely stared, but always they left it to the last minute to get out of the way. The chickens were especially nonchalant. They were quite handsome creatures here, brightly coloured, but with no feathers on any part of the length of their necks. Presumably they'd come up with this idea themselves over the centuries, to help them cope with the terrible heat.

While all this was interesting to me, it was a bleak landscape that surrounded us. Everywhere were the skeletons of tall whitened trees that had been defoliated, or by some other method killed. They led up to the edge of the surviving rainforest. It was a tremendous thing to see.

This was a place that looked like the Somme, a landscape from the First World War, but then above us, suddenly, on the ridge of a hill, was the rainforest itself, and the first line of its defence. It is so shocking to see the destruction and the magnificence just yards apart. The great trees, those that had survived here because the last ridge of the mountain was too difficult to climb, were starkly dramatic. They looked like the ridge on the back of a great prehistoric creature. I asked Miguel if he would stop the van for a moment. I got out and leant against the side.

'I know what you will say now,' he said. 'It's what everyone says when they come here and they see this.'

'I will say', I said, 'that I hadn't known it was so terrible, what has been done?'

'Yes,' he said, 'and you haven't even been in the forest yet to see how beautiful it is, and it isn't even your home like it is mine.'

As we drove I stared at the ridge of trees and could hear shrieks of life from within them, but the road curled around it, between the world and beyond.

It took us until lunchtime to get to Frontera Cruz, where we would board our little boat to get into the real Lacandon country upriver. Frontera Cruz was a small town and unlike any that I'd seen in the country. The buildings were single-storey log cabins with corrugated roofs gleaming in the sun. I didn't know what made the place look so virgin at first until I realised that there were no garish billboards or signs on the shops provided by the Coca-Cola and Fanta companies. There was no advertising anywhere at all. The whole place looked entirely unreached by MTV. Even the roads were green here: they were so unused to traffic that a thick lawn had grown across them. People stopped to wave and stare as our old Dormobile rolled down the grassy streets.

We pulled up to a small concrete hut with a pole flying the Mexican flag. I turned to Miguel sharply.

'Where the hell are we?' I said.

'The border post,' he said, smiling. 'We have to go into the office.' I got out of the van warily. 'The border with where? Guatemala?' I asked.

'Yes, Guatemala,' he said brightly. We walked into the office. Miguel showed the officer a card which identified him as an authorised guide, or something, then the officer asked to see my passport. I hesitated for just a few seconds and then explained that I didn't have it with me. I'd hidden it the night I'd arrived behind the cistern of the lavatory in my room.

'Then it is not possible to go any further,' he said, in Spanish. I reached into my money belt and pulled out a roll of pesos.

'Is it possible to buy a temporary passport from you?' I asked, as innocently as I could. He smiled in a matter-of-fact way and took my money.

'In this case I will make an exception,' he said. I stood for a few moments not knowing whether he was going to go through any formalities pertaining to the temporary passport, but the mere action of placing the peso notes in his back pocket seemed to take care of it all, cutting through the red tape with remarkable ease.

Then he asked where we were bound. When Miguel told him, he shook his head. 'I have to tell you that the border with Guatemala is closed because of the coup. You cannot travel up the Usumacinta today.' The river itself was the border, and it made no difference to the guard that we would not be setting one foot actually into Guatemala.

Miguel looked at me, motioning again to my money belt. I pulled out a few more notes and handed them over. The guard put his hand to his ear, as if listening. Then he smiled. 'No gunshots on the border today,' he said. We took this as a cue to get back in the van and drive on our way.

The border with Guatemala is formed by a mighty river, the Usumacinta. Miguel wanted to take me deep into the rainforest and the only way to get there was along this river. I'd read about this route in one of my guidebooks and I knew full well that it had been closed to tourists for years because of the fondness the Guatemalan guerrillas have for foreigners, either taking them hostage or simply picking them off in the boats as they passed. It wasn't so long before that the Mexican army had turned back Salvadorean refugees at gunpoint on these banks. El Salvador was only two hundred miles to the south. Refugees from all over South America tried to cross the border here. It was quite ironic, really, that the Mexicans had the same problem on their southern border as the United States has in California.

I stood on the banks of the Río Usumacinta while Miguel parked the van, for safety, with a family he knew. I stared across the water. It was a wide river and because of the rains it was swollen and brown now, flowing fast with eddies and whirlpools lying on its surface. The current of the river was so strong that it was higher in some places than in others. Whole trees, up to a hundred feet long, that had been washed from the banks were sweeping past.

I stood there on the crumbling southern edge of Mexico looking across to Guatemala and remembered that night on the northern border. The terrible crossing, the awful hotel, the rows with Lucinda. We were both different people now. I felt as if my father had forced me to cross the whole country before I would be allowed to meet him. My head was beginning to flood with all sorts of doubts, doubts about my father, doubts about the wisdom of hiring Miguel. He had gone strangely quiet and thoughtful, as if he was hatching some terrible plan.

We made our way down to a narrow thatched riverboat by way of some steps cut into the mud of the bank. Miguel hired the boatman. The boat was something like a wagon on water, but quite elegant with a sharp prow like a swordfish.

We pushed out into the river fighting against the current. Our boatman was a silent old character perched like a wizened kingfisher watching the water for any logs and obstacles that might overturn us. His dark Indian eyes were concentrated solely on the precariousness of the river.

The banks on both sides were impenetrably green with no sign of habitation. We sped along the middle of the river on the rapid current. After about forty minutes Miguel went up and spoke to the boatman. Suddenly he changed course as Miguel sat beside him, looking back at me, where I was squatting in the stern hanging onto the seat. There was a glint in his eye. What was happening? My stomach thudded as I realised that we were heading across the river towards Guatemala. I looked up at Miguel, shaking my head from side to side, puzzled. But he said nothing.

I stared into the trees on the far bank, still quite a way off. I couldn't see anything there but the emerald darkness beneath the canopy of the forest. A large tree trunk swept past us, almost hitting the boat. The boatman looked down at Miguel, shaking his head, but Miguel urged him on. We took the river in an arc, battling all the way against the current to keep on course.

The sweat was dripping from my every pore and my shirt and trousers were sodden. I had a stabbing pain in my neck, and I was afraid.

It suddenly dawned on me. What if Miguel had discovered that I had been asking about someone called Morgan? Perhaps he was playing me at my own game. If Miguel and my father had decided that I was one of the people after him it would be the easiest thing to lose me here and now. They might even think that I was Gregor. All it would need was a bullet in the back of my head on that far bank. The chances of my body being found were slim. Even if it was I would merely be a tourist shot in the head during a *coup d'état*, in a place I'd been expressly forbidden to visit by the Mexican authorities. It would make two inches in the British broadsheets, and what did I expect? Damn fool backpacker. My mind was racing.

We began to approach the bank and the boatman threw out a rope with a grappling iron on the end of it, to pull us in.

I put my hand on my gun.

Miguel got out of the boat. I had to think very quickly. What would I do about the boatman? Would I have to shoot him too? I certainly wouldn't be able to return to Frontera Cruz. I'd have to take the boat, I supposed, as far as it went, to the sea, to Villahermosa, but that was hundreds of miles away. My head was as busy and as full as the current of the river.

The boatman stayed by his tiller. I got out and followed Miguel up the bank. We were in the middle of nowhere.

'What the fuck are we doing illegally entering Guatemala, Miguel?' I said, angrily.

Miguel laughed. 'I have a big surprise for you. Get your money out.' I put my hand on my gun. Then I opened my fanny pack. I drew the gun, 'No,' I said. 'I have a big surprise for you.'

'My God!' screamed Miguel. 'Why are you doing this? What do you want? What have I done?'

We stared at each other for a few moments, silently, the forest rasping and shrieking around us as I pointed my gun at his belly.

'Why have you brought me here? Tell me, what are you up to?' I said.

Miguel pointed nervously to a small hut just visible now through the trees. 'There,' he said. On the side of the hut was a small tin sign which read TECATE.

'It is the only place for many miles where they've got beer.'

33

When we were back in the boat I felt terrible. Miguel stacked the beer into a coolbox he'd brought with him. The boatman took us back over to hug the bank along the Mexican side of the river.

'I'm sorry, Miguel,' I said, finally. 'It's this heat. It must have got to me. And all that rain last night, pounding on the roof.'

'You would have shot me,' he said, hanging his head down as if he were broken-hearted. 'Don't you trust me?' he asked quietly.

'Of course I do. It's just you didn't say where we were going and I got nervous. I've been robbed so many times in Mexico,' I said, lying. He shook his head sadly.

'And you think all people like me are the same?'

'No, no, not at all,' I said. 'I should never have bought that bloody gun. It makes a person paranoid.'

'Yes,' he said, then suddenly he smiled, looked up at me and laughed, imitating my voice, 'No, I've got a big surprise for you!' he repeated. 'You were like an American!' he said, shaking his head and laughing. I tried a smile. I took the gun out again and went to throw it into the river.

'No, no,' he said. 'It's a nice gun. Don't throw it away! You never know, with all the trouble here you might need it yet . . .'

We travelled on the river for another hour and gradually I stopped shaking. Every now and then Miguel would look up at me and laugh. I didn't like it – it made me feel ashamed – but at the same time I had to pay for the outrageous act of pulling a gun on him. By the time we moored against the bank he seemed to have erased the whole incident from his mind. Every time I thought about it the whole episode seemed ever more Gothic and ridiculous.

As we got out of the boat Miguel turned to me and patted me reassuringly on the arm. 'This time,' he said, 'I will tell you where we are going. We are going to the village of the Hach Winik, the village where I was born.'

We left the boatman, instructing him to come and pick us up in the morning. Miguel handed me a folded hammock, which I slung over my shoulder, and we began the walk into the forest. The track was very narrow, made by feet in single file. The great canopy of trees filtered out most of the light and the forest floor by the track was quite clear in places. But the moment I began to breathe among the trees it was like inhaling the steam in a shower cubicle. The intense humidity of the place was tangible and quite overwhelming. I was immediately soaked in sweat. When I pulled out my packet of Marlboros from my trouser pocket, it almost disintegrated.

The noise of the insects was incredible. I had found the jungle noisy, and I suppose just as I had imagined it to sound, but this was something else entirely. It was ten times the volume for a start and made up of sounds that I'd never imagined. It came in waves, searing, ominous waves, and sounded as if all the insects on the forest floor had started up together with circular saws. It was a ghostly place in some respects, especially when we came across the remains of a small Mayan building jutting, dark and lichen-covered, out of the undergrowth. Its serpents and hook-nosed rain gods looked fearsome, as they lurked in the middle of huge vine-dripping trees.

The plants, the ferns and the orchids that suspend themselves from the trees were as fresh and vibrant as if they had just been created whole and perfect.

When it began to rain it was a sudden great torrent, as if someone had released it from a tank above. We were soaked in an instant and leant against the trunk of a tree made up of columns of vines like a cathedral. Once I learnt to give up breathing through my mouth, and just let the rain slide off my nose, I began to enjoy the thrashing the warm water gave me. Several bugs drowned in my turnups. The shower was like a welcome to the forest. We stayed against the tree trunk for a while. You couldn't rush things here. When the rain was at its most torrential it was impossible to see because our eyes were full of water. We cupped our hands over our noses so that we could breathe.

The rain abated to a sort of steam and we pressed on along the mushy track. Above us, from the canopy, there'd be sudden crashings about, the screeching of monkeys, and the squawks of exotic birds mad with desire for each other. Everywhere there was the sudden slap of leaves falling, like sodden paper plates, and from within the steaming darkness the sound of a mighty insect, its teeth ripping through rotting wood, and in the distance the awful wrenching, shattering sound of a great hard wood falling to the floor, tearing vines down with it, and scattering the creatures for whom it had been home.

I began to understand why tropical vegetation is the way it is. Every leaf was expressly designed to deal with the rain in some way. They parted like springs and flicked back again like knives as the drops passed through. Bulbous plants had great cups to catch it, and with which to drown their feast of bugs.

It became quieter as we approached the village of Lacan-Har, the home of the Hach Winik. The sun was beating down, and where the land was cleared it was already dry. Miguel seemed a little apprehensive, and he was looking at me to see what I thought of the place. There was a small grassy area with a few huts around it. One of them was an abandoned health clinic outpost. There was a strip of grass that looked as if it could be used for an airstrip, but most of the dwellings were tucked away among the trees.

There was a small plaque by the health clinic which read, HACH WINIK: LOS HOMBRES VERDADERES, and I asked Miguel what it meant.

'When most of the Maya were made Christians by the Spanish my people moved into the forest and so the other Maya called us Lacandon. It means "the people who set up idols", but we said, no, we will call ourselves Hach Winik, which means "the Real People". We are the Real People,' he said smiling.

'But most Lacandon are Christians now,' I said. Miguel smiled and his eyes twinkled mischievously. 'Of course,' he said, 'we believe in Jesus. We believe he died on a tree and rose again. He became the sun.' I smiled too. This seemed to be a very neat way round the whole business of being Christianised.

There had been great fights, and expulsions, from a lot of the villages, he told me, after American evangelicals had come down to convert them. There were whole villages that were now Seventh Day Adventists. It was a miracle that this village had survived at all.

To walk around the village we had to pass through their gardens – not that people who live in a forest such as this would call them gardens. They were places planted with avocado and banana, and they had irrigation channels drawing on the water from the river that flowed down into the Usumacinta. We stood for a while staring up into an avocado tree where a howler monkey was playing. He was black and furry, and quite sizable, like a little gorilla. He swung from branch to branch, repeating the same passage between the trees over and over again. The circuit included a spectacular leap and a swing on a low branch before us. And all of this was done solely for our benefit.

'He's showing off for you,' said Miguel. The monkey kept his eyes fixed on me as if I was a fascination to him. When I looked around a small girl was gripping onto a nearby sapling and staring at us as well, at our western clothes, and the way I was fascinated by the monkey. She wore a simple white smock and had long dark hair, down to her waist. She spoke to us, shyly.

'She says, "there are many more monkeys by the river,"' said Miguel, amused. Perhaps we wanted to go and stare at them too. Miguel asked her what her name was and she replied, 'Pancho, like my father.' Behind her a middled-aged man, dressed like the girl, was peering at us from behind a fence, but he wasn't as bold as his daughter was. He wouldn't approach us.

Miguel took me into a hut that served as the general store. The shop was a simple wood-planked hut, surrounded by pyramids of drying corn cobs and with a couple of shelves of tinned food and batteries inside. There was a marked absence of the Virgin of Guadalupe, or pictures of Jesus or saints in mortal agony. We sat on a wooden bench by the door. The shop was owned by a broad-faced man with long dark hair that fell over his bare chest. All he was wearing was a pair of Manchester United football shorts.

He didn't move once from his hammock throughout our transaction. We had asked for guava juice, and one of three little girls, or possibly boys, sitting on a bench behind him got up to get a jug from a primitive coolbox and served us. I stepped towards him and gave him the money. He took it and I went back to my seat. He held the money out in his hand and one of the children came over, took it from him, and crossed the room to put it in a biscuit tin.

We sat in silence. The little children began giggling as we caught them staring at us, and they'd dip down to hide behind their father's hammock. I was an object of extraordinary fascination to them, so much so that I had to be careful not to make any sudden movements, which caused a bit of panic. They all wore simple white smocks made from a plain square of cloth that had been hemmed and patched. Their dark hair, parted dramatically in the middle, didn't look as if it had ever been cut.

I reached into my pocket for a cigarette and pulled out my pack of disintegrating Marlboros. The man's eyes lit up and he stared at the packet. It was still sodden and, as I pulled a cigarette out, it collapsed in my hands. I managed to find a couple that were still partially dry, albeit pretty bent. I offered him one. He smiled and accepted it. He swung in his hammock, staring up at the ceiling, persisting with the damp tobacco until he had smoked it all. Then he nodded to me in recognition of the pleasure it had given him.

As we left, the children tentatively whispered 'adios' and then hid under the hammock. As I closed the door behind me I heard them shriek 'touristos!' in excitement. They seemed very pleased about our visit.

We walked through one of their milpas, the square fields where they grow maize, papaya and tobacco. We saw no one else at all. The milpa silently got on with its business. We followed the small river around until we came to a place where it formed a natural pool. White smocks that had been washed in it were hung on poles to dry. We stripped off and got into the pool to cool down.

'Why didn't anyone speak to you?' I asked.

'They wouldn't recognise me,' said Miguel, 'not in these town clothes. It wouldn't even occur to them that I was Hach Winik. They wouldn't think that I was a Real Person. I am as American as you.'

We spent the best part of the afternoon lying in the washing pool, talking. Every now and then young men would pass by, smiling at us, and carrying fish that they'd hooked in the river. They all wore the same style of simple white smock. I wondered if at any moment my father might just suddenly appear. I was determined, now that I trusted Miguel, not to rush things. Softly, softly, catchee monkey.

It was the most idyllic of afternoons, and slowly but surely, as we sipped the beers from the coolbox we'd brought with us, I heard the story of Miguel's life.

Five years before, when he was eighteen, the crops in their *milpa* had failed. It was at the height of the colonisation boom when people from the towns were taking over much of the indigenous Indians' ancestral land. He now suspected that their *milpa* had been poisoned. He and his father had gone to work for one of the new *hacendados* who were clearing the rainforest and trying to harvest chicle, the crop from which they make bubble gum. His father had been a strong man. In the village he was revered for his ability to move the heaviest of boulders single-handed out of the riverbank for the making of their dykes.

'Working for the *hacendados* crippled his spirit,' said Miguel. 'His powerful muscles began to shrink and his heart was dying. They brought a new tractor down the river and he was sent to unload it. The other men were relying on his strength, but as it came off the raft he couldn't hold it. It crushed him on the riverbed.'

Miguel had then attacked one of the foremen, incensed, and had to take to his heels, making the long trek to San Cristóbal. He'd always been known in the village for the things he'd made with his hands. He'd made the masks for the fiestas, and he'd heard that the tourists in the town would pay cash for things like this.

'It wasn't so much of a change', he said, 'from making masks to drawing portraits of tourists.'

That was when he'd met my father. He'd shown an interest in his talents.

'But it was hard', he said, 'to make enough money to keep myself in San Cristóbal and to send money back to feed my mother and my sister. Seeing all the wonderful things in the houses, I took to stealing some of them.'

I was glad of his admission, and, if anything it made me trust him more. Miguel had evidently become something of a cat burglar. He spoke with undisguised pride about his ability to enter a building through its air ducts because of his slight frame. He was pretty agile, nipping from roof to roof as well.

'That was', he said, 'until I was caught and put in prison.'

He hung his head for a moment.

'But then Morgan came and paid the bail and got me out,' he said, happily, 'and hired me a lawyer, too. The case against me collapsed in court. They couldn't have imagined that a Lacandon would ever have anyone to defend them so they hadn't even bothered to collect any evidence against me. They expected me to rot in jail and be forgotten.'

When Miguel got out of prison he heard that a diphtheria epidemic, brought by the American evangelists, had decimated his village and that his mother and sister were dead.

I looked at him as he lay in the water of the washing pool. He was staring sadly at the flapping *huipiles* and smocks as they hung drying on their poles.

'The injustice against the people here is so terrible,' I said. 'It makes you want to lash out at something. And it's been going on for hundreds of years.'

'Yes,' said Miguel. 'One day we will snap. We won't take it any more. We will be like other small peoples in the world. We will gas them in their offices, and bomb them on buses.'

I smiled. I felt it was very unlikely that these gentle people would ever do anything more than stand in the *zócalo* and cry, with an immortal sadness in their eyes.

'Your friend, the Englishman, he's been very good to you,' I said.

'Yes, yes, very good.'

If I hadn't heard the sad story of his life I would have been very jealous of him, and I felt ashamed to admit that to myself.

'I would love to meet him,' I said.

Miguel laughed.

'Ah yes,' he said, 'he is what we call a *Nagules*.'

'What the hell is that?' I asked.

'In the Lacandon religion the elders can sometimes become *Nagules*. It means that they can take on the form of an animal and disappear into the forest, or they can take on the shape of another person if they wish.'

I smiled a very broad grin, and nodded.

'Some people have *Tonas* too,' said Miguel. 'The *tona* is the animal version of your soul. Guess what mine is?'

I shook my head, 'A magpie?' I said.

He smiled.

'No, my *tona* is a gecko, because just when you go to catch him he flicks away like lightning.'

'And is pretty good at sticking to the side of walls too,' I said.

'My friend Morgan is a mountain jaguar.'

I nodded my head. 'And me? what do you think I am?'

Miguel smiled politely. He obviously didn't like to say what he had seen behind my face.

We left the pool and the village and walked back through the forest to where the boat had left us on the banks of the Usumacinta, ready to be collected in the morning. I was terribly happy and sprang through the forest as if I was on a country walk. A bit like a Jack Russell in fact. I felt certain now that Miguel would introduce me to my father. I just had to let him do it in his own time. To rush it would be dangerous, but, nevertheless, I could feel that the meeting was imminent.

As night came down we made a fire and Miguel produced some tortillas and cheese from a bag that he'd stashed in a bush when we'd landed. Then we hung our hammocks, and talked as we swayed, watching a thunderstorm over Guatemala. We counted the seconds between the flash and the thunder as it moved towards us. Upriver, under the flashes, the water turned white with the torrential downpour. Very soon we would both be drenched in our hammocks, but it was so peaceful gently swaying there that neither of us could be bothered to do anything about it at all. We'd had a couple of beers and we were happy.

'And have you brought your friend Morgan here to see all this?' I asked.

Miguel laughed. '*He* brings *me* most times,' he said. 'He is well known in all the villages now. When we first met in San Cristóbal he paid me, like you did, to guide him up here. Sometimes we come for many weeks at a time, going into the deeper parts of the forest.'

'You seem to like being with him.'

'Well, yes, now that I'm his son, it's good to be with my father and work together.'

I looked towards him as the lightning caught his face.

'What do you mean?' I asked.

'Oh,' said Miguel, 'he adopted me last year. The lawyer drew up the papers and so I'm now Mr Morgan too,' he laughed.

I could hear the rain in the trees.

'Miguel Morgan . . .' he repeated with pride.

The cloud burst overhead and the rain came down. Miguel jumped up to take cover, squatting beneath the polythene that the hammocks had been wrapped in. I stayed in my hammock, getting drenched. I was numb with shock. The only solace I could take from the situation was the fact that Miguel was around the same age as I was and in some ways, I hoped, my father's adoption of him had been an act of contrition because of me. I was glad of the rain – it hid the welling of tears in my eyes.

In the morning, when the boat came, Miguel was busy packing up.

'Are you all right?' he asked, touching my arm lightly.

'I'm always quiet in the morning,' I said, obliquely. I let him do most of the work. I was too possessed of the most persistent dull ache I'd felt on this whole escapade so far. Why should a man abandon one son only to adopt another? I wondered. I knew the answers to that question now, of course, but it didn't stop me asking it again. In many ways I should be pleased. I'd meet my father now – there was no doubt. I hadn't reckoned on finding a brother too. I began to fantasise about how I'd break this news to Miguel. I really had no idea how to go about it.

As I got out of the hammock several of the buttons fell off my shirt where the humidity had rotted the cotton in the night.

I got into the boat. Our boatman looked particularly miserable this morning. The river was higher after the night's rains and filled with even more logs and full-sized trees. It was still only about six o'clock in the morning and the entire forest was levelled by a thick mist which hung in the trees in Guatemala, and in Chiapas, but above the river the sky was clear, just a steamy film swirling on its surface.

'I should tell you where we are going,' said Miguel brightly, trying but failing to make me laugh. 'I thought that on the way back I would take you to see Yaxchilán. It is our ancient city here along the river.'

I looked at the river and despised it. It was alive and awake and I felt as dead as the logs and trees that lay on it heading towards the sea.

34

Our boat pulled up at Yaxchilán. The ancient Mayan city had been built on a large mound that jutted out into the wide river. We climbed out onto the bank and the struggling sound of the outboard motor gave way again to the searing rasps and shrieks of the rainforest. There was a clearing where there were two small and very basic bungalows that had been built for archaeologists. They stood empty with the vines crawling in. There was a shelter, just a corrugated-iron roof supported by poles from which visitors could hang their hammocks. There was no one else here today, just ourselves and some sort of semi-official person who'd also just arrived by boat. Miguel seemed keen to show me the place. Maybe, I thought, my father would be there.

Everywhere there were wonderful butterflies going about their paradisiacal business, playing at mating, sipping nectar, landing innocently on my hand. I could reach down and pick them up without their attempting to fly away. Miguel reached out towards some exotic blooms that flowered from a plant that grew on a low bough of a tree. He picked something out of the air. He turned to me and opened his hand. Sitting in his palm was a tiny, shimmering, blue humming bird. It had no fear of him whatsoever.

The semi-official person came to take us into the undergrowth for the short walk to the ruins. He walked ahead of us, trimming the exuberant daily growth of the forest with his machete. He took us up to show us an overview of the town.

From the pinnacle of a set of ancient stone towers, built on the top of a hill, we looked out over the canopy of the rainforest. My eyes went forever, across the miles of green. Up there it was bright sunshine and the lid of the canopy gently swayed in the breeze like an endless sea made of lush green leaves, with delicate orchids spotted among it, flowering at altitude. As one's head comes out above the canopy the damp, dripping, darkness of the forest is obliterated by the light. It is like that moment when flying on a winter's day the plane banks above the layer of cloud, and there is a perpetual summer and a gleaming white blanket of snowy cloud below.

The stillness of the place was broken by the loud lionlike roars of the howler monkeys. At times they sounded like cows in labour. Or a great tiger attacking a hunting party. The howler monkeys imitate, it's said, the sound of the great cats, and if you didn't know anything about the nature of the forest here you would believe you were in danger of your life.

We descended into the ancient city. The place had been entirely unknown to anyone but the Lacandon Indians until recently, when a young American pilot had found their village and lived with them. One day, when he'd gained their confidence, they took him to the place where they still held their religious ceremonies. And so he discovered Yaxchilán. He drowned three years later in the swells of the Usumacinta.

The atmosphere of Yaxchilán was remarkable. There were mighty carved faces of Chac the rain god, and the stories of the lives of the city's nobility of a thousand years ago were carved on standing stelae. I asked Miguel who these dignified-looking men were.

'Two of our greatest kings,' he said. 'Jaguar Shield and his son, Bird Jaguar.'

Looking down on the thousand-year-old city, lost here in the forest, was a remarkable experience and I was mesmerised by it all. The great stone edifices were wrapped around with vines and jungle, the rasping of the insects, and the calls of the monkeys in the canopy, and the heat, the intense heat.

Miguel bent down and laid his ear against the rotting trunk of a tree. A smile came across his face.

'Listen to this,' he said. 'Put your ear against that small hole in the bark.'

I placed my ear against the trunk. At first all I could hear was a low hum, until Miguel thwacked the hilt of the machete against the bark. Then it erupted into a deafening buzzing. I leapt back.

'Bees!' I yelled. 'It's a bloody bees' nest. I could have been stung in the ear.'

'No,' said Miguel laughing, 'these bees wouldn't sting you. Our ancestors who built this city also bred a strain of bee that had no sting, and look, they still live here.'

I smiled, but it was deeply sad to realise that all that remained of such magnificence was a scattering of Lacandon Indians in their poor villages and these stingless bees that had reverted to the wild.

We climbed up to the most spectacular monument, the palace of the great kings. The palace had a terrace in front of it, with a hundred stone steps leading up. The building stood almost vertical, rising above the trees, with a great ornately carved 'comb' surmounting it. We climbed the steps to the top where the palace had a dozen entrance ways, and above each one a lintel carved with the most wonderful bas reliefs. I walked along them, gazing into the darkness of the vaulted palace within. Great stone sculptures of their gods still lay on the floor. A body here, and a couple of yards away a dismembered stone head lay where it had fallen. I shone my torch in and my feet faltered on the debris, causing great fruit bats to scatter among the vaulting, and a cascade of swallows burst out into the light. I went inside. The air was filled with a musty cave dampness. Suddenly right in front of my face clinging to the stone was a cave scorpion about ten inches across, its crablike legs twitching and vibrating. I leapt back. I retreated to the light of the lintel, and stared up at the wonderful carvings that surrounded the deep doorway. I went back out and then began to venture into the next chamber, where I came across a lintel that had no carvings at all, just bare virgin stone bearing the marks of a chisel.

The guide looked away from me. Miguel began walking back down the steps.

'There's no lintel here,' I said.

'No, señor,' said the guide, 'it has gone.'

'What do you mean, gone?'

'Many of them are. A few months ago you would have seen them, but they are gone.'

'To a museum?' I asked.

'No, not to a museum. They have been stolen by thieves. They come at night on the river, in a ship, and in the morning more of the city was gone.'

I walked on to the next lintel in the palace frontage, which was intact, and stared at it for a few moments.

Now I knew where I'd seen these stones before. I could never forget those marks on the rock, and the square flatness of the stone. My eyes had been so alive with panic when I saw them before. They were the stones I'd seen in the *Karina* when the current had dashed my head against them. The stones that Todd had taken for ballast to scuttle it. They were its cargo. It was my father who had stolen them, these priceless ancient sculptures. I daresay, I thought, that Miguel had helped him. Led him to them, aided and abetted. That was why my father had made it his business to befriend the Lacandon: to steal their inheritance. And Miguel had been crucial to his ends.

I shook again. I had been cheated. My father was an art thief. No wonder the British Embassy were concerned. I felt sick. I felt as if *I'd* been robbed of something.

When I got to the bottom of the steps I took Miguel firmly by the arm.

'It's time', I said, 'to get back to San Cristóbal. We should go.'

I wanted to leave Yaxchilán immediately.

35

We began the long journey back to San Cristóbal and I was rather silent. I liked Miguel; I liked him enormously.

I was an only child and consequently the revelation that I had a 'brother' of sorts, and such an exotic one as this, had rather turned my mind. It wasn't his fault that such a stake had been driven between us. I was forming a notion in my mind that my father had saved the little thief's life to use him for an even greater theft. The removal of the treasures of Yaxchilán. It wasn't his fault. Maybe he didn't even know. I didn't know.

I realised also that I'd misjudged Gregor and the British Embassy. It was a crime on a par with the removal of the Elgin Marbles, after all. God knows what other treasures Miguel had led him to that were still under the canopy of the forest.

It was late at night when we got back to San Cristóbal. Just a few sodden Indians were shuffling through the streets and trying to sell brocade work to a smattering of drunken backpackers. Candles were burning in the windows. We decided to drop in at the small restaurant in the Square of the Forgotten General for a nightcap and *tortas*. Miguel's rations had run out hours before. As we turned down a dark street Miguel suddenly brightened up.

'Look!' he said, pointing to a light burning in an upper window of a house up on the hillside. 'My father is back in town!'

Miguel asked me if I would like to join them at the house for dinner the next evening. I was silent for a moment, and then I nodded.

'I'd be delighted,' I said. We went into the square.

As we sat eating our sandwiches and drinking the hot sweet coffee there was a sudden commotion in the street on our side of the square. I turned to see a riderless horse rearing up in the centre of the road, a look of fearsome anger in its eyes. A small dog stood on the pavement barking at it. The horse was struck on the head by the young Mexican leading it, and the dog was pulled, violently, by the scruff of the neck by a shopkeeper into his doorway. It continued to howl from inside. As the boy pulled the horse on, its hooves grinding on the road, it swung its head towards me and its large brown eye looked for a moment directly into mine.

Miguel turned back to his coffee. I was shaking.

'The horse startled you?' he said.

'Yes.' I could barely hold my coffee cup. Miguel looked up into the trees where hundreds of birds were noisily roosting, flying in flocks from one tree to the next, up to the cornices of the buildings, and then down again. They couldn't settle.

'All the animals seem uneasy tonight,' he said. 'Perhaps it's the heat.'

I said goodnight to Miguel.

I walked slowly back to my hotel. I'd achieved my goal. My father was up there in the burning lights of the house on the hill and I could meet him, as a friend of Miguel's, quite innocently. But the victory, I felt, was pyrrhic.

There was an uneasiness in the air tonight. I could sense the tension beneath the surface in this town. The desk clerk was sitting in semi-darkness.

'Candles again,' I said.

'*Vibraciónes*,' he replied, wearily. He reached for a scrap of paper from under the desk.

'The señora has called yesterday,' he said. 'You have a message in your pigeonhole.' He reached behind the desk and handed me the piece of paper. I looked at it. It said, 'The Señora has called.' I nodded my head wearily and went up to my room.

I lay for some time thinking about what it would be like to have dinner at my father's house the next evening. I wasn't even sure, at that moment, if I'd go. I reached out my hand to the bedside table where I'd laid my gun. It gleamed in the moonlight. I held it up in front of my face and then I felt its hard metal between my teeth. I thought of Miguel and wondered why my father had gone to such lengths to make him his son when he had obviously found it so easy to walk away from me, and never sent me so much as a ten-pence piece. I thought of the bloodstained Harry Koch and how this journey had destroyed my relationship with Lucinda. I wondered if Gregor, or anyone, would do anything if I took the gun along to dinner the following evening, and shot my father. It would be painlessly in the temple, for all the grief he caused me. I could get away with patricide, easily. Some would even thank me for it. One small clean hole. I wanted to hear the sound of the thing going off.

I closed my eyes and buried my face into the hard pillow trying to wipe my mind free of everything. I didn't want any more of that day. I breathed deep on the musky damp taste of the feathers.

I woke early and opened my eyes to look out of my window at the slither of a dawn sky where the sun was struggling to clear a bank of low cloud. I lay there enjoying the smell of the pillow and the rare morning chill. I lay dozing for an hour or more.

Then at seven-thirty I was woken abruptly by the sound of dogs howling in the street outside, and the macaws in their cage shrieking wildly. Birds were fluttering in the trees and I could hear horses and mules kicking and baying.

Four seconds later the earthquake hit the town. I leapt naked from the bed, pulling my blanket around me. The room was swaying as if the walls, and their component parts, had turned to liquid. I began to sway with the movement of the room. I was thrust towards the window. I watched with horror as a hotel a few streets away lurched sideways, masonry falling from its upper floors, glass showering down into the street. There was the awful sound of wrenching metal, a searing, frightening noise, like a building in pain. Then a lower floor of the building collapsed and the whole thing sank in a jolt. I tried to cover my ears to the sound of the screams from the people inside. The upper floors seemed to hesitate for a moment before they quivered and the whole building dropped down, like an epileptic collapsing helplessly in a public place. I began to panic.

There was a moment's silence and then there was more screaming, everywhere screaming. At this time in the morning men would be gathering on the street corner outside, waiting for the casual-labour trucks to come and pick them up for a day's work. Mothers would be getting their children ready for school. I could hear the men on the corner screaming and shouting as they saw the town, and their houses, collapsing around them. Then, after a few seconds, came the second part of the shock. The glass in my window simply imploded on me. Several of the heavy ceiling beams in my room sprang away from the walls. One of them glanced off my head. I don't remember any more. I was knocked out cold.

People who were conscious through those first minutes of the quake said later that the worst thing about it wasn't the screaming, but when the screaming from a building suddenly stopped and you knew that those inside were dead.

Then the town began to fill with an acrid stench, a mixture of escaping gases from the mains pipes and leaking chemicals. The air was almost yellow with it. The shit from the drains was thrown up into the streets; electrical sparks were spluttering under the water cascading from ruptured pipes and water tanks.

Then the fires and explosions began. Most of the devastation happens after the shaking has stopped. A chain of destruction is set in motion. Fuel tanks explode in fireballs, rats dash from the bowels of old buildings like black marbles cast on a polished floor. Worst of all is the panic of the people running, bleeding, amid the smell of burning human flesh. A smell like no other, inspiring abject fear and horror.

I was trapped, and still unconscious, in my room but the worst hopelessness was outside. People were wandering hysterically. Who could help? Where were the people to help them? Where were the saviours, the emergency services? Where was the outside world?

The hospital with the only people who could help was largely destroyed. It was one of the few new buildings in the town, but, because of its poor construction, it had killed its staff. It had been built from second-rate materials by corrupt contractors. Fire tenders had been destroyed. Ambulances with their crews had been crushed under the faulty beams of the Institutional Revolution.

The people were lost. There was no one to take charge. A policeman who'd been on duty in the street, opposite the apartment block where he lived, fell to his knees. Knowing that his wife and child would be dead inside, he took his service revolver and shot himself through the roof of the mouth. His body lay there in the street untouched. He became a symbol of the hopelessness.

36

I came round on the floor of the foyer of the American-owned hotel. I had no idea how I'd got there, and at first didn't know where I was.

It was the middle of the night and all I could hear were the groans of people lying around me. I think the man beside me was already dead because when I began waving my arm to attract attention a couple of guys came over and quickly pulled him away across the marble.

A young woman in a hotel uniform came over and sat beside me. I stared up at her name tag. My eyes remained fixed on the phrase 'Beverley – Guest Services' for some time. There was blood smeared around the cuffs of her blouse. Her hair was tied up but it flopped in strands across her face. Her eyes were red.

'Please sir,' she said in an American accent as she pulled out a notebook, 'can you tell me your name, your nationality and your religion?' Her voice quivered with exhaustion. She looked like an ex-cheerleader, one of those Barbie-doll girls that American corporations employ with the promise of exotic foreign travel. She'd lost a cap from one of her front teeth and she lisped as she spoke.

'Jay,' I said, 'Jay Morgan, British, C. of E.'

She sighed deeply and slouched down onto her haunches. She began to sob.

'I'm sorry, I'm just so sorry . . .' she said. 'I don't know what that is. I don't know what C. of E. is.' She gripped her notebook in her hand.

'Church of England,' I said quietly. 'I'm sure it doesn't matter.'

'I don't know if it's important,' she said weakly, 'we're just trying to do everything properly, but it's chaos. I've only been at this hotel two weeks . . .' She tried to pull herself together. She had most probably been employed as one of those people who are supposed to keep everyone jolly, get them to go on day trips, join the exercise class. She was in a state of shock. I reached out and took her hand.

'I was rescued from the Santa Clara?' I asked.

'Yeah, I guess so. I don't know. I haven't got any details. I'm sorry, I'm so sorry, it's chaos . . .'

All I wanted to do at that moment was to get out of the building, get out into fresh air, into fields and wide open spaces. I stared up at the roof supports above me and quivered with fear of them.

I must have passed out again because the next I knew I was being led out by a couple of guys onto the glass-strewn and blood-splattered steps of the hotel. I'd been naked when I was rescued and I looked down at what I was wearing. I was dressed in all that the hotel probably had to hand: a waiter's uniform. Golden epaulets and brass buttons glimmered on my white tunic. I had a cake of blood on the side of my head and my arm hurt badly. Apart from that I had escaped remarkably well. The Santa Clara was a solid building.

The acrid stench of the escaping gases of the town hit me and I was close to fainting again. I began to stagger, and my arm was caught by one of the men. They were leading a small group of us out to a waiting truck. Beverley was helping. We were all dazed and zombie-like.

'Where am I going?' I asked Beverley.

'The Red Cross have got here,' she said. 'They've set up a camp. We have to take you there. We can't cope here anymore.' It was then that I realised that my other arm was linked to an elderly woman I took to be American. She was silently staring ahead of her. She was shaking and there was blood on her face. She was still wearing her nightgown under a man's coat. Her arm was in a sling and she was in severe shock. She was in her late sixties. She'd probably been on a tour of the monuments. She walked heavily. She was wearing a large pair of men's black shoes. She gripped my arm tightly as we staggered towards the back of the truck. Her nails dug into my flesh.

The camp was just a grid of military tents, gloomy and green, flapping in the pall of smoke that lay over the town. I think we all felt happier in a tent. A young doctor came round and sedated us. We now had plastic labels, with our names and nationalities written on, secured to our ankles.

I was woken the next day by the sound of helicopters. They were flying out the most critical cases. I felt that I couldn't just lie there any longer.

I dismissed myself from the tent discreetly, sneaking out under cover of the mayhem, and wandered back into the debris of the town. I joined some people in a chain gang moving lumps of concrete and metal beams away from a collapsed apartment under which there had been a pharmacy. The emergency services needed the drugs. It was a hopeless task and the gang worked silently. I stayed with them for a couple of hours but I could see the frustration on the face of the man to whom I was passing my lumps of concrete. My right arm wasn't good and if anything I was more of a hindrance than a help. I was slowing things down as I struggled with the weight and frequently dropped lumps dangerously near to his bare feet.

Like everyone who had lived through the quake I was suffering from nausea and every now and then I sank to my knees and threw up. We had bits of cloth tied around our faces for masks, but the sulphurous smell still seeped through, as if someone had opened up hell. Every so often it would rain and, though it cleared the air momentarily, it didn't put out the fires. The torrential water built up in twisted ducts and caused further collapse to the buildings. We knew that people trapped in the basements of the buildings were being drowned by it. It gave us a hopeless sense of frustration. People openly cursed God in the streets.

I dropped another piece of masonry, a lump of stucco moulding in the shape of the wing of the Mexican eagle, and I couldn't lift it again. The man beside me lost his temper with me. I left them and walked into the town, unhappy that there was nothing I could do to help. It was a hopeless, helpless feeling.

Everywhere buildings were burning, as if in a dream, no tenders around them, no attempt at all to put them out. No way of doing so.

The army had arrived but they were reluctant to join in with the rescue operations. They were only concerned with guarding the banks against looters and they stood outside them like sentries in a siege town. People cursed them as if they were an occupying force, but no matter what appeals were made to them they remained resolutely at their posts. I saw one old man, with a badly damaged leg, hit with the butt of a rifle as he remonstrated with them. It was reported later that many of the soldiers had looted the banks themselves.

Small shrines had been set up by the people. Candles burned around the images of saints, and offerings of bread were laid out for the dead. Saddest of all among the rubble were the small personal items that flapped in the wind: family photographs; a baby's rattle; underwear; a pornographic magazine of large-breasted women. Things that had been private, and part of a person's life, were mixed with oil, and blood, and the debris of the town. Even money fluttered, untouched, sticking out from the fractured concrete and stucco.

The most terrible sight was the group of men and old women who stood all day and all night before the remains of the maternity wing of the hospital. They stood there silently staring at the hissing rubble. The maternity wing had contained twenty women and ten babies when the earthquake hit. Not one of them had been rescued. The building had collapsed in on itself. The substandard cement and badly designed structure had simply given way. Young husbands stood weeping in their mothers' arms. Several of them had tried to climb up onto the debris but had been forced back by the Red Cross workers. Not only were they a danger to themselves in their distraught state but the weight of their bodies could have caused further collapse to the structure. The people found this the most frustrating thing of all. That they could not even make a gesture towards saving those trapped below.

As I stood and watched them I heard singing in the street behind me. A procession of choirboys in ragged vestments were parading down the street, carrying a cross before them. Behind them were the priests, some of them with their heads bandaged, some just wearing a white sheet around them as makeshift vestments. Some were hobbling, and supporting each other by linking arms. At the end of the procession they carried the wax figures of Christ and the disciples that I had seen, sitting around at the last supper, in the church. The disciples were equally battered by it all, and the head of Christ, where the wax had melted, hung sorrowfully to one side. As the procession approached the hospital the people dropped to their knees, crossing themselves and fingering their rosaries. They set down a figure of the Virgin and Child in front of the hospital where the women and babies were trapped.

I began to weep.

I walked back into the centre of town. It was remarkable to see that all the other buildings, those built of stone like the cathedral, were still standing, almost untouched by it all. It was the newer, jerry-built places, and the houses of the poor, that had suffered. The head of Benito Juarez lay in the main street but the statue of the Forgotten General still stood, perfectly intact and still as imperious.

I walked back to the Red Cross encampment to ask if they had any lists of those who had survived.

There was a trestle table where people could enquire about their loved ones. The queue was about fifty long. I stood in line, but after an hour I wavered and collapsed. I was picked up by some volunteers.

'None of the names you have given us are registered,' they said, when they came back to where I lay on a canvas bed. 'It doesn't mean anything,' they said. 'Information is very difficult to collate.'

'May I use the phone?' I asked. I wanted to see if I could get through to Stevo's place in Yelapa and speak to Jody.

'We only have the one line at the moment and it's tied up with the critical cases,' I was told. I nodded my head and set off out into the town again. It was night.

I turned a corner and heard a trumpet wailing and in front of me was a makeshift cover where men were drinking together under a length of polythene lashed up to poles. I recognised some of the salvaged chairs and tables.

Leaning against a length of planking that was serving as a counter was Jeff, the owner of the Bamboo Bar. He had a battered panama pushed back on his head. He was polishing glasses, and as he breathed I could see that he too had lost some of his front teeth.

I walked in. He looked grey and his chin was rough with stubble and cuts. One of his hands was bandaged. On the planking he had a cash register. I pulled up the one stool he had and sat down. He didn't seem to recognise me.

'You want a drink sir?' he said, I closed my eyes for a moment.

'No, no, just some water,' I said.

'Water's at a premium right now. Beer's cheaper,' he said. I bought a bottle of water from him. 'I'm looking for Miguel. You know if he survived?'

Jeff laughed. 'You know where the motherfucker was when the quake hit? He was in the Bank of fucking Mexico, man. That's our Miguel, always the first in the bank in the morning with his night's takings.'

Miguel would have been paying in the money I had given him for our trip into the forest.

'The whole bank collapsed, man,' continued Jeff. 'Came down like a pack of frigging cards, crushed everyone dead.'

I stared down into my plastic bottle of water.

'But you know what?' Jeff went on. 'They say he tunnelled his way out through the frigging air vents! Can you believe that? A fucking thief tunnels his way *out* of a bank!'

'He's alive?'

'So they say.'

I smiled. 'I don't know how you manage to carry on like this, Jeff,' I said.

'Guess I'm just glad to be alive and still have a bar,' he said, 'not that I'm going to let my folks know that. I'm gonna try and get my name on the dead lists, and disappear. A real good plan, yeah? I get off the paternity suit. I get no hassles for the rest of my life on account of I'm dead. Neat, eh?'

I shook my head.

'What about Miguel's friend, Morgan? Have you hear anything about him?'

'No, I don't think I have.'

'I've been trying to make a phone call. Any idea where I can find a phone that works?'

'You want to go to the American hotel. They got some kinda centre set up there for the press guys. They'll have a phone, fax, the lot. Those guys always do, somehow, don't they?'

So I went back to the hotel where I'd been taken after my rescue and asked for the press centre. I was shown upstairs. There they were, not many of them, but they were most definitely the press, sitting about in the mezzanine champagne bar. The glass in the picture frames was shattered, coffee tables were propped up with books, there was glass on the carpets. It was like the dance hall on the *Titanic*. But apart from this the bar still seemed to be functioning; people had drinks in their hands. There were bottles of Scotch lying about, even peanuts in bowls. A handful of reporters had set up a card school. As I walked in a young, clean-cut, under-manager rushed up to stop me going any further.

'Can I help you, sir?' he said.

'Yes,' I said. 'I'd like to use the press facility.' He looked me up and down.

'I'm sorry, sir, this area is reserved for the international press corps only.'

'I'm a reporter,' I said. 'I have to file my copy with my news desk.' He didn't believe me. He gave me one of those withering looks that they must teach them at hotel management school.

'I have to see your accreditation,' he said.

'I'm sorry,' I said. 'I was here in the quake and I've lost them. I'm from the *Guardian* in the UK.'

'Would you like to speak to the manager? And perhaps your journal could fax us with your accreditation. Do you have your passport?'

'No I don't!' I shouted. 'I was in the quake. I don't have anything. That's why I'm dressed as a fucking waiter.' I was about to take a swing at him when a voice I recognised piped up from the corner of the room.

'Just a moment, there. I can vouch for him. He can be my guest,' he said.

The under-manager looked at me and smiled.

'I'm so sorry, sir. Do come in. Use any of the facilities you may require,' he said, and gave a short sharp bow of his head.

I crossed the room and sat down.

'Thanks, thanks,' I said, 'I need to use the phone. What are you doing here Mr Gregor?'

He looked at me with a faint twinkle in those dead-rabbit eyes, and offered me a Scotch and soda.

'Choppered in this morning, Mr Morgan. To mastermind the wellbeing of our nationals.'

'Very decent of you. As far as I know I'm your only customer.'

'Well, that's what I'm here to establish,' he said wryly. 'You do manage to get yourself into some dreadful scrapes.'

'I'd call this a bit more than a scrape,' I said coldly.

'I know, I know,' he said, his voice suddenly becoming sympathetic. He pressed me again to take a glass of Scotch. I refused it.

'No, go on,' he said. 'It'll do you good. You've had one hell of a shock.'

'Yeah.' I took a slug of the whisky.

'I heard they rescued you from the Santa Clara and brought you here. Good job you were there. It's a solid-built place. Once again San Cristóbal survives, but, as ever, it's hit the ordinary people hardest. As it always does in this country.'

Even Gregor had been moved by what he'd seen.

'Perhaps you can help me,' I said. 'I want to let my friends in Puerto Vallarta know that I'm okay.'

'Yes, yes, of course, and then maybe I can help you with your repatriation. We've got a flight leaving from Oaxaca.'

'No, thank you,' I said. 'I'm not quite ready to go home yet.'

'Certainly,' he said, and he patted my hand. It was patronising but he seemed to be genuinely concerned about me.

'I've lost the number of their phone in Yelapa,' I said. 'You haven't still got it have you?'

Gregor pulled out a small notebook and flicked it open.

'I'll dial it for you shall I?'

We walked over to the phone. When he handed me the receiver Stevo was on the line. He sounded exactly as I imagined he would with a lazy, laid-back drawl. When I said who I was he was shocked.

'God, man,' he said, 'we been kinda worried here. You wanna speak to Lucinda?'

'Yes.'

'She's out by the pool. I'll just go get her.'

She came on the line. She sounded stoned, but screeched when she heard my voice. She was relieved that I was alive. It was an oddly disjointed feeling, hearing her voice, so far away. While she was smoking hash I could have been dead up in the mountains. It annoyed me.

'Is Jody okay?' she said. 'Is she with you?'

'No. Why should she be?' I asked, bemused.

'She left for San Cristóbal a couple of days ago, before the earthquake, to come and see you,' she said.

I was thrown into a sudden panic. She could have arrived while I was in the forest. Please God Jody hadn't been killed.

'How did she come here? Did she come by bus?'

There was a chance she wouldn't have made it before the quake.

'No, she flew to . . . I can't remember, ugly-sounding place . . .'

'Tuxtla Gutiérrez?'

'Sounds like it.'

She could have got to San Cristóbal in under twenty-four hours. I couldn't talk to Lucinda anymore. It was too strange. I replaced the receiver and turned to Gregor. 'You know where I am,' I said, and left.

I went back to the Red Cross station to check the dead lists again, this time for Jody's name. I couldn't find it, but in the chaos that meant very little.

37

I asked everyone I could if they had seen anyone fitting Jody's description. No one could help me.

As I queued for something to eat at the Red Cross station there was a feeling of excitement in the air among the rescuers. I asked what had happened.

'They've begun the rescue at the hospital,' they told me. A young man had got a group of teenagers together, kids who were light enough to scramble over the rubble, and last night they'd made their first successful descent into the destruction. They'd all but stripped themselves naked and covered themselves with butter and oil so that they could slip through the air ducts. Then their leader had called for silence from the crowd that had been chanting prayers together. Sounds had been heard from the depths of the destruction, the groans of women, and the cry of a baby, they said. The people were praying for a miracle.

I went over to the press centre at the American hotel again. I needed Gregor's help, I felt, to find Jody. Gregor wasn't there, but the pressmen were fighting to use the fax and the phone. They were excited too. They had a new story to file. I asked one of them what was going on at the hospital and he confirmed the story I'd heard at the camp.

'The people are calling these kids *los topos* – the moles – because of the way they're slipping down into the earth. No equipment, nothing, just butter on their bodies,' he told me.

It was a story the press liked. CNN had arrived. They'd already erected a scaffold to illuminate the site with arc lamps.

As I sat there Gregor walked in. He looked unusually grave and came straight over to me.

'I just missed you over at the camp,' he said. 'I came to speak to you. I've some news.' Standing behind him was Cynthia.

'Hello, again,' she said, smiling, but there was a pained look on her face.

'Shall we go somewhere quieter?' said Gregor. He seemed serious. I stood up and followed them both to the door.

As we walked across the *zócalo* Cynthia took my arm briefly.

'So how have you been?' she asked. 'You seem to be bearing up considerably well under the circumstances. We'll have to think about giving you a medal.' She spoke to me as if I was an eight-year-old who had grazed his knee.

'You're here as well, then, looking after us nationals,' I said.

'All hands to the pump once again,' she said, squeezing my waist. They were walking me towards the church of San Domingo. I stopped as we approached. They both looked at me.

'I'm sorry,' I said. 'Can we stop for a moment?' I looked around me. 'It's been so terrible,' I said. I was breathing very heavily, and shaking, as I thought of the things I'd seen here, and watched the Indians wandering about, picking over the remains, some of them ragged and hopeless, their eyes staring, their hair matted with blood. Cynthia looked at me, concern in her eyes.

'We'll see if we can't get you out of that waiter's jacket,' she said. 'I'm sure Giles will lend you something.'

We sat in the back pew of the church. Candles were burning everywhere and people sat, gently rocking; others were sleeping in the aisle. A few groups had lit small fires on the flagstones to cook on and the church was full of the smell of wood smoke.

'Why have you been following me?' I asked. 'I suppose you checked me out and found out I was genuine.'

'Yes, eventually we managed to do that,' said Gregor. There seemed to be real compassion in his voice.

'And will I ever know what this has all been about?'

'Well, sometimes it's best to let sleeping dogs lie.'

'Oh, absolutely,' said Cynthia. 'Not always best to rake things over.'

They stared up into the gilded stucco of the ceiling. Gregor coughed and braced himself. 'This time,' he said, 'I'm afraid your father didn't make it. He was killed in the earthquake. It would have been very quick.'

I gasped and fought for breath.

'You must be awfully disappointed,' said Cynthia. 'We will, of course, make all the necessary arrangements for the removal of the body to the UK. You can't be worried, we realise, with anything of that nature. We are most terribly sorry. You made such an effort to find him.'

I watched the Indians shuffling about, making tortillas on the stone floor. Gregor put his arm round me. I sat for a few moments, breathing heavily. Of all the emotions I felt, I suppose it was a sorrow for Miguel that I felt most keenly at that moment. He was the one, after all, who had really lost a father, not I.

'I want to see his body,' I said. 'Where is he?'

'In the basement of the old governor's palace,' said Cynthia. 'It's all quite dignified. Despite everything, the authorities here have really quite risen to the occasion. We have to thank them for that.'

I nodded my head slowly. In some ways my mind was more on the living than the dead now and I found their sympathy rather cloying. I felt a sudden rush of energy.

'So, for God's sake, can't you tell me now what it was he had done?'

They smiled at me.

'Not now,' said Gregor, 'not just now.' They patted my hand again. I felt slightly sick.

'So I led you to my father after all,' I said.

'Yes, yes, you did,' said Gregor.

That evening I went to join the crowds standing around the hospital. The news crews were there and the whole building was illuminated under arc lamps. The debris glowed like the lava from a volcano.

After a little while I saw Miguel standing at the top of the debris and I gave a silent cheer to see him alive. When I'd heard, in the press facility, that a young guy had organised the rescue at the hospital, I'd hoped against hope that it was Miguel. Now that I saw it was him I was deeply moved. I watched Miguel as he led his 'moles' down into the building again. His head was bloodstained and his half-naked body was pitted with wounds from where sharp parts of the building had obstructed him on his way. I stood and watched him in awe. He must also have known that his adoptive father was dead, and as I watched the heroism of his efforts I could feel nothing but pride in the fact that in some distant way he was my brother.

I watched as he emerged from the building again. He stood at the summit of the devastation, under the arc lamps, and called for silence from the mass of people. Then he craned his head downwards into the shafts that his moles had excavated. I fancied I heard the groans of the women and the cries of the babies too. Then he darted down, his body shining with the oil, into the building. I stayed for hours watching him as he returned to the surface exhausted. But no one was saved.

The next morning Gregor and Cynthia took me to the old governor's palace to see my father's body. As we stood in the damp, dark basement, where he was laid out in a body bag, I had so many questions that they all came brimming up at once.

'Who killed Harry Koch?' I asked as a man unzipped the body bag. 'Was it the Mexican authorities?'

'We now think it was most probably the *hacendados*,' said Gregor. 'They believed that he was the money behind your father's opposition to them here. They are the landowners—'

'Yes I know,' I interrupted. 'I guessed that much. And they sank the *Karina* too?'

'No, we don't think so,' said Cynthia. 'We expect that *was* the Mexican authorities. It looks to have been a bit of a botched-up job all round. The ship contained certain items that we imagine your father was going to ransom.'

I turned to look at her. 'The art works from Yaxchilán, you mean? He was going to *ransom* them? He didn't steal them from the Indians?'

'Good heavens no,' said Cynthia. 'We wouldn't want you to go home with that kind of impression. Good Lord no. Your father was very well thought of in intelligence circles. He was a holder of the Military Cross.'

She sighed heavily. 'Your father and I go back a long way. I've worked with him on many an occasion. Cyprus, Angola, a spell down in Belize.'

I turned to look at Cynthia. I had entirely misjudged her. I hadn't imagined for a moment that she was anything more than a flunky of the consul. I was rather startled to discover she was obviously rather high up in MI6. It was bizarre.

She continued. 'He was one of the old school. As far as we know the Lacandones gave him the artworks from Yaxchilán. They stole them themselves in a misguided bid to . . . well, I suppose, try and secure their future with their past. Sweet, really. But the revenue they hoped to generate was most probably for the purchase of arms.'

The body bag was unzipped and I saw his face. It had been so badly battered that there were really no features remaining. I turned toward the wall and fought the urge to throw up. I'd puked so much in the last days that I was steeled against it. My stomach muscles were exhausted. My hand was wet from the dripping slime where I gripped the wall. I turned back. They had unzipped him to the waist and his right hand was swinging limply from the marble slab. His arm was striped with dried blood, his hand wasn't complete, his thumb was missing.

'You seem to have a certain respect for him anyway,' I said.

'Oh yes,' said Cynthia, 'a certain fascination. It was just that in this instance we were on opposing sides of the question in hand.'

'Opposing sides?'

'He fell in love with the Lacandon Indians,' said Gregor.

'Yes, I know,' I said, thinking of his adoption of Miguel.

'But of course things like that can be dangerous. Have you heard of the North American Free Trade Agreement?'

'Yes I have, constantly,' I said. The attendant began zipping the body bag up again, then he walked over with a small plastic bag and handed it to me.

I opened the bag. Inside were a few credit card slips, signed with my father's name, and his passport. The effects of the deceased. I stared at my father's photograph. He was a handsome man, and I could see where he looked like me: he had a fleck in his eye. I liked the quizzical expression on his face, as he suffered the indignity of a passport photograph.

'He was planning to supply arms to the local Indians,' said Gregor, 'and encourage them to insurrection. It would have been an embarrassment to the Mexican President. It's his crowning achievement, this trade treaty. An uprising would have been a spanner in the works, discouraged investment in the country, that kind of thing.'

I turned now to look at Gregor. Of, course, I thought to myself, and the British government couldn't be seen to be involved, even in the person of a former employee like my father.

'Perhaps we should go now. You have his effects?' said Gregor.

'Yes, thank you,' I said. We began walking back up into the paper-strewn governor's palace.

'What I don't understand at all', I said as we hit the dull light of the *zócalo*, 'is why you were involved. Why didn't you just let the Mexicans or the Americans get on with it?'

'Whatever affects American interests affects the world's economic interests,' said Gregor. 'And, as he was one of ours, it was a little bit of professional pride to get there first. Vanity, I suppose.'

'And if you *had* got to him first, you would have killed him?' I asked.

They were silent.

'Shall we take you for some lunch?' he replied.

I stared at Gregor in disbelief for a moment. 'No,' I said. 'I can't actually face lunch right now.'

38

The rescue at the hospital had caught the imagination of the world's press. I spent a great deal of time there standing in the silent crowd watching for Miguel to climb back to the surface. But it was now ten days since the earthquake and all hope was fading. Some newspapers had run stories saying that the sounds of crying that the crowds heard when Miguel called for silence was nothing but mass hysteria. A kind of hypnotism.

On the morning of the eleventh day I went back to the mezzanine floor of the American hotel to use the telephone. I wanted to see if they had any news of Jody back in Yelapa. The press facility was buzzing with activity. It was obvious that something had happened at the hospital.

I caught the arm of a guy from the *Daily Mail*.

'What's the big story?' I asked.

'Haven't you heard?' he said. 'This Miguel chap?'

'What about him?'

The journalist laughed. 'Turns out he's something of a thief. A common thief. A proper con merchant . . .'

I walked away and sat down on one of the endless sofas that lined the smoke-filled room. It saddened me that they should sit there in the luxury of the mezzanine digging up dirt on the people's 'little hero'.

I got through to Stevo. There had been no word from Jody.

I felt sick at heart. I thought of the night we'd sat on the balcony together watching the Mardi Gras parade in Mazatlán when she'd told me how scared she'd been living in San Francisco. I prayed to God that I hadn't been the cause of drawing her into her worst nightmare.

I returned to work with the heavy lifting gangs over the next couple of days. Slowly the air was beginning to clear. I got a message, from the Red Cross people at the camp, to go over to the Hotel Santa Clara. They wanted to see me urgently. I dashed straight over.

'Ah, good to see you, señor,' said the desk clerk as I walked in. There was the sound of repairs being carried out in the rooms. The glass and the mud had been cleared from the lobby. There was even a semblance of service in the dining room. More service, in fact, than there had been before the quake, journalists and TV crews mainly, eating their way through the menu.

'I got an urgent message to come over,' I said to the clerk.

'Ah yes!'

He smiled and reached under the fractured reception desk.

'Are these your trousers, sir?' he said, bringing up a pair of beige turnups. They were. They'd even managed, somehow, to press them for me.

'And this,' said the clerk. He pulled out my Delsey suitcase. 'This has been recovered from your room.'

I laughed. It was perfectly intact.

'I can't believe it,' I said. 'It survived the earthquake. The bloody thing's indestructible.'

'Not entirely, señor: we searched and searched, but I'm afraid we couldn't find the wheels.'

When I got back to the Red Cross camp I opened up the case. The first thing I saw was my old toiletry bag. It was bulging. I unzipped it, and there, lying on top of the little sewing kit I'd taken from the Holiday Inn, was my gun, and the small cardboard box of bullets. I smiled.

That evening I wandered the streets again until I came to the hospital. I stood for hours, mesmerised, with the crowd. Most of the TV crews had given up and gone home. Just one arc lamp remained trained on the pinnacle of the debris.

People sat around little fires feeling their rosaries and rocking inconsolably on their haunches. Then, at about one o'clock in the morning, there was a shout and people began rushing towards the foot of the rubble. All around me people were either jumping up and shrieking, or falling to their knees, weeping and reciting prayers. I pushed my way to the front. There, right at the top, under the arc lamp was Miguel, holding a baby aloft in his hands. He called for quiet and the crowd fell silent.

All we could hear was the whimpering of the baby. Miguel looked up into the light of the arc lamp.

'They are alive!' he shouted. Then, I felt myself running with the crowd, involuntarily, forward. I began to scrabble up onto the scaffolding that held the arc lamp to get a better view of Miguel. I hung from the scaffolding, cheering and applauding with the others. Then behind him one of his little moles crawled out, blood across her face, a baby in her arms. There were gasps, and then silence, and then the sound of weeping as the sense of what had happened sank in.

Miguel began walking down the face of the debris, with the baby in his arms, to the waiting ambulances. I turned back to look into the crowd and the lights from other re-illuminated TV arc lamps caught me in the face, almost blinding me. News crews were scrabbling onto the tops of their vans for a vantage point, and reporters were presenting their pieces-to-camera.

I heard a shout from the crowd. I heard my name being called. I shielded my eyes and found my way back down. Until I got to the ground I hadn't realised how far up the scaffolding I had climbed.

I pushed my way through the exultant crowd. I could see Jody, standing on a beam of twisted metal, calling to me. As I got to her she jumped down and threw her arms around my neck. Tears were streaming down her face. There she stood, her hair all over her face, tears splashing about her eyes and cheeks.

That evening we sat in the room that she'd managed to get at the American hotel. She told me how she had been sure that I was dead. She had been planning to leave the next morning, returning home to San Francisco. She had searched for me for several days, but had then found the name Morgan on the dead lists and had presumed it was me.

She had been in San Cristóbal for only a few days. She had, in fact, flown only as far as Oaxaca, and had then got a bus to Tuxtla. She was there when the earthquake had struck and had got through it with no more than a bruised backside from when she was thrown out of bed. After the quake no buses were making the journey up into the mountains and she had been stuck for a week, but was still determined to reach me.

She opened her suitcase and pulled out a bag. She handed it to me.

'I brought you this,' she said. I put my hand into the bag. It was a carved wooden jaguar head from Isobel.

I asked her how things were with Todd. She looked down to the floor and then back up at me and laughed.

'There was an argument,' she said. 'When I said that I was coming to find you here, Todd packed up his things. By now he must be back in Pittsburgh, organising for the sale of our house.'

'And you're going to move back to San Francisco together, or something?' I asked.

'I think I will go to San Francisco,' she said, 'but not with Todd. Paradise has done for us.'

We prepared ourselves to leave Mexico and the next day Jody arranged for a Red Cross jeep to pick us up at the American hotel and drive us out to the airstrip. They would fly us out to the airport at Oaxaca, where we intended spending a few days together before each of us flew on home. I was ready to go now.

We sat together in the back of the jeep as we drove through town. I was holding the jaguar head on my lap as we hit against the potholes and rocks. As we turned the corner into the Square of the Forgotten General I pulled on the driver's shoulder and asked him to stop.

I looked across the square to where the restaurant was functioning again. People sat around drinking coffee as if nothing had happened. Since the 'miracle' at the hospital the evening before, journalists were beginning to flood back into the town.

'Look,' I said to Jody, 'you see who's sitting at that table? It's the pair from the embassy. That's Gregor and Cynthia.'

They were drinking coffee in the morning sunshine, looking satisfied with themselves. They had their bags with them beneath the table and it looked as if they, too, were preparing to leave. I smiled at them, but they didn't see me.

The driver turned around to see if we wanted to get out and

speak to them. Just as I was about to tell him to drive on I saw Miguel. He was sitting on the other side of the square, outside Jeff's makeshift bar. Standing around him was a group of journalists holding out their micro-recorders. The waiters were fawning. He was a *somebody* in this town now. I decided to go over and say goodbye to him. Jody came with me and we pushed our way through the gaggle of reporters. When we got to the table he looked up and smiled as he saw me.

Sitting beside him, with an espresso coffee in his hand, was a man with a shock of silver hair. I stared at him for a moment. It was my father. He looked remarkably well.

I froze for a moment.

'This is my friend, Jay,' said Miguel, to break the impasse.

'Nice to meet you,' said my father, holding out his hand to shake mine.

'How do you do?' I said. I shook his hand. He had a firm grip and my hand felt weak and lifeless inside his. My hand slipped away.

'Well, Miguel,' I said. 'I just came to say goodbye. I'm getting on the plane now.'

'Goodbye, my friend,' he said.

My father was sipping his coffee and staring out across the square. I couldn't be sure if he had seen anything in my face that he recognised at all.

I reached into my fanny pack and took out my passport and my wallet and stuffed them into my trouser pocket. I held the fanny pack out to Miguel.

'I want you to have this, to remember me by,' I said. He took it, smiling. Jody and I walked back to the jeep.

We began driving out of town. I was shocked into silence. Finally Jody turned to me.

'It was him, wasn't it?' she said.

'Yes,' I said. 'I have his passport photograph, and it was him.'

'My God,' she said. 'So who was it in the governor's wine cellar?'

'You remember that Frenchman I told you about that I had dinner with in Mexicali, the one with the missing thumb?'

'Yes?'

'I guess he must have been killed in the quake and my

father bribed someone to get his own name on the dead lists.'

'Well, I got to say, your father's got style. Had himself laid out in the governor's palace at least.'

'Certainly has.'

'And you really don't want to stay? You don't want to talk to him?'

'Let's get to that airstrip,' I said.

'What was in the fanny pack you gave Miguel?'

'My gun,' I said.

We drove out of town.

Epilogue $\int$

England, 1st January 1994.

When I returned home I found it strangely difficult to get back into the way of things. I found myself sitting quite mesmerised in front of the television set watching all the new commercials. I felt that I wanted to go up to strangers in the street and say, 'Have you any idea what it was like there?'

I had rented a flat on the seafront at Brighton, where I spent a great deal of time looking at the sea, or re-reading Jody's letters to me.

On the evening of New Year's Day I was watching the evening television news. I was startled as they announced reports of an uprising in Chiapas, Mexico.

Two thousand Mayan Indians had 'formed a ragtag army' and had marched out of the jungle. At dawn they had taken, 'with little resistance and little loss of life', four towns in Chiapas. They had captured Ocosingo; Las Margaritas; Altamirano, and San Cristóbal de Las Casas.

I ran up to the television set as I saw pictures of the square in San Cristóbal. It was covered in debris and papers. The rebels had raided the governor's palace and destroyed all the files that had been kept on suspected Indian insurgents. I saw the helicopter gunships of the Mexican army as they fired into the surrounding hillsides. I saw the window of my room at the Hotel Santa Clara, with smoke pouring out of it. There were bodies in the street.

The newscaster came back on.

'The Zapatista Army of National Liberation has proclaimed its intention of marching on to Mexico City to topple the

325 •

government of President Carlos Salinas. The uprising has been timed to coincide with the New Year's Day implementation of President Salinas' greatest political achievement: the creation, with the United States and Canada, of the world's largest free-trade zone. It is intended to catapult Mexico into the First World. The North American Free Trade Agreement.'

Over the next days I watched every news bulletin. On 8th January the government forces recaptured the centre of San Cristóbal. A spokesman for the President gave a press conference in the courtyard of the Posada Diego, dressed in battle fatigues.

'The rising', he said, 'has been controlled by foreign elements.' They showed a photograph of one of the Zapatistas. The face was obscured by a ski mask, but he took great delight in pointing out that the insurgent had blue eyes. Blue eyes with what I thought to be a small brown fleck.

Although forced back into their rain forest, the indigenous people of Chiapas continue their fight.